THE WRECK OF THE
GROSVENOR

OTHER NAUTICAL FICTION
PUBLISHED BY McBOOKS PRESS

THE WRECK OF THE GROSVENOR

by
W. Clark Russell

AN ACCOUNT OF THE MUTINY OF THE CREW
AND THE LOSS OF THE SHIP WHEN TRYING
TO MAKE THE BERMUDAS

CLASSICS OF NAUTICAL FICTION SERIES

McBOOKS PRESS
ITHACA, NEW YORK

Book and cover design by Paperwork.
Cover painting is *The Shipwreck* by Joseph Mallord William Turner, courtesy of Clore Collection, Tate Gallery, London/Art Resource, NY.

Library of Congress Cataloging-in-Publication Data

Russell, William Clark, 1844–1911.
   The wreck of the Grosvenor : an account of the mutiny of the crew
and the loss of the ship when trying to make the Bermudas / by W.
Clark Russell.
         p.   cm. — (Classics of nautical fiction series)
   ISBN 0-935526-52-8 (pbk.)
   I. Title. II. Series.
   PR5282.W74 1998
   823'.8—dc21   98-38970
                                                            CIP

The Wreck of the Grosvenor was first published by Low in London in 1877. This text is based on the 1899 edition published by Charles Scribner's Sons, New York. A few corrections were made for consistency and clarity, but most of the original spelling and punctuation remain intact.

Distributed to the book trade by:

Login Trade, 1436 West Randolph, Chicago, IL 60607, 800-626-4330

Additional copies of this book may be ordered from any bookstore or directly from McBooks Press, 120 West State Street, Ithaca, NY 14850. Please include $3.00 postage and handling with mail orders. New York State residents must add 8% sales tax. All McBooks Press publications can also be ordered by calling toll-free 1-888-BOOKS11 (1-888-266-5711).

Visit the McBooks Press website at http://www.McBooks.com.

Printed in the United States of America

9 8 7 6 5 4 3 2 1

FOREWORD

By Herman Melville

THIS SHORT appreciation of W. Clark Russell first appeared in 1888 as a dedication ("Inscription Epistolary") to Russell in Herman Melville's *John Marr and Other Sailors,* a privately published collection of nautical poetry.

To
W. C. R.

Health and Content:

Hilary, my companionable acquaintance, during an afternoon stroll under the trees along the higher bluffs of our Riverside Park last June, entertained me with one of those clever little theories, for the originating and formulating whereof he has a singular aptitude. He had but recently generalised it—so, at least, I inferred—from certain subtler particulars which, in the instances of sundry individuals, he flattered himself his perspicacity had enabled him to discern.

Let me communicate to you this theory; not that I imagine you will hail it as a rare intellectual acquisition; hardly that, but because I am much mistaken if it does not attract your personal interest, however little it may otherwise, and with other people, win consideration or regard.

Briefly put, it is this. Letting alone less familiar nationalities, an American born in England, or an Englishman born in America, each in his natural

make-up retains through life, and will some way evince, an intangible something imbibed with his mother's milk from the soil of his nativity.

But for a signal illustration hereof, whom, think you, he cites? Well, look
into any mirror at hand and you will see the gentleman. Yes, Hilary thinks he
perceives in the nautical novels of W. C. R. an occasional flavour as if the
honest mid-sea brine, their main constituent, were impregnated with a dash
of the New World's alluvium—such, say, as is discharged by our Father of
Waters into the Gulf of Mexico. "Natural enough," he observes; "for, though
a countryman of the Queen—his parentage, home, and allegiance all English—this writer, I am credibly informed, is in his birthplace a
New-Worlder; ay, first looked out upon life from a window here of our island of Manhattan, nor very far from the site of my place in Broadway, by
Jove!"

Now, Hilary is that rare bird, a man at once genial and acute. Genial, I
mean, without sharing much in mere gregariousness, which, with some,
passes for a sort of geniality; and acute, though lacking more or less in cau-
tionary self-scepticism. No wonder then that, however pleasing and
instructive be Hilary's companionship, and much as I value the man, yet as
touching more than one of his shrewder speculations I have been reluctantly led to distrust a little that penetrative perspicacity of his, a quality
immoderately developed in him, and perhaps (who knows?) developed by
his business; for he is an optician, daily having to do with the microscope,
telescope, and other inventions for sharpening and extending our natural
sight, thus enabling us mortals (as I once heard an eccentric put it) liberally
to enlarge the field of our original and essential ignorance.

In a word, my excellent friend's private little theory, while, like many a
big and bruited one, not without a fancifully plausible aspect commending
it to the easy of belief, is yet, in my humble judgment—though I would not
hint as much to him for the world—made up in no small part of one element inadmissible in sound philosophy—namely, moonshine.

As to his claim of finding signal evidence for it in the novels aforemen-
tioned, that is another matter. That, I am inclined to think, is little else than
the amiable illusion of a zealous patriot eager to appropriate anything that in
any department may tend to reflect added lustre upon his beloved country.

But, dismissing theory, let me come to a fact, and put it fact-wise; that is to say, a bit bluntly: By the suffrages of seamen and landsmen alike, *The Wreck of the Grosvenor* entitles the author to the naval crown in current literature. That book led the series of kindred ones by the same hand; it is the flagship, and to name it implies the fleet.

Upon the *Grosvenor's* first appearance—in these waters, I was going to say—all competent judges exclaimed, each after his own fashion, something to this effect: The very spit of the brine in our faces! What writer, so thoroughly as this one, knows the sea and the blue water of it; the sailor and the heart of him; the ship, too, and the sailing and handling of a ship? Besides, to his knowledge he adds invention. And, withal, in his broader humane quality he shares the spirit of Richard H. Dana, a true poet's son, our own admirable Man before the Mast.

Well, in view of those unanimous verdicts summed up in the foregoing condensed delivery, with what conscientious satisfaction did I but just now, in the heading of this inscription, salute you, W. C. R., by running up your colours at my fore. Would that the craft thus embravened were one of some tonnage, so that the flag might be carried on a loftier spar, commanding an ampler horizon of your recognising friends.

But the pleasure I take in penning these lines is such that, did a literary inscription imply aught akin to any bestowment, say, or benefit—which it is so very far indeed from implying—then, sinner though I am, I should be tempted to repeat that divine apothegm which, were it repeated forever, would never stale: "It is more blessed to give than to receive." And though by the world at large so unworldly a maxim receives a more hospitable welcome at the ear than in the heart—and no wonder, considering the persistent deceptiveness of so many things mundane—nevertheless, in one province—and I mean no other one than literature—not every individual, I think, at least not every one whose years ought to discharge him from the minor illusions, will dispute it, who has had experience alike in receiving and giving, in one suggestive form or other, sincere contemporary praise. And what, essentially, is such praise? Little else indeed than a less ineloquent form of recognition.

That these thoughts are no spurious ones, never mind from whomsoever proceeding, one naturally appeals to the author of *The Wreck of the Grosvenor*, who, in his duality as a commended novelist and liberal critic in his more especial department, may rightly be deemed an authority well qualified to determine.

Thus far as to matters which may be put into type. For personal feeling the printed page is hardly the place for reiterating that. So I close here as I began, wishing you from my heart the most precious things I know of in this world—Health and Content.

CHAPTER I

THERE WAS every appearance of a south-westerly wind. The coast of France, which had been standing high and shining upon the horizon on the port bow, and so magnified by the clear northerly air that you could discern, even at that distance, the dim emerald sheen of the upper slopes and the streaky shadows thrown by projecting points and elbows on the white ground, was fast fading, though the sun still stood within an hour of its setting beyond the bleak Foreland. The north wind which had rattled us, with an acre of foam at our bows, right away down the river, and had now brought us well abreast of the Gull Light-ship, was dropping fast. There was barely enough air to keep the royals full; and the ship's number, which I had just hoisted at the peak—a string of gaudy flags which made a brilliant figure against the white canvas of the spanker—shook their folds sluggishly.

The whole stretch of scene, from the North Foreland down to the vanishing French headlands miles away yonder, was lovely at that moment, full of the great peace of an ocean falling asleep, of gentle moving vessels, of the solemn gathering of shadows. The town of Deal was upon the starboard bow, a warm cluster of houses, with a windmill on the green hills turning drowsily; here and there a window glittering with a sudden beam of light; an inclined beach in the foreground, with groups of boats high and dry upon it, and a line of foam at its base, which sung upon the shingle so that you could hear it plainly amid intervals of silence on board the ship. The evening sun, shining over the giant brow of the South Foreland, struck the gray outline of the cliff deep in the still water; but the clear red blaze fell far and wide over the dry white downs of Sandwich, and the outlying plains, and threw the distant country into such bold relief against the blue sky that, from the sea, it looked close at hand, and but a short walk from the shore.

There were three or four dozen vessels at anchor in the Downs, waiting for a change of wind or anticipating a dead calm for some hours. A few others, like ourselves, were swimming stealthily over the slack tide, with every foot of their canvas piled upon them to reach safe anchorage before the wind wholly failed and the tide turned. A large ship with her sails stowed, and her masts and rigging showing with the fineness of ivory tracing against the sky, was being towed up Channel, and the slapping of the water by the paddles of the tug, in fast, capricious revolutions, was quite audible, though both ship and steamer were a long league distant. Here and there small boats were rowing away from the anchored ships for the shore. Now and again you could hear the faint distant choruses of the seamen furling a big sail or paying out more cable, the *clank, clank* of which was as pretty as music. Down in the east the heavens were a deep blue, flecked along the water-line with white sails, which glowed in the sunshine like beacons.

I was in a proper mood to appreciate this beautiful, tranquil scene. I was leaving England for a long spell; and the sight of this quiet little town of Deal and the grand old Foreland cliffs shutting out the sky, and the pale white shores we had left far astern, went right to my heart. Well, it was just a quiet leave-taking of the Old Country without words or sobs.

"The pilot means to bring up. I have just heard him tell the skipper to stand by for a light sou'-westerly breeze. This is a *most* confounded nuisance! All hands, perhaps, in the middle watch to get under way."

"I expected as much," said I, turning and confronting a short, squarely built man, with a power of red hair under his chin, and a skin like yellow leather through thirty years' exposure to sun and wind and dirt all over the world. This was the chief mate, Mr. Ephraim Duckling, confidently assumed by me to be a Yankee, though he didn't talk with his nose. I had looked at this gentleman with some doubt when I first met him in the West India Docks. He had blue eyes, with a cast in the port optic. This somehow made him humorous, whether or no, when he meant to be droll, so he had an advantage over other wits. He had hair so dense, coarse, and red withal, that he might safely have been scalped for a doormat. His legs were short, and his body very long and broad, and I guessed his strength by the way his arm filled out, and threatened to burst up the sleeve of his coat when he bent it. So far he had been polite enough to me, in a mighty rough fashion indeed; and as to the men, there had been little occasion for him to give orders as yet.

"I expected as much," said I. "I have been watching the coast of France for the last quarter of an hour, and the moisture has nearly shut it out altogether. I doubt if we'll fetch the Downs before the calm falls."

"There is a little wind over the land, though, or that mill wouldn't be turning."

He turned his eyes up aloft, then went to the ship's side and looked over. I followed him. The clear, green water was slipping slowly past, and now and again a string of seaweed went by, or a big transparent jelly-fish, or a great crab floating on the top of the water. A thin ripple shot out in a semi-circle from the ship's bow, and, at all events, we might tell that we were moving by watching the mast of the Gull Light-ship sliding by the canvas of a vessel hull below the horizon to the eastward of the Sands.

Some of the hands were on the forecastle, looking and pointing toward the shore. Others stood in a group near the galley, talking with the cook, a fat, pale man, with flannel shirt-sleeves rolled above his elbows. The pigs in the long-boat grunted an accompaniment to the chatter of a mass of hens cooped under the long-boat. There was a movement in the sea, and the great sails overhead hung without flapping, and nothing stirred aloft but the light canvas of the royals, which sometimes shook the masts lazily, and with a fine distant sound.

The skipper stood on the weather side of the poop, against the starboard quarter-boat, conversing with the pilot.

Have before you a tall, well-shaped man, with iron-gray hair, a thin aquiline nose, a short, compressed mouth, small dark eyes, which looked at you imperiously from under a perfect hedge of eyebrow, and whitish whiskers, which slanted across his cheeks, dressed in a tall hat, a long monkey-jacket, and square-toed boots.

Captain Coxon was a decidedly good-looking man, not in the smallest degree approaching the conventional notion of the merchant skipper. Happily, it is no condition of good seamanship that a man should have bow-legs, and a coppery nose, and groggy eyes; and that he should prefer a dish of junk to a savory kickshaw, and screeching rum to good wine. I had heard before I joined the "Grosvenor" that Coxon was a smart seaman, though a bully to his men. But this did not prejudice me. I thought I knew my duties well enough to steer clear of his temper; and for the rest, knowing what a sea-faring life is, and how scarcely an hour ever comes without bringing some kind of peril of its own, I would rather any day take service under a bashaw who knew his work than a mild-natured creature who didn't.

The pilot was a little dusky-faced man, with great bushy whiskers, and a large chocolate-colored shawl round his throat, though we were in August. I was watching these two men talking, when Duckling said:

"It's my belief that we shall have trouble with those fellows forward. When we trimmed sail off the North Foreland, did you notice how they went to work?"

"Yes, I did. And I'll tell you what's the matter. As I was going forward after dinner, the cook stopped me, and told me the men were grumbling at the provisions. He said that some of the pork served out stunk, and the bread was moldy and full of weevils."

"Oh, is that it?" said Duckling. "Wait till I get them to sea, and I'll give them my affidavit now, if they like, that *then* they'll have something to cry over. There's a Portuguese fellow among them, and no ship's company can keep honest when one of those devils comes aboard. He'll always find out something that's wrong, and turn and tumble it about until it sets all hands on fire."

He went to the break of the poop and leaned, with his arms squarely set, upon the brass rail, and stared furiously at the group of men about the galley. Some of them grew uneasy, and edged away and got round to the other side of the galley; others, of those who remained, folded their arms and stared at him back, and one of them laughed, which put him in a passion at once.

"You lazy hounds!" he bellowed, in a voice of thunder, "have you nothing to get about? Some of you get that cable range there more over to windward. You, there, get some scrubbing-brushes and clean the long-boat's bottom. Forecastle, there, come down out of that and see that your halyards are clear for running! I'll teach you to palaver the cook, you grumbling villains!" and he made a movement so full of menace that the most obstinate-looking of the fellows got life into them at once, and bustled about.

I looked at the skipper to see what he thought of this little outbreak;

but neither he nor the pilot paid the smallest attention to it; only when Duckling had made an end, the pilot gave an order which was repeated by the chief mate with lungs of brass.

"Aft here, and clew up the mainsail and furl it!"

The men threw down the scrubbing-brushes and chain-hooks which they had picked up, and came aft to the main-deck in a most surly fashion. Duckling eyed them like a mastiff a cat. I noticed some smart-looking hands among them, but they all to a man put on a lubberly air; and as they hauled upon the various ropes which snug a ship's canvas upon the yard preparatory to its being furled, I heard them putting all manner of coarse, violent expressions, having reference to the ship and her officers, into their songs.

They went up aloft slowly and laid out along the yard, grumbling furiously. And to show what bad sailors they were, I suppose, they stowed the sail villainously, leaving bits of the leech sticking out, and making a bunt that must have blown out to the first capful of wind.

I was rather of opinion that Duckling's behavior was founded on traditions which had been surrendered years ago by British seamen to Yankee skipper and mates. He had sailed a voyage in this ship with Coxon, and the captain therefore knew his character. That Coxon should abet Duckling's behavior toward the men by his silence was a bad augury. I reckoned that they understood each other, and that the whole ship's company, including myself, might expect a very uncomfortable voyage.

Meanwhile, Duckling waited until the men were off the yard and descending the rigging; he then roared out, "Furl the mainsail!"

The men stopped coming down, and looked at the yard and then at Duckling; and one of them said, in a sullen tone, "It is furled."

I was amazed to see Duckling hop off the deck on to the poop-rail and spring up the rigging; I thought he was going to thrash the man who had answered; and the man evidently thought so too, for he turned pale, and edged sideways, along the ratline on which he stood, while he held one of his hands clinched. Up went Duckling, shaking the shrouds violently with his ungainly, sprawling way of climbing, and making the men dance upon the ratlines. In a moment he had swung himself upon the foot-rope, and was casting off the yard-arm gaskets. I don't think half a dozen men could have loosed the sail in the time taken by him to do so. Down it fell, and down he came, hand over fist along the main-topsail sheet against the mainmast, bounded up the poop-ladder, and without loss of breath, roared out:

"Furl the mainsail!"

The men seemed inclined to disobey; some of them had already reached the bulwark; but another bellow, accompanied by a gesture, appeared to decide them. They mounted slowly, got upon the yard, and this time did the job in a sailor-like fashion.

"I'm only beginning with them," he said, in his rough voice, to me; and he glanced at Coxon, who gave him a nod and a smile.

The pilot now told me to go forward and see that everything was ready for bringing up. We were drawing close to the Downs, but the air had quite died out and the sea stretched like oil to the horizon. I don't know what was giving us way, for the light sails aloft hung flat, and the smoke of a steam-boat, with its two funnels only showing away across the Channel, went straight up into the sky. There must however have been a faint, imperceptible tide running, but it took us another half hour to reach the point where the pilot had resolved to bring up, and by that time the sun had sunk behind the great headland beyond Deal, and was casting a broad crimson glare upon the sea.

The royals and top-gallantsails were clewed up and furled, and then the order was given to let go the top-sail halyards. Down came the three heavy yards rumbling along the masts, with the sound of chain rattling over sheaves. The canvas fell into festoons, and the pilot called:

"All ready forrard?"

"All ready."

"Let go the anchor!"

"Stand clear of the cable!" I shouted.

Whack! whack! went the carpenter's driving-hammer. A moment's pause, then a tremendous splash, and the cable rushed with a hoarse outcry through the hawser-hole.

When this job was over I waited on the forecastle to superintend the stowing of the sails forward. The men worked briskly enough, and I heard one of them who was stowing the fore-topmast stay-sail say "that it was good luck the skipper had brought up. He didn't think he'd be such a fool."

This set me wondering what their meaning could be; but I thought it best to take no notice, nor repeat what I had heard, as I considered that the less Mr. Duckling had to say to the men the better we should all get on.

It was half past seven by the time the sails were furled, and the decks cleared of the ropes. The hands went below to tea, and I was walking aft when the cook came out of the galley, and said:

"Beg your pardon, sir; would you mind tasting of this?" And he handed me a bit of the ship's biscuit. I smelled it and found it moldy, and put a piece in my mouth, but soon spit it out.

"I can't say much for this, cook," said I.

"It's not fit for dogs," replied the cook. "But so far as I've seen, all the provisions is the same. The sugar's like mud, and the molasses is full of grit; and though I have been to sea, man and boy, two and twenty year I never saw tea like what they've got on board this ship. It ain't tea—it makes the liquor yaller. It's shavings, and wot I say is, regular tea *ain't* shavings."

"Well, let the men complain to the captain," I answered. "He can report to the owners, and get the ship's stores condemned."

"It's my belief they was condemned afore they came on board," answered the cook. "I'll bet any man a week's grog that they wos bought cheap in a dock-yard sale o' rotten grub by order o' the Admirality."

"Give me a biscuit," said I, "and I'll show it to the captain."

He took out one from a drawer in which he kept the dough for the cuddy's use, and I put it in my pocket and went aft.

CHAPTER II

I WILL here pause to describe the ship, which, being the theater of much that befell me which is related in this book, I should place before your eyes in as true a picture as I can draw.

The "Grosvenor," then, was a small, full-rigged ship of five hundred tons, painted black with a single white streak below her bulwarks. She was a soft-wood vessel, built in Halifax, Nova Scotia. Her lines were very perfect.

Indeed, the beauty of her hull, her lofty masts, stayed with as great perfec-
tion as a man-of war's, her graceful figure-head, sharp, yacht-like bows, and
round stern had filled me with admiration when I first beheld her. Her decks
were white and well-kept. She had a poop and a top-gallant forecastle, both
of which I think the builder might have spared, as she was scarcely big
enough for them. There was a good deal of brass work on her after-decks,
and more expense than she deserved, from the perishable nature of the
material of which she was constructed, had been lavished upon her in respect of deck ornamentation. Her richly carved wheel, brass belaying pins,
brass capstan, brass binnacle, handsome sky-lights, and other such details,
made her look like a gay pleasure-vessel rather than a sober trader. Her cuddy,
however, was plain enough, containing six cabins, including the pantry. The
wood-work was cheaply varnished mahogany; a fixed table ran from the
mizzen-mast to within a few feet of the cuddy front, and on either side this
table was a stout hair-covered bench. Abaft the mizzen-mast were the two
cabins respectively occupied by Captain Coxon and Mr. Duckling. My own
cabin was just under the break of the poop, so that from the window in it
I could look out upon the main deck. A couple of broad sky-lights, well protected with brass wire fenders, let plenty of light into the cuddy; and
swinging trays and lamps, and red curtains to draw across the sky-lights when
the sun beat upon them, completed the furniture of this part of the vessel.

We could very well have carried a few passengers, and I never learned
why we did not; but it may, perhaps, have happened that nobody was going
our way at the time we were advertised to sail.

We were bound to Valparaiso with a general cargo, consisting chiefly of
toys, hardware, Birmingham and Sheffield cutlery, and metal goods, and a
stock of piano-fortes. The ship, to my thinking, was too deep, as though the
owners had compensated themselves for the want of passenger-money by
"taking it out" in freight. I readily foresaw that we should be a wet ship, and
that we should labor more than was comfortable in a heavy sea. The steerage was packed with light goods—bird-cages, and such things—but space
was left in the 'tween deck, though the cargo came flush with the deck in
the hold.

However, in spite of being overloaded, the "Grosvenor" had beaten
everything coming down the river that day. Just off the Reculvers, for example, when we had drawn the wind a trifle more abeam, we overhauled a

steamer. She was pretty evidently a fast screw, and her people grew jealous when they saw us coming up astern, and piled up the fires, but could not stop us from dropping her, as neatly as *she* dropped an old coal brig that was staggering, near the shore, under dirty canvas. But she smothered us with her smoke as we passed her to leeward and I dare say they were glad to see the dose we got for our pains.

I came aft, as I have said, after leaving the baker, with the biscuit in my pocket, and got upon the poop. The skipper had gone below with the pilot, and they were having tea. Duckling was walking the poop, swearing now and again at a couple of ordinary seamen, whom he had set to work to flemish-coil the ropes along the deck, for no other reason than that he might put as much work on them as he could invent—for this flemish-coiling was of no use under the circumstances, and is only fit for Sundays on passenger ships, when you want to please the ladies with "tidy" effects, or when a vessel is in port. A watch had been set forward, and having cast a look up aloft to see that everything was trim, I went down the companion-ladder to the cuddy, followed by Duckling.

The interior of the cabin looked like some old Dutch painting, for the plain mahogany wood-work gave the place an antique air. The lamps were alight, for it was dusk here, though daylight was still abroad upon the sea; and the lamplight imparted a grave, old-fashioned coloring to the things it shone upon. The skipper sat near the mizzen-mast, stirring the sugar in a cup of tea. He looked better without than with his hat; his forehead was high, though rather peaked, and his iron-gray hair, parted amidships and brushed carelessly over his ears, gave him a look of dignity. The coarse little pilot was eating bread and butter voraciously, his great whiskers moving as he worked his jaws.

Duckling and I seated ourselves at the table, and I had some difficulty to prevent myself from laughing at the odd figures Duckling and the pilot made side by side—the one with his whiskers working like a pair of brushes, and the other with that door-mat of red hair on his head, and the puzzling cast of the eye that made me always doubt which one I should address when I tried to look him full in the face.

"There's a breeze coming up from the sou'west, sir," said Duckling to the captain. "The water's darkish out in that quarter, but I don't think there's enough of it to swing the ship."

"Let it come favorable, and we'll get under way at once," answered Coxon. "I had a spell of this sort of thing last year—for ten days, wasn't it, Duckling?—because I neglected a light air that sprung up south-easterly. I thought it couldn't have held ten minutes, but it would have carried me well away to the French side before it failed, and made me a free passage down, for the wind came fresh from south by west and deadlocked me here. Mr. Royle, what's going forward among the men? I heard them cursing pretty freely when they were up aloft."

"They are complaining of the ship's provisions, sir," I replied. "The cook gave me a biscuit just now, and I promised to show it to you."

Saying which, I pulled the biscuit out of my pocket and put it upon the table. He contracted his bushy eyebrows, and without looking at the biscuit, stared angrily at me.

"Hark you, Mr. Royle!" said he, in a voice I found detestable for the sneering contempt it conveyed, "I allow no officer that sails under me to become a confidant of my crew. Do you understand?"

I flushed up as I answered that I was no confidant of the crew; that the cook had stopped me to explain the men's grievance, and that I had asked him for a biscuit to show the captain as a sample of the ship's bread which the steward was serving out.

"It's very good bread," said the obsequious pilot, taking up the biscuit while he wiped the butter out of the corners of his mouth.

"Eat it then!" I exclaimed.

"Damnation! eat it yourself!" cried Coxon, furiously. "You're used to that kind of fare, I should think, and like it, or you wouldn't be bringing it into the cuddy in your pocket, would you, sir?"

I made him no answer. I could see by the expression in Duckling's face that he sided with the skipper, and I thought it would be bad lookout for me to begin the voyage with a quarrel.

"I'll trouble you to put that biscuit where you took it from," the captain continued, with an enraged nod in the direction of my pocket, "and return it to the blackguard who gave it, and tell him to present Captain Coxon's respects to the men, and inform them that if they object to the ship's bread, they're welcome to take their meals along with the pigs in the long-boat. The butcher'll serve them."

"Mr. Royle tells me they find the meat worse than the bread," said Mr. Duckling. "I guess the hounds who grumble most are men who have shipped out of workhouses, where their grub was burned burgoo twice a day, and a lick of brimstone to make it easy."

He laughed loudly at his own humor, and was joined by the pilot who rubbed his hands, and swore that he hadn't heard a better joke for years.

I made what dispatch I might with my tea, not much desiring to remain in company with Coxon in his present temper. I fancy he grew a little ashamed of himself presently, for he softened his voice and now and again glanced across at me. The pilot looking up through the sky-light called attention to the vane at the main-royal mast-head which was fluttering to a light air from the south-west, as had been predicted, and as I could tell by referring to the tell-tale compass, which was swung just over where Coxon was seated. Then Coxon and his chief mate talked of the time they meant to occupy in the run to Valparaiso. I understood the former to say that his employers had given him eight weeks to do it in. I should like to have said that, had they added another two to that, they would still have been imposing enough upon us all to keep us alive. But at this point I quitted the table, giving Coxon a bow as I rose which he returned with a sort of half-ashamed stiffness, and repaired to my cabin to get my pipe for a half-hour's enjoyment of the beautiful autumn evening on deck.

I don't think tobacco has the same flavor ashore that it has at sea. Something in the salt air brings out the full richness and aroma of it. A few whiffs on the main-deck came like oil upon the agitation of my mind, ruffled by Coxon's impertinence and temper. I stepped on to the forecastle to see that the riding lamps were all right, and that there was a man on the lookout. The crew were in the forecastle talking in subdued voices, and the hot air that came up through the fore-scuttle was intolerable as I passed it. I then regained the poop, and seated myself on the rail among the shadows of the backstays leading from the main-royal and top-gallant masts.

The sun had gone down some time now, and only faint traces of daylight lowered in the westward. The light on the South Foreland emitted a most beautiful, clear, and brilliant beam, and diffused a broad area of misty radiance on the land around. The light-beacons were winking along the Goodwin Sands, and pretty close at hand were the lights of Deal, a pale, fine constellation, which made the country all the darker for their presence. The moon would not rise until after nine, but the heavens were spangled with stars, some so lustrous that the calm sea mirrored them in cones of silver; and from time to time flashing shooting-stars chased across the sky, and with their blue fires offered a peculiar contrast to the eye with the yellow and red lights on the water.

There was a little air moving from the southward, but so light as scarcely to be noticeable to any man but a sailor awaiting a change. The vessels at anchor near us loomed large in the starlighted gloom that over-spread the face of the sea. Lights flitted upon them; and the voices of men singing, the jingling of a concertina or a fiddle, the rumbling of yards low-ered aboard some new-comers which could not be descried, and now and again the measured splash of oars, were sounds which only served to give a deeper intensity to the solemn calm of the night.

The inmates of the cuddy still kept their seats, and their voices came out through the open sky-lights. I heard Captain Coxon say,

"I should like to know what sort of a fellow they have given me for a second mate. He strikes me as coming the gentleman a trifle, don't he, Duckling?"

To which the other replied, "He seems a civil-spoken young man, and up to his work. But I guess there's too much molasses mixed with his blood to suit my book. He wants a New Orleans training, as my old skipper used to say. Do you know what that means, sir?" evidently addressing the pilot. "Well, it means a knife in your ribs when you're not disposed to hurry, and a knuckle-duster in the shape of a marline-spike down your throat if you stop to arguefy."

The pilot laughed, and said, "Here's your health, sir. Men of your kind are wanted nowadays, sir."

It was plain from this speech that the pilot had exchanged his tea for something stronger. The captain here began to speak, but I couldn't catch his words, though I strained my ears, as I was anxious to gain all the insight I could into his character, that I might know how to shape my behavior.

I say this for a very weighty reason—I was entirely dependent on the profession I had adopted. I knew it was in the power of any captain I sailed with to injure me, and perhaps ruin my prospects. Everything in sea-faring life depends upon reports and testimonials; and in these days, when the demand for officers is utterly disproportionate to the immense supply, owners are only too willing to listen to objections, and take any skipper's word as an excuse to decline your services or get rid of you.

Neither the captain nor Mr. Duckling appeared on deck again. The pilot came up shortly after one bell (half past eight) and looked about him for a few minutes. The tide had swung the ship with her stern up Channel. He went and looked over the side, and then had a stare at Deal, but took no notice of me, whom he could very plainly see, and returned below.

I lingered three-quarters of an hour on deck, during which time the little sigh of wind that had come from the south-west died out, and a most perfect calm fell. The large stars burned with amazing brilliancy and power, and I thought it possible that the wind might go to the eastward. This idea detained me on deck longer than I had meant to stop, as I thought it would do me no ill service if I should be the first to report a fair wind to the skipper, and show myself smart in getting the hands up. Perhaps the moon would bring a breeze with her, and as she rose at twenty minutes past nine, I filled another pipe to await her coming.

As I struck a match, the steward came half-way up the poop-ladder to tell me the spirits were on the table.

"Did the captain send you?" I asked.

"No, sir," he answered. "I thought I'd let you know, as they'll be cleared away after nine, and my orders are not to serve them again when once they're stowed away for the night. That's the captain's rule."

"All right," said I. Another time I should have gone below and had my glass of grog; but I considered it my best policy to keep clear of Coxon until the temper that had been excited by unfortunate production of the ship's biscuit was cooled down.

I took some turns along the deck, and shortly after nine one of the lamps in the cuddy was extinguished, and on looking through the sky-light I found that the three men had left the table. There was a man pacing to and fro the forecastle, and I could just make out his figure against the stars which gleamed and throbbed right down to the horizon. The rest of the crew had evidently turned in, for I heard no voices; and now that the talking which had been going on in the cuddy no longer vexed the ear with rough accents, a profound silence and peace came down upon the ship. Around me the anchored vessels gloomed like phantoms; the sea unrolled its dark unbreathing surface into the visionary distances; nothing sounded from the shore but the murmur of the summer surf upon the shingle. One might have said that the spirit of life had departed from the earth; that nothing lived but the stars, which looked down upon a scene as impalpable and elusive as a dream.

At last up rose the moon. She made her coming apparent by paling the stars in the southern sky, then by projecting a white mist of light over the horizon. Anon her upper limb, red as fire, jetted upward, and the full orb, vast and feverish as the setting sun, sailed out of the sea, most slowly and solemnly, lifting with her a black mist, that belted her like a circle of smoke; this vanished, and by degrees, perceptible to the eye, her color changed; the red chastened into pearl, her disk grew smaller and soon she was well above the horizon, shining with a most clear and silvery splendor, and making the sea beneath her lustrous with mild light. But not a breath of air followed her coming. The ships in the Downs caught the new light, and their yards showed like streaks of pearl against the night. The red lights of the Goodwin Sands dwindled before the pure, far-reaching radiance into mere floating sparks of fire. The heavens were cloudless, and the sea wonderfully calm. I might keep watch all night, and still have nothing to report; so, knocking the ashes out of my pipe, I descended the poop-ladder and entered my cabin.

CHAPTER III

I HAD slung a cot, although there was a good mahogany bunk in the cabin. No sensible person would sleep in a bunk at sea when he could swing in a hammock or cot. Suppose the bunk is athwartship; when the vessel goes about you must shift your pillow; and very often she will go about in your watch below and catch you asleep, so that when you wake you find your feet are in the air, and all the blood in your body in your head. When I first went to sea I slept in a 'thwartship bunk. The ship was taken aback one night when I was asleep, and they came and roared, "All hands shorten sail!" down the booby-hatch. I heard the cry and tried to get out of my bed, but my head was jammed to leeward by the weight of my body, and I could not move. Had the ship foundered, I should have gone to the bottom, in bed, helpless. Always after that I slept in a hammock.

The watch on deck had orders to call the captain if a change of wind came; also I knew that the pilot would be up, sniffing about, off and on through the night; so I turned in properly and slept soundly until two; when waking up, I drew on my small clothes and went on deck, where I found Duckling mousing about in the moonshine in a pair of yellow flannel drawers, he having, like myself, come up to see if any wind was stirring. He looked like a new kind of monkey in his tight white rig and immense head of hair. "No wind, no wind!" he muttered, in a sleepy grumble, and then went below with a run, nearly tumbling, in fact, head over heels down the companion-ladder.

I took a turn forward to see if the riding lights burned well and the man on the lookout was awake. The decks were wet with dew, and the moon was now hanging over the South Foreland. The sky was still cloudless, and not a breath of air to be felt. This being the case I went back to my cot.

When I next awoke I found my cot violently swinging. I thought for the moment that we were under way and in a heavy sea; but on looking over I saw Mr. Duckling, who exclaimed, "Out with you, Mr. Royle! There's a good breeze from the east'ard. Look alive and call the boatswain to pipe all hands."

Hearing this, I was wide awake at once, and in a few minutes was making my way to the boatswain's cabin, a deck-house on the port side against the forecastle. He and the carpenter were fast asleep in bunks placed one over the other. I laid hold of the boatswain's leg, which hung over the bunk—both he and the carpenter had turned in "all standing," as they say at sea—and shook it. His great, brown, hairy face came out of the bolster in which it was buried; he then threw over his other leg and sat upright.

"All hands, sir?"

"Yes; look sharp, bo's'n."

He was about to speak, but stopped short and said, "Ay, ay, sir"; whereupon I hurried aft.

It was twenty minutes past five by the clock in the cuddy. The sun had been risen half an hour, and was already warming the decks. But there was a fine breeze; not from the eastward, as Duckling had said, but well to the northward of east—which brought ripe, fresh morning smells from the land with it, and made the water run in little leaps of foam against the ship's side.

Captain Coxon and the pilot were both on the poop, and as I came up the former called out,

"Is the boatswain awake yet?"

"Yes, sir," I answered, and dived into my cabin to finish dressing. I heard the boatswain's pipe sound, followed by the roar of his voice summoning the hands to weigh anchor. My station was on the forecastle, and thither I went. But none of the hands had emerged as yet, the only man seen being the fellow on the lookout. All about us, the outward bound vessels were taking advantage of the wind; some of them were already standing away, others were sheeting canvas; the clinking of the windlasses was incessant, and several Deal boats were driving under their lugs among the shipping.

"Mr. Royle," cried out the captain, "jump below, will you, and see what those fellows are about."

I went to the fore-scuttle and peered into it bawling, "Below there!"

"There's no use singing out," said a voice; "we don't mean to get the ship under way until you give us something fit to eat."

"Who was that who spoke?" I called. "Show yourself, my man."

A fellow came and stood under the fore-scuttle, and looking up, said, in a bold, defiant way:

"I spoke—'Bill Marling, able seaman.'"

"Am I to tell the captain that you refuse to turn to?"

"Ay! and tell him we'd rather have six months of chokee than one mouthful of his d——d provisions," he answered; and immediately a lot of voices took up the theme, and as I left the forecastle to deliver the message, I heard the men cursing and abusing us all violently, the foreigners particularly—that is, the Portuguese and a Frenchman, who was a half negro —swearing in the worst English words and worst English pronunciation, shrilly and fiercely.

Coxon pretty well knew what was coming. He and Duckling stood together on the poop, and I delivered the men's message from the quarter-deck.

Coxon was in a great rage, and quite pale with it. The expression in his face was really devilish. His lips became bloodless, and when he glanced his eyes around and saw the other ships taking advantage of the fine breeze and sailing away, he seemed deprived of speech. He had sense enough, however, with all his fury, to know that in his case no good could come from passion. He seized the brass rail with both hands, and made a gesture with his head to signify that I should draw nearer.

"Who was the man who gave you that message, sir?"

"A fellow who called himself Bill Marling."

"Do they refuse to leave the forecastle?"

"They refuse to get the ship under way."

"Is the boatswain disaffected?"

"No, sir; but I fancy he knows the men's minds."

He turned to Mr. Duckling.

"If the boatswain is sound, we four ought to be able to make the scoundrels turn to."

This was like suggesting a hand-to-hand fight—four against twelve, and Duckling had the sense to hold his tongue. The boatswain was standing near the long-boat, looking aft, and Coxon suddenly called to him, "Lead the men aft."

I now thought proper to get upon the poop; and in a short time the men came aft in twos and threes. They were thirteen in all, including the carpenter, four ordinary seamen, the cook, and the cook's mate. The boatswain kept forward.

There was a capstan just abaft the mainmast, and here the men assembled. There was not much in the situation to move one's gravity, and yet I could scarcely forbear smiling when I looked down upon their faces fraught with expressions so various in kind, though all denoting the same feelings. Some were regular old stagers, fellows who had been to sea all their lives, with great bare arms tattooed with crucifixes, bracelets, and other such devices, in canvas or blanket breeches and flannel shirts, with the invariable belt and knife around their middle. Some, to judge from their clothes, had evidently signed articles in an almost destitute condition, their clothes being complete suits of patches, and their faces pale and thin. The foreigners were, of course, exceedingly dirty; and the "Portugee's" wonderfully ugly countenance was hardly improved by the stout silver ear-rings with which his long ears were ornamented.

The first movement of mirth in me, however, was but transient. Pity came uppermost in a few moments. I do think there is something touching in the simplicity of sailors, in the child-like way in which they go about to explain a grievance and get it redressed. They have few words and little experience outside the monotonous life they follow; they express themselves ill, are subdued by a harsh discipline on board, or by acts of cruelty which could not be tolerated in any kind of service ashore; the very negroes and savages of distant countries have more interest taken in them by the people of England than sailors, for whom scarcely a charity exists; the laws which deal with their insubordination are unnecessarily severe; and of the persons who are appointed to inquire into the causes of insubordination, scarce five in the hundred are qualified by experience, sympathy, or disinterestedness to do sailors justice.

Some such thoughts as these were in my mind as I stood watching the men on the quarter-deck.

Coxon, with his hand still clutching the rail, said: "The boatswain has piped you out to get the ship under way. Do you refuse?"

The man named Bill Marling made a step forward. The men had evidently constituted him spokesman.

"We don't mean to work this here ship," said he, "until better food is put aboard. The biscuits are not fit for dogs; and I say that the pork stinks, and that the molasses is grits."

"That's the truth," said a voice; and the Portuguese nodded and gesticulated violently.

"You blackguards!" burst out the captain, losing all self-control. "What do you know about food for dogs? You're not as good as dogs to know. Aren't you shipped out of filthy Ratcliffe Highway lodgings, where the ship's bread and meat and molasses would be eaten by you as d——d fine luxuries, you lubbers? Turn to at once and man the windlass, or I'll find a way to make you!"

"We say," said the spokesman, pulling a biscuit out of his bosom and holding it up, "that we don't mean to work the ship until you give us better bread than this. It's moldy and full of weevils. Put the bread in the sun and see the worms crawl out of it."

"Will the skipper pitch the cuddy bread overboard and eat ourn?" demanded a rough voice.

"And the cuddy meat along with it!" exclaimed a man, a short, powerfully built fellow with a crisp, black beard and woolly hair, holding up a piece of pork on the blade of a knife. "Let Captain Coxon smell this."

The captain looked at them for a few moments with flashing eyes, then turned and walked right aft with Duckling. Here they were joined by the pilot, and a discussion took place among them that lasted some minutes. Meanwhile I paced to and fro athwart the poop. The men talked in low tones among themselves, but none of them seemed disposed to give in. For my own part, I rather fancied that though their complaint of the provisions was justifiable enough, it was advanced rather as a sound excuse for declining to sail with a skipper and chief mate whose behavior so far toward them was a very mild suggestion of the treatment they might expect when they should be fairly at sea, and in these two men's power. I heard my name mentioned among them, and one or two remarks made about me, but not uncomplimentary. The cook had probably told them I was well-disposed, and I believe that some of them would have harangued me had I appeared willing to listen.

Presently Mr. Duckling left the captain and ordered the men to go forward. He then called the boatswain, and turning to me, said that I was to be left in charge of the ship with the pilot while he and the captain went ashore.

The boatswain came aft and got into the quarter-boat which Duckling and I lowered; and I then towed her by her painter to the gangway, where Duckling and the captain got into her.

As no signal was hoisted, I was at a loss to conceive what course Captain Coxon proposed to adopt. Duckling and the boatswain, each took an oar while Coxon steered, and away they went, sousing over the little waves which the fresh land breeze had set running along the river.

By this time all the outward bound ships had got their anchors, up, and were standing down Channel. Some of them which had got away smartly were well around the Foreland, and we were the only one of them all that still kept the ground. Captain Coxon's rage and disappointment were, of course, intelligible enough; for time to him was not only money, but credit—I mean that every day he could save in making the run to Valparaiso would improve him in his employers' estimation.

The men peered over the bulwarks at the departing boat, wondering what the skipper would do. There was a tide running to the southward, and they had to keep the boat heading toward Sandwich. Strong as the boatswain was, I could see what a much stronger oar Duckling pulled, by the way the boat's head swerved under the strokes.

I stood watching them for some time, and then joined the pilot, who had lighted a pipe and sat smoking on the taff-rail. He gave me a civil nod, being well disposed enough, now that Coxon was not by, and made some remark about the awkwardness of the men refusing work when the breeze was so good.

"True," said I; "but I think you'll find that the magistrates will give it in their favor. There's some mistake about the ship's stores. Such bread as the men have had served out to them ought never to have been put on board, and the steward has owned to me that it's all alike."

"The captain don't intend to let it come before the magistrates," answered the pilot, with a wink, and pulling his pipe from his mouth to inspect the bowl. "He wants to be off, and means to telegraph for another crew and turn those fellows yonder adrift."

"Won't he ship some better provisions?"

"I don't know, sir. Preehaps he's satisfied that the provisions is good enough for the men, and preehaps he isn't. Leastways he'll not be persuaded contrarily to his belief."

"So, then, the police are to have nothing to do with this matter, and the stores will be retained for another crew?"

"That's as it may be."

"There will be a mutiny before we get to Valparaiso."

"Something'll happen, I dare say."

I not only considered the captain's behavior in this matter bad morally, but extremely impolitic. His motives were plain enough. The stores had been shipped as a cheap lot for the men to eat; and I dare say the understanding between Coxon and the owners was that the stores should not be

changed. This view would account for his going on shore to telegraph for a
new crew, since sending the old crew about their business would promise
a cheaper issue than signaling for the police and bringing the offenders
before the magistrates, and causing the vessel to be detained while inquiries
were made. But that he would be imperiling the safety of his vessel by shipping a fresh crew without exchanging the bad stores for good, was quite
certain, and I wondered that so old a sailor as he should be such a fool as
not to foresee some disastrous end to his own or his owner's contemptible
cheese-paring policy.

However, I had not so good an opinion of the pilot's taciturnity as to
make him a confidant in these thoughts; we talked on other matters for a
few minutes, and he then went below, and after a while, on passing the
sky-light, I saw him, stretched on one of the cuddy benches sound asleep.

The Downs now presented a very different appearance from what they
had exhibited an hour before. There were not above four vessels at anchor,
and of those which had filled and stood away scarce half a dozen were in
sight. These were some lumbering old brigs with a bark among them, with
the water almost level with their decks; picturesque enough, however, in
the glorious morning light, as they went washing solemnly away, showing
their square sterns to the wind. A prettier sight was a fine schooner yacht
coming up fast from the southward, with her bow close to the wind; and
over to the eastward the sea was alive with smacks, their sails shining like
copper, standing apparently for the North Sea.

The land all about Walmer was of an exquisite soft green, and in the
breezy summer light Deal looked the quaintest, snuggest little town in the
world.

A little after eight the steward called me down to breakfast, where I
found the pilot impatiently sniffing an atmosphere charged with the aroma
of broiled ham and strong coffee. I own, as I helped myself to a rasher and
contrasted the good provisions with which cuddy table was furnished with
the bad food served to the men, I was weak enough to sympathize very
cordially with the poor fellows. The steward told me that not a man among
them had broke his fast; this he had been told by the cook, who added that
they would rather starve than eat the biscuit that had been served out to
them. Such was their way of showing themselves wronged; and the steward

declared that he did not half like bringing our breakfast from the galley, for the men, when they smelled the ham and saw him going aft with a tin of hot rolls, became so forcible in their language that he every moment, during his walk along the main deck, expected to feel himself seized behind and pitched overboard.

"It's the old story, sir," said the Pilot, who was making an immense breakfast, "and it's true enough what Mr. Duckling said last night, which I thought uncommonly good. They ship sailors out of places where there's nothing to be seen but rags and rum—rum and rags, sir; they give 'em a good cabin to sleep in, pounds sterling a month, grog every day at eight bells, plenty of good livin', considering what they was, where they come from, and what they desarves; and what do they do but turn up their noses at food which they'd crawl upon their knees to get in their kennels ashore, and swear that they won't do ne'er a stroke of work unless they're bribed by the very best of everything. What do they want?—lobsters for breakfast, and wenison and plum-duff for dinner and chops and tamater-sauce for supper? It's the ruination of owners, sir, are these here new-fangled ideas; and I don't say—mind, I don't say that it don't go agin pilots as a body. A pilot can't do his dooty as he ought when he's got such crews as sarve nowadays to order about. Here am I stuck here, with a job that I knows of waitin' and waitin' for me at Gravesend; and all because this blessed ship's company wants wenison and plum-duff for dinner!"

He helped himself to a large slice of broiled ham and devoured it with sullen energy.

I could have said a word for the men, but guessed that my remarks would be repeated to the skipper; and since I could not benefit them, there was no use in injuring myself.

After breakfast I went upon deck, and saw a Deal boat making for the ship. She came along in slashing style, under her broad lug—what splendid boats those Deal luggers are, and how superbly the fellows handle them!— and in a short time was near enough to enable me to see that she towed our quarter-boat astern, and that Coxon and Duckling were among her occupants. I went to the gangway to receive her; she fell off, then luffed, running a fine semicircle; down dropped her lug, her mizzen brought her right to, and she came alongside with beautiful precision, stopping under the gangway like a carriage at your door.

I caught the line that was flung from her, took a turn with it, and then Coxon and the chief mate stepped on board. The moment he touched the deck, Coxon called to his men, who were hanging about the forecastle.

"Get your traps together and out with you! If ever a man among you stops in my ship five minutes, I'll fling him overboard."

With which terrible threat he walked into the cuddy. Duckling remained at the gangway to see the crew leave the ship. The poor fellows were all ready. They had made up their minds to go ashore, but hardly knew under what circumstances. I had noticed the pressing forward to look into the boat when she came alongside no doubt expecting to see the uniform of a police superintendent there. The presence of such an official would, of course, have mean imprisonment to them; they would have been locked up until brought before the magistrates. They were clearly disappointed by the skipper's procedure, for as they came to the gangway, carrying their bags and chests, all kinds of remarks, expressive of their opinion on the matter, were uttered by them.

"The old blackguard!" said one flinging his bag into the boat, and lingering before Duckling and myself in order to deliver his observations, "he hasn't the pluck to have us tried. Pitch us overboard! let him try his (etc.) hand upon the littlest of us! I'd take six months and thank 'em, just to warm my fist on his (etc.) face!" and so forth.

Duckling was wise to hold his peace. The men were furious enough to have massacred him had he opened his lips.

The older hands got into the boat in silence, but none of the rest left the ship without some candid expression of his feelings. One said he'd gladly pay a pound for leave to set fire to the ship. Another called her a floating workhouse. A third hoped that the vessel would be sunk, and the brutes commanding her drowned before this time to-morrow. Every evil wish that malice and rage could invent was hurled at the vessel and at those who remained in her. In after days I recalled that beautiful morning, the picture of the lugger alongside the ship, the hungry, ill-used men with their poor packs going over the vessel's side, and the curses they pronounced as they left us.

An incident followed the entry of the last of the men in the boat.

The sail was hoisted, the rope that held the boat let her go, and her head was shoved off; when the "Portugee," in the excitement and fury of his feelings, drew in his breath and his cheeks, and spit with tremendous energy at Duckling, who was watching him; but the missile fell short; in a word, he spit full in the face of one of the old hands, who instantly knocked him down. He tumbled head over heels among the feet of the crowd of men, while Duckling roared out, "If the man who knocked that blackguard down will return to his duty, I'll be his friend." But all the answer he got was a roar which resembled in sound and character the mingled laughter and groans of a large mob. The fresh wind caught and filled the sail, the boat bounded away under the pressure, and in a few minutes was a long distance out of hail.

CHAPTER IV

A FRESH crew came down from London the following morning in charge of a crimp.

Duckling went ashore to meet them at the railway station, and they came off in the same boat that had landed the others on the previous day.

They appeared much the same sort of men as those who had left us; badly clothed for the most part, and but four of them had sea-chests, the rest bringing bags. There was one very big man among them, a fellow that dwarfed the others; he held himself erect, wore good boots, and might very well have passed for an escaped Life Guardsman, were it not for an indescribable *something* in his gait and the way in which he hung his hands, that marked him for a Jack.

Another fellow I noticed, as he scrambled over the ship's side and sung out, in tones as hoarse as a raven's, to pitch him up "blooming portmantey," had a very extraordinary face, altogether out of proportion with his head, being, I dare say, a full third too small. The back of the skull was immense, and was covered with hair coarser than Duckling's—as coarse as hemp-yards. This grew down beside his ears, and got mixed up with his streaky whiskers which bound up the lower part of his face like a tar poultice. Out of this circle of hair looked a face as small as a young boy's; little closed Chinese eyes, a bit of a pug-nose, and a square mouth, open so as to show that he wanted four front teeth. The frame belonging to this remarkable head and face was singularly vigorous, though grievously misshapen. His long arms went far down his legs; his back, without having a hump, was as round as a shell, and he looked as if he measured a yard and a half from shoulder to shoulder. I watched this strange-looking creature with great curiosity until I lost sight of him in the forecastle.

The men bustled over the side with great alacrity, bawling for their bags and property to be handed up in a great variety of accents. There were two Dutchmen, and a copper-colored man, with African features, among them; the rest were English.

The crimp remained in the boat, watching the men go on board. He was from the other side of Jordan. His woolly hair was soaked with oil, and shone resplendent in the sun; the oil seemed to have got into his hat, too, for that had a most fearful polish. He wore a great-coat that came down to his shins, and beneath this he exhibited a pair of blue serge breeches, terminating in boots as greasy as his hat. He was genteel enough to wear kid gloves; but the imagination was not to be seduced by such an artifice from picturing the dirt under the gloves.

I knew something of crimps, and amused myself with an idle speculation or two while watching the man. This was a fellow who would probably keep a lodging-house for sailors in some dirty little street leading out of the West India Dock Road. His terms would be very easy; seven shillings a week for board and lodging, and every gentleman to pay for extras. He would probably have two or three amiable and obliging sisters, daughters, or nieces living with him, knowing the generous and blind confidence Jack reposes in the endearments of the soft sex, and how very prodigally he will pay for them.

So this greasy miscreant's dirty West India Dock Road lodging-house for sailors would always be pretty full, and he would never have much difficulty in mustering a crew when he got an order to raise one. Of course it would pay him, as it pays other crimps, to let lodgings to sailors, so as to have them always about him when a crew is wanted: for will he not obligingly cash their advance notes for them, handing them say, thirty shillings for three pounds ten? "What do I do with this dirty risk?" he will exclaim, when Jack expostulates. "Supposing you cut stick? I lose my money. I only do this to obleege you. Go into the street," he cries, pretending to get in a passion, "and see what you'll get for your dirty piece of paper. You'll be comin' back to me on your bended knees, with tears a-tricklin' and runnin' over your cheeks, axing my parding for me and willin' to say a prayer of thankfulness for me bein' put in your way. You'll want a bag for your clothes, and here's one, dirt cheap, five and a 'arf. And you can't go to sea with one pair o' brigs, and you shall have these beauties a bargain—come, fourteen and six, for you, and I'll ask you not to say what you gave for 'em, or I shall have four hundred and fifty-vun customers comin' in a rage to tell me I'm a villin for charging of 'em a guinea for the same article. And here's a first-class knife and belt—something fit for the heye to rest upon—honestly vorth 'arf a sovrin, which I'll make you a present of for a bob; and if you say a word I'll take everything back, for I *can't* stand ingratitood."

Our friend watched the crew over the vessel's side with jealous eyes, for had they refused at the last moment to remain in the ship, he would have been a loser to the amount he had given them for their advance notes. He looked really happy when the last man was out of the lugger and her head turned for the shore. He raised his greasy hat to Duckling, and his hair shone like polished mahogany in the sun.

"Aft here, some of you, and ship this gangway. Boatswain, pipe all hands to get the ship under way," cried Duckling; and turning to me with a wink, he added, "If the grub is going to bring more rows, we must fight 'em on the high seas."

There was a little breeze from the south-east; quite enough to keep the smaller sails full and give us headway against the tide that was running up Channel. The men, zealous as all new comers are, hastened briskly out of the forecastle on hearing Duckling's voice and the boatswain's whistle, and manned the windlass. The pilot was now on the poop with the skipper, the latter looking lively enough as he heard the quick clanking of the palls. The men broke into a song and chorus presently and the rude strains chimed in well with the hoarse echo of the cable coming link by link inboard.

Presently I reported the cable up and down. Then from Duckling, the pilot's mouth-piece, came the familiar orders:

"Loose the outer jib."

"Lay aloft, some of you, and loose the top-sails."

"Up with that jib smartly my lads."

"A hand aft here to the wheel."

The ship lay with her head pointing to the direction in which she was going: there was nothing more to do than sheet home the top-sails and trip the anchor. The men were tolerably nimble and smart. The three top-sails were soon set, the windlass again manned, and within a quarter of an hour from the time when the order was given, the ship was under way, and pushing quietly through a tide that raced in a hundred wrinkles around her bows.

We set the fore and maintop-gallant-sails and spanker presently; the yards were braced sharp up, for we were heading well south, so as to give the Foreland a wide berth. This extra canvas sent us swirling past the red-hulled light-ship off this point, and soon the Dover pier opened, and the great white cliffs with their green heights. Anon, our course bringing the wind more aft, we set the mainsail and main-royal and mizzen-top-gallant-sail, with the stay-sails and jibs.

The breeze freshened as we stretched seaward—the ship was now carrying a deal of canvas, and the men seemed pleased with her pace.

The day was gloriously fine. The sea was of an emerald green, alive with little leaping waves, each with its narrow thread of froth. The breeze was strong enough to lay the vessel over just so far as to enable one looking over the weather side to see her copper, shining red below the green line of water. The brilliant sunshine illuminated the brasswork with innumerable glories, and shone with fluctuating flashes in the glass of sky-lights, and made the decks glisten like a yacht's. The canvas, broad and white, towered nobly to the sky; and the main-royal against the deep blue of the sky seemed like a cloud among the whiter clouds which swept in quick succession high above. It was a sight to look over the ship's bows, to see her keen stem shredding the water, and the permanent pillar of foam leaning away from her weather-bow.

This part of the Channel was full of shipping, and I know, by the vividness with which my memory reproduces the scene, how beautiful was the picture impressed upon it. All on our right were the English shores, made delicate and even fanciful by distance; here and there fairy-like groups of houses, standing on the heights among trees or embosomed in valleys, with silver sands sloping to the sea; deep shadows staining the purity of the brilliant chalk; and a foreground of pleasure boats, with sails glistening like pearl, and bright flags streaming. And to our right and left vessels of different rigs and sizes standing up or down Channel, some running, like ourselves, free, with streaming wakes, others coming up close-hauled, some in ballast high out of water, stretching their black sides along the sea, and exposing to windward shining surfaces of copper.

At half past two o'clock in the afternoon, all sail that was required having been made, and the decks cleared, the hands were divided into watches, and I, having charge of the port watch, came on deck. The starboard watch went below; but, as the men had not dined, a portion of my own watch joined the others in the forecastle to get their dinner.

I now discovered that the copper-faced man, to whom I have drawn attention, was the new cook. I heard the men bandying jokes with him as they went in and out of the galley, carrying the steaming lumps of pork and reeking dishes of pea-soup into the forecastle, whence I concluded that they had either not yet discovered the quality of the provisions, or that they were more easily satisfied than their predecessors had been.

Among the men in my own watch was the great, strapping fellow whom I had likened to a Life Guardsman. I had thought the man too big to be handy up aloft, but was very much deceived, for in all my life I never witnessed such feats of activity as he performed. His long legs enabled him to take two ratlines at a time, and he saved himself the trouble of getting over the futtock shrouds by very easily making two steps from the main shrouds to the mainyard, and from the mainyard to the maintop. I watched him leave the galley, carrying his smoking mess; but I also noticed, before I lost sight of him, that he took a suspiciously long sniff at the steam under his nose, and then violently expectorated.

The breeze was now very lively; the canvas was stretching nobly to it; and the shore all along our starboard beam was a gliding panorama, brilliant with color and sunshine. They were having dinner in the cuddy; and as often as I passed the sky-light, I could see the captain glancing upward at the sails with a well pleased expression.

I presently noticed the cook's copper face, crowned with an odd kind of knitted cap, protruding from the galley, and his small eyes gazed intently at me. I paced the length of the poop, and when I returned, the cook's head was still at its post; and then his body came out, and he stood staring in my direction.

I had to turn abruptly to hide my mirth, for his face was ornamented with an expression of disgust exquisitely comical with the wrinkled nose, the arched, thick mouth, and the screwed-up eyebrows.

When I again looked, he was coming along the deck, swinging a piece of very fat pork at the end of a string. He advanced close to the poop-ladder, at the top of which I was standing, and holding up the pork, said:

"You see dis, sar?"

"Yes," I answered.

"Me belong to a country where we no eat pork," he exclaimed, with great gravity, still preserving his wrinkled nose and immensely disgusted expression.

"What country is that?" I asked.

"Hot country, sar," he answered. "But me will eat pork on board ship."

"Very proper."

"But me will *not* eat stinking pork on board ship or any where else!" he cried, excitedly.

"Is that piece of pork tainted?" I inquired.

"Don't know nuffen 'bout tainted, sar," he replied, "but it smells kinder strong. But not so strong as the liquor where t'other porks was biled in. Nebber smelled de like, sar. Most disgusting. Come and try it, sar. Make you feel queer."

"Pitch the water overboard, then."

"No good, sar. Fork'sle full of stinks, and men grumblin' like hell. Me fust-rate cook, too—but no make a stink sweet. Dat beats me." He held up the pork, with an expression on his face as if he were about to sneeze, shook his finger at it as though it were something that could be affected by the gesture, and flung it overboard.

"Dat's my rations," said he. "Shouldn't like to eat de fish dat swallers it."

And turning jauntily in his frocked canvas breeches, he walked off.

A few moments afterward the extraordinary-looking man with the small face and large head and shell-shaped back came out of the forecastle, walking from side to side with a springing, jerky action of the legs, they being evidently moved by a force having no reference to his will.

"Ax your pardon, sir," he said, twirling up his thumb in the direction of his forehead; "but the meat's infernal bad aboard of this here wessel."

"I can't help it," I answered, annoyed to be the recipient of these complaints, which seemed really to justify Coxon's charge of my being the crew's confidant. "You must talk to the captain about it."

"Ne'er a man among us can eat of the pork; and the cook, as is better acquainted than us with these here matters, says he'd rather be biled alive than swaller a ounce of it."

"The captain is the proper person to complain to."

"That may be, sir," said the man, dropping his chin, so that by projecting his beard, his face appeared to withdraw and grow smaller still; "but the boatswain says there'll not be much got by complaining to the skipper."

"I can't make the ship's stores better than they are," I replied, moving a step, for I now perceived that some of the crew were watching us, and I did not want the captain to come on deck and find me talking to this man about the provisions. But it so happened that at this particular moment the captain emerged from the companion hatchway. The man did not stir, and the captain said:

"What does that fellow want?"

"He is complaining of the pork, sir. I have referred him to you."

He gave me a sharp look, and leaning forward, said, in a quiet, mild voice:

"What's the matter, my man?"

"Why sir, I've been asked to come and say that the pork that's been served to the men is in a werry bad state, to be sure. It's more smell than meat, and what ain't smell is brine."

"I am sorry to hear that," said the captain, in a most benignant manner. "Look into the cuddy and tell the steward I want him."

The steward stepped on to the quarter-deck, and looked up at his master in a way that made me suspect he had got his cue.

"What's the matter with the pork, steward?"

"Nothing, sir, that I know of."

"The men say it smells strong—that's what you say, I think?" remarked the captain, addressing the man.

"Werry strong, sir—strong enough to sit upon, sir."

"I don't know how that can be," exclaimed the steward, looking very puzzled indeed. "It's sweet enough in the cask. Perhaps it's the fault of the biling."

"Nothing to do with the biling, mate," said the man, shaking his extraordinary head, at the same time surveying the steward indignantly. "Biling clears away smells, as a rule."

"Perhaps you've opened a bad cask. If so," said the captain, "fling it overboard, for I'll not have the men poisoned. Let the cook boil me a sample from the next cask you open, and put it upon my table—do you hear?"

"Yes, sir."

"That will do," continued the captain, addressing the man. "You may go forward and tell your mates what I have said."

And away straggled the man to inform the crew, no doubt, that the skipper was a brick, and that he'd like to punch the steward's head.

At seven o'clock next morning, we were abreast the Isle of Wight, having carried a strong south-easterly breeze with us as far as Eastbourne, when the wind lulled and remained light all through the middle watch; but after four it freshened again from the same quarter, and came on to blow strong; but we kept the fore and main-royals on her all through, and only furled them to heave the ship to off Ventnor, where we landed the pilot.

There was a nasty lump of a sea on just here, and some smacks making Portsmouth carried half sails soaking and their decks running with water. The "Grosvenor," owing to her weight, lay steady enough; a little too steady, I thought, for she shipped water over her starboard bow without rising, reminding me of a deep-laden barge, along which you will see the swell running and washing, while she herself goes squashing through with scarcely a roll.

A dandy-rigged boat put off in response to our signal, and I enjoyed the pretty picture she made as she came foaming, close hauled, toward the ship, burying herself in spray as she shoved her keen nose into the sea, and hopping nimbly out of one trough into another, so that sometimes you could see her forefoot right out of water.

I was glad when the pilot got over the side. He was a mean toady, and had done me no good with the captain. The gangway ladder had been thrown over to enable him to descend, and the boat washed high and low, up and down, alongside, some times level with the deck, sometimes twelve or fourteen feet in a hollow.

"Now's your time," said I, mischievously, as he hung on to the manrope with one leg out to catch the boat as she rose. He took me at my word and let go; but the boat was sinking, and down he went with her, and I had the satisfaction of seeing him roll right into the boat's bottom, and there get so hopelessly entangled with the pump and some trawling gear, that it took two boatmen to pull him out and set him on his feet.

Then away they went, the pilot waving his hat to the skipper, who cries:

"Man the lee main braces."

The great yards were swung around, and the ship lay over to the immense weight of canvas.

"Ease off those jib-sheets there, and set the mainsail."

The ship, feeling the full breeze, surged slowly forward, parting the toppling seas with thundering blows of her bows. She had as much sail on her as she could well carry and a trifle to spare, for the breeze had freshened while we had been lying to: a couple of vessels to windward were taking in their fore and mizzen-top-gallant-sails, and ahead was a smart brig with a single reef in her foretop-sail. The wind was well abeam, perhaps half a point abaft, and every sail was swollen like the cheeks of rude Boreas in the picture of the bleak worthy.

This cracking on delighted Duckling, whose head turned so violently about, as he stared first at these sails, then at those, then forward, then aft, that I thought he would end in putting a kink into his neck.

"This is proper!" he exclaimed, in his hoarse voice, after ordering some hands "to cap the watch-tackle on to the main-tack and rouse it down. We'll teach 'em how to froth this blessed Channel! I guess we've had enough of calms, and if the Scilly ain't some miles astern by the second dog-watch to-morrow I'll turn a monk, you see!"

We were heading well west-south-west, and the water was flying in sheets of foam from the ship's bows. By this time it was dark, and the sky thick with the volume of wind that swept over it; and the stars shone hazily, but it was as much as I could do to trace the outlines of the main-royal and top-gallant sail.

The vessel was rushing through the water at a great pace. I felt as exhilarated as one new to the life when I looked astern and saw the broad path of foam churned by the ship rising and falling and fading upon the desolate gloom of the hilly horizon. Blue fires burned in the water; but, by and by, when by stretching out we had got into the broader sea, and the vessel plunged to the heavier waves which were running, big flakes of phosphorescent light were hurled up with the water every time the ship pitched, and for twenty fathoms astern the water was as luminous as the Milky Way. The roaring of the wind on high, the creaking of the spars, the clanking and grinding of the chain-sheets, the squeal of sheaves working on rusty pins, the hissing and spitting of the seething foam, and ever and anon the sullen thunder of a sea striking the ship, filled the ear with a wonderful volume of sound. The captain was cracking on to make up for the lost time, and he was on deck when I went below at ten o'clock to get some rest before relieving Duckling at midnight. There were then two hands at the wheel, and a couple on the lookout; our lamps were burning bravely, but we had long ago outrun all sight of shore and of lights ashore.

I slept soundly, and at eight bells Duckling roused me up. The unpleasantest part of a sailor's life is this periodical turning out of warm blankets to walk the deck for four hours. The rawness of the night air is anything but stimulating to a man just awake and very sleepy. Let the wind be ever so steady, the decks are full of powerful draughts rushing out of the sails, and blowing into your eyes and ears, and up the legs of your trousers, and down the collar of your shirt, turn where you will: and you think, as your hair is blown over your eyes and a shower of spray comes pattering upon your oilskins and annoying your face, of your sheltered cabin and warm cot, and wonder what, in the name of common sense, caused you to take to this uncomfortable profession. The crew in this respect are better off than their officers; for the watch on deck at night can always manage to sneak into the forecastle and doze upon their chests, or on the deck and keep under shelter; whereas the mate in charge must be always wide awake and on his legs throughout his watch, and shirk nothing that the heavens may choose to pour upon his defenseless person.

I had four hours before me when I went on deck, and I may perhaps have wished myself ashore in a quiet bed. The captain stood near the wheel.

It was blowing very fresh indeed, the wind about east-south-east, with a strong following sea. The yards had been braced further aft, but no other alteration had been made since I had gone below. If I had thought that the vessel was carrying too much sail then, I certainly thought that she was carrying a great deal too much sail now. She could have very well dispensed with the main-royal and top-gallant-sails, and in my opinion would have made the same way with a single reef in the top-sails. The press of canvas was burying her. Well aft as the wind was, the vessel lay over to starboard under it, and was dragging her heavy channels sluicing and foaming through the water. The moon was weak, with a big ring round her and the sky was obscured by the scud which fled away to the north-west. The horizon was thick, and the troubled sheen of the moon upon the jumping seas made the dark waters, with their ghastly lines of phosphorescent foam, a most wild and weird panorama.

I mustered the watch, and a couple of them went to relieve their mates on the forecastle. A night-glass lay on one of the sky-lights, and I swept the horizon with it, but nothing was to be seen. I walked aft to see how she was steering, for these heavy following seas lumping up against a ship's quarter play the deuce with some vessels, making the compass-card swing wildly and setting the square sails lifting; but found her steering very steadily, though the rush of some of the seas under her counter might have bewildered a two-thousand-ton ship. She rose, too, better than I thought she would, though she was sluggish enough, for some of the seas ran past her with their crests curling above her lee bulwarks, and she had received one souser near the galley; but her decks to windward were dry.

Coxon was smoking a big Dutch pipe, holding it with one hand and the rail with the other. He had a hair cap on with flaps *over his ears,* and sea-boots, and all that he was doing was first to blow a cloud and then look up at the sails and then blow another cloud and then look up again; this would appear to have been going on since nine o'clock. I thought he must be pretty tired of his diversion by this time.

"She bears her canvas well, sir," said I.

"Yes," he answered gruffly, "I have lost twenty-four hours. I ought to have been clear of the Channel by this."

"She is a fast vessel, sir. We are doing a good twelve, I should say."

He cast his eyes over the stern, then looked up aloft, but made no answer. I was moving away when he exclaimed:

"Go forward and tell the men to keep a bright look-out. And keep your weather-eye lifting yourself, sir."

I did as he bade me, and got upon the forecastle. I found the two men, who were indistinguishable from the poop, wrapped in oil-skins leaning against the forecastle rail. It blew harder here than it did aft for a power of wind rushed slanting from the fore-topmast stay-sail and whirled up from under the foot of the foresail. The crashing sound of the vessel's bows, urged through the heavy water by the great power that was bellowing overhead, was wonderful to hear: an uproar of thunder was all around, mingled with wild shrieking cries and the strange groaning of straining timbers. The moon stood away to windward of the mizzen-royal-masthead, and it was a sight to look up and see the gray canvas, full like balloons, soaring into the sky, and to hear the mighty rush of the wind among the rigging as the vessel rolled against it, making the moon whirl across her spars to and fro, to and fro.

I had been on deck three-quarters of an hour when, feeling the wind very cold, I dived into my cabin for a shawl to wrap round my neck.

I had hardly left the cuddy door to return, when I heard a loud cry from the forecastle, and both hands roared out simultaneously, "A sail right ahead!"

Coxon walked quickly forward to the poop-rail to try to see the vessel to windward; then he went over to the other side and peered under the mainsail; after which he said, "I see nothing. Where is she?"

I shouted through my hands, "On which bow is she?"

"Right ahead!" came the reply.

There was a short pause, and then one of the men roared out, "Hard over! we're upon her! She's cutter rigged. She's a smack."

"Hard a-port! hard a-port!" bawled Coxon.

I saw the spokes of the wheel fly round, but almost at the same moment I felt a sudden shock—an odd kind of *thud,* the effect of which upon my senses was to produce the impression of a sudden lull in the wind.

"God Almighty!" bellowed a voice, "we've run her down!"

In a second I had bounded to the weather-side of the poop and looked over, and what I saw sliding rapidly past was a mast and a dark-colored sail, which in the daylight would probably be red, stretched flat upon the wilderness of foam which our ship was sweeping off her sides. Upon this ghastly white ground sail and mast were distinctly outlined—for a brief moment only; they vanished even as I watched, swallowed up in the seething water. And then overhead the sails of the ship began to thunder, and the rigging quivered and jerked as though it must snap.

"Hard over! hard over!" bellowed Coxon.

I saw him rush to the wheel, thrust away one of the men, and pull the spokes over with all his force. The vessel answered splendidly, swerved nobly round like a creature of instinct, and was again rushing headlong with full sail over the sea.

This was a close shave. At the speed at which she was traveling she had obeyed the rudder in the first instance so promptly as to come round close to the wind. A few moments more and she would have been taken back; and this, taking into consideration the amount of canvas she was carrying, must infallibly have meant the loss of most, if not of all, her spars. Horrified by the thoughts of living creatures drowning in our wake, I cried out to the skipper:

"Won't you make an effort to save them, sir?"

"Save them be hanged!" he answered, fiercely. "Why the devil didn't they get out of our road?"

I was so much shocked by the coarse inhumanity of this reply that I turned on my heel, but yet was constrained by an ugly fascination to turn again and cast shuddering glances at the spot where I pictured the drowning wretches battling with the waves.

Captain Coxon was too intent upon the compass to notice my manner; he was giving directions to the men in a low voice, with his eyes fixed on the card.

Presently be exclaimed, in his gruffest voice, "Call the carpenter to sound the well."

This was soon dispatched, and I returned and reported a dry bottom.

"Heave the log, sir."

I called a couple of hands aft and went through the tiresome and tedious job of ascertaining the speed by the measured line and sand-glass. The reel rattled furiously in the hands of the man who held it; I thought the whole of the line would go away overboard before the fellow who was holding the glass cried, "Stop!"

"What do you make it?" demanded Coxon.

"Thirteen knots, sir."

He looked over the side as though to assure himself that the computation was correct, then called out:

"Clew up the main-royal, and furl it!"

This was a beginning, and it was about time that a beginning was made. The breeze had freshened into a strong wind, this had grown into half a gale, and the look of the sky promised a whole gale before morning. The main-royal halyards were let go, and a couple of hands went up to stow the bit of canvas that was thumping among the clouds.

Presently, "Furl the fore and mizzen-top-gallant-sails."

This gave occupation to the watch; and now the decks began to grow lively with the figures of men running about, with songs and choruses, with cries of "Belay, there!"—"Up with it smartly, my lads!" and with the heavy flapping of canvas.

All this, however, was no very great reduction of sail. The "Grosvenor" carried the old-fashioned single topsails, and these immense spaces of canvas were holding a power of wind. Overhead the scud flew fast and furious, and all to windward the horizon was very thick. We took in the maintop-gallant-sail; and while the hands were aloft we came up hand over fist with a big ship, painted white. She was to leeward, stretching away under double-reefed top-sails, and showed out quite distinctly upon the dark sea beyond, and under the struggling moonshine. We ran close enough to take the wind out of her sails, and could easily have hailed her had there been any necessity to do so; but we could discern no one on deck but a single hand at the wheel. She showed no lights, and with her white hull and gleaming sails, and fragile naked yards and masts, she looked as ghostly as anything I ever saw on water. She rolled and plunged solemnly among the seas, and threw up her own swirling outline in startling relief upon the foam she flung from her side, and which streamed away in pyramid-shape. She went astern like a buoy, and in a few minutes had vanished as utterly from our sight as if she had foundered.

I now stood waiting for an order, which I knew must soon come. It is one thing to "carry on," but it is another thing to rip the masts off a ship. I don't think we had lost half a knot in speed through the canvas that had been taken in; the vessel seemed to be running very nearly as fast as the seas. But the wind was not only increasing, but increasing with squalls, so that there were times when you would have thought that the inmates of forty madhouses had got among the rigging and out upon the yards, and were screeching, yelling, and groaning with all the force they were master of.

At last the captain gave the order I awaited:

"All hands reef top-sails."

In a few minutes the boatswain's pipe sounded, and the watch below came tumbling out of the forecastle. Now came a scene familiar to every man who has been to sea, whether as a sailor or a passenger. In a ship of war the crew go to work to the sound of fiddles or silver whistles; every man knows his station; everything is done quickly, quietly and completely. But in a merchantman the men go to work to the sound of their own voices; these voices are, as a rule, uncommonly harsh and hoarse, and every working party has its own solo and chorus, and as all working parties sing together, the effect upon the ear, to say the very least, is hideous. But also in a merchantman the crew is always less in number than they ought to be. Hence, when the halyards are let go, the confusion below and aloft becomes overwhelming; for not more, perhaps, than a couple of sails can be handled at a time, and, meanwhile, the others waiting to be furled are banged about by the wind, and fling such a thunder upon the ear that orders are scarce audible for the noise.

All this happened to a certain degree in the present instance.

The captain, having carried canvas with foolhardy boldness, now ran to the other extreme. The quick, fierce gusts which ran down upon the ship frightened him, and his order was to let go all three top-sail halyards, and double-reef the sails. The halyards were easily let go; but then, the working hands being few, confusion must follow. The yards down upon the caps, the sails stood out in bellies hard as iron. A whole watch upon each reef-tackle could hardly bring the blocks together. When the mizzentop-sail was reefed, it was found that the foretop-sail would require all hands; the helm had to be put down to shake the sail, so as to enable the men to make the reef-points meet. The maintop-sail lifted as well as the foretop-sail, and both sails rattled in unison; and the din of the pealing canvas, furiously shaken by the howling wind, the cries of the men getting the sail over to windward, the booming of the seas against the ship's bows, the groaning of her timbers, the excited grunting of terrified pigs, and the trembling of an empty water-cask, which had broken from its lashings and was rolling to and fro on the main-deck, constituted an uproar of which no description, however elaborate, could even faintly express the overwhelming character.

When the dawn broke it found the "Grosvenor" under reefed topsails, fore-top masts, stay-sail, fore-sail, maintry-sail, and spanker, snug enough, but with streaming decks, for the gale had raised a heavy beam sea, and the deep-laden ship was sluggish, and took the water repeatedly over her weather bulwarks.

The watch below had turned in again, but it was already seven bells, and at four o'clock my turn would come to go to bed. I had charge of the ship, for the captain, having passed the night in observing his vessel's sailing powers under all canvas, had gone below, and I was not sorry to get rid of him, for his continued presence aft had become a nuisance to my eyes.

The sea under the gathering light in the east was a remarkable sight. The creaming, arching surfaces of the waves took the pale illumination, but the troughs or hollows were livid, and looking along the rugged surface as the ship rose, one seemed to behold countless lines of yawning caverns opening in an illimitable waste of snow. Nothing could surpass the profound desolation of the scene surveyed in the faint struggling dawn; the pallid heaven, bearing its dim and languishing stars, over which were swept long lines of smoke-colored clouds torn and mangled by the wind; the broken ocean pouring and boiling away to a melancholy horizon, still dark, save where the dawn was creeping upward with its chilly light, and making the eastern sea and sky leaden-hued.

I had now leisure to recall the fatal accident I have related, and the inhumanity of Captain Coxon's comment upon it. I hugged myself in my thick coat as I looked astern at the cold and rushing waters, and thought of the bitter, sudden deaths of the unfortunates we had run down. With what appalling rapidity had the whole thing happened! not even a dying shriek had been heard amid the roar of the wind among the masts. For many a day the memory of that dark-colored sail, prone upon the foaming water, haunted me. The significance of it was awful to think upon. But for the men on the lookout, never a soul among us would have known that living beings had been hurled into sudden and dreadful death; that the ship in which we sailed had perchance made widows of sleeping wives, had made children fatherless, and that ruin and beggary and sorrow had been churned up out of the deep by our unsparing bows.

Our voyage had begun inauspiciously enough, God knows; and as I looked toward the east, where the morning light was kindling over the livid, rugged horizon, a strange depression fell upon my spirits, and the presentiment then entered my mind, and never afterward quitted it, that perils and suffering and death were in store for us, and that when I had looked on the English coast last night I was unconsciously bidding farewell to scenes I should never behold again.

CHAPTER V

I WAS on deck again at eight o'clock. It was still blowing a gale, but the wind had drawn right aft, and though the top-sails were kept reefed, Duckling had thought fit to set the maintop-gallant-sail, and the ship was running bravely.

Yet, though her speed was good, she was rolling abominably; for the wind had not had time to change the course of the waves, and we had now all the disadvantage of a beam sea, without the modifying influence over the ship's rolling of a beam wind.

I reckoned that we had made over one hundred and thirty knots during the twelve hours, so that if the gale lasted we might hope to be clear of the Scilly Isles by next morning. There was a small screw steamer crossing our bows right ahead, possibly hailing from France and bound to the Bristol Channel. I watched her through a glass, sometimes breathlessly, for in all my life I never saw any vessel pitch as she did, and live. Sometimes she seemed to stand clear out of the water, so as to look all hull, then down she would go and leave nothing showing but a bit of her funnel sticking up, with black smoke pouring away from it. Several times when she pitched I said to my-self, "Now she is gone!" Her bows went clean under, heaving aloft a prodigious space of foam; up cocked her stern, and, with the help of the glass, I could see her screw scurrying around in the air. Her decks were lumbered with cattle-pens, but the only living thing I could see on board was a man steering her on the bridge. She vanished all on a sudden, amid a Niagara of spray; but some minutes after I saw her smoke on the horizon. Had I not seen her smoke I should have been willing to wager that she had foundered. These mysterious disappearances at sea are by no means rare, but are difficult to account for, since they sometimes happen when the horizon is clear. I have sighted a ship and watched her for some time; with-drawn my eyes for a minute, looked again, and perceived no signs of her. It is possible that mists of small extent may hang upon the sea, not noticeable at a distance, and that they will shut out a vessel suddenly and puzzle you as a miracle would. The fascinating legend of the "Phantom Ship" may have originated in disappearances of this kind, for they are quite complete and surprising enough to inspire superstitious thoughts in such plain unlettered minds as sailors'.

They were breakfasting in the cuddy and in the forecastle, and I was waiting for the skipper to come on deck that I might go below and get something to eat. But before he made his appearance, the confounded copper-colored cook, accompanied by a couple of men, came aft.

"Sar," said this worthy, who looked lovely in a pink striped shirt and yellow overalls, "me ask you respeckfly to speak to de skipper and tell him biscuit am dam bad, sar."

"I'm messman for the starboard watch, sir," exclaimed one of the men, "and the ship's company says they can't get the bread down 'em nohow."

"Why do you come to me?" I demanded of them, angrily. "I have already told you, cook, that I have nothing to do with the ship's stores. You heard what Captain Coxon said yesterday?"

"Can't the steward get up a fresh bag of bread for breakfast?" exclaimed the third man.

"He's in the cuddy," I replied, "ask him."

They bobbed their heads forward to see through the cuddy windows, and at that moment Duckling came on deck up through the companion.

"You can get your breakfast," he said to me. "I'll keep watch until you've done."

"Here are some men on the quarter-deck complaining of the bread," said I. "Will you speak to them?"

He came forward at once very briskly, and looked over.

"What's the matter?" he called out.

"We've come to complain of the ship's bread, sir," said one of the men, quite civilly.

"Dam bad bread, sar! Me honest man and speak plain truff," exclaimed the cook, who possibly thought that his position privileged him to be both easy and candid on the subject of eating.

"Get away forward!" cried Duckling, passionately. "The bread's good enough. You want to kick up a shindy."

The men made a movement, the instinct of obedience responding mechanically to the demand. But the cook held his ground, and said, shaking his head and convulsing his face:

"De bread am poison, sar. All de flour's changed into worms. Nebber see such a t'ing. It get here"—touching his throat—"and make me—yaw!"

"Go forward, I tell you, you yellow-faced villain!" shouted Duckling. "D'ye hear what I say?"

"Dis chile is a cook," began the fellow; but Duckling sprung off the poop, and with his clinched fist struck him full under the jaw; the poor devil staggered and whirled round, and then up went Duckling's foot, and cook was propelled at a great pace along the main-deck toward the galley. He stopped, put his hand to his jaw, and looked at the palm of it; rubbed the part that had been kicked, turned and held up his clinched fist, and went into the galley. The two other men disappeared in the forecastle.

"Curse their impudence!" exclaimed Duckling, remounting the poop-ladder, and polishing his knuckles on the sleeves of his coat. "Now, Mr. Royle, get you down to your breakfast. I want to turn in when you've done."

I entered the cuddy, not greatly edified by Duckling's way of emphasizing his orders, and made a bow to the captain who was still at table. He condescended to raise his eyes, but for some minutes afterward took no notice of me whatever, occupying himself glancing over a bundle of slips which looked like bill-heads in his hand.

The vessel was rolling so heavily that the very plates slid to and fro on the table; and it not only required dexterity, but was no mean labor, to catch the coffee-pot off the swinging tray, as it came like a pendulum over to my side, and to pour out a cup of coffee without capsizing it. The mahogany paneling and cabin doors all around creaked incessantly, and in the steward's pantry there was a frequent rattle of crockery.

"What was going forward on the main-deck just now?" demanded Coxon, stowing away the papers in his pocket, and breaking fragments from a breakfast roll.

I explained.

"Ah!" said he; "they're still at that game, are they?"

"Mr. Duckling punched the cook's head—"

"I saw him, sir. Likewise he kicked him. Mr. Duckling knows his duty, and I hope he has taught the cook his. Steward!"

"Yes, sir?" responded the steward, coming out of the pantry.

"See that a piece of the pork you are serving out to the men is put upon my table to-day."

"Yes, sir."

The captain fell into another fit of silence, during which I ate my breakfast as quickly as I could, in order to relieve Duckling.

"Mr. Royle," said he, presently, "when we ran that smack down this morning, what were you for doing?"

"I should have hove the ship to," I replied, meeting his eyes.

"Would you have hove her to had you been alone on deck, sir?"

"Yes, and depended on your humanity to excuse me."

"What do you mean by my humanity?" he cried, dissembling his temper badly. "What kind of cant is this you have brought on board my ship? Humanity! D——n it!" he exclaimed, his ungovernable temper blazing out, "had you hove my ship to on your own hook, I'd have had you in irons for the rest of the voyage!"

"I don't see the use of that threat, sir," said I, quietly. "You have to judge me by what I did do, not by what I might or would do."

"Oh, confound your distinctions!" he went on, pushing his hair over his ears. "You told me that you would have hove the ship to, had you been alone, and that means that you would have whipped the masts out of her.

Do you mean to tell me that you knew what sail we were carrying, to talk like this?"

"Perfectly well."

My composure irritated him more than my words, and I don't know what savage answer he was about to return; but his attention was on a sudden arrested and diverted from me. I turned my eyes in the direction in which he was staring, and beheld the whole ship's company advancing along the main deck, led by the big seaman, whose name was Johnson, and by the tortoise-backed, small-faced man, who was called Fish—Ebenezer Fish.

The moment the captain observed them, he rose precipitately and ran up the companion-ladder; and, as I had finished breakfast, I followed him.

By the time I had reached the break of the poop the hands were all gathered around the mainmast. A few of them held tin dishes in their hands, in which were lumps of meat swimming in black vinegar. One carried some dozen biscuits supported against his breast. Another held a tin pannikin filled with treacle, and another grasped a salt-jar, or some such utensil, containing tea.

The *coup d'œil* from the poop was at this moment striking. All around was a heavy sea, with great waves boiling along it; overhead a pale blue sky, along which the wildest clouds were sweeping. The vessel running before the wind under double-reefed top-sails, rolled heavily both to port and to starboard, ever and anon shipping a sheet of green water over her bulwarks, which went rushing to and fro the decks, seething and hissing among the feet of the men, and escaping with loud, bubbling noises, through the scupper-holes.

I was almost as soon on deck as Coxon, and therefore heard the opening address of Johnson, who, folding his arms upon his breast, and "giving" on either leg, so as to maintain his equilibrium while the deck sloped to and fro under him, said, in a low, distinct voice:

"The ship's company thinks it a dooty as they owe theirselves to come aft all together to let you know that the provisions sarved out to 'em ain't eatable."

"Out, all hands, with what you've got to say," replied Coxon, leaning against the rail; "and when you've done I'll talk to you."

"Now then, mates, you hear what the skipper says," exclaimed Johnson, turning to the others.

Just then I noticed the copper face of the cook, who was skulking behind the men, with his eyes fixed, flashing like a madman's, upon Duckling.

The fellow with the biscuits came forward, but a heavy lurch at that moment made him stumble, and the biscuits rolled out of his arms. They were collected officiously by the others, and placed again in his hands, all sopping wet; but he said, in a collected voice:

"These here are the starboard watch's bread. Ne'er a man has tasted of them. We've brought 'em for you to see, as so be it may happen that you aren't formiliar with the muck the steward sarves out."

"Hand up a dry one," said the skipper.

A man ran forward, and returned with a biscuit, which the captain took, broke, smelled, and tasted. He handed it to Duckling, who also smelled and tasted. He (the captain) said, "Fire away!"

The fellow with the biscuits withdrew, and one of the men, bearing the pork swimming in vinegar, advanced. He was a Dutchman, and was heard and understood with difficulty.

"My mates they shay tat tiss pork is tam nashty, and it ishn't pork ash I fanshy; but Gott knowsh what it iss; an' I shwear it gifs me ta shtomach-ache—by Gott, it does, sir, ass I am a man."

This speech was received with great gravity by the men as well as Coxon, who answered: "Hand it up."

The mess was shoved through the rail and poked at by the skipper with a penknife; he even jabbed a piece of it out and put it into his mouth. I watched for a grimace, but he made none. He handed the tin dish, as he had the biscuit, to Duckling, who looked at it closely and put it on the deck.

"The next," said the captain.

The Dutchman, looking as a man who is conscious of having discharged a most important duty, hustled back among the others, and the man with the treacle came out.

"This, sir, is what the steward's givin' us for molasses," said he, looking into the pannikin.

The captain made no answer.

"And though his senses are agin him, he goes on a-callin' of it molasses."

Another pause.

"But to my way of thinkin' it ain't no more molasses than it's oysters.

It's biled black beetles, that's what I call it, and you want a tooth-pick as thick as a marline-pike to get the shells out o' your teeth arter a meal of it."

"Hand it up," said the captain, from whom every moment I was expecting an expression of temper. He did not offer to taste the stuff, but inspected it with apparent attention, and tilted the vessel first this way and then that, that the treacle might run.

"Here's your molasses," said he, handing down the pannikin. "What else is there?"

"We're willin' to call this tea," said a man, holding up an earthenware jar filled with a black liquid; "but it ain't tea like what they sells ashore, and tain't tea like what I've bin used to drink on board other vessels. It's tea," continued he, looking first into the jar and then at the skipper, "and yet it ain't. May be it was growed in England, for there isn't no flavor of Chaney about it. It's too faint for 'bacca leaves, and tain't sweet enough for licorice. Fish here says it's the mustiness as makes it taste like senna."

Here followed a pause, during which the men gazed eagerly at the skipper. I noticed some angry and even sinister countenances among them; and the cook looked as evil as a fiend, with his hard yellow face and gleaming eyes staring upward under his eyebrows. But so far there had been nothing in the men's speeches and behavior to alarm the most timid captain; and I thought it would require but little tact and a few kindly concessions to make them, on the whole, a hard-working and tractable crew.

The captain having kept silence for some time, exchanged looks with Duckling, and called to know if the men had any more complaints to make. They talked among themselves, and Johnson answered, "No."

"Very well, then," said he. "I can do nothing for you here. There are no bake-houses yonder," nodding at the sea, "to get fresh bread from. You must wait till we get to Valparaiso."

A regular growl came up from the men, and Johnson exclaimed:

"We can't live on nothing till we get to Valparaiso."

"What do you want me to do?" cried the skipper, savagely.

"It's not for us to dictate," replied Johnson. "All that the crew wants is grub fit to eat."

"Put into Brest," exclaimed a voice. "It ain't far off. There is good junk and biscuit to be got at Brest."

"Who dares to advise me as to what I'm to do?" shouted the skipper in his furious way. "By Heaven, I'll break every bone in the scoundrel's body if he opens his infernal mutinous mouth again! I tell you I can't change the provisions here, and I'm not going to alter the ship's course with this wind astern, not if you were all starving in reality." But having said this, he pulled up short, as if his temper was diverging him from the line of policy he had in his mind to follow; he lowered his voice and said: "I'll tell you what, my lads; you must make the provisions last you for the present, and if I can make fair wind of it, I'll haul round for some Spanish port; or if not there, I'll see what land is to be picked up."

"You hear what the captain says, don't you?" growled Duckling.

"It isn't us that minds waiting, it's our stomachs," said Fish, the small-faced man.

"Do you mean to tell me you can't get a meal out of the food in your hands?" demanded the captain, pointing among them.

"We'd rayther drink cold water than the tea," said one.

"And the water ain't overdrinkable, neither," exclaimed another.

"The cook shays te pork'll gif us te cholera," said one of the Dutchmen.

"We wouldn't mind if the bread and molasses was right," cried Fish. "But they aren't. Nothen's right. The werry weevils ain't ordinary; they're longer and fatter than common bread-worms."

"Hold your jaw!" bawled Duckling. "The captain has spoken to you fairer than any skipper that I ever sailed under would have spoke. So now cut forward—do you hear?—and finish your breakfast. Cook, come from behind the mainmast, you loafing nigger, and leave the main-deck, or I'll make you trot to show the others the road."

He pulled a brass belaying-pin out of the rail and flourished it. The captain walked aft to the wheel, leaving Duckling to finish off with the men. They moved away, talking in low grumbling tones among themselves, manifestly dissatisfied with the result of their conference, and presently were all in the forecastle.

"I tell you what it is, Mr. Royle," said Duckling, turning impudently upon me; "you must wake up, if you please, and help me to keep those fellows in their places. No use in staring and listening. You must talk to 'em and curse 'em, damme! do you understand, Mr. Royle?"

"No, I don't understand," I replied. "I don't believe in cursing men. I've seen that sort of thing tried, but it never answered."

"Oh, I suppose you are one of those officers who call all hands to prayer before you reef down, are you?" he asked, with a coarse, sneering laugh. "I don't think Captain Coxon will appreciate your services much if that's your kind."

"I am sorry you should misunderstand me," I said, gravely. "I believe I can do my work, and get others to do theirs, without foul language and knocking men down."

"Thunder and lightning! what spoony skipper nursed *you* at his breast? Could you knock a man down if you tried?"

I glanced at him with a smile, and saw him running his eyes over me, as though measuring my strength. There was enough of me, perhaps, to make him require time for his calculations. Sinewy and vigorous as his ill-built frame was, I was quite a match for him—half a head taller, and weighed more, with heavier arms upon me and a deeper chest than he; and was eight-and-twenty, while he was nearly fifty.

"I think," said I, "that I *could* knock a man down if I tried. Perhaps two. But then I don't try. The skipper who nursed me was not a New Orleans man but an Englishman, and something better—an English gentleman. That means that no one on board his ship ever gave him occasion to use his fists."

He muttered something about my thinking myself a fine sort of bird, no doubt, but I could not catch all that he said, owing to the incessant thundering of the gale; he then left me and joined the captain, who advanced to meet him, and they both went below.

It was now pretty plain that I was unsuited for the taste and society of the two men with whom I was thrown. The captain saw that I was not likely to help his paltry views, and that my sympathy was with the crew; and, try as I might, I could *not* disguise my real contempt for Duckling. They were great chums, and thoroughly relished each other's nature. They were both bullies, and, in addition, Duckling was a toady. Hence it was inevitable—but less from the subordinate position that I filled than from the dislike I had of these men's characters—that I should be an outsider, distrusted by the skipper as to objecting to his dealings with the crew and capable of opposing them, and hated by Duckling for the contempt of him

I could not disguise. Much as I regretted this result, and had done what I could to avert it, now that it was thrust upon me, I resolved to meet it quietly. For the rest of that watch, therefore, I amused myself by shaping my plans, which simply amounted to a determination to do my duty as completely as I could, so as to deprive Coxon of all opportunity of making my berth more uncomfortable than it was; to hold my tongue, to take no notice of the skipper's doings, to steer clear of Duckling as much as possible, and to quit the ship, if possible, at Valparaiso. How I kept these good resolutions you shall hear.

CHAPTER VI

THE WEATHER mended next day, and we made all sail with a fine breeze, steering south-south-west. We had left the Downs on Tuesday, the 22d of August, and on the 25th we found by observation that we had made a distance of over nine hundred miles, which, considering the heavy seas the ship had encountered and the depth to which she was loaded, was very good sailing.

However, though we carried the strong northwesterly wind with us all day, it fell calm toward night, then shifted ahead, then drew away north, and then fell calm again. We were now well upon the Bay of Biscay, and the heavy swell for which that stretch of sea is famous did not fail us. All through the night we lay like the ship in the song, rolling abominably, with Coxon in a ferocious temper on deck, routing up the hands to man first the port and then the starboard braces, bousing the yards about to every whiff of wind, like a madman in the Doldrums, until both watches were exhausted. All this work was put upon us merely because the skipper was in a rage at the calm, and, not caring to rest himself, determined that his crew should not; but for all the good this sluing the yards about did, he might as well have laid the mainyards aback, and waited until some wind really came.

Early in the morning a light breeze sprung up aft, and the foretop-mast-stun'sail was run up, and the ship began to move again. This breeze held steady all day and freshened a bit at night, but, being right aft, scarcely gave us more than six knots when liveliest. However, it saved the men's arms and legs, and enabled them to go about other and easier work than manning braces, stowing sails, and set them again.

And so till Thursday the 31st of August, on which day we were, to the best of memory, in latitude 45° and longitude about 10°.

The men during this time had been pretty quiet. The boatswain told me that grumbling among them was as regular as meal-times; but no murmurs came aft, no fresh complaints were made to the skipper. The reason was, I think, the crew believed that the skipper meant to touch at Madeira or one of the more southerly Canary Islands. That this was their notion was put into my head by a question asked me by a hand at the wheel when I was alone on deck: would I tell him where the ship was?

I gave him the results of the sights taken at noon.

"That's to the east'ard of Madeery, ain't it, sir?"

"Yes."

He bent his eyes on the compass-card, and seemed to be reflecting on the ship's course. The subject dropped; but after he had been relieved, and was gone forward, I saw him talking to the rest of the watch; and one of them knelt down and drew some kind of figure with a piece of chalk upon the deck (it looked to me, and doubtless was, a rude chart of the ship's position), whereupon the cook began to jabber with great vehemence, extending his hands in the wildest way, and pulling one of the men close to him and whispering in his ear. They noticed me watching them, presently, and broke up.

Had I been on friendly terms with Coxon or Duckling, I should have made no delay in going to one or the other of them and communicating my misgivings; for misgivings I had, and pretty strong misgivings they were. But I perfectly well foresaw the reception my hints would meet with from both Duckling and the captain. I really believed that the latter disliked me enough now to convert my apprehension of trouble into some direct charge against me. He might swear that I had sympathized all along with the crew—and this I admitted—and that if the mutiny which my fears foreboded broke out, I should be held directly responsible for it and treated as the ringleader. Besides, there was another consideration that influenced me: and my misgivings *might* be unfounded. I might make a report which would not only imperil my own position, but provoke him into assuming an attitude toward the men which would produce in reality the mutiny that might, as things went, never come to pass. This consideration, more than anything else, decided me to hold my tongue, to let matters take their course, and to leave the captain and his chief mate to use their own eyesight, instead of obtruding mine upon them.

When I left the deck at four o'clock on the Wednesday afternoon, there was a pleasant breeze blowing directly from astern, and the ship was carrying all the canvas that would draw. The sky was clear, but pale, like a winter's sky, and there was a very heavy swell rolling up from the southward. The weather, on the whole, looked promising, and, despite the northeasterly wind, the temperature was so mild that I could have very well dispensed with my pilot-jacket.

There was something, however, about the aspect of the sun which struck me as new and strange. Standing high over the western horizon, it should be brilliant enough; and yet it was possible to keep one's eyes upon it for several moments without pain. It hung, indeed, a fluctuating molten globe in the sky, without any glory of rays. This seemed to me a real phenomenon, viewed with respect to the *apparent* purity of the sky; but of course I understood that a mist or fog intervened between the sight and the sun, though I never before remembered having seen the sun's disk so dim in brilliancy and at the same time so clean in outline in a blue sky.

I looked at the barometer before entering my cabin and found a slight fall. Such a fall might betoken rain, or a change of wind to the southward. In truth, there is no telling what a rise or fall of the barometer *does* betoken beyond a change in the density of the atmosphere. I would any day rather trust an old sailor's or an old farmer's eye: and as to weather forecasts, based upon a thousand fantastic hobbies, I liken them to dreams, of which every one remembers one or two that were verified, and forgets the immense number were never fulfilled.

Through the dog-watches the weather still held fair; but the glass had fallen another bit, and the wind was dropping. Captain had very little to say to me now, and I to him. I was just civil, and he was barely so; but when I was taking a glass in the cuddy preparatory to turning in for three hours, he asked me what I thought of weather.

"It's difficult to know what this swell means, sir," I answered. "Either it comes in advance of a gale or it follows a gale."

"In advance," he said. "If you are going to turn in, keep your clothes on. There was a thundering gale in the sun this afternoon, and if you clap your nose over the ship's side you'll smell it coming."

Oddly as he expressed himself, he was quite serious, and I understood him.

As the wind grew more sluggish the vessel rolled more heavily. I never was in a cuddy that groaned and strained more than this, owing to the mahogany fittings having shrunk and warped away from their fixings. Up through the sky-lights it was pitch-dark, from the effect of the swinging lamps within; and though both sky-lights were closed, I could hear the sails flapping like sharp peals of artillery against the masts, and the gurgling, washing sob of the water as the roll of the ship brought it up through the scupper-holes.

Just then Duckling overhead sung out to the men to get the foretop-mast-stun'sail in; and Coxon at once quitted the cabin and went on deck. There was something ominous in the calm and darkness of the night and the voluminous heaving of the sea, and I made up my mind to keep away from my cabin awhile longer. I loaded a pipe, and posted myself in a corner of the cuddy front. Had this been my first voyage, I don't think I should have found more difficulty in keeping my legs. The roll of the vessel was so heavy that it was almost impossible to walk. I gained the corner by dint of keeping my hands out and holding on to everything that came in my road; but even this nook was uncomfortable enough to remain in standing, for, taking the sea-line as my base, I was at one moment reclining at an angle of forty degrees; the next, I had to stiffen my legs forward to prevent myself from being shot like a stone out of the corner and projected to the other side of the deck.

The men were at work getting in the foretop-mast-stun'sail, and some were aloft rigging in the boom. There was no air to be felt save the draughts wafted along the deck by the flapping canvas. Even where I stood I could hear the jar and shock of the rudder struck by the swell, and the grinding of the tiller-chains as the wheel kicked. The sky was thick, with half a dozen stars sparely glimmering upon it here and there. The sea was black and oily, flashing fitfully with spaces of phosphorescent light which gleamed below the surface. But it was too dark to discern the extent and bulk of the swell; that was to be felt.

Duckling's voice began to sound harshly, calling upon the men to bear a hand, and *their* voices, chorusing up in the darkness, produced a curious effect. So far from my being able to make out their figures, it was as much as I could do to trace the outlines of the sails. After awhile they came down, and immediately Duckling ordered the fore and main-royals to be furled. Then the fore and mizzentop-gallant halyards were let go, and the sails clewed up ready to be stowed when the men had done with the royals. So by degrees all the lighter sails were taken in, and then the whole of the watch was put to close-reef the mizzentop-sail.

As I knew one watch was not enough to reef the other top-sails, and that all hands would soon be called, I put my pipe in my pocket and got upon the poop. Duckling stood holding on to the mizzen-riggings, vociferating, bully fashion, to the men. I walked to the binnacle and found that the vessel had no steerage way on her, and that her head was lying west, though she swung heavily four or five points either side of this to every swell that lifted her. The captain took no notice of me, and I went and stuck myself against the companion-hatch-way and had a look around the horizon, which I could not clearly see from my former position on the quarter-deck.

The scene was certainly very gloomy. The deep, mysterious silence, made more impressive by the breathless rolling of the gigantic swell, and by the impenetrable darkness that overhung the water circle, inspired a peculiar awe in the feelings. The rattle of canvas overhead had been in some measure subdued; but the great top-sails flapped heavily, and now and then the bell that hung just abaft the mainmast tolled with a single stroke.

It was a relief to turn the eye from the black space of ocean to the deck of the ship catching a luster from the cuddy lights.

Duckling, perceiving my figure leaning against the hatchway, poked his nose into my face to see who I was.

"I believed you were turned in," said he.

"I thought all hands would be called, and wished to save myself trouble."

"We shall close-reef at eight bells," said he, and marched away.

This was an act of consideration toward the men, as it meant that the watch below would not be called until it was time for them to turn out. At all events, the ship was snug enough now, come what might, even with two whole top-sails on her. Having close-reefed the mizzentop-sail, the hands were now furling the mainsail, and only a little more work was needful to put the ship in trim for a hurricane. So I took Duckling's hint and lay down to get some sleep, first taking a peep at the glass and noting that it was dropping steadily.

Sailors learn to go to sleep smartly and to get up smartly; and they also learn to extract refreshment out of a few winks, which is an art scarce any landsman that I am acquainted with ever succeeded in acquiring. I was awakened by one of the hands striking eight bells, and at once tumbled up and got on deck.

The night was darker than it was when I had gone to my cabin; no star was now visible; an inky blackness overspread the confines of the deep, and inspired a sense of calm that was breathless, suffocating, insupportable. The heavy swell still rose and sunk the vessel, washing her sides to the height of the bulwarks, and making the rudder kick furiously.

The moment Coxon saw me he told me to go forward and set all hands to close-reef the fore-top sail. I did his bidding, calling out the order as I went stumbling and sprawling along the main-deck, and letting go the halyards to wake up the men, after groping for them. Indeed, it was *pitch*-dark forward. I might have been stone-blind for anything I could see, barring the thin rays of the forecastle lamp glimmering faintly upon a few objects amidships.

Owing to this darkness, it was a worse job to reef the top-sails than had it been blowing a hurricane in daylight. It was a quarter to one before both sails were reefed, and then the watch that had been on deck since eight o'clock turned in.

Here were we now under almost bare poles, in a dead calm; and yet, had the skipper ordered both the fore and mizzentop-sails to be furled, he would not have been doing more than was justified by the extraordinary character of the night—the strange and monstrous sub-swell of the ocean, the opacity of the heavens, the sinister and phenomenal breathlessness and heat of the atmosphere.

Duckling was below, lying at full length upon one of the cuddy benches, ready to start up at the first call. I glanced at him through the sky-light, and wondered how on earth he kept himself steady on his back. I should have been dislodged by every roll as surely as it came. Perhaps he used his shoulder-blades as cleats to hold on to the sides of the bench; and to so widely proportioned a man as Duckling a great deal was possible.

The card was swinging in the binnacle as before, and just now the ship's head was north-west. With more canvas upon the vessel, her position would have been perilous by the impossibility of guessing from what quarter the wind would come—if it came at all. Even to be taken aback under close-reefed top-sails might prove unpleasant enough, should a sudden gale come down and find the ship without way on her.

The captain, who was on the starboard side of the wheel, called me over to him.

"Are the decks clear?"

"All clear, sir."

"Foretop-sails sheets?"

"Ready for running, sir."

"How's her head now?" to the man at the helm.

"Nor'-west, half north."

"Keep a brisk lookout to the south'ard, sir," he said to me; "and sing out if you see the sky clearing."

I saw him, by the binnacle light, put his finger in his mouth and hold it up. But there was no other air to be felt than the short rush first one way, then another, as the ship rolled.

Scarcely ten minutes had passed since he addressed me, when I saw what I took to be a ship's light standing clear upon the horizon, right astern.

I was about to call out when another light sprung up just above it.

Then a small, faint light, a little to the westward of these, then another.

Owing to the peculiar character of the atmosphere these lights looked red, and so completely was I deceived by their appearance that I hallooed out.

"Do you see those lights astern, sir? They look like a fleet of steamers coming up."

But I had scarcely spoken when I knew that I had made a fool of myself.

They were not ship's lights, but stars, and at once I comprehended the import of this sudden astral revelation.

"Stand by the starboard braces!" roared the skipper; and the men, awake to a sense of a great and perhaps perilous change close at hand, came shambling and stumbling along the deck.

A wonderful panorama was now being rapidly unfolded in the south.

All down there the sky was clearing as if by magic, and the stars shining; but as I watched, great flying wreaths like mighty volumes of smoke pouring out of gigantic factory chimneys, came rushing over and obscuring them, though always leaving a few brightly burning in a foreground which advanced with astonishing rapidity toward the ship. To right and left of this point of the horizon the sky cleared only to be obscured afresh by the flying clouds. Soon, amid the solemn pauses falling upon the ship between the intervals of her pitching, for she had now swung right before the swell, we could hear the coming whirlwind screeching along the surface of the water. The contrast of its approach with the oily, breathless, heaving surface of the sea around us and all ahead, and the utter stagnation of the air, produced an effect upon my mind, and, I believe, upon the minds of all others who were witnesses of the sight, to which no words could give expression—an emotion, if you like, of suspense that was almost terror, and yet terror deprived of pain by a wild and tingling curiosity.

But such a gale as I am describing travels quickly; all overhead the sky was first cleared and then massed up with whirling clouds, before the wind struck us; the white surface of the sea, cleanly lined like the surf upon a beach, was plainly seen by us, even when the water all around was still unruffled; and *then,* with a prolonged and pealing yell, the gale and the spray it was lashing out of the sea were upon us. In a moment our decks were soaking—the masts creaked, and every shroud and stay sung to the sudden, mighty strain; the vessel staggered and reeled—stopped, as a heavy swell rolled under her bows and threw her all aslant against the hurricane, which screeched and howled through the rigging, and then fled forward under the yards, which had squared themselves as the starboard braces were slackened.

It was lucky for the "Grosvenor" that the gale struck her astern. So great was its fury that, had it taken her aback, I doubt if she would have righted.

This furious wind had cleared the horizon, and the waterline all around was distinctly figured against the sky. The sea was a sheet of foam, and what will scarcely seem credible, the swell *subsided* under the lateral pressure of the wind, so that for a short time we seemed to be racing along a level surface of froth. Large masses of this froth, bubbly and crackling like wood in a fire, were jogged clean off the water and struck the decks or sides of the ship with reports like the discharge of a pistol; and no more than a handful of water blown against my face hit me with such force that for some moments I suffered the greatest torment, as though my eyes had been scalded, and I hardly knew whether I had not lost my sight.

The wind was blowing true from the south, and we were bowling before it due north, losing as much ground every five minutes as had taken us an hour to get during the day. Coxon, however, was *feeling* the gale before he brought the ship close; at any moment, you see, the wind might chop round and blow a hurricane; though, to be sure, the sky with its torn masses of skurrying clouds had too wild an aspect to make us believe that this gale was likely to be of short duration.

The sea now began to rise, and it was strange to watch it. First it boiled in short waves, which the wind shattered and blew flat. But other waves rose, too solid for the wind to level; they increased in bulk as they ran, and broke in coils of spray; while fresh and larger waves succeeded, and the ship began to pitch quickly in the young sea.

The wonderful violence of the wind could not be well appreciated by us who were running before it; but when the crew manned the braces and the helm was put to starboard, it seemed as if the wind would blow the ship out of the water. She came to slowly, laying her main-deck level with the sea, and the screeching of the wind was diabolical and absolutely terrifying to listen to. With the weather-leeches just lifting, she was still well away from her course, and her progress under all three top-sails was all leeway.

But I soon saw that she could not carry two of the three top-sails, owing to the tremendous sudden pressure put upon the masts by her lurches to windward; and, sure enough, Duckling (who had turned out along with all hands when the gale had first struck the ship) roared through a speaking-trumpet to clew up and furl the fore and mizzentop-sails.

It took all hands to deal with each sail separately, and I helped to stow the foretop-sail.

To be up aloft in weather of the kind I am describing is an experience no landsman can realize by imagination. To begin with, it is an immense job to *breathe,* for the wind stands like something solid in your mouth and up your nostrils, and makes the expelling of your breath a task fitter for a one-horse engine than a pair of human lungs. Then you have two remorseless forces at work in the shape of the wind and the sail doing their utmost to hurl you from the yard. The foretop-sail was snugged as well as bunt-lines and clew-lines, hauled taut as steel bars, could bring it; and, besides, there were already three reefs in it. And yet it stood out like cast-iron, and all hands might have danced a hornpipe upon it without putting a crease into the canvas with their united weight. We had to roar to Duckling to put the helm down, and spill the sail, before we could get hold of it; and so fiercely did the canvas shake in the hurricane as the ship came to, that I, who stood in the bunt, expected to see the hands out at the yard-arms shaken off the foot-ropes and precipitated into the sea.

But what a wildly picturesque scene was the ocean, surveyed from the height of the foremast! The sea was now heavy, and furiously lashing the weather-bow; avalanches of spray ran high up the side, and were blown in a veil of hurtling sleet and froth across the forecastle. Casting my eyes backward, the ship looked forlornly naked with no other canvas on her than the close-reefed maintop-sail, with the bare outlines of her main and after yards, and the slack ropes and lines blown to leeward in semicircles, surging to and fro in long sweeps against the stars, which glimmered and vanished between the furiously whirling clouds. The hull of the vessel looked strangely narrow and long, contemplated from my elevation, upon the boiling seas; the froth of the water made an artificial light, and objects on deck were clear now, which, before the gale burst upon us, had been wrapped in impenetrable darkness.

When the sail was furled, all hands lay down as smartly as they could; but just under the foretop the rush of wind was so powerful that when I dropped my leg over the edge to feel with my foot for the futtock shrouds, my weight was entirely sustained and buoyed up, and I believe that, had I let go with my hands, I should have been blown securely against the fore-shrouds and there held.

The ship was now as snug as we could make her, hove to under close-reefed maintop-sail and foretop-mast-stay-sail, riding tolerably well, though, to be sure, the wind had not yet had time to raise much of a sea. The crew were fagged by their heavy work, and the captain ordered the steward to serve out a tot of grog apiece to them, more out of policy than pity, I think, as he would remember what was in their minds respecting their provisions, and how the ship's safety depended on their obedience.

CHAPTER VII

ALL THAT night it blew terribly hard, and raised as wild and raging a sea as ever I remember hearing or seeing described. During my watch—that is, from midnight until four o'clock—the wind veered a couple of points, but had gone back again only to blow harder, just as though it had stepped out of its way a trifle to catch extra breath.

I was quite worn out by the time my turn came to go below, and though the vessel was groaning like a live creature in its death-agonies, and the seas thumping against her with such shocks as kept me thinking that she was striking hard ground, I fell asleep as soon as my head touched the pillow, and never moved until routed out by Duckling four hours afterward.

All this time the gale had not bated a jot of its violence, and the ship labored so heavily that I had the utmost difficulty in getting out of the cuddy on to the poop. When I say that the decks fore and aft were streaming wet, I convey no notion of the truth; the main deck was simply *afloat,* and every time the ship rolled, the water on her deck rushed in a wave against the bulwarks and shot high in the air, to mingle sometimes with fresh and heavy inroads of the sea, both falling back upon the deck with the boom of a gun.

I had already ascertained from Duckling that the well had been sounded and the ship found dry; and therefore, since we were tight below, it mattered little what water was shipped above as the hatches were securely battened down fore and aft, and the mast-coats unwrung. But still she labored under the serious disadvantage of being overloaded; and the result was her fore parts were being incessantly swept by seas which at times completely hid her forecastle in spray.

Shortly after breakfast Captain Coxon sent me forward to dispatch a couple of hands on to the jib-boom to snug the inner jib, which looked to be rather shakily stowed. I managed to dodge the water on the main-deck by waiting until it rolled to the starboard scuppers, and then cutting ahead as fast as I could; but just as I got upon the forecastle, I was saluted by a green sea which carried me off my legs, and would have swept me down on the main-deck had I not held on stoutly with both hands to one of the fore-shrouds. The water nearly drowned me, and kept me sneezing and coughing for ten minutes afterward. But it did me no further mischief, for I was incased in good oilskins and sou'-wester, which kept me as dry as a bone inside.

Two ordinary seamen got upon the jib-boom, and I bade them keep a good hold, for the ship sometimes danced her figure-head under water and buried her spritsail-yard; and when she sunk her stern, her flying jib-boom stood up like the mizzen-mast. I waited until this job of snugging the sail was finished, and then made haste to get off the forecastle, where the seas flew so continuously and heavily that had I not kept a sharp lookout I should several times have been knocked overboard.

Partly out of curiosity and partly with a wish to hearten the men, I looked into the forecastle before going aft. There were sliding doors let into the entrance on either side the windlass, but one of them was kept half open to admit air, the fore-scuttle above being closed. The darkness here was made visible by an oil-lamp, in shape resembling a tin coffee-pot with a wick in the spout, which burned black and smokily. The deck was up to my ankles in water, which gurgled over the pile of swabs that lay at the open entrance. It took my eye some moments to distinguish objects in the gloom, and then by degrees the strange interior was revealed. A number of hammocks were swung against the upper deck, and around the fore-castle were two rows of bunks, one atop the other. Here and there were sea-chests lashed to the deck, and these, with the huge windlass, a range of chain-cable, lengths of rope, odds and ends of pots and dishes, with here a pair of breeches hanging from a hammock, and there a row of oilskins swinging from a beam, pretty well made up all the furniture that met my eye.

The whole of the crew were below. Some of the men laying smoking in their bunks, others in their hammocks with their boots over the edge; one was patching a coat, another greasing his boots, others were seated in a group talking, while under the lamp were a couple of men playing at cards upon a chest, three or four watching and holding on by the hammocks over their heads.

A man, lying in his bunk with his face toward me, started up and sent his legs, incased in blanket trousers and brown woolen stockings, flying out.

"Here's Mr. Royle, mates!" he called out. "Let's ask him the name of the port the captain means to touch at for proper food, for we aren't goin' to wait much longer."

"Don't ask me any questions of that kind, my lads," I replied, promptly, seeing a general movement of heads in the bunks and hammocks. "I'd give you proper victuals if I had the ordering of them; and I have spoken to Captain Coxon about you, and I am sure he will see this matter put to rights."

I had difficulty in making my voice heard, for the striking of the seas against the ship's bows filled the place with an overwhelming volume of sound, and the hollow, deafening thunder was increased by the uproar of the ship's straining timbers.

"Who the devil thinks," said a voice from a hammock, "that we're going to let ourselves be grinded as we was last night without proper wittles to support us? I'd rather have signed articles for a coal-barge with drowned rats to eat from Gravesend to Whitstable than shipped in this here cursed wessel, where the bread's just fit to make savages retch!"

I had not bargained for this, but had merely meant to address them cheerily, with a few words of approval of the smart way in which they had worked the ship in the night. Seeing that my presence would do no good, I turned about and left the forecastle, hearing, as I came away, one of the Dutchmen cry out:

"Look here, Mister Rile, vill you be pleashed to shay ven we are to hov' something to eat?—for, by Gott! ve vill kill te dom pigs in the long-boat, if the skipper don't mindt—so look out!"

As ill-luck would have it, Captain Coxon was at the break of the poop, and saw me come out of the forecastle. He waited until he had got me alongside of him, when he asked me what I was doing among the men.

"I looked in to give them a good word for the work they did last night," I answered.

"And who asked you to give them a good word, as you call it?"

"I have never had to wait for orders to encourage a crew."

"Mind what you are about, sir!" he exclaimed, in a voice tremulous with rage. "I see through your game, and I'll put a stopper upon it that you won't like."

"What game, sir? Let me have your meaning."

"An infernal mutinous game!" he roared. "Don't talk to me, sir! I know you! I've had my eye upon you! You'll play false if you can, and are trying to smother up your d——d rebel meanings with genteel airs! Get away, sir!" he bellowed, stamping his foot. "Get away aft! You're a lumping, useless encumbrance! But, by thunder! I'll give you two for every one you try to give me! So stand by!"

And, apparently half mad with his rage, he staggered away in the very direction in which he told me to go, and stood near the wheel, glaring upon me with a white face, which looked indescribably malevolent in the fur cap and ear-protectors that ornamented it.

I was terribly vexed by this rudeness, which I was powerless to resist, and regretted my indiscretion in entering the forecastle after the polite resolutions I had formed. However, Captain Coxon's ferocity was nothing new to me; truly I believed he was not quite right in his mind, and expected, as in former cases, that he would come round a bit by and by, when his insane temper had passed. Still, his insinuations were highly dangerous, not to speak of their offensiveness. It was no joke to be charged, even by a madman, with striving to arouse the crew to mutiny. Nevertheless, I tried to console myself as best I could by reflecting that he could not prove his charges; that I need only to endure his insolence for a few weeks, and that there was always a law to vindicate me and punish him, should his evil temper betray him into any acts of cruelty against me.

The gale, at times the severest that I was ever in, lasted three days, during which the ship drove something like eighty miles north-west. The sea on the afternoon of the third day was appalling: had the ship attempted to run, she would have been pooped and smothered in a minute; but lying close, she rode fairly well, though there were moments when I held my breath as she sunk in a hollow like a coal-mine, filled with the astounding noise of boiling water, really believing that the immense waves which came hurtling towards us with solid, sharp, transparent ridges, out of which the wind tore lumps of water and flung them through the rigging of the ship, must overwhelm the vessel before she could rise to it.

The fury of the tempest and the violence of the sea, which the boldest could not contemplate without feeling that the ship was every moment in more or less peril, kept the crew subdued, and they ate as best they could the provisions without complaint. However, it needed nothing less than a storm to keep them quiet; for on the second day a sea extinguished the galley-fire, and until the gale abated no cooking could be done; so that the men had to put up with the cold water and biscuit. Hence all hands were thrown upon the ship's bread for two days, and the badness of it, therefore, was made even more apparent than heretofore when its wormy moldiness was in some degree qualified by the nauseousness of bad salt pork and beef, and the sickly flavor of damaged tea.

As I had anticipated, the captain came round a little a few hours after his insulting attack upon me. I think his temper frightened him when it had reference to me. Like others of his breed he was a bit of a cur at the bottom. My character was a trifle beyond him, and he was ignorant enough to hate and fear what he could not understand. Be this as it may, he made some rough attempts at a rude kind of politeness when I went below to get some grog, and condescended to say that when I had been to sea as long as he, I would know that the most ungrateful rascals in the world were sailors; that every crew he had sailed with had always taken care to invent some griev-ance to growl over—either the provisions were bad, or the work too heavy, or the ship unseaworthy; and that long ago he had made up his mind never to pay attention to their complaints, since no sooner would one wrong be redressed than another would be coined and shoved under his nose.

I took this opportunity of assuring him that I had never willingly lis-tened to the complaints of the men, and that I was always annoyed when they spoke to me about the provisions, as I had nothing whatever to do with that matter; and that, so far from my wishing to stir up the men into rebellion, my conduct had been uniformly influenced by the desire to con-ciliate them and represent their conditions as very tolerable, so as to repress any tendency to disaffection which they might foment among themselves.

To this he made no reply, and soon we parted; but all the next day he was sullen again, and never addressed me save to give an order.

On the evening of the third day the gale broke; the glass had risen since the morning, but until the first dog-watch the wind did not abate one iota of its violence, and the horizon still retained its stormy and threatening aspect. The clouds then broke in the west, and the setting sun shone forth with deep crimson light upon the wilderness of mountainous waters. The wind fell quickly, then went round to the west, and blew freshly; but there was a remarkable softness and sweetness in the feel and taste of it. A couple of reefs were at once shaken out of the maintop-sail, and a sail made. By mid-night the heavy sea had subsided into a deep, long, rolling (strangely enough) coming from the south; but the fresh westerly wind held the ship steady, and for the first time for nearly a hundred hours we were able to move about the decks with comparative comfort. Early the next morning the watch were sent to wash down and clear up the decks, and when I left my cabin at eight o'clock, I found the weather bright and warm, with a blue sky shining among heavy, white, April-looking-clouds, and the ship making seven knots under all plain sail. The decks were dry and comfortable, and the ship had a habitable and civilized look by reason of the row of clothes hung by the seamen to dry on the forecastle.

It was half-past nine o'clock, and I was standing near the taffrail looking at a shoal of porpoises playing some hundreds of feet astern, when the man who was steering asked me to look in the direction to which he pointed—that was, a little to the right of the bowsprit—and say if there was anything to be seen there; for he had caught sight of something black upon the horizon twice, but could not detect it now.

I turned my eyes toward the quarter of the sea indicated, but could discern nothing whatever; and, telling him that what he had seen was probably a wave, which, standing higher than his fellows, will sometimes show black a long distance off, walked to the fore part of the poop.

The breeze still held good and the vessel was slipping easily through the water, though the southerly swell made her roll, and at times shook the wind out of the sails. The skipper had gone to lie down, being pretty well exhausted, I dare say, for he had kept the deck for the greater part of three nights running. Duckling was also below. Most of my watch were on the forecastle, sitting or lying in the sun, which shone very warm upon the decks; the hens under the long-boat were chattering briskly, and the cocks crowing and the pigs grunting with the comfort of the warmth.

Suddenly, as the ship rose, I distinctly beheld something black out away upon the horizon, showing just under the foot of the foresail. It vanished instantly; but I was not satisfied, and went for the glass which lay upon the brackets just under the companion. I then told the man who was steering to keep her away a couple of points for a few moments, and resting the glass against the mizzen-royal back-stay, pointed it toward the place where I had seen the black object.

For some moments nothing but sea or sky filled the field of the glass as the ship rose and fell; but all at once there leaped into this field the hull of a ship, deep as her main-chains in the water, which came and went before my eye as the long seas lifted or dropped in the foreground. I managed to keep her sufficiently long in view to perceive that she was totally dismasted.

"It's a wreck," said I, turning to the man; "let her come to again and luff a point. There may be living creatures aboard of her."

Knowing what sort of man Captain Coxon was, I do not think that I should have had the hardihood to luff the ship a point out of her course had it involved the bracing of the yards; for the songs of the men would certainly have brought him on deck, and I might have provoked some ugly insolence. But the ship was going free, and would head more westerly without occasioning further change than slightly slackening the weather-braces of the upper yards. This I did quietly, and the dismantled hull was brought right dead on end with our flying jib-boom. The men now caught sight of her, and began to stare and point, but did not sing out, as they saw by the telescope in my hand that I perceived her. The breeze unhappily began to slacken somewhat, owing, perhaps, to the gathering heat of the sun; our pace fell off, and a full hour passed before we brought the wreck near enough to see her permanently, for up to this she had been constantly vanishing under the rise of the swell. She was now about two miles off, and I took a long and steady look at her through the telescope. It was a black hull with painted ports. The deck was flush fore and aft, and there was a good-sized house just before where the mainmast should have been. This house was uninjured, though the galley was split up, and to starboard stood up in splinters like the stump of a tree struck by lightning. No boats could be seen aboard of her. Her jib-boom was gone, and so were all three masts, clean cut off at the deck, as though a hand-saw had done it; but the mizzen-mast was alongside, held by the shrouds and backstays, and the port main and foreshrouds streamed like serpents from her chains into the water. I reckoned at once that she must be loaded with timber, for she never could keep afloat at that depth with any other kind of cargo in her.

She made a most mournful and piteous object in the sunlight, sluggishly rolling to the swell which ran in transparent volumes over her sides and foamed around the deck-house. Once, when her stern rose, I read the name, *Cecilia,* in broad, white letters.

I was gazing at her intently in the effort to witness some indication of living thing on board, when, to my mingled consternation and horror, I witnessed an arm projecting through the window of the deck-house, and frantically wave what resembled a white handkerchief. As none of the men called out, I judged this signal was not perceptible to, the naked eye, and in my excitement I shouted—

"There's a living man on board of her, my lads!" I dropped the glass, and ran aft to call the captain.

I met him coming up the companion-ladder. The first thing he said was, "You're out of your course," and looked up at the sails.

"There's a wreck yonder!" I cried, pointing eagerly, "with a man on board signaling to us."

"Get me the glass," he said, sulkily, and I picked it up and handed it to him.

He looked at the wreck for some moments, and, addressing the man at the wheel, exclaimed, making a movement with his hand:

"Keep her away! Where in the devil are you steering to?"

"Good Heaven!" I ejaculated; "there's a man on board—there may be others!"

"Damnation!" he exclaimed, between his teeth; "what do you mean by interfering with me? Keep her away!" he roared out.

During this time we had drawn sufficiently near to the wreck to enable the sharper-sighted among the hands to remark the signal, and they were calling out that there was somebody flying a handkerchief aboard the hull.

"Captain Coxon," said I, with as firm a voice as I could command—for I was nearly in as great a rage as he, and rendered insensible to all consequences by his inhumanity—"if you bear away and leave that man yonder to sink with that wreck when he can be saved with very little trouble, you will become as much a murderer as any ruffian who stabs a man asleep."

When I had said this Coxon turned black in the face with passion. His eyes protruded, his hands and fingers worked as though he were under some electrical process, and I saw for the first time in my life a sight I had always laughed at as a bit of impossible novelist description—a mouth foaming with rage. He rushed aft, just over Duckling's cabin, and stamped with all his might.

"Now," thought I, "they may try to murder me!" And without a word, I pulled off my coat, seized a belaying pin, and stood ready, resolved that, happen what might, I would give the first man who should lay his fingers on me something to remember me by while he had breath in his body.

The men, not quite understanding what was happening, but seeing that a "row" was taking place, came to the forecastle and advanced by degrees along the main-deck. Among them I noticed the cook, muttering to one or the other who stood near.

Mr. Duckling, awakened by the violent clattering over his head, came running up the companion-way with a bewildered, sleepy look in his face. The captain grasped him by the arm, and, pointing to me, cried out, with an oath, "that that villain was breeding a mutiny on board, and, he believed, wanted to murder him and Duckling."

I at once answered, "Nothing of the kind! There is a man miserably perishing on board that sinking wreck, Mr. Duckling, and he ought to be saved. My lads!" I cried, addressing the men on the main-deck, "is there a sailor among you all who would have the heart to leave that man yonder without an effort to rescue him?"

"No, sir!" shouted one of them. "We'll save the man, and if the skipper refuses, we'll make him!"

"Luff!" I called to the man at the wheel.

"Luff at your peril!" screamed the skipper.

"Aft here, some hands," I cried, "and lay the main-yard aback. Let go the port main-braces!"

The captain came running toward me.

"By the living God!" I cried, in a fury, grasping the heavy brass belaying-pin, "if you come within a foot of me, Captain Coxon, I'll dash your brains out!"

My attitude, my enraged face, and menacing gesture produced the desired effect. He stopped dead, turned a ghastly white looked round at Duckling.

"What do you mean by this (etc.) conduct, you (etc.) mutinous scoundrels?" roared Duckling, with a volley of foul language.

"Give him one for himself, if he says too much, Mr. Royle!" sung out some hoarse voice on the main-deck; "we'll back yer!" And then came cries of "They're a cursed pair o' murderers!" "Who run the smack down?" "Who lets men drown?" "Who starves honest men?" This last exclamation was followed by a roar.

The whole of the crew were now on deck, having been aroused by our voices. Some of them were looking on with a grin, others with an expression of fierce curiosity. It was at once understood that I was making a stand against the captain and chief mate, and a single glance at them assured me that by one word I could set the whole of them on fire to do my bidding even to shedding blood.

In the meantime the man at the wheel had luffed until the weather leeches were flat and the ship scarcely moving. And at this moment, that the skipper might know their meaning, a couple of hands jumped aft and let go the weather main-braces. I took care to keep my eyes on Coxon and the mate, fully prepared for any attack that one or both might make on me. Duckling eyed me furiously, but in silence, evidently baffled by my resolute air and the position of the men. Then he said something to the captain, who looked exhausted and white and haggard with his useless passion. They walked over to the leeside of the poop, and after a short conference, the captain, to my surprise, went below, and Duckling came forward.

"There's no objection," he said, "to your saving the man's life, if you want. Lower away the starboard quarter-boat, and you go along in her," he added to me, uttering the last words in such a thick voice that I thought he was choking.

"Come along, some of you!" I cried out, hastily putting on my coat; and in less than a minute I was in the boat with the rudder and hole-pins shipped and four hands ready to out oars as soon as we touched the water.

Duckling began to fumble at one end of the boat's falls.

"Don't let him lower away!" roared out one of the men in the boat. "He'll let us go with a run. He'd like to see us drowned!"

Duckling fell back, scowling with fury, and, shoving his head over as the boat sunk quietly into the water, he discharged a volley of execrations at us, saying that he would shoot some of us, if he swung for it, before he was done, and especially applying a heap of abusive terms to me.

The fellow pulling the boat oar laughed in his face, and another shouted out, "We'll teach you to say your prayers yet, you ugly sinner!"

We got away from the ship's side cleverly, and in a short time were rowing fast for the wreck. The excitement under which I labored made me reckless of the issue of this adventure. The sight of the lonely man upon the wreck, coupled with the unmanly, brutal intention of Coxon to leave him to his fate, had goaded me into a stab to *compel* Coxon to save him. He might call it mutiny, but I called it humanity, and I was prepared to stand or fall by my theory. The hate the crew had for their captain and chief mate was quite strong enough to guarantee me against any foul play on the part of Coxon, otherwise I might have prepared myself to see the ship fill and stand away, and leave us alone on the sea with the wreck. One of the men in the boat suggested this; but another immediately answered, "They'd pitch the skipper overboard if he gave such an order and glad o' the chance. There's no love for 'em among us, I can tell you; and by ———! there'll be bloody work done aboard the 'Grosvenor' if things aren't mended soon, as you'll see."

They all four pulled at their oars savagely as these words were spoken, and I never saw such sullen and ferocious expressions on men's faces as came into theirs as they fixed their eyes as with one accord upon the ship.

She, deep as she was, looked a beautiful model on the mighty surface of the water, rolling with marvelous grace to the swell, the strength and volume of which made me feel my littleness and weakness as it lifted the small boat with irresistible power. There was wind enough to keep her sails full upon her graceful, slender masts, and the brass-work upon her deck flashed brilliantly as she rolled from side to side.

Strange contrast, to look from her to the broken and desolate picture ahead! My eyes were riveted upon it now with new intense emotion, for by this time I could discern that the person who was waving to us was a female—woman or girl I could not yet make out—and that her hair was like a veil of gold behind her swaying arm.

"It's a woman!" I cried in my excitement; "it's no man at all. Pull smartly, my lads! pull smartly, for God's sake!"

The men gave way stoutly, and the swell favoring us, we were soon close to the wreck. The girl, as I now perceived she was, waved her handkerchief wildly as we approached; but my attention was occupied in considering how we could best board the wreck without injury to the boat. She lay broadside to us, with her stern on our right, and was not only rolling heavily with wallowing, squelching movements, but was swirling the heavy mizzen-mast that lay alongside through the water each time she went over to starboard, so that it was necessary to approach her with the greatest caution to prevent our boat from being stove in. Another element of danger was the great flood of water which she took in over her shattered bulwarks, first on this side, then on that, discharging the torrent again into the sea as she rolled. This water came from her like a cataract, and in a second would fill and sink the boat unless extreme care were taken to keep clear of it.

I waved my hat to the poor girl to let her know that we saw her and had come to save her, and steered the boat right around the wreck that I might observe the most practical point for boarding her.

She appeared to be a vessel of about seven hundred tons. The falling of her masts had crushed her port bulwarks level with the deck, and part of her starboard bulwarks was also smashed to pieces. Her wheel was gone, and the heavy seas that had swept her deck had carried away capstans, binnacle, hatchway gratings, pumps—everything, in short, but the deck-house and the remnants of the galley. I particularly noticed a strong iron boat's davit twisted up like a cork-screw. She was full of water, and lay as deep as her main-chains, but her bows stood high, and her fore-chains were out of the sea. It was miraculous to see her keep afloat as the long swell rolled over her in a cruel, foaming succession of waves.

Though these plain details impressed themselves upon my memory, I did not seem to notice anything in the anxiety that possessed me to rescue the lonely creature in the deck-house. It would have been impossible to keep a footing upon the main-deck without a lifeline or something to hold on by; and seeing this, and forming my resolutions rapidly, I ordered the man in the bow of the boat to throw in his oar and exchange places with me, and head the boat for the starboard port-chains. As we approached I stood up with one foot planted on the gunwale ready to spring; the broken shrouds were streaming aft and alongside, so that if I missed the jump and fell into the water there was plenty of stuff to catch hold of.

"Gently—'vast rowing—ready to back astern smartly!" I cried, as we approached. I waited a moment: the hull rolled toward us, and the succeeding swell threw up our boat; the deck, though all aslant, was on a line with my feet. I sprung with all my strength, and got well upon the deck, but fell heavily as I reached it. However, I was up again in a moment, and ran forward out of the water.

Here was a heap of gear—stay-sail, and jib-halyards, and other ropes, some of the ends swarming overboard. I hauled in one of the ends, but found I could not clear the raffle; but looking round, perceived a couple of coils of line—spare stun'sail tacks or halyards I took them to be—lying close against the foot of the bowsprit. I immediately seized the end of one of these coils and flung it into the boat, telling them to drop clear of the wreck astern; and when they had backed as far as the length of the line permitted, I bent on the other end of the other coil and paid that out until the boat was some fathoms astern. I then made my end fast, and sung out to one of the men to get on board by the starboard mizzen-chains, and to bring the end of the line with him. After waiting a few minutes the boat being hidden, I saw the fellow come scrambling over the side with a red face, his clothes and hair streaming, he having fallen overboard. He shook himself like a dog, and crawled with the line, on his hands and knees, a short distance forward, then hauled the line taut and made it fast.

"Tell them to bring the boat round here," I cried, "and lay off on their oars until we are ready. And you get hold of this line and work yourself up to me."

Saying which, I advanced along the deck, clinging tightly with both hands. It very providentially happened that the door of the deckhouse faced the forecastle within a few feet of where the remains of the galley stood. There would be, therefore, less risk in opening it than had it faced beamwise; for the water, as it broke against the sides of the house, disparted clear of the fore and after parts; that is, the great bulk of it ran clear, though, of course, a foot's depth of it at least surged against the door.

I called out to the girl to open the door quickly, as it slid in grooves like a panel, and was not to be stirred from the outside.

The poor creature appeared mad, and I repeated my request three times without inducing her to leave the window. Then, not believing that she understood me, I cried out, "Are you English?"

"Yes," she replied. "For God's sake, save us!"

"I cannot get you through that window," I exclaimed. "Rouse yourself, and open that door, and I will save you."

She now seemed to comprehend, and drew in her head. By this time the man out of the boat had succeeded in sliding along the rope to where I stood, though the poor devil was nearly drowned on the road; for when about half-way the hull took in a lump of swell which swept him right off his legs, and he was swung hard a-starboard, holding on for his life. However, he recovered himself smartly when the water was gone, and came along hand over fist, snorting and cursing in wonderful style.

Meanwhile, though I kept a firm hold of the life-line, I took care to stand where the inroads of water were not heavy, waiting impatiently for the door to open. It shook in the grooves, tried by a feeble hand; then a desperate effort was made, and it slid a couple of inches.

"That will do!" I shouted. "Now, then, my lad, catch hold of me with one hand, and the line with the other."

The fellow took a firm grip of my monkey-jacket, and I made for the door. The water washed up to my knees, but I soon inserted my fingers in the crevice of the door, and thrust it open.

The house was a single compartment, though I had expected to find it divided into two. In the center was a table that traveled on stanchions from the roof to the deck. On either side were a couple of bunks. The girl stood near the door. In a bunk to the left of the door lay an old man with white hair. Prostrate on his back, on the deck, with his arms stretched against his ears, was the corpse of a man, well dressed; and in a bunk on the right sat a sailor, who, when he saw me, yelled out and snapped his fingers, making horrible grimaces.

Such, in brief, the *coup d'œil* of that weird interior as it met my eyes. I seized the girl by the arm.

"You first," said I. "Come, there is no time to be lost."

But she shrunk back, pressing against the door with her hand to prevent me from pulling her, crying in a husky voice, and looking at the old man with the white hair. "My father first! my father first!"

"You shall all be saved, but you must obey me. Quickly, now!" I exclaimed, passionately, for a heavy sea at that moment flooded the ship, and a rush of water swamped the house through the open door, and washed the corpse on the deck up into a corner.

Grasping her firmly, I lifted her off her feet, and went staggering to the life-rope, slinging her light body over my shoulder as I went. Assisted by my man, I gained the bow of the wreck, and, hailing the boat, ordered it alongside.

"One of you," cried I, "stand ready to receive this lady when I give the signal."

I then told the man who was with me to jump into the fore-chains, which he instantly did. The wreck lurched heavily to port. "Stand by, my lads!" I shouted. Over she came again, with the water swooping along the main-deck. The boat rose high, and the fore-chains were submerged to the height of the man's knees. "Now," I called and lifted the girl over. She was seized by the man in the chains, and pushed toward the boat; the fellow standing in the bow of the boat caught her and at the same moment down sunk the boat, and the wreck rolled wearily over. But the girl was safe.

"Hurrah, my lad!" I sung out. "Up with you—there are others remaining"; and I went sprawling along the line to the deck-house, there to encounter another rush of water, which washed as high as my thighs, and fetched me such a thump in the stomach that I thought I must have died of suffocation.

I was glad to find that the old man had got out of his bunk, and was standing at the door.

"Is my poor girl safe, sir?" he exclaimed, with the same huskiness of voice that had grated so unpleasantly in the girl's tone.

"Quite safe; come along."

"Thanks be to Almighty God!" he ejaculated, and burst into tears.

I seized hold of his thin, cold hands, but shifted my fingers to catch him by the coat-collar, so as to exert more power over him, and handed him along the deck, telling my companion to lay hold of the seaman and fetch him away smartly. We managed to escape the water, for the poor old gentleman bestirred himself very nimbly, and I helped him over the fore-chains, and when the boat rose, tumbled him into her without ceremony. I saw the daughter leap toward him and clasp him in her arms, but I was soon again scrambling on to the deck, having heard cries from my man, accompanied with several loud curses, mingled with dreadful yells.

"He's bitten me, sir!" cried my companion, hauling himself away from the deck-house. "He's roaring mad."

"It can't be helped," I answered. "We must get him out."

He saw me pushing along the life-line, plucked up heart, and went with myself through a sousing sea to the door. I caught a glimpse of a white face glaring at me from the interior: in a second a figure shot out, fled with incredible speed toward the bow, and leaped into the sea just where our boat lay.

"They'll pick him up," I exclaimed. "Stop a second"; and I entered the house and stooped over the figure of the man on the deck. I was not familiar with death, and yet I knew it was here. I can not describe the signs in his face; but such as they were they told me the truth. I noticed a ring upon his finger, and that his clothes were good. His hair was black, and his features well-shaped, though his face had a half-convulsed expression, as if something frightful had appeared to him, and he had died of the sight of it.

"This wreck must be his coffin," I said. "He is a corpse. We can do no more."

We scrambled for the last time along the life-line and got into the fore-chains, but to our consternation saw the boat rowing away from the wreck. However, the fit of rage and terror that possessed me lasted but a moment or two; for I now saw they were giving chase to the madman, who was swimming steadily away. Two of the men rowed, and the third hung over the bows, ready to grasp the miserable wretch. The "Grosvenor" stood steady, about a mile off, with her main-yards backed; and just as the fellow over the boat's bows caught hold of the swimmer's hair, the ensign was run up on board the ship and dipped three times.

"Bring him along!" I shouted. "They'll be off without us if we don't bear a hand."

They nearly capsized the boat as they dragged the lunatic, streaming like a drowned rat, out of the water; and one of the sailors tumbled him over on his back, and knelt upon him, while he took some turns with the boat's painter round his body, arms and legs. The boat then came alongside, and, watching our opportunity, we jumped into her and shoved off.

I had now leisure to examine the persons whom we had saved.

They—father and daughter, as I judged them by the girl's exclamation on the wreck—sat in the stern-sheets, their hands locked. The old man seemed nearly insensible, leaning backward with his chin on his breast and his eyes partially closed. I feared he was dying, but could do no good until we reached the "Grosvenor," as we had no spirits in the boat.

The girl appeared to be about twenty years of age, very fair, her hair of golden straw color, which hung wet and streaky down her back and over her shoulders, though a portion of it was held by a comb. She was deadly pale and her lips blue, and in her fine eyes was such a look of mingled horror and rapture as she cast them around her, first glancing at me, then at the wreck, then at the "Grosvenor," that the memory of it will last me to my death. Her dress, of some dark material, was soaked with salt water up to her hips, and she shivered and moaned incessantly, though the sun beat so warmly upon us that the thwarts were hot to the hand.

The mad sailor lay at the bottom of the boat, looking straight into the sky. He was a horrid-looking object, with his streaming hair, pasty features, and red beard, his naked shanks and feet protruding through his soaking, clinging trousers, which figured his shin-bones as though they clothed a skeleton. Now and again he would give himself a wild twirl and yelp out fiercely; but he was well-nigh spent with his swim, and, on the whole, was quiet enough.

I said to the girl, "How long have you been in this dreadful position?"

"Since yesterday morning," she answered, in a choking voice painful to hear, and gulping after each word. "We have not had a drop of water to drink since the night before last. He is mad with thirst, for he drank the water on the deck," and she pointed to the man in the bottom of the boat.

"My God!" I cried to the men, "do you hear her? They have not drunk water for two days! For the love of God, give way!"

They bent their backs to the oars, and the boat foamed over the long swell. The wind was astern and helped us. I did not speak again to the poor girl, for it was cruel to make her talk when the words lacerated her throat as though they were pieces of burning iron.

After twenty minutes, which seemed as many hours, we reached the vessel. The crew pressing round the gangway cheered when they saw we had brought people from the wreck. Duckling and the skipper watched us grimly from the poop.

"Now, then, my lads," I cried, "up with this lady first. Some of you on deck get water ready, as these people are dying of thirst."

In a few minutes both the girl and the old man were handed over the gangway. I cut the boat's painter adrift from the ring-bolt so that we could ship the madman without loosening his bonds, and he was hoisted up like a bale of goods. Then four us got out of the boat, leaving one to drop her under the davits and hook on the falls.

At this moment a horrible scene took place.

The old man, tottering on the arms of two seamen, was being led into the cuddy, followed by the girl, who walked unaided. The mad man, in the grasp of the big sailor named Johnson, stood near the gangway, and as I scrambled on deck one of the men was holding a pannikin full of water to his face. The poor wretch was shrinking away from it, with his eyes half out of their sockets; but suddenly tearing his arms with a violent effort from the rope that bound him, he seized the pannikin and bit clean through the *tin;* after which, throwing back his head, he swallowed the whole draught, dashed the pannikin down, his face turned black, and he fell dead on the deck.

The big sailor sprung aside with an oath, forced from him by his terror, and from every looker-on there broke a groan. They all shrunk away and stood staring with blanched faces. Such a piteous sight as it was, lying doubled up, with the rope pinioning the miserable limbs, the teeth locked, and the right arm uptossed!

"Aft here and get the quarter-boat hoisted up!" shouted Duckling, advancing on the poop; and, seeing the man dead on the deck, he added, "Get a tarpaulin and cover him up, and let him lie on the forehatch."

"Shall I tell the steward to serve out grog to men who went with me?" I asked him.

He stared at me contemptuously, and walked away without answering.

"You shall have your grog," said I, addressing one of them who stood near, "though it should be my own allowance." And thoroughly exhausted after my exertion, and wet through, I turned into my cabin, to put on some dry clothes.

CHAPTER VIII

While I was in my cabin I heard the men hoisting up the quarter-boat, and this was followed by an order from Duckling to man the lee main braces. The ship, hove to, was off her course; but when she filled, she brought the wreck right abreast of the port-hole in my cabin. I stood watching for some minutes with peculiar emotions, for the recollection of the dead body in the deck-house lent a most impressive significance to the mournful object which rolled from side to side. It comforted me, however, to reflect that it was impossible I could have left anything living on the hull, since nothing could have existed below the deck, and any one above must have been seen by me.

The ship, now lying over, shut the wreck out, and I shifted my clothes as speedily as I could, being anxious to hear what Captain Coxon should say to me. I was also curious to see the old man and girl, and learn what treatment the captain was showing them. I remember it struck me, just at this time, that the girl was in a very awkward position; for here she was on board a vessel without any female to serve her for a companion and lend her clothes, which she would stand seriously in need of, as those she had on her were wringing wet. And even supposing she could make shift with these for a time, she would soon want a change of apparel, which she certainly would not get until we reached Valparaiso, unless the skipper put into some port and landed them. The memory of her refined and pretty face, with the amber hair about it, and her wild, soft, piteous blue eyes, haunted me; and I tried to think what could be done to make her comfortable in this matter of dress if the captain refused to go out of his way to set them ashore.

Thus thinking, I was pulling on a boot when there came an awkward knock at the door of the cabin, and in stepped the carpenter, Stevens by name, holding in his hand a bar of iron with a collar at either end, and one collar fastened with a padlock. Close behind the carpenter came Duckling, who let the door close of itself, and who immediately said:

"Captain Coxon's orders are to put you in irons. Carpenter clap those belayers, on his d——d shins!"

I jumped off the chest on which I was seated, not with the intention of resisting, but of remonstrating; but Duckling, mistaking the action, drew a pistol out of his side-pocket, and, presenting it at my head, said, right through his nose, which was the first time I had heard him so speak, "By the Eternal! If you don't let the carpenter do his work, I'll shoot you dead—so mind!"

"You're a ruffian and a bully!" said I; "but I'll keep my life if only to punish you and your master!"

Saying which I reseated myself, folded my arms resolutely and suffered the carpenter to lock the irons on my ankles, keeping my eyes fixed on Duckling with an expression of the utmost scorn and dislike in them.

"Now," said he, "you infernal mutinous hound! I reckon you'll not give us much trouble for the rest of the voyage."

This injurious language was more than my temper could brook. Scarcely knowing what I did, I threw myself against him, caught his throat, and dashed him violently down upon the deck. The pistol exploded in his hand as he fell.

"Carpenter," I cried, furiously, "open that door!"

The fellow obeyed me instantly, and walked out of the cabin. Duckling lay pretty well stunned upon the deck; but in a few moments he would have been up and at me, and, hampered as I was by the irons, he must have mastered me easily. I shambled over to where he lay, dragged him upright, and pitched him with a crash through the open door against the cuddy table. He struck it heavily and rolled under it, and I then slammed the door and sat down, feeling faint and quite exhausted of breath.

The door had not been closed two minutes when it was partially opened, and a friendly hand (the boatswain's, as I afterward learned) placed a pannikin of rum and water on the deck, and a voice said, "They'll not let you be here long, sir!" The door was then shut again; and, very thankful for a refreshment of which I stood seriously in need, I got hold of the pannikin and swallowed the contents.

I now tried to reflect upon my situation, but found it impossible to do so, as I could not guess what intentions the captain had against me and what would be the result of my conflict with Duckling. For some while I sat expecting to see the chief mate rush in on me; and, in anticipation of a struggle with a coward who would have me almost at his mercy, I laid hold of a sea-boot, very heavy, with an iron-shod heel, and held it ready to strike at the bully's head should he enter. However, in about a quarter of an hour's time I saw him through my cabin window pass along the main-deck, with a blue lump over his right eye, while the rest of his face shone with soap, which he must have used without stint to rid his features of the blood that had smeared them. Whether the report of the pistol had been heard or not I could not tell; but no notice appeared to be taken of it. I noticed a number of the crew just under the forecastle conversing in a very earnest manner, and sometimes looking toward my cabin.

There was something very gross and brutal in this treatment to which I was subjected, and there was a contempt in it for me, suggested by the skipper sending Duckling to see me in irons, instead of logging to my face and acting in a ship-shape fashion in putting me under arrest, which galled me extremely. The very irons on my legs were not such as are ordinarily used on board ship, and looked as if they had been picked up cheap in some rag-and-slop shop in South America or in the West Indies, for I think I had seen such things in pictures of truculent negro slaves. I was in some measure supported by the reflection that the crew sympathized with me, and would not suffer me to be cruelly used; but the idea of a mutiny among them gave me no pleasure, for the skipper was sure to swear that I was the ringleader, and Duckling would of course back his statements; and my calling upon the men to help me put off to the wreck, against the captain's orders, my going thither, and my confinement in irons, would all tell heavily against me in any court of inquiry; so that, as things were, I not only stood the chance of being professionally ruined, but of having to undergo a term of imprisonment ashore.

These were no very agreeable reflections; and if some rather desperate thoughts came into my head while I sat pondering over my misfortunes, the reader will not greatly wonder.

I was growing rather faint with hunger, for it was past my usual dinner hour, and I had done enough work to account for a good appetite.

The captain was eating his dinner in the cuddy; for I not only smelled the cooking, but heard his voice addressing the steward, who was, perhaps, the only man in the ship who showed any kind of liking for him. I tried to hear if the old man or the girl were with him, but caught no other voice. I honestly prayed that the captain would act humanely toward them; but I had my doubts, for he was certainly a cold-blooded, selfish rascal.

By and by I heard Duckling's voice, showing that the captain had gone on deck. This man, either wanting the tact of his superior or hating me more bitterly (which I admit was fair, seeing how I had punished him), said in a loud voice to the steward:

"What fodder is that mutinous dog yonder to have?"

The steward spoke low and I did not hear.

"Serve the skunk right," continued the chief mate. "By glory! if there were only a pair of handcuffs on board they should be on him. How's this lump?"

The steward replied, and Mr. Duckling continued:

"I guess the fellow at the wheel grinned when he saw it. But I'll be raising bigger lumps than this on some of 'em before I'm done. This is the most skulking, sniveling, mutinous ship's crew that ever I sailed with; I'd rather work the vessel with four Lascars; and as to that rat in the hole there, if it wasn't for the color of the bunting we sail under, I reckon we'd have made an ensign of him at the mizzen-peak some days ago, by the Lord! with the signal halyards round his neck, for he's born to be hanged; and I guess, though he knocked me down when I wasn't looking, I'm strong enough to hoist *him* thirty feet, and let him drop with a run."

All this was said in a loud voice for my edification, but I must own it did not frighten me very greatly. To speak the truth, I thought more of the old man and his daughter than I did of myself; for if they should hear this bragging bully from their cabins, they would form very alarming conclusions as to the character of the persons who had rescued them, and scarcely know, indeed, whether we were not all cut-throats.

Shortly after this, Duckling came out on to the main-deck, and, observing me looking through the window, bawled at the top of his voice for the carpenter, who presently came, and Duckling, pointing to my window, gave him some instructions, which he went away to execute. A young ordinary seaman—an Irish lad named Driscoll—was coiling a rope over one of the belaying-pins around the main-mast. Duckling pointed up aloft, and his voice sounded, though I did not hear the order. The lad waited to coil the rest of the rope—a fathom or so—before obeying; whereupon Duckling hit him a blow on the back, slued him round, caught him by the throat, and backed him savagely against the starboard bulwarks, roaring, in language quite audible to me now, "Up with you, you skulker! Up with you, I say, or I'll pound you to pieces!"

At this moment the carpenter approached my window, provided with a hammer and a couple of planks, which he proceeded to nail upon the framework. Duckling watched him with a grin upon his ugly face, the lump over his eye not improving the expression, as you may believe. I was now in comparative darkness, for the port-hole admitted but little light, and, unlike the rest of the cuddy berths, my cabin had no bull's-eye.

I reached the door with a great deal of trouble, for the iron bar hampered my movements excessively, and found it locked outside; but by whom and when I did not know, for I had not heard the key turned. But I might depend that Duckling had done this with catlike stealthiness, and that he probably had the key in his pocket.

I was hungry enough to have felt grateful for a biscuit, and had half a mind to sing out to the steward to bring me something to eat but reflected that my doing so might only provoke an insulting answer from the fellow. With same difficulty I pulled the mattress out of the cot and put it into the bunk, as my pinioned legs would not enable me to climb or spring, and lay down and presently fell asleep.

I slept away the greater part of the afternoon, for when I awoke, the sky, as I saw it through the port-hole, was dark with the shadow of evening. A strong wind was blowing and the ship laying heavily over to it, by which I might know she was carrying a heap of canvas.

I looked over the edge of the bunk, and saw on the deck near the door a tin dish, containing some common ship's biscuit and a can of cold water. I was so hungry that I jumped up eagerly to get the biscuit, by doing which I so tweaked my ankles with the irons that the blood came from the broken skin. I made shift to reach the biscuit, which proved to be the ship's bread as served to the men, and ate greedily, being indeed famished; but speedily discovered the substantial ground of complaint the sailors had against the ship's stores; for, the biscuit was intolerably moldy and rotten, and so full of weevils that, nothing but hunger could have induced me to swallow the abomination. I managed to devour a couple of these things, and drank some water; and then pulled out my pipe and began to smoke, caring little about the skipper's objection to this indulgence in the saloon, and heartily wishing he would come to the cabin that I might tell him what I thought of his behavior.

How long was this state of things going to last with me? Would the crew compel Captain Coxon to put into some near port where I should be handed over to the authorities, or would we proceed direct to Valparaiso?

The probability of his touching anywhere was, in my opinion, now smaller than before, as the delays, and inquiry into my conduct, and the complaints of the men, would seriously enlarge the period of the voyage. Nor could I imagine that the poor persons we had rescued would prevail upon him to go out of his way to land them. As for myself, looking back on my actions, I did not believe that any court would judge me severely for obliging Coxon to send a boat to the wreck; for I had the evidence of the crew to prove that a human being had been seen signaling to us for help before I ordered the ship to be hove to, and that therefore my determination to board the wreck had not been speculative, but truly justified by the spectacle of human distress. Still, such anticipations scarcely consoled me for the inconvenience I suffered in my feet being held in irons, and in my being locked up in a gloomy cabin, where such fare as I had already eaten would probably be the food I should get until the voyage out was ended.

As the evening advanced the wind freshened, and I heard the captain give orders just over my head, and the hands shortening sail. The skipper was again straining the ship heavily; the creaking and groaning in the cuddy were incessant; and every now and again I heard the boom of a sea against the vessel's side and the sousing rush of water on deck. But after the men had been at work some time, the vessel labored less and got upon a more even keel.

Two bells (nine o'clock) had been struck, when I was suddenly attracted by a sound of hammering upon the dead-light in my cabin. I turned my head hastily; but as it was not only dark inside, but dark without, I could discern nothing, and concluded that the noise had been made on the deck overhead.

After an interval of a minute the hammering was repeated, and now it was impossible for me to doubt that it was caused by something hard, such as the handle of a knife, being struck upon the thick glass of the port-hole. I was greatly astonished; but remembering that the main-chains extended away from this port-hole, I easily concluded that some one had got down into them and was knocking to draw my attention.

I hoisted my legs out of the bunk with very great difficulty, and having got my feet upon the deck, drew myself to the port-hole, but with much trouble, it being to windward, and the deck sloping to a considerable angle.

Not a glimmer of light penetrated my cabin from the cuddy; and whether the sky outside was clear or not, I only know that the prospect seen through the port-hole, buried in the thickness of the ship's wall, was pitch-dark.

I untwisted the screw that kept the dead-light closed, and it blew open, and a rush of wind, concentrated by the narrowness of the aperture through which it penetrated, blew damp with spray upon my face.

Fearful of my voice being heard in the cuddy—for this was the hour when the spirits were put upon the table, and it was quite likely that Coxon and Duckling might be seated within, drinking alone—I muffled my voice between my hands and asked who was there?

The fellow jammed his face so effectually into the port-hole as to exclude the wind, so that the whisper in which he spoke was quite distinct.

"Me—Stevens, the carpenter. I've come from the crew. But you're to take your solemn oath you'll not split upon us if I tell you what's going to happen?"

"I am not in a position to split," I replied. "But I can make no promises until I know your intention."

The man was a long time silent. Several times he withdrew his face, as I knew (for I could not see him) by the rush of wind that came in, to shake himself free of the spray that broke over him.

"It's just this," he said, bunging up the port-hole again. "We'd rather take a twelve months' imprisonment ashore, in the worst jail in England, than work this vessel on the rotten food we're obliged to eat. What we want to know is, will you take charge o' the ship, and carry her where we tell yer, if we give you command?"

I was too much startled by this question to reply at once. Influenced by the long term of confinement before me if Captain Coxon remained in control, by my bitter dislike of him and his bully factotum, by the longing to be free, and the hundred excuses I could frame for cooperating with the crew, my first impulse was to say yes. But there came quickly considerations of the danger of mutiny on board ship, of the sure excesses of men made reckless by liberty and freed from the discipline which though their passions might protest against it, their still stronger instincts admitted and obeyed.

"Give us your answer," said the man. "If the chief mate looks over, he'll see me."

"I can not consent," I replied. "I am as sorry for the crew as I for myself. But things are better as they are."

"By———!" exclaimed the man, in a violent, hoarse whisper, "we don't mean to let 'em be as they are. We've put up with a bit too much as it is. We'll find a way of making you consent—see to that! And if you peach on us, we're still too strong for you—so mind your life!"

Saying which, he withdrew his head; and after waiting a short time to see if he remained, I closed the port and shuffled into my bunk again.

I tried to think how I should act.

If I acquainted the captain with the carpenter's disclosure, the men would probably murder me. And though they withheld from bloodshed, my putting the captain on his guard would not save the ship if the men were determined to seize her, because he could not count on more than two men to side with him, and the crew would overpower them immediately.

However, I will not seem more virtuous and upright than I was; and I may therefore say that, after giving this matter some half hour's thinking, I found that it would suit my purpose better if the crew mutinied than if the captain continued in charge, because it might open large opportunities for my future, and relieve me from the disgraceful position in which I was placed by the malice and injustice of my two superiors. The one thing I heartily prayed for was that murder might not be done; but I did not anticipate great violence, as I imagined that the crew had no other object in rebelling than to compel the captain to put into the nearest port to exchange the stores.

The night wore away very slowly, and I counted every bell that was struck. The wind decreased at midnight, and I heard Duckling go into the captain's cabin and rouse him up, the captain evidently having undertaken my duties. Duckling reported the weather during his watch, and said: "The wind is dropping, but it looks dirty to the south'ard.—If we lose the breeze we may get it fresh from t'other quarter, and she can't hurt under easy sail until we see what's going to do."

They then went on deck together, and in about ten minutes' time Duckling returned and went into his cabin, closing the door noisily.

A little after one o'clock I fell into a doze, but was shortly after awakened by hearing the growl of voices close against my cabin, apprehensions making my hearing very sensitive even in sleep.

In a few moments the voices of the men were silenced, and I then heard the tread of footsteps in the cuddy going aft, and some one as he passed tried the handle of my door.

Another long interval of silence followed, and as I did not hear the men who had entered the cuddy return, I wondered where they had stationed themselves, and what they were doing. As to myself, the irons on my legs made me quite helpless.

The time that now passed seemed an eternity, and I was beginning, to wonder whether the voices I had heard might not have been Coxon's and the steward's—all was so quiet—when a step sounded overhead, and the captain's voice rung out, "Lay aft, some hands, and brail up the spanker!"

Instantly several men ran up the starboard poop-ladder, proving that they must have been stationed close against my cabin, and their heavy feet clattered along the deck, and I heard their voices singing. Scarcely were their voices hushed when a shrill whistle, like a sharp, human squeal, was raised forward, and immediately there was a sharp twirl and a shuffle of feet on the deck, followed by a groan and a fall. At the same moment a door was forced open in the cuddy, and, as I might have judged by what followed, a body of men tumbled into the chief mate's cabin. A growling and yelping of fierce human voices followed. "Haul him out of it by the hair!" "You black-guard! you'll show fight, will yer! Take that for yourself!" "Over the eyes next time, Bill! Let me get at the ———"

But, as I imagined, the muscular, infuriate chief mate would not fall an easy prey, fighting as he deemed for his life. I heard the thump of bodies swung against the paneling, fierce execrations, the smash of crockery, and the heavy breathing of men engaged in deadly conflict.

It was brief enough in reality, though Duckling seemed to find them work for a good while.

"Don't kill him now! Wait till dere's plenty of light!" howled a voice, which I knew to be the cook's. And then they came along the cuddy dragging the body, which they had either killed or knocked insensible, after them, and got upon the main-deck.

"Poop ahoy!" shouted one of them. "What cheer up there, mates?"

"Right as a trivet!—ready to sling astern!" came the answer directly over my head, followed by some laughter.

As I lay holding my breath, scarcely knowing what was next to befall, the handle of my door was tried, the door pushed, then shaken passionately, after which a voice, in tones which might have emanated from a ghost, exclaimed:

"Mr. Royle, they have killed the captain and Mr. Duckling! For God Almighty's sake, ask them to spare my life! They will listen to you, sir! For God's sake, save me!"

"Who are you?" I answered.

"The steward, sir."

But as he said this, one of the men on the quarter-deck shouted,

"Where's the steward? He's as bad as the others! He's the one that swore the pork was sweet!"

And then I heard the steward steal swiftly away from my cabin door and some men come into the cuddy. They would doubtless have hunted him down there and then, but one of them unconsciously diverted the thoughts of the others by exclaiming:

"There's the second mate in there. Let's have him out of it."

My cabin door was again tried, and a heavy kick administered.

"It's locked, can't you see?" said one of the men.

As it opened into the cuddy, it was not to be forced, so one of them exclaimed that he would fetch a mallet and a calking-iron, with which he returned in less than a couple of minutes, and presently the lock was smashed to pieces and the door fell open.

Both swinging lamps were alight in the cuddy, and one, being nearly opposite my cabin, streamed fairly into it. I was seated erect in my bunk when the men entered, and I immediately exclaimed, pointing to the irons, "I am glad you have thought of me. Knock those things off, will you?"

I believe there was something in the cold way in which I pronounced those words that as fully persuaded them that I was intent upon the mutiny as any action I could have committed.

"We'll not take long to do that for you," cried the fellow who held the mallet (a formidable weapon by the way, in such hands). "Get upon the deck, and I'll swaller this iron if you aren't able to dance a break-down in a jiffy!"

I dropped out of the bunk, and with two blows the man cut off the staple, and I kicked the irons off.

"Now, my lads," said I, beginning to play the part I had made up my mind to act while listening to the onslaught on the captain and Duckling, "what have you done?"

The fellow who had knocked off the irons, and now answered me, was named Cornish, a man in my own watch.

"The ship's ourn—that's what we've done," he said.

"The skipper's dead as a nail up there, I doubt," exclaimed another, indicating the poop with a movement of the head; and if you'll step on to the main-deck, you'll see how we've handled Mister Duckling."

"And what do *you* mean to do?" exclaimed a man, one of the four who had accompanied me to the wreck. "*We're* masters now, I suppose you know, and so I hope you ar'n't agin us."

At this moment the carpenter, followed by a few others, came shoving into the cuddy.

"Oh, there he is!" he cried.

He grasped me by the arm and led me out of the cabin, and bidding me stand at the end of the table, with my face looking aft, ran to the door, and bawled at the top of his voice, "Into the cuddy, all hands!"

Those who were on the poop came scuffling along, dragging something with them, and presently rose a cry of "One—two—three!" and there was a soft thud on the main-deck—the body of the captain, in fact, pitched off the poop—and then the men came running in and stood in a crowd on either side of the table.

This was a scene I am not likely ever to forget, nor the feelings excited in me by it.

The men were variously dressed, some in yellow sou'-westers, some in tight-fitting caps, in coarse shirts, in suits of oilskin, in liberally patched monkey-jackets. Some of them with black beards and moustaches and burned complexions, looked swarthy and sinister enough in the lamplight; some were pale with the devilish spirit that had been aroused in them; every face, not excepting the youngest of the ordinary seamen, wore a passionate, reckless, malignant look. They ran their eyes over the cuddy as strangers would, and one of them took a glass off a swinging tray, and held it high, saying grimly, "By the Lord! we'll have something fit to swaller now! No more starvation and stinking water!"

I noticed the boatswain—named Forward—the only quiet face in the crowd. He met my eye, and instantly looked down.

"Now, Mr. Royle," said the carpenter, "we're all ekals here, with a fust-rate execootioner among us" (pointing to the big sailor Johnson), "as knows, when he's axed, how to choke off indiwiduals as don't make theirselves sootable to our feelin's. What we're all here collected for to discover is this—are you with us or agin us?"

"With you," I replied, "in everything but murder."

Some of them growled, and the carpenter exclaimed hastily:

"We don't know what you call murder. We ar'n't used to them sort o' expressions. What's done has happened, ain't it? And I *have* heerd tell of accidents, which is the properest word to convey our thoughts."

He nodded at me significantly.

"Look here," said I. "Just a plain word with you before I am asked any more questions. There's not a man among you who doesn't know that I have been warm on your side ever since I learned what kind of provisions you were obliged to eat. I have had words with the captain about your stores, and it is as much because of my interference in that matter as because of my determination not to let a woman die upon a miserable wreck that he clapped me in irons. I don't know what you mean to do with me, and I'll not say I don't care. I do care. I value my life, and in the hope of saving it, I'll tell you this, and it's God's truth—that if you take my life, you'll be killing a man who has been your friend at heart, who has sympathized with you in your privations, who has never to his knowledge spoken harshly to you when he had the power to do so, and who, had he commanded this vessel, would have shifted your provisions long ago."

So saying I folded my arms and looked fixedly at the carpenter.

They listened to me in silence, and when I had done broke into various exclamations.

"We know all that."

"We don't owe *you* no grudge."

"We don't want your life. Just show us what to do—that's what it is."

I appeared to pay no attention to their remarks, but kept my eyes resolutely bent on Stevens, the carpenter, that they might see I accepted him as their mouth-piece, and would deal only with him.

"Well," he began, "all what you say is quite correct, and we've no fault to find with you. What I says to you this evenin' through the port-hole I says now—will you navigate this here vessel for us to the port as we've agreed on? And if you'll do that, you can choose officers out of us, and we'll do your bidding as though you was lawful skipper, and trust to you. But I say now, I says it before all hands here, that if you takes us where we don't want to go, or put us in the way of any man-o'-war, or try in any manner to bring us to book for this here job, so help me, Mr. Royle, and that's your name, as mine is William Stevens, and I say it before all hands, we'll sling you overboard as sartain as there's hair growin' on your head—we will; we'll murder you out and out. All my mates is a-followin' of me—so you'll please mind that!"

"I hear you," I replied, "and will do your bidding, but on this condition—that having killed the captain, you will swear to me that no more lives shall be sacrificed."

"By Gor, no!" shouted the cook. "Don't swear dat! Wait till by-um-by."

"Be advised by me!" I cried, seizing the fellow's frightful meaning, and dreading the hideous scene it portended. "We have an old man and young girl on board. Are they safe?"

"Yes," answered several voices; and the cook jabbered, "yes, yes!" with horrid contortions of the face, under the impression that I had mistaken his interruption.

"We have the steward and the chief mate?"

"Dat's dey! dat's dey!" screamed the cook. "No mercy upon 'em. Had no mercy upon us! Him strike me on de jaw and kick me! T'oder one poison us! No mercy!" he howled, and several joined in the howl.

"Look here! I am a single man among many," I said, "but I am not afraid to speak out—because I am an Englishman speaking to Englishmen, with one blood-thirsty yellow savage among you!" There was a shout of laughter. "If you wish it, I will go on my knees to you, and implore you not to stain your hands with these men's blood. You have them in your power—you cannot better your position by killing them—be merciful! Mates, how would you kill them—in cold blood? Is there an Englishman among you who would slaughter a defenseless man? who would stand by and see a defenseless man slaughtered? There is an Almighty God above you, and he is the God of vengeance! Hear me!"

"We'll let the steward go!" cried a voice; "but we want our revenge on Duckling, and we'll have it. D——n your sermons!"

And once again the ominous growling of angry men muttering altogether arose; in the midst of which the fellow who was steering left the wheel to sing out through the sky-light:

"It's as black as thunder to the leeward. Better stand by, or the ship'll be aback!"

"Now what am I to do?" I exclaimed.

"We give you command. Out with your orders—we'll obey 'em," came the answer.

In a few moments I was on the poop. By the first glance I threw upward I saw that the ship was already aback.

"Port your helm—hard a-port!" I shouted. "Let go your port-braces fore and aft! Round with the yards smartly!"

Fortunately, not only was the first coming of the wind light, but the canvas on the ship was comparatively small. The main-sail, cross-jack, the three royals, two top-gallant-sails, spanker, flying and outer jibs were furled, and there was a single reef in the fore and mizzentop-sails. The yards swung easily and the sails filled, and not knowing what course to steer, I braced the yards up sharp and kept her close.

The sky to the south looked threatening, and the night was very dark. I ran below to look at the glass, and found a slight fall, but nothing to speak of. This being so, I thought we might hold on with the top-sails as they were for the present, and ordered the topgallant-sail to be furled. The men worked with great alacrity, singing out lustily; indeed it was difficult for me, standing on the poop and giving orders, to realize the experiences of the last hour; and yet I might know, by the strange trembling and inward and painful feeling of faintness which from time to time seized me, that both my moral and physical being had received a terrible shock, and that I should feel the reality more keenly when my excitement was abated and I should have no other occupation than to think.

The only food I had taken all day was the two ship's biscuits; and, feeling the need of some substantial refreshment to relieve me of the sensation of faintness, I left the poop to seek the carpenter, in order to request him to keep watch while I went below.

When on the quarter-deck, and looking toward the cuddy, I perceived two figures huddled together just outside the cuddy door. There was plenty of light here from the lamps inside, and I at once saw that the two bodies were those of Duckling and Coxon.

I stepped up to them. Coxon lay on his back with his face exposed, and Duckling was right across him, breast downward, his head in the corner and his feet toward me. There was no blood on either of them. Coxon had evidently been struck over the head from behind, and killed instantly; his features were composed, and his gray hairs made him look a reverend object in death.

Some men on the main-deck watched me looking at the bodies, and when they saw me take Duckling by the arm and turn him on his back one of them called, "That's right; keep the beggar alive! He's cookee's portion, he is!"

These exclamations attracted the attention of the carpenter, who came aft immediately and found me stooping over Duckling.

"He's dead, I reckon," he said.

"Dead, or next door to it," I replied. "Better for him if he is dead. The captain's a corpse, killed quickly enough, by the look of him," I continued, gazing at the white, still face at my feet. "You had better get him carried forward and covered up. Where's the body of the sailor I brought on board?"

"Why, pitched him overboard like a dead rat, by orders of this Christian," he answered, giving the captain's body a kick. "He had a good deal of feelin', this pious gentleman. Why do you want him covered up? Let him go overboard now, won't 'ee? Hi, mates!" he called to the men who were looking on. "Here's another witness agin us for the Day o' Judgment! Heave him into the sea, my hearties! We don't want to give him no excuse to soften the truth for our sakes when he's called upon to spin his yarn!"

The men flocked round the bodies, and while three of them caught up the corpse of the skipper as if it had been a coil of rope, others of them began to handle Duckling.

"Him too?" asked one.

"What do you say, Mr. Royle?" demanded the carpenter.

"It ain't Mr. Royle's consarn—it's cookee's!" cried one of the men. And he began to bawl for "cookee."

Meantime the fellows who held the captain's body, not relishing their burden, went to leeward; and, two of them taking the shoulders and one the feet, they began to swing him, and at a given word shot him over the bulwarks. They then came back quite unconcernedly, one of them observing that the devil ought to be very much obliged to them for their handsome present.

The cook now approached, walked aft by some men who held him by the arms. They were laughing uproariously, which was explained when I saw that the cook was drunk.

"Here's your friend, Mr. Cookee," said Stevens, stirring Duckling with the toe of his boot. "He's waitin' for you to know wot's to become of him."

"Him a berry good gentleman," returned the cook, pulling off his cap with drunken gravity, and making a reeling bow to the body. "Me love dis gentleman like my own son. Nebber knew tenderer-hearted man. Him gib me a nice blow here," holding his clinched fist to his jaw, "and anoder one here," clapping his hand to his back. Then, after a pause, he kicked the dying or dead man savagely in the head, yelling in a hideous falsetto, "Oh, I'll skin urn alive! Oh, I'll pull his eyes out and make um swaller dem! He kick an' strike honest English cook! Oh, my golly! I'll cut off his foot! Gib me a knife, sar," looking round him with a wandering, gleaming eye. "Gib me a knife, I say, an' you see what I do!"

One of the ruffians actually gave him a knife.

I grasped the carpenter's arm.

"Mr. Stevens," I exclaimed, in his ear, "you'll not allow this! For God's sake, don't let this drunken cannibal disgrace our manhood by such brutal deeds before us! Living or dead, better fling the body overboard! Don't let him be tortured if living; and if dead, is not our revenge complete?"

The carpenter made no answer, and sick with horror and disgust I was turning away, feeling powerless to deal with these wretches, when, the cook already kneeling and baring his arm for I know not what bloody work, Stevens sprung forward and fetched him such a thump under the chin that he rolled head over heels into the lee-scuppers.

The men roared with laughter.

"Now, then, overboard with this thing!" the carpenter shouted; "and if cookee wants more wengeance, fling him overboard arter him!"

They seized Duckling as they had seized Coxon, and slung him overboard just as they had slung the other. Some of them ran to the cook, and it was impossible to judge whether they were in earnest or not when they shrieked out, "Overboard with him too! We can't separate the friends!" The cook, at all events, believed they meant no joke, for uttering a prolonged yell of terror, he wriggled with incredible activity out of their hands, and rushed forward like a steam engine. They did not offer to pursue him; and, ill with these scenes of horror, I called to the carpenter and asked him to step on the poop while I went into the cuddy.

"What to do there?" he inquired, suspiciously.

"To get something to eat. I have had nothing all day but two of the ship's bad biscuits."

"Right," he said. "But, before I go, I'll tell you what's agreed among us. You're to take charge, and sarve with me and the bo's'n, turn and turn about on deck. That's agreeable, ain't it?"

"Quite."

"You're to do all the piloting of the ship, and navigate us to where the ship's company agrees upon."

"I understand."

"We three live aft here, and the ship's company forrard; but all the ship's stores'll be smothered, and the cuddy provisions sprung, d'ye see? likewise the grog and whatsomever there may be proper to eat and drink. We're all to be ekals, and fare and fare alike, though the crew'll obey orders as usual. You're to have the skipper's berth, and I'll take yourn; and the bo's'n he'll take Duckling's. That we've all agreed on afore we went to work, and so I thought I'd let you know."

"Well, Mr. Stevens," I replied, "as I told you just now, I'll do your bidding. I'll take the ship to the place you may name; and as I sha'n't play you false, though I have no notion of your intentions, so I hope you won't play me false. I have begged for the steward's life, and you have promised to spare him. And how are the two persons we saved to be treated?"

"They're to live along with us here. All that's settled, I told yer. But I'm not so sure about the steward. I never made no promise about sparing him."

"Look here!" I exclaimed, sternly. "I am capable of taking this ship to any port you choose to name. There is not another man on board who could do this. I can keep you out of the track of ships, and help you in a number of ways to save your necks. Do you understand me? But I tell you, on my oath, if you murder the steward, if any further act of violence is committed on board this ship, I'll throw up my charge, and you may do your worst. These are my terms, easier to you than to me. What is your answer?"

He reflected a moment and replied, "I'll talk to my mates about it."

"Do so," I said. "Call them aft now. But you had better get on deck, as the ship wants watching. Talk to them on the poop."

He obeyed me literally, calling for the hands to lay aft, and I was left alone.

I went into the steward's pantry, where I found some cold meat and biscuit and a bottle of sherry. These things I carried to the foremost end of the table. Somehow I did not feel greatly concerned about the debate going on overhead, as I knew the men could not do without me; nor did I believe the general feeling against the steward sufficiently strong to make them willing to sacrifice my services to their revengeful passions.

I fell to the meat and wine as greedily as a starving man, and was eating very heartily, when I felt a light touch on my arm. I turned hastily and confronted the girl whom I had brought away from the wreck. Her hair hung loose over her shoulders, and she was pale as marble. But her blue eyes were very brilliant, and fired with a resolved and brave expression, and I thought her beautiful as she stood before me in the lamp-light with her hair shining about her face.

"Are you Mr. Royle?" she asked, in a low but most clear and sweet voice.

"I am," I replied, rising.

She took my hand and kissed it.

"You have saved my father's life and mine, and I have prayed God to bless you for your noble courage. I have had no opportunity to thank you before. They would not let me see you. The captain said you had mutinied and were in irons. My father wishes to thank you—his heart is so full that he can not rest—but he is too weak to move. Will you come and see him?"

She made a movement toward the cabin next the pantry.

"Not now," I said. "You should be asleep, resting after your terrible trials."

"How could I sleep?" she exclaimed, with a shudder. "I have heard all that has been said. I heard them killing the man in that cabin there."

She clasped her hands convulsively.

"Frightful things have happened," I said, speaking quickly, for I every moment expected the men to come running down the companion-ladder, near which we were conversing; "but the worst has passed. Did you not hear them answer me that you and your father were safe? Go, I beg you, to your cabin and sleep if you can, and be sure that no harm shall befall you while I remain in this ship. I have a very difficult part before me, and wish to reflect upon my position. And the sense that *your* security will depend upon my actions," I added, moved by her beauty and the memory of the fate I had rescued her from, "will make me doubly vigilant."

And as she kissed my hand on meeting me, so now I raised hers to my lips; and, obedient to my instructions, she entered her cabin and closed the door.

I stood for some time engrossed, to the exclusion of all other thoughts, by the picture impressed on my mind by the girl's sweet face. It inspired a new kind of energy in me. Whatever qualms my conscience may have suffered from my undertaking to navigate the ship for the satisfaction and safety of a pack of ruffians, merely because I stood in fear of my life, were annihilated by the sight of this girl. The profound necessity enjoined upon me to protect her from the dangers that would inevitably come upon her should my life be taken, so violently affected me as I stood thinking of her, that my cowardly acquiescence in the basest proposals which the crew could submit would have been tolerable to my conscience for her lonely and helpless sake.

The voices of the men overhead, talking in excited tones, awoke me to a sense of my situation. I took another draught of wine, and entered the captain's cabin, wishing to inspect the log-book that I might ascertain the ship's position at noon on the preceding day. The shadow of the mizzen-mast fell right upon the interior as I opened the cabin door. I looked about me for a lamp, but was suddenly scared by the spectacle of a man crawling on his hands and knees out of a corner.

"Oh, my God!" cried a melancholy voice. "Am I to be killed? Will they murder me, sir? Oh, sir, it is in your power to save me! They'll obey you. I have a wife and child in England, sir. I am a miserable sinner, and not fit to die!"

And the wretched creature burst into tears, and crawled close to my legs and twined his arms around them.

"Go back to your corner," I said. "Don't let them hear or see you. I can make no promises, but will do my best to save your life. Back with you now. Be a man, for God's sake! Your whining will only amuse them. Be resolute; and should you have to face them, meet them bravely."

He went crawling back to his corner, and I, seeing the log-book open upon the table, carried it under the lamp in the cuddy. There I read off the sights of the previous day, replaced the book, and mounted to the poop.

The dawn was breaking in the east, and the sky heavy, though something of its threatening character had left it. There was a smart sea on, but the ship lay pretty steady, owing to the wind having freshened enough to keep the vessel well over. We were making no headway to speak of, the yards being against the masts, and but little canvas set. The fellow steering lounged at the wheel, one arm through the spokes, and his left leg across his right shin, letting all hands know by his free-and-easy attitude that we were all equals now, and that he was only there to oblige. He was watching the men assembled round the forward saloon sky-light, and now and then called out to them.

There were eight or nine of the crew there and on the top of the sky-light, and in the center of the throng were squatted the boatswain and the carpenter.

Many of them were smoking, and some of them laid down the law with their forefingers upon the palms of their hands. I saw no signs of the cook, and hoped that the fright the evil-minded scoundrel had undergone would keep him pretty quiet for a time.

Not thinking it politic to join the men until they summoned me, I walked to the compass to see how the ship's head lay; whereupon the man steering, out of a habit of respect too strong for him to control, drew himself erect, and looked at the sails, and then at the card, as a man intent upon his work. I made no observation to him, and swept the horizon through my hands, which I hollowed to collect the pale light, but could discover nothing save the rugged outline of waves.

Just then the men saw me, and both the carpenter and the boatswain scrambled off the sky-light, and they all came toward me.

A tremor ran through me which I could not control, but strength was given me to suppress all outward manifestations of emotion, and I awaited their approach with a forced tranquillity which, as I afterward heard, gave the more intelligent and better-disposed among them a good opinion of me.

The carpenter said, "Most of us are for leaving the steward alone; but there's three of us as says that he showed hisself so spiteful in the way he used to sarve out the rotten stores, and swore to such a lie when he said the pork was sweet before it went into the coppers, that they're for havin' some kind of rewenge."

"None of you want his life, do you?"

"D——n his life!" came a growl. "Who'd take what ain't of no use even to him as owns it?"

"Which of you wants revenge?" I asked.

There was a pause; and Fish, projecting his extraordinary head, said, "Well, I'm one as dew."

"Suppose," said I, "you were to see this wretched creature groveling on his hands and knees, weeping and moaning like a woman, licking the deck in his agony of fear, and already half dead with terror. Would not such a miserable sight satisfy your thirst for revenge? What punishment short of death that you can inflict would make him suffer more dreadful tortures than his fear has already caused him? Fish, be a man, and leave this haunted wretch alone."

He muttered something under his breath, though looking, I was glad to see, rather shamefaced; and the boatswain said:

"There's something more, Mr. Royle. He knows where to lay his hands on the cuddy provisions; and if we knock him on the head we shan't be able to find half that'll be wanted. What I woted was that we should make him wait upon us, and let him have nothing but the ship's stores to eat, while he sarves us with the cuddy's."

"Won't that do?" I exclaimed, addressing the others, at the same time receiving a glance from the boatswain which showed me that I should have an ally in him, as indeed I had expected; for this was the only one of the forecastle hands who had come from London with us, and I was pretty sure he had joined in the mutiny merely to save his life.

"Oh, yes, that'll do," some of them answered impatiently; and one said, "Wot's the use of jawing about the steward? We want to talk of ourselves. Where's the ship bound to? I don't want to be hanged when I get ashore."

This sensible observation was delivered by Johnson.

"Now, then, if you like we'll come to that," said I, immensely relieved; for I not only knew that the steward's life was safe, but that, in their present temper, no further act of violence would be perpetrated. "Mr. Stevens, you told me that all your plans were prepared. Am I to have your confidence?"

"Sartinly," replied the fellow, looking around upon the assembled faces fast growing distinguishable in the gathering light. "You're a scholard, and can sail the ship for us; and we look to you to get us out o' this mess, for we've treated you well, and made you skipper."

"Go ahead!" I exclaimed, seating myself in a nonchalant way on one of the gratings abaft the wheel.

"This here mutiny," began the carpenter, after casting about in his mind for words, "is all along o' bad treatment. Had the captain acted fair and proper, *we'd* ha' acted fair and proper. He as good as swore that he'd put in for fresh stores, but never altered the ship's course, and we wouldn't starve no longer: so we up and did the business. But we never meant to kill him. We was afraid he'd ha' had pistols on him, and so some of us knocked him down unaweers, and knocked too hard, that was all. And t'other one, he struggled so, instead of givin' up when he saw we was too many for ten o' the likes of him, that he died of his own doin'; and that's a fact, mates, ain't it?"

"Ay," responded a gruff voice. "He'd ha' gouged my eye out. He had his thumb in my mouth, workin' away as if he thought my tooth was my eye. He drawed blood with his thumb, and I had to choke it out of my mouth, or he'd ha' tore my tongue out!"

So saying, he expectorated wildly.

"To come back to wot I was saying," resumed the carpenter; "it's this: when me and my mates made up our minds to squench the skipper and his bully mate for their wrongful dealings with us, one says that our plan was to run the ship to the North Ameriky shores somewheeres. One says Floridy way; and another, he says round into the Gulf o' Mexico, within reach o' New Orleans; and another, he says, 'Let's go south, mates, upon the coast of Africa'; and another, he says he's for making the ice right away north, up near Baffin Land. But none was agreeable to that. We aren't resolved yet, but we're most all for Ameriky because it's a big place pretty nigh big enough to hide in."

Some of the men laughed.

"And so," continued the carpenter, "our plan is this—as easy as sayin' your prayers: we'll draw lots and choose upon the coast for you to run us to; and when we're a day's sail of them parts, leavin' you to tell us and to keep us out o' the way of ships, d'ye mind, Mr. Royle?"—with stern significance: I nodded—"some of us gets into the long-boat and—some into the quarter-boats, and we pulls for the shore. And what we do and says when we gets ashore needn't matter, eh, mates? We're shipwrecked mariners, destitoot and forlorn, and every man's for hisself. And so that's our plan."

"Yes, that's our plan," said one; "but it ain't all. You're putting everything to Mr. Royle, mate."

"Look here, Bill," answered the carpenter, savagely, "either I'm to manage this here business or I'm not. If *you're* for carryin' of it on, good and well—say the word, and then well know the time o' day. But either it must be you or it must be I—there ain't room for two woices in one mouth."

"I've got nothen to say," rejoined the man addressed as "Bill," extending his arms and turning his back; "only I thought you might ha' forgot."

What the carpenter was holding back I could not guess; but I exhibited no curiosity. Neither did I tell him that our course to the "American shores," as they called it, would bring us right in the road of vessels from all parts of the world. My business was to listen and to act as circumstances should dictate, with good judgment, if possible, for the preservation of my own and the lives of the old man and his daughter.

The carpenter now paused to hear what I had to say. Finding this, I exclaimed:

"I know what you want me to do; and the sooner you fix upon a point to start for the better."

"Can't you advise us?" said one of the men. "Give us some place easily fetched."

"I was never on the North American coast," I answered.

"Well, Ameriky ain't the only place in the world," said Fish.

"You'd best not say that when you're there," exclaimed Johnson.

"Most of the hands want to go ashore in Ameriky, and so that's settled, mates," said the carpenter, sharply.

"Let's keep south, anyhow, say I. If we can make New Orleans there's plenty of vessels sailing every day from that port, paying good wages," said Johnson.

"And every man can choose for hisself where he'll sail for," observed Fish.

"Make up your minds," I exclaimed, "and I'll alter the ship's course."

So saying, I got off the grating and walked to the other end of the poop.

I was much easier in my mind, now that I had observed the disposition of the men. They were unquestionably alarmed by what they had done, which was tolerable security against the commission of further outrages. Their project of quitting the ship when near land and making for the shore, where, doubtless, they would represent themselves as shipwrecked seamen, was practicable and struck me as ingenious; for as soon as they got ashore they would disperse and ship on board fresh vessels, and so defy inquiry even should suspicion be excited, or one of them peach upon his fellows. These I at least assumed to be their plans. But how far they would affect my own safety I could not tell. I doubted if they would let me leave the ship, as they might be sure that, on my landing, I should hasten to inform against them. But I would not allow my mind to be troubled with considerations of the future at that time. All my energies were required to deal with the crisis of the moment, and to guard myself against being led, by too much confidence in their promises, into any step which might prove fatal to me and those I had promised to protect.

The dawn was now bright in the east and the wind strong from the southward. The ship was chopping on the tumbling seas with scarcely any way upon her; but the menacing aspect of the sky was fast fading, and there was a promise of fair weather in the clouds, which ranged high and out of the reach of the breeze that was burying the ship's lee channels.

Presently the carpenter called me, and I went over to the men.

"We're all resolved, Mr. Royle," said he, in a pretty civil voice, "and our wotes is for New Orleans. Plenty of wessels is wrecked in the gulf of Mexico, as I've heeard tell; and when we're about fifty miles off you'll say so, and give us the bearings of the Mississippi, and we'll not trouble you any more."

"How's her head?" I asked the man at the wheel.

"Sou'-west," he replied.

"Keep her away!" I exclaimed, for the weather leeches were flat.

"What's our true course for New Orleans?" asked the carpenter, suspiciously.

"Stop a bit and I'll show you," I answered, and went below to captain's cabin to get the chart.

"Steward!" I called.

"Yes, sir," replied the miserable whining voice. It was still too dark for me to see the man.

"Make your mind easy—they'll not hurt you," I said.

He started up and rushed toward me like a madman.

"May God in Heaven bless you!" he cried, delirious with joy.

"Hold off!" I exclaimed, keeping him away with my outstretched hand. "Get your wits about you, and remain here for the present. Don't let them hear you, and don't show yourself until I call you."

I could have said nothing better to repress his violent manifestations of delight; for he at once went cowering again into the gloom of the corner.

I struck a wax match, and after a short search found the chart of the North Atlantic upon which the ship's course, so far as she had gone up to noon on the preceding day, was pricked off. I took this on deck, spread it on the sky-light, and showed our whereabouts to the men.

"Our course," said I, "is south-west and by west."

They bent their faces over the chart, studying it curiously.

"Are you satisfied, Mr. Stevens?" I asked him.

"Oh, I suppose it's all right," answered he.

"Slacken away the lee braces," I said. "Put your helm up" (to the man at the wheel).

The men went tumbling off the poop to man the braces, and in a few minutes we were making a fair wind.

Both the carpenter and the boatswain remained on the poop.

"Some hands lay aloft and loose the fore and maintop-gallantsails!" I called out. And, turning to the carpenter, I said, "I'll navigate this ship for you and your mates to within fifty miles of the mouth of the Mississippi, as you wish, but on the conditions I have already named. Do you remember?"

"Oh, yes," he growled "We've done enough—too much, I dessay, though not more than the beggars desarved. All that we want is to get out o' this cursed wessel."

"Very well," I said. "But I won't undertake to pilot this ship safely unless my orders are obeyed."

"The men are quite willin' to obey you, so long as you're true to 'em," he rejoined.

"You may do what you like with the cuddy stores, though if you take my advice you will let the steward serve them out in the regular way that they may last; otherwise you will eat them all up before we reach our journey's end and have to fall back upon the bad provisions. But I must have control of the spirits."

"And what allowance do you mean to put us on?" demanded the carpenter.

"I shall be advised by you," said I.

This was turning the tables. He pulled off his cap and scratched his head.

"Three tots a day?" he suggested.

"Very well," I said; "but you'll stop at that?"

'Well, perhaps we can do on three tots a day," he answered, after deliberating.

"And you engage that the steward will be protected against any violence while serving out the men's allowance?"

"Mates!" he suddenly called out to the men who were standing by to sheet home the top-gallant-sails; "will three tots o' grog a day keep you alive?"

"Are we to have it all at once?" one of them answered.

"No," I replied; "three times a day."

"Now then, my lads, let's know your minds," cried the boatswain.

A young ordinary seaman answered, "Three ain't enough." But one of the older hands turned upon him, exclaiming:

"Why, you bit of a snuffler! where will *you* stow away all that rum?

Don't go answering for your betters, my young scaramouch, or may be you'll be findin' yourself brought up with a round turn. That'll do!" he called out to us.

"Right you are!" replied the carpenter.

"Sheet home!" I cried, as the sails fell from the top-gallant yards, anxious to clinch this matter of the grog.

And so it rested.

CHAPTER IX

AS THE men had been up all night, I recommended the carpenter to go to them and tell them that the watches would not be altered, and that the watch whose spell it was below should turn in.

Some, it appeared, asked that rum should be served out to them; but the carpenter answered that none should be given them until breakfast-time, and that if they got talking too much about the drink, he'd run a brad-awl into the casks and let the contents drain out; for if the men fell to drinking, the ship was sure to get into a mess, in which case they might be boarded by the crew of another vessel and carried to England, where nothing less than hanging or transportation awaited them.

This substantial advice from the lips of the man who had been foremost in planning the mutiny produced a good effect, and the fellows who had asked for spirits were at once clamorously assailed by their mates; so that, in their temper, had the carpenter proposed to fling the rum casks overboard, most of the hands would have consented and the thing been done.

All this I was told by the boatswain, who had left the poop with the carpenter, but returned before him. I took this opportunity of being alone with the man to ask him some questions relative to the mutiny, and particularly inquired if he could tell me what was that intention which the man named "Bill" had asked the carpenter to communicate to me, but which he had refused to explain. The boatswain, who was at the bottom a very honest man, declared that he had no notion of the intention the carpenter was concealing, but promised to try and worm the secret out of Johnson or others who were in it, and impart it to me.

He now informed me that he had come into the mutiny because he saw the men were resolved, and also because they thought he took the captain's part, which was a belief full of peril to him. He said that he could not foresee how this trouble would end; for though the idea of the men to quit the ship and make for the shore in open boats was feasible, yet they would run very heavy risks of capture any way; for if they came across a ship while in the boats, they could not refuse to allow themselves to be taken on board, where, some of the mutineers being very gross and ignorant men, the truth would certainly leak out; while as to escaping on shore, it was fifty to one if the answers they made to enquiries would not differ so widely one from another as to betray them.

But at this point our conversation was interrupted by the carpenter coming aft to ask me to keep watch while he and the boatswain turned in, as he, for one, was "dead beat," and would not be of any service until he had rested.

It was now broad daylight, the east was filled with the silver splendors of the rising sun. I descried a sail to windward, on the starboard tack, heading eastward. I made her out through the glass to be a small top-sail schooner; but as we were going free with a fresh breeze, we soon sunk her hull.

The sight of this vessel, however, set me thinking on my own position. What would be thought and how should I be dealt with when (supposing I should ever reach land) I should come to tell the story of this mutiny? But this was a secondary consideration. My real anxiety was to foresee how the men would act when I had brought them to the place they wished to arrive at. Would they give such a witness against their murderous dealings as I was a chance to save my life? I, whose plain testimony could set justice on the hunt for every one of them. I could not place confidence in their assurances. The oaths of such ruffians as many of them undoubtedly were, were worthless. They would murder me without an instant's scruple if by so doing they could improve their own chances of escape; and I was fully persuaded that I should have shared the fate of Coxon and Duckling, in

spite of the sympathy I had shown them, and their declaration that they did
not want my life, had they not foreseen that they would stand in need of
some competent person to navigate the ship for them, and that I was more
likely to come into their projects than either of the men they had murdered.

My agitation was greater than I liked to admit; and I turned over in my
mind all sorts of ideas for my escape, but never forgetting the two helpless
persons whose lives I considered wholly dependent on my own preservation.

At one moment I thought of taking the boatswain into my confidence,
stealthily storing provisions in one of the quarter-boats, and watching an
opportunity to sneak off with him and our passengers under cover of night.

Then I thought of getting him to sound the minds of the crew, to judge
if there was any who might assist us should we rise upon the more desperate of the mutineers.

Another notion was to pretend to mistake the ship's whereabouts, and
run her into some port.

But such stratagems as these, easily invented, were in reality impracticable.

To let the men see that I stood to my work, I never quitted the deck
until six o'clock. The morning was then very beautiful, with a rich and
warm aroma in the glorious southerly breeze, and the water as blue as the
heavens.

On arousing the carpenter in the cabin formerly occupied by me (I
found him in the bunk on my mattress with his boots on, and a pipe belonging to me in his hand), I told him that the ship could now carry all plain sail,
and advised him to make it. He got out of the bunk in a pretty good temper,
and went along the cuddy; but as he was about to mount the
companion-ladder I called to know if he would see the steward, and speak
to him about serving out the cuddy stores, as I preferred that he should give
the man instructions, since they would best represent the wishes of the
crew. But the truth was, I wanted to pack all the responsibility that I could
upon him, so as to make myself as little answerable as possible to the men.

"Yes, yes. Fetch him out. Where is he?" he replied, turning round.

"Steward!" I called.

After a pause the door of the captain's cabin opened, and the figure of the steward stepped forth. Such a woe-begone object, with bloodless lips and haggard expression, and red eyes and quivering mouth, hands hanging like an idiot's, his hair matted, his knees knocking together as he walked, I never wish to see again.

"Now, young fellow," said the carpenter (the steward, by the way, was about forty years old), "what do you think ought to be done to you, hey? Is hangin' too mild, or is drownin' more to your fancy? or would you like to be dissected by the cook, who is reckoned a neat hand at carving?"

The steward turned his blood-shot eyes upon me, and his lips moved.

"Mr. Stevens is only joking," I exclaimed, feeling that I would give a year's pay to strike the ruffian to the earth for his brutal playing with the miserable creature's terror. "He wants to talk to you about the cuddy provisions."

The carpenter stared at him grimly, out of a mean tyranny and relish of his fears; and the poor creature said "Yes, sir!" lifting his eyes humbly to the carpenter's face, and folding his hands in an involuntary attitude of supplication.

"You'll understand, young fellow," said the carpenter, thrusting his hands into his pockets, and leaning against the mizzenmast, "that we're all equals aboard this here wessel, now. No one's above t'other, barring yourself, who's just nowheeres at all, owin' to your keepin' in tow of the skipper when he was pisoning us with the stores which you, d——n yer! took joy in sarving out! Now you understand this: you're to turn to and sarve out the cuddy stores to me at the proper time, and three tots o' grog every day to each man. Mr. Ryle'll tell you how long our passage'll last, and you're to make calkilation of the live-stock so as each watch gits a share of the pigs an' poultry. But you," he continued, squirting some tobacco-juice from his mouth, "aren't to touch any other provisions but the stores which the crew's been eatin' of; mind that! If we catch you tastin' so much as half a cuddy biscuit, by the living thunder! we'll run you up to the fore yard-arm!"

He shook his fist in the steward's face and addressing me said:

"That's all to be said, ain't it?"

"That's all," I replied; and the steward went cringing and reeling toward the pantry, while the carpenter mounted the companion-ladder.

I entered the cabin, which, to save confusion, I will continue to call the captain's cabin, and seated myself in a chair screwed down to the deck before a wide table. This cabin was comfortably furnished with hanging book-shelves, a fine map of the world, a few colored prints of ships, a handsome cot, and mahogany lockers cushioned on top to serve for seats.

Among some writing materials, a case of mathematical instruments, a boat's compass, and a variety of other matters which covered the table, I observed an American five-chambered revolver, which, on examining, I found was loaded. I at once put this weapon in my pocket, and, after searching awhile, discovered a box of cartridges, which I also pocketed.

This I considered a very lucky find, as I never knew the moment when I might stand in need of such a weapon; and, whether I should have occasion to use it or not, it was certainly better in my possession than in the hands of the men.

I now left my chair to examine the lockers, in the hopes of finding other fire-arms; and I cannot express the eagerness with which I prosecuted the search, because I considered that, should the boatswain succeed in winning even one man over from the crew, three resolute men, each armed with a revolver or fire-arm of any kind, might, by carefully waiting their opportunity, kill or wound enough of the crew to render the others an easy conquest.

However, to my unspeakable disappointment, my search proved fruitless; all that I found in the lockers were clothes belonging to Captain Coxon, a quantity of papers, old charts and log-books, some parcels of cigars, and a bag containing about thirty pounds in silver.

While engaged in these explorations, a knock fell on the door, and on my replying, the girl came in. I bowed and asked her to be seated, and inquired how her father did.

"He is still very weak," she answered; "but he is not worse this morning. I heard your voice just now, and watched you enter this cabin. I hope you will let me speak to you. I have much to say."

"Indeed," I replied, "I have been waiting impatiently for this opportunity. Will you first tell me your name?"

"Mary Robertson. My father is a Liverpool merchant, Mr. Royle, and the ship in which we were wrecked was his own vessel. Oh!" she exclaimed, pressing her hands to her face, "we were many hours expecting every moment to die. I can not believe that we are saved; and sometimes I can not believe that what has happened is real! I think I was going mad when I saw your ship. I thought the boat was a phantom, and that it would vanish suddenly. It was horrible to be imprisoned with the dead body and that mad sailor! The sailor went mad on the first day, and soon afterward the passenger—for he was a passenger who lay dead on the deck—sat up in his bed and uttered a dreadful cry, and fell forward dead! The mad sailor pointed to him and howled; and neither papa nor I could get out of the house, for the water swept against it and would have swept us overboard."

She told me all this with her hands to her face, and her fair hair flowing over her shoulders, and made a sweet and pathetic picture in this attitude.

Suddenly she looked up with a smile of wonderful sweetness, and, seizing my hand, cried:

"What do we not owe for your noble efforts? How good and brave you are!"

"You praise me too warmly, Miss Robertson. God knows there was nothing noble in my efforts, nor any daring in them. Had I really risked my life to save you, I should still have barely done my duty. How were you treated yesterday? Well, I hope."

"Oh, yes. The captain told the steward to give us what we wanted. I think the wine he sent us saved papa's life. He was sinking, but rallied after he had drunk a little of it. I am in a sad plight," she added, while a faint tinge of red came into her cheeks. "I have not even a piece of ribbon to tie up my hair with."

She took her beautiful hair in her hands, and smiled.

"Is there nothing in this cabin that will be of use to you?" I said. "Here is a hair brush—and it looks a pretty good one. I don't know whether we shall be able to muster a bit of ribbon among us, but I just now came across a roll of serge, and if you can do anything with that and a needle and thread, which I'll easily get for you, I'll see that they are put in your cabin. Here are enough clothes to rig your father, at all events, until his own are made ship-shape. But how am I to help *you?* That has been on my mind."

"I can use the serge, if I may have it," she replied, in the prettiest way imaginable.

"Here it is," I said, hauling it out of the locker; "and I'll get needles and thread for you presently. No sailor goes to sea without a housewife, and you shall have mine. And if you will wait a moment, I think I can find something else that may be useful."

Saying which, I hurried to my old cabin, unlocked my chest, and took out a new pair of carpet slippers.

"A piece of bunting or serge fitted into these will make them sit on your feet," I explained, handing them to her. "And I have other ideas, Miss Robertson, all which I hope will help to make you a little more comfortable by and by. Leave a sailor alone to find out ways and means."

She took the slippers with a graceful little smile, and put them along side the roll of serge; and then, with a grave face and in an earnest voice, she asked me what the men meant to do with the ship, now that they had seized her.

I freely told her as much as I knew, but expressed no fears as to my own, and her, and her father's safety. Indeed, I took the most cheerful view I could of our situation.

"My notion," said I, "is that when the time comes for the men to leave the ship they will not allow us to go with them. They will oblige us to remain in her, which is the best thing that could happen; for I am sure that the boatswain will stay, and with his and the steward's help there is nothing to prevent us taking the ship into the nearest port, or lying to until we meet a vessel and then signaling for help."

I fancy she was about to express her doubts of this result, but exclaimed instead:

"No matter what comes, Mr. Royle, we shall feel safe with you." And then, suddenly rising, she asked me to come and see her father.

I followed her at once into the cabin.

The old man lay in an upper bunk, with a blanket over him. He looked like a dead man, with his white face rendered yet more deathlike in appearance by the disheveled white hair upon his head, and the long white beard. He was lying perfectly still, with his eyes closed, his thin hands folded outside the blanket.

I thought he slept, and motioned to his daughter; but she stooped and whispered, "Papa, here is Mr. Royle"; whereupon he opened his eyes and looked at me. The sense of my presence appeared to be very slowly conveyed to his mind, and then he extended his hand. I took it, and saw with emotion that tears streamed from his eyes.

"Sir," he said, in a weak, faltering voice, "I can only say, God bless you!"

I answered cheerfully, "Pray say no more, Mr. Robertson. I want to see you recover your strength. Thank God, your daughter has survived her horrible trials, and will soon quite recover from the effects of them. What now can I do for you? Have you slept?"

"Yes, yes, I have slept—a little, I thank you. Sir, I have witnessed shocking scenes."

I whispered to Miss Robertson.

"Let me prescribe some medicine that will do you both good. What you require is support. I will be with you in a minute."

So saying, I quitted the cabin and entered the pantry. There I found the steward sitting on the plate chest, with his hands to his temples.

"Now then, my lad," said I, "rouse up. You are not dead yet. Have you any brandy here?"

He pointed in a mechanical way to a shelf, where were several bottles. I found what I wanted, and gave him a dose to put heart into him, and asked him for some eggs. Four or five, the gathering of yesterday from the kindly hens under the long-boat, lay in the drawer, which he pulled open. I proceeded to mix two tumblers of eggs and brandy, which I carried to the next cabin.

"That is my physic, Miss Robertson," I exclaimed, putting one of the tumblers into her hand; "oblige me by drinking it; and you, sir," I continued, addressing the old gentleman, "will not wait for her example."

They both, to my great satisfaction, swallowed the contents of the glasses, the effect of which, after some moments, upon Mr. Robertson was decidedly beneficial, for he thanked me for my kindness in a much stronger voice, and even made shift to prop himself on his elbow.

"It is the best tonic in the world," said I, taking Miss Robertson's glass, "and I am very much obliged to you for your obedience."

The look she gave me was more eloquent than any verbal reply; at least, I found it so. Her face was so womanly and beautiful, so full of pathos in its pallor, with something so brave and open in its whole expression, that it was delightful to me to watch it.

"Now," said I to the old gentleman, "allow me to leave you for a little. I want to see what the 'Grosvenor' can furnish in the shape of linen and drapery. Isn't that what they call it ashore? We have found some serge, and needles and thread are easily got; and I'll set what wits the unfortunate steward has left in him to work to discover how Miss Robertson may be made comfortable until we put you both ashore."

"Do not leave us," cried the old man. "Your society does me good, sir. It puts life into me. I want to tell you who we are, and about our shipwreck, and where we were going. The 'Cecilia' was my own vessel. I am a merchant, doing most of my trade with the Cape—the Cape of Good Hope. I took my daughter—my only child, sir—to Cape Town, last year, for a change of scene and air; and I should have stopped another year, but Mary got tired and wanted to get home, and—and—well, as I was telling you, Mr.—Mr.—"

"Royle," said Miss Robertson.

"Mr. Royle, as I was telling you, Mary got tired; and as the 'Cecilia' was loading at Cape Town—she was a snug, sound ship—yes, indeed; and we went on board, we and a gentleman named—named—"

"Jameson," his daughter suggested.

"Ay, poor Jameson—poor, poor fellow!"

He hid his face, and was silent, I should say, a whole minute, neither Miss Robertson nor myself speaking. Presently, looking up, he continued:

"It came on to blow very heavily, most suddenly, a dreadful gale. It caught the ship in a calm, and she was unprepared, and it snapped all three masts away. Oh, God, what a night of horror! The men went mad, and cried that the ship was going stern down, and crowded in the boats. One went whirling away into the darkness, and one was capsized; and then the captain said the ship was sinking, and my daughter and I ran out of the cabin on to the deck. Well, sir," continued the old man, swallowing convulsive sobs as he spoke, "the ship's side had been pierced, the captain said, by one of the yards; and she was slowly settling, and the water came over the deck, and we got into the house where you found us, for shelter. I put my head to the window and called the captain to come, and as he was coming the water hurled him overboard; and there was only myself and my poor girl and Mr. Jameson and—and—tell him the rest!" he suddenly cried, hiding his eyes and stretching out his hand.

"Another time, Miss Robertson," I suggested, seeing the look of horror that had come into her face during her father's recital of the story. "Tell me where you live in England, and let us fancy ourselves in the dear old country, which, so it please God we shall all reach safely in a little time."

But they were both too overcome to answer me. The old man kept his face concealed, and the girl drew long, sobbing breaths with dry eyes.

However, she plucked up presently, and answered that they lived just out of Liverpool, but that her father had also an estate at Leamington, near Warwick, where her mother died, and where she spent most of her time as she did not like Liverpool.

"Tell me, sir," cried Mr. Robertson, "did you bring the body of poor Jameson with you? I forget."

"If that was Mr. Jameson whose body lay in the deck-house," I replied, "I left him on the wreck. There was his coffin, Mr. Robertson, and I dared not wait to bring off a dead man when living creatures stood in peril of their lives."

"To be sure, sir!" exclaimed the old gentleman. "You were very right. You acted with great nobleness, and are most kind to us now—most kind, Mary, is he not? Let me see!" knitting his brows. "You are not captain of this ship? I think, my dear, you said this gentleman was the mate? Who is the captain, sir?"

His daughter put her finger to her mouth, which puzzled me until I considered that she either did not want him to know that the captain was murdered, or, supposing he knew of the murder, that the circumstances should not be revived in his memory, which was just now very feeble.

He did not wait for his question to be answered, but asked me where the ship was bound to.

"New Orleans," I answered, with a glance at his daughter.

"New Orleans!" he exclaimed. "Let me think—that is beyond the West Indies." And with great eagerness he said, "Will you put into one of the West India Islands? I am known at Kingston; I have shipped largely to a firm there, Messieurs Raymondi & Company. Why, my dear, we shall be very well received, and we shall be able to purchase fresh clothes," he continued, holding up his arm and looking at it with a smile, "and go home in one of the fine mail packets. Ha! ha! ha! how things come about!"

He lay back upon his pillow with this short mirthless laugh, and remained silent. I do not say that his mind was unhinged, but his intellect was unquestionably impaired by the horrors he had witnessed and the sufferings he had endured. But, then, he was an old man—nearer seventy than sixty, I took him to be; while his daughter, whom a little rest had put upon the high-road to recovery, did not appear to be above twenty years old.

As the time was passing rapidly, I determined to seize the opportunity of the carpenter being on deck to do what I could to make these sufferers comfortable. I therefore left them and sung out to the steward, who came with terrified promptitude, casting the while and almost at every step fearful glances in the direction of the main-deck, where some of the hands were visible.

I gave him the captain's hair-brush to wash, and covered a tray with the various toilet conveniences with which the ill-fated skipper had provided himself. These I dispatched by the steward to Miss Robertson, and I then made the man prepare a tray with a substantial breakfast, consisting of cold fowl, fine white biscuit, ham, preserved fruit, and some tea, which I boiled in the pantry by means of a spirit-lamp that belonged to me.

I took an immense pleasure in supplying these new friends' wants, and almost forgot the perilous situation I was in, in the agreeable labor of devising means to comfort the girl, whose life and her father's, thanks to God! I had been instrumental in preserving.

I made a thorough overhaul of Coxon's effects, holding myself fully privileged to use them for the benefit of poor Mr. Robertson, and sent to his cabin a good suit of clothes, some clean linen, and a warm overcoat.

The steward obeyed me humbly and officiously. He considered his life still in great danger, and that he must fall a sacrifice to the fury of the crew if he quitted the cuddy. However, I found him very useful, for he furnished me with some very good hints, and among other things he, to my great delight, informed me that he had in the steerage a box of women's underclothing, which had been made by his wife's hand for a sister living in Valparaiso, to whom he was taking out the box as a gift, and that I was very welcome to the contents.

I requested him at once to descend with me and get the box out; but this job took us over twenty minutes, for the box was right aft and we had to clear away upward of five hundred bird cages, and a mass of light wooden packages of toys and dolls, to come at it. We succeeded at last in hauling it into the cuddy, and he fetched the key and raised the lid; but burst into tears when he saw a letter from his wife, addressed to his sister, lying on top of the linen.

I told him to put the letter in his pocket, and to be sure that his sister would be liberally compensated, if all went well with us, for this appropriation of his property.

"I'm not thinking of the clothes, sir," whined the poor fellow, "but of my wife and child, who I may never see again."

"Nonsense!" I exclaimed; "try to understand that a man is never dead until the breath is out of his body. You are as well off as I am and those poor people in the cabin there. What we have to do now is to help each other, and put a bold face on our troubles. The worst hasn't arrived yet, and it won't do to go mad with anticipating it. Wait till it comes, and if there's a road out of it, I'll take it, trust me. Cock this box under your arm, and take it to Miss Robertson."

I had now done everything that was possible, and to my perfect satisfaction; for, besides having furnished the old gentleman with a complete change of clothes, I had supplied his daughter with what I knew she would appreciate as a great luxury—a quantity of warm, dry underclothing.

It may strike the reader as ludicrous to find me descending into such trivialities, and perhaps I smiled myself when I thought over the business that had kept me employed since six o'clock. But shipwreck is a terrible leveler, and cold and hunger and misery know but little dignity. How would it seem to Miss Robertson, the daughter of a man obviously opulent, to find herself destitute of clothing, and accepting with gratitude such rude articles of dress as one poor work-woman would make for another of her condition? She, with the memory in her of abundant wardrobes, of costly silks, and furs, and jewelry, of rich attire, and the plentiful apparel of an heiress! But the sea pays but little attention to such claims, and would as lief strip a monarch as a poor sailor, and set him afloat naked to struggle awhile and drown.

CHAPTER X

AT SEVEN bells—that is, half an hour before eight—I heard the carpenter's voice shouting down the companion for the steward. I instantly opened the cabin door to tell the man to go at once, as I believed that Stevens merely called to give him orders about the men's breakfast.

This proved to be the case, as I presently learned on going on deck, whither I repaired (although it was my watch below) in order to see what the carpenter was about.

I found him lying upon one of the sky-lights, with a signal flag under his head, smoking a pipe, while three or four of the men sat round him smoking also. All plain sail had been made, as I had directed, and the ship heading west-south-west under a glorious sky, and all around a brilliantly clear horizon and an azure sea.

Away on our lee quarter was a large steamer steering south, brig-rigged, bound, I took it, to the west coast of Africa. The men about the carpenter made a movement when they saw me, as though they would leave the poop, but one of them made some remark in a low voice, which kept them all still. The carpenter, seeing me watch the steamer, called out:

"She wouldn't take long to catch us, would she? I hope there's no man on board this wessel as 'ud like to see her alongside, or would do anything to bring her near. I wouldn't like to be the man 'ud do it—would you, Joe?"

"Well, I'd rather ha' made my vill fust than forget it, if so it were that I was that man," responded the fellow questioned.

"We're glad you've come up," continued the carpenter, addressing me, though without shifting his posture, "for blowed if I knowed what to do if she *should* get askin' us any questions. What'll *you* do, Mr. Royle?"

"Let her signal us first," I replied, quite alive to the sinister suggestiveness of these questions.

"Put the helm up and go astern of her—that's what my advice is," said one of them.

"You'll provoke suspicion if you do that," I exclaimed. "However, you can act as you please."

"Mr. Royle's quite right," said the man addressed as Joe. "Why can't you leave the man alone?— He knows more about it than us, mates."

"She's going twelve knots," I said, "and will cross our bow soon enough. Let her signal; we're not bound to answer."

The men, in spite of themselves, watched her anxiously, and so did others on the forecastle, such cowards does conscience make of men. As for myself, I gazed at her with bitter indifference. The help that I stood in need of was not likely to come from such as she, or, indeed, from any vessel short of an inquisitive government ship. Moreover, the part I was playing was too difficult to permit me to allow any impulse to inspire me. The smallest distrust that I should occasion might cost me my life. My rôle, then, surely was to seem one with the men, heart and soul.

"Let her go off a point," I shouted to the man steering. "They'll not notice that, and she'll be across us sooner for it!"

We were slipping through the water quickly, and by the time she was on our weather-bow the steamer was near enough to enable us to see the awning stretched over her after-deck, and a crowd of persons watching us. She was a great ocean steamer, and went magnificently through the water. In a few minutes she was dead on end, dwindling, the people watching us, but leaving such a long wake astern of her that we went over it.

What would I have given to be on board of her!

"Let her come to again!" I sung out.

The carpenter now got off the sky-light.

"I've told the steward to turn to and get the men's breakfast," said he. "Ourn's to be ready by eight; and I reckon I'll show that sniveling cockney what it is to be hungry. You don't call this a mutiny, do yer, Mr. Royle? Why the men are like lambs."

"Yes, so they are," I answered. "All the same, I shall be glad to feel dry land under me. The law always hangs the skipper of a mutiny, you know; and I'm skipper by your appointment. So the sooner we all get out of this mess the better, eh, Mr. Stevens?"

"That's right enough," said he; "and we look to you to get us out of it."

"I'll do as you ask me—I won't do more," I answered.

"We don't want more. Enough's what we want. You'll let us see your reckonings every day—not because we doubt you—but it'll ease the minds of the men to know that we ar'n't like to foul the Bermudas."

"The Bermudas are well to the nor'ard of our course," I answered promptly.

"All right, Mr. Royle, we look to you," he said, with a face on him and in a tone that meant a good deal more than met the ear. "Now, mates," addressing the others, "cut for'ard and get your breakfast, my lads. It's eight bells. Mr. Royle, I'll go below and call the boatswain; and shall him and me have our breakfast and you arterward, or you fust? Say the word. I'm agreeable vichever way it goes."

"I'll stop on deck till you've done," I replied, wishing to have the table to myself.

Down he went, and I advanced to the poop-rail, and leaned over it to watch the men come aft to receive their share of the cuddy stores.

I will do them the justice to say that they were quiet enough. Whether the perception that they no longer recognized any superiors would not presently prevail; whether quarrels, deeds of violence, and all the consequences which generally attend the rebellion of ignorant men would not follow, was another matter. They were decent enough in their behavior now, congregating on the main-deck, and entering the cuddy one by one to receive the stores which the steward was serving out.

These stores, as far as I could judge by the contents of the tin dishes which the men took forward, consisted of butter, white biscuit, a rasher of ham to each man, and tea or cocoa; excellent for men who have been starved on rotten provisions. I also found that every man had been served with a glass of rum. They did not seem to begrudge the privilege assumed by the carpenter and boatswain of occupying the cuddy, and eating at the table there. The impression conveyed to me, on the whole, by their aspect and demeanor was that of men subdued and to a certain extent alarmed by the position in which they had placed themselves. But for the carpenter, I believe that I at that time, and working upon their then state of mind, could have won them over to submission, and made them willing to bring the ship into port and face an inquiry into the circumstances of the revolt. But though I believe this *now,* I conceived the attempt too full of peril to undertake, seeing that my failure must not only jeopardize my own, but the lives of poor old Mr. Robertson and his daughter, in the safety of whom I was so concerned that I do not say that my profound anxiety did not paralyze the energy with which I should have attempted my own rescue had I been alone.

How the men treated the steward I could not tell, but I noticed that

Master Cook was very quiet in his manner. This was the sure sign of the efficacy of the fright he had received, and it pleased me greatly, as I feared he would prove a dangerous and blood-thirsty mutineer, and a terrible influence in the councils of the men.

The carpenter was the first to come on deck. I had seen him (through the sky-light) eating like a cormorant, his arms squared, his brown tattooed hands busy with his mouth, making atonement for his long fast in the forecastle. He kept his cap on, but the boatswain had better manners and looked, as he faced his mate, a quite superior and different order of man altogether.

I went below as soon as Stevens appeared, and the boatswain had the grace to rise, as though he would leave the table when he saw me. I begged him to keep his seat, and calling to the steward, asked to know how the men had treated him.

"Pretty middling, sir, thank you, sir," he replied, with a trifle more spirit in his manner. "They're not brutal, sir. The cook never spoke, sir. Mr. Stevens is rather unkind, but I dare say it's only a way he has."

The boatswain laughed, and asked him if he had breakfasted.

"No sir—not yet. I can wait, sir."

"There's plenty to eat and drink," said the boatswain, pointing to the table.

"Yes, sir, plenty," responded the steward, who, looking on the boatswain as one of the ringleaders, was as much afraid of him as of the carpenter.

"Well, then," continued the boatswain, "why don't you tuck in? Mr. Royle won't mind. Sit there, or take what you want in the pantry."

The steward turned pale, remembering the threats that had been used toward him if he touched the cuddy stores, and looked upon the boatswain's civility as a trick to get him hanged.

"Thank you, sir," he stammered; "I've no happetite. I'd rather not eat anything at present, sir. I'll take a ship's biscuit shortly, sir, with your leave."

Saying which, and with a ghastly face, he shuffled into the pantry, no doubt to escape from what he would consider highly murderous attentions.

"Rum customer, that steward, Mr. Royle," said the boatswain, rubbing his mouth on the back of his hand.

"So should I be had I undergone his sensations," I replied

"Well, I don't know about that. You see there ain't nothing regular about a steward. He isn't a sailor and he isn't a landsman; and when you come to them kind o' mongrels, you can't expect much sperrit. It isn't fair to expect it. It's like fallin' foul of a marmozeet, because he isn't as big as a monkey. What about them passengers o' yours, sir? They've not been sarved with breakfast since I've been here."

"I have seen to them," I answered. "What has Stevens been talking about?" As I said this I cast my eyes on the open sky-light to see that our friend was not within hearing.

He shook his head, and after a short pause exclaimed:

"He's a bad 'un! he's a bad 'un! he's an out and outer!"

"Do you know which of them struck the captain down?"

"He did," he answered at once.

"I could have sworn it, by the way in which he excused the murderer."

"Stevens," continued the boatswain, "is at the bottom of all this here business—him and the cook. I suppose he didn't want the cook for a chum, and so knocked him over when he was going to operate on Duckling's body. But Duckling was a bad 'un, too, and so was the skipper. They've got to thank theirselves for what they got. The crew never would ha' turned had they been properly fed."

"I believe that," I said. "But I'll tell you what's troubling me, boatswain. The carpenter has some design behind all this, which he is concealing. Does he really mean that I should navigate to within fifty miles of New Orleans?"

"Yes, sir, he do," answered the boatswain, regarding me steadfastly.

"And he means then to heave the ship to, lower away the boats, and make for one of the mouths of the Mississippi, or land upon some part of the coast, and represent himself and his companions as castaway sailors?"

"Quite right," said the boatswain, watching me fixedly.

"If that is really his intention," I proceeded, "I can not believe that he will allow me to land with the others. He distrusts me. He is as suspicious as all murderers are."

The boatswain continued eyeing me intently, as a man might who strives to form a resolution from the expression in another's face.

"He means to scuttle the ship," he said, in a low voice.

"Ah!" I exclaimed, starting. "I should have foreseen this."

"He means to scuttle her just before he puts off in the boats," he added, in a whisper.

I watched him anxiously, for I saw that he had more to tell me. He looked up at both sky-lights, then toward the cuddy door, and then toward the companion-ladder, bent over to me, and said:

"Mr. Royle, he don't mean to let you leave the vessel."

"He means to scuttle her, leaving me on board?"

He nodded.

"Did he tell you this?"

He nodded again.

"When?"

"Just now."

"And them?" I exclaimed, pointing toward the cabin in which were Mr. Robertson and his daughter.

"They'll be left too," he replied.

I took a deep breath, and closed the knife and fork on my plate.

"Now, then, mate!" bawled the carpenter's voice, down the companion; "how long are you goin' to be?"

"Coming," answered the boatswain.

A thought had flashed upon me.

"There must be others in this ship whom Stevens distrusts as well as me," I whispered. "Who are they? Give me but two other men and yourself, and I'll engage that the ship will be ours! See! if these men whom he distrusts could be told that, at the last moment, they will be left to sink in a scuttled ship, they would come over on my side to save their lives. How are they to be got at?"

He shook his head without speaking, and left the table; but turned to say, "Don't be in a hurry. I've got two hours afore me, and I'll turn it over." He then went on deck.

I remained at the cuddy table, buried in thought. The boatswain's communication had taken me utterly by surprise. That Stevens, after the promise he had made me that there should be no more blood shed, after the sympathy I had shown the men from the beginning, should be base enough to determine upon murdering me and the inoffensive persons we had rescued, at the moment when we might think our escape from our heavy misfortunes certain, was so shocking that the thought of it made me feel as one stunned. An emotion of deep despair was bred in me, and then this, in its turn, begot a wild fit of fury. I could scarcely restrain myself from rushing on deck and shooting the ruffian as he stood there.

To escape from my own insanity, I ran into the captain's cabin and locked the door, and plunged into deep and bitter reflection.

It was idle for me to think of resistance in my then condition.

Upon whom could I count? The boatswain? I could not be sure that he would aid me single-handed, nor hope that he would try to save my life at the risk of his own. The steward? Such a feeble-hearted creature would only hamper me, would be of less use, even, than old Mr. Robertson. Many among the crew, if not all of them, indeed, must obviously be acquainted with Stevens' murderous intentions, and would make a strong and desperate gang to oppose me; and though I should discover the men who were not in the carpenter's confidence, how could I depend on them at the last moment?

The feeling of helplessness induced in me by these considerations was profound and annihilating. I witnessed the whole murderous process as though it were happening: the ship hove to, the boats shoving away, one, perhaps, remaining to watch the vessel sink, that they might be in no doubt of our having perished. All this would happen in the dark, too, for the departure of the men from the ship would only be safe at night, that no passing vessel might espy them. An idea that will sound barbarous, though I should not have hesitated to carry it out could I have seen my way to it, occurred to me. This was to watch an opportunity when the carpenter was alone, to hurl him overboard. But here, again, the chances against me were fifty to one. To destroy the villain without risk of detection, without the act being witnessed, without suspicion attaching to me on his being missed, would imply such a host of favoring conditions as the kindliest fortune would scarcely assemble together.

What, then, was to be done?

I had already pointed out the course the ship was to steer, and could not alter it. But though I should plausibly alter her course a point or two, what could follow? The moment land was sighted, let it be what coast it would, they would know I had deceived them; or, giving me credit of having mistaken my reckonings, they would heave the ship to themselves, and then would come the dastardly crime. I dared not signal any passing vessel. Let my imagination devise what it would, it could invent nothing that my judgment would adopt; since being single-handed in this ship, no effort I could make to save the lives of the persons it was my determination to stand by but must end in our destruction.

By such confessions I show myself no hero; but then I do not want to be thought one. I was, and am, a plain man, placed in one of the most formidable situations that any one could find himself in. In the darkness and horror of that time, I saw no means of escape, and so I admit my blindness. A few strokes of the pen would easily show me other than I was, but then I should not be telling the truth, and should falsely be taking glory to myself, instead of truly showing it to be God's, by whose mercy I am alive to tell the story.

My clothes and other things belonging to me being in the cabin now occupied by Stevens, I opened the door and desired the steward to bring them to me. My voice was heard by Miss Robertson, who came round the table to where I stood and thanked me for my kindness to her and her father.

She had made good use of the few conveniences I had been able to send her. Her hair was brushed and most prettily looped over the comb, and she wore a collar that became her mightily, which she found in the steward's box. She looked a sweet and true English girl, her death-like pallor gradually yielding to a healthy white, with a tinge of color on her cheeks.

"Papa seems better," she said, "and is constantly asking for you; but I told him" (with the prettiest smile) "that you require rest as well as others, and that you have plenty to occupy you."

Then looking earnestly at me for some moments, while her face grew wonderfully grave, she exclaimed:

"What is wrong, Mr. Royle? What makes you look so anxious and worried?"

"There is plenty to trouble me," I answered, not carelessly, but not putting too much significance into my tone, for at that moment I did not think I ought to tell her the truth. "You know the men have mutinied, and that my position is a difficult one. I have to be careful how I act, both for my sake and yours."

"Yes, I know that," she said, keeping her clear and thoughtful eyes on me. "But then you said you did not fear that the men would be violent again, and that they would leave us on board this ship when we were near New Orleans."

I watched her face some time without speaking, asking myself if I should take her into my confidence, if I ought to impart the diabolical scheme of Stevens, as told me by the boatswain. Certainly I should have put her off without telling her the truth had not the courageous expression in her eyes, her firm and beautiful mouth, her resolute voice and manner told me she would know how to bear it.

"I will not conceal that I have heard something just now which has affected me very much," I said to her. "Will you step into my cabin? We can talk there without being seen," I added, having observed Stevens walk along the main-deck, and expecting that he would return in a few moments to his cabin, it being his watch below.

She followed me in silence, and I closed the door.

"I will tell you in a few words," I at once began, "what I heard just now. I told the boatswain that I questioned whether the men would let me land with them, for fear of the evidence I could give. He replied that he had gathered from the carpenter, while at breakfast, that the men intended to scuttle the ship when they quitted her, and to leave us on board."

"To drown?"

"That is their idea."

She pursed up her mouth tightly, and pressed her hand to her forehead. That was all. Whatever emotion my statement inspired was hidden. She said in a low voice:

"They are fiends! I did not think them so cruel. My poor father!"

"This is what I am told they mean to do; and I know Stevens to be a ruffian, and that he will carry out his project if he can. I have spent time alone here in trying to think how we can save ourselves. As yet I see no remedy. But wait," I said; "it will take us three weeks, sailing well every day, to reach the Gulf of Mexico. I have this time before me; and in that time not only something must, but something shall be done."

She did not answer.

"I will hazard nothing; I will venture no risks. What I resolve to do must be effectual," I went on, "because my life is dearer to me now than it was three days ago, for you and your father's sake. You must be saved from these ruffians, but no risk must attend your deliverance. This is why I see no escape before us as yet, but it will come—it will come! Despair is very fruitful in expedients, and I am not beaten because I find myself flung like a dog in a hole!"

She looked up at this, and said: "What is to be done?"

"I must think."

"I will think, too. We need not tell papa?" she added, toning her voice to a question, with an appealing look in her eyes.

"No, certainly not. Remember, we are not supposed to question the men's honest intentions toward us. We must appear utterly ignorant."

"Are they armed?" she inquired.

"No."

She cast her eyes round the cabin, and said, "Have you no guns?"

"Nothing but a pistol. But though we had twenty guns, we have no hands to use them. So far as I know yet, there is no man that would stand with me—not even the boatswain, unless he were sure he would conquer the ruffians."

"Could I not use a pistol? Ah, I remember, you have only one."

She sunk her chin on her hand and looked downward, lost in thought.

"Why should you not steer the ship for some near port?" she asked, presently.

"I could not alter the course without being challenged. Remember, that my policy is not to excite suspicion of my honesty."

"If a gale would rise like that which wrecked the 'Cecilia,' it might drive us near the land, where we would get help."

"No, we shall have to depend upon ourselves. I do not want to pin my faith on chance."

I began to pace to and fro, torn by the blind and useless labors of my mind.

Just then a step sounded along the cuddy. The cabin door was pushed open roughly, and Stevens walked in. He stared at Miss Robertson, and cried:

"Sorry to interrupt. Didn't know you was here, ma'am, I'm sure. I thought," addressing me, "I should find you turned in. I've come to have a look at that chart of yours. How long d'ye make it to New Orleans?"

"About three weeks."

"Well, there's live stock enough for three weeks anyways. I've just told the cook to stick one of them porkers. All hands has a fancy for roast pork to-day. Sarvant, miss. You was pretty nigh drowned, I think."

"My father and I owe our lives to the noble fellows in this ship. They must be brave and good men to risk their lives to save ours," she answered, with a smile of touching sweetness, looking frankly into the face of the miscreant who stood, cap on head, before her.

"Lor' bless yer!" he exclaimed; "there wasn't no risk. I'd ha' swum the distance in such a sea for five shilling."

She shook her head with another smile (I judged the effort this piece of acting cost her), as she said:

"I know that English sailors undervalue their good deeds. But happily my father is a rich man, and when you land us he will take care that no man on board of this ship will complain of his gratitude."

"Oh, he's rich!" exclaimed the carpenter, as though struck with a new idea.

"Very rich."

"How rich might he be, ma'am?"

"Well, he owned the ship that you saved us from—cargo and ship."

She could not have offered a better illustration of her father's wealth to the man, for he would appreciate the value of a vessel of that size.

"And what do you think he'll give the men—them as saved him, I suppose?"

"Oh, he won't make any difference. He is indebted to you all, for I have heard that the captain would not have stopped for us had he not been obliged to do so by the crew."

"That's true enough," rejoined the carpenter with an oath, looking at me.

"Perfectly true," I made haste to say.

"My father would not certainly offer less than one hundred pounds to each man," she said, quite simply.

He pulled off his cap at this and twirled it and let it drop; picked it up so slowly that I thought he would never bend his body sufficiently to enable him to recover it; looked at her sideways as he put it on his head again, and then said to me, with offensive abruptness:

"Come, master, let's have a look at that blooming chart."

I opened the door to let Miss Robertson pass out, exchanging one glance with her as she left, and addressed myself to the carpenter.

He pored over the chart with his dirty forefinger upon it.

"Whereabouts are we now?" he inquired.

I pointed to the spot, as near as I could judge from yesterday's reckoning.

"What's this here line?" he asked.

"That's the longitude."

He ran his eye to the bottom of the chart, and exclaimed:

"Thirty. Is that it?"

"Call it thirty."

"But what do *you* call it?"

"Thirty, I tell you—thirty degrees west longitude."

"And this here line's the latitude, I suppose?"

"Yes."

"That's forty."

"Call it forty-four."

"Will that make it right?"

"Pretty nearly."

"What are all these dots and streaks!" said he, after squinting with his nose close to the chart. "Blowed if ever I could them read small words."

"They are the Azores."

"Oh, we're to the nor'ard o' them, ar'n't we?" he inquired, sharply.

"You can see for yourself," I answered, putting my finger on the chart.

"Where's this blessed Gulf of Mexico?" he inquired, after casting his eyes all over the chart.

"There."

He ran his dirty thumb nail in a line to the Gulf, and asked me what that blot was.

"Bermuda."

"You'll keep south o' that, will yer?"

"If I can, certainly."

"It's a man-o'-war station, I've heerd."

"I believe it is."

"All right," he said, and, looking at the boat's compass on the table, and asked if it were true.

I told him it was; whereupon he set it upon the chart and compared its indications with the line he had run down the chart, and was going away, when I said:

"What do you think of the young lady's idea? I should like to earn a hundred pounds."

"So should I," he answered, gruffly, pausing.

"It would pretty well pay me for what I have had to put up with from Coxon."

He gave me an indescribable look, full of fierceness, suspicion, and cunning.

"I dessay it would, if you got it," he said, and walked out, banging the door after him.

CHAPTER XI

I HAD been greatly struck by the firmness with which Miss Robertson had received the ghastly bit of information I gave her, and not more by this than by her gentle and genial manner toward the carpenter, wherein she had shown herself perfectly well qualified to act with me in this critical, danger-ous time. She had only just been rescued from one trial frightful enough in character to have driven one, at least, of the male sufferers mad; and now fate had plunged her into a worse situation, and yet she could confront the terrors of it calmly, and deliberate collectedly upon the danger.

Such a character as this was, I thought, of the true type of heroine, with nothing in it that was strained; calm in emergency, and with a fruitful mind scattering hope around it—even though no more than hope—as the teem-ing flower sheds its perfume.

I had especially noted the quickness with which she had conceived and expressed that idea about her father rewarding the men; it inspirited me, in spite of the reception Stevens had given it. One hundred pounds a man was a promise that might move them into a very different thought from what Stevens had induced and was sustaining.

Having heard the carpenter enter his cabin, I determined to step on deck and take the boatswain's sense on this new idea. But before quitting the cuddy, I knocked lightly on Miss Robertson's cabin door.

She opened it instantly.

"Will you come on deck?" I asked her.

"Yes, if I can be of any use there."

"The air will refresh you after your confinement to this cabin, and will do your father good."

"He is sleeping now," she answered, opening the door fully, that I might see the old man.

"Let him sleep," said I; "that will do him more good. But you will come?"

"Yes, with pleasure."

"You have nothing to fear from the men," I said, wishing to reassure her. "They are willing to acknowledge the authority of the persons they have put over them—the bo's'n, Stevens, and myself."

"I should not mind if they spoke to me," she exclaimed. "I should know what to say to them, unless they were brutal."

She turned to look at her father, closed the door softly, and accompanied me on deck.

The morning was now advanced. The day was still very bright; and the wonderful blue of the heavens lost nothing of its richness from contrast with the stately and swelling clouds—pearl-colored where they faced the sun, and with here and there a rainbow on their skirts, and centers of creamy white—which sailed solemnly over it.

The breeze had freshened, but the swell had greatly subsided, and the sea was almost smooth, with brilliant little waves chasing it. The ship was stretching finely along the water, all sail set, and every sail drawing.

On our lee beam was the canvas of a big ship, her hull invisible; and astern of her I could just make out the faint tracing of the smoke of a steamer upon the sky. The sun shone warm, but not too warm; the strong breeze was sweet and soft; the ship's motion steady, and her aspect a glorious picture of white rounded canvas, taut rigging delicately interlaced,

and gleaming decks and glittering brasswork. The blue waters sung a racing chorus at the bows, and the echo died upon the broad bubbling wake
astern.

I ran my eye forward upon the men on the forecastle. Most of the
crew were congregated there, lounging, squatting, smoking—no man doing any work. I wondered, not at this, but that they should be so orderly
and keep their place. They might have come aft had they pleased,
swarmed into the cuddy, occupied the cabins; for the ship was theirs.
Since they acted with so much decency, could they not be won over from
their leader's atrocious project? If I went among them, holding this girl,
now at my side, by the hand, and pleaded for her life, if not for my own,
would they not spare her? would not some among them be moved by her
beauty and her helplessness?

Nothing would seem more rational than such conjectures, always providing that I ceased to remember these men were criminals, that their one
idea now was how to elude the law, and that I who should plead, and those
for whom I pleaded, could by a word, when set on shore, procure the conviction of the whole gang, charge them with their crimes, prove their
identity, and secure their punishment. Would not Stevens keep them in
mind of this? Knowing what they knew, knowing what they meditated, I say
that in the very orderliness of their behavior I witnessed something more
sinister than I should have found in violent conduct. I alone could carry
them to where they wished to go. I must be conciliated, pleased, obeyed,
and my fears tranquilized. If I failed them, their doom was inevitable; shipwreck or capture was certain. All this was plain to me as the fingers on my
hand; and during the brief time I stood watching them, I found myself re-
peating again and again the hopeless question, "What can I do?"

Miss Robertson walked up and down the deck. The boatswain glanced
at her respectfully, and the men forward stared, and some of them laughed,
but none of the remarks they indulged in were audible.

Fish was at the wheel. I went to the binnacle, and said:

"That's our course. Let this wind hold, and we'll soon be clear of this
mess."

"Three weeks about, I give us," answered the man.

"And long enough, too, " said I.

He spit the quid in his mouth overboard, and dried his lips on his cuff. As he did not seem disposed to talk, I left him and joined the boatswain, and at my request he came and stood with me near Miss Robertson.

"I have told this lady what you repeated to me at breakfast," I said, in a low voice. "She's full of courage, and I have asked her to come on deck that we may talk before her."

"If she's as brave as she is pretty, I reckon not many'll carry stouter hearts in 'em than her," he said, addressing her full, with an air of respectful gallantry that was very taking.

She looked down with a smile.

"Boatswain," said I, "every hour is precious to us, for at any moment Stevens may change the ship's course for a closer shore than the American; and though we should hold on for the Gulf, it may take us all our time to hit on a scheme to save ourselves and work it out. I have come to tell you an idea suggested by this lady, Miss Robertson. Her father is a rich man, owner of the vessel he was wrecked in—"

"Robertson & Co., of Liverpool, ship brokers?" he interrupted, addressing her.

"Yes," she replied.

"Why, I sailed in one of the firm's vessels as bo's'n's mate, three years ago—the 'Albany' she was called, and a very comfortable ship she was, well found and properly commanded."

"Indeed!" she exclaimed, brightening up and looking at him eagerly. And then, reflecting a little, she said, "The 'Albany'—that ship was commanded by Captain Tribett."

"Quite right, miss; Tribett was the name. And the first mate's name was Green, and the second's Gull, and the third—ah! he were Captain Tribett's son—same name, of course. Well, blow me if this ain't wot the Italians call a cohincidence."

He was as pleased as she, and stood grinning on her.

"Mr. Royle," she suggested, raising her fine eyes to mine, "surely there must be others like the boatswain in this ship. They can not all be after the pattern of that horrible carpenter."

"We ought to be able to find that out, bo's'n," I said.

"Look here, miss," he answered, with a glance first at the men forward and then at Fish at the wheel, "the circumstances of this affair is just this: the crew have been very badly treated, fed with rotten stores, and starved and abused by the skipper and chief mate until they went mad. I don't think myself that they meant to kill the captain and Mr. Duckling; but it happened, and no man barrin' Stevens was guiltier than his mate, and that's where it is. The carpenter knocked the skipper down, and others kicked him when he was down, not knowing he was dead; and four or five set on Mr. Duckling, and so you see it's a sin as they all shared alike in. If one man had killed the skipper, and another had killed the chief mate, why then, so be, miss, the others might be got to turn upon 'em to save their own necks. But here it's all hands as did the job. And the only man who kept away, though I pretended to be one with 'em hearty enough, was me; and wot's the consequence? Stevens don't trust me; and I'm sartin in my own mind that he don't mean to let me into the boats when the time comes any more than you."

So saying, he deliberately walked aft, looked at the compass, then at the sails, and patrolled the poop for several minutes, for the very obvious reason that the men should not take notice of our talking long and close together.

Presently he rejoined us, standing a little distance away, and in a careless attitude.

"Bo's'n," said I, addressing him with my eyes on the deck, so that from a distance I would not appear to be speaking. "Miss Robertson told Stevens that her father would handsomely reward every man on board this ship on her arrival in port. He asked her what her father would give, and she said a hundred pounds to each man. If this were repeated to the crew, what effect would it produce?"

"They wouldn't believe it."

"My father would give each man a promise in writing," she exclaimed.

"They wouldn't trust him," said the boatswain, without reflecting. "They'd think it a roose to bring 'em together to give them into custody. If I was one of them, that's what I should think, and you may be sure I'm right."

"But he would give them written orders on his bankers; they could not think it a ruse," she said, eagerly, evidently enamored of her own idea, since she saw that I entertained it.

"Sailors don't know anything about banks and the likes of that, miss. There are thirteen men in the ship's company, counting the cook and the steward. Call 'em twelve. If your father had a bag of sovereigns on board this vessel, and counted out a hundred to each man, then they'd believe him. But I'd not believe *them*. They'd take the money and scuttle the ship all the same. Don't make no mistake. They're fond o' their wagabon' lives and the carpenter's given 'em such a talkin' to that they're precious keen in gettin' away and cuttin' off all evidence. It 'ud take more than a hundred pounds each to a man to make 'em willing to risk their lives."

He walked away once more and stood lounging aft, chatting with Fish.

"I am afraid the bo's'n is right," said I. "Having lived among them and heard their conversation, he would know their characters too well to be deceived in the consequences of your scheme."

"But papa would pay them, Mr. Royle. He would give them any pledge they might choose to name, that they would run no risk. The money could be sent to them—they need not appear—they need not be seen."

"*We* know they would run no risks; but could we get them to believe us?"

"At least let us try."

"No—forgive me—we must not try. We must have nothing more to say. You have spoken to Stevens; let *him* talk among the men. If the reward tempts them, be sure they will concert measures among themselves to land you. But I beg you to have no faith in this project. They are villains, who will betray you in the end. The boatswain's arguments respecting them are perfectly just—so just that he has inspired me with a new kind of faith in him. He owns that his own life is in jeopardy, and I believe he will hit upon some expedient to save us. See how he watches us! He will join us presently. I, too, have a scheme dawning in my head, but too imperfect to discuss as yet. Courage!" I said, animated by her beauty and the deep, speaking expression of her blue eyes; "the bo's'n's confession of his own danger makes me feel stronger by a man. I have greater confidence in him than I had. If I could muster a few fire-arms—for even the steward might be made a man of, fighting for his life with a revolver in his hand—there is nothing I would not dare. But twelve to two!—what is our chance? It must not be thought of, with you and your father depending for your lives on ours."

"No," she answered, firmly. "There must be other and better ways. I will think as well as you."

The boatswain came sauntering toward us. He flung a coil of rope over a belaying-pin, looked over the ship's side approached us nearer, and pulled out a pipe and asked me for a light. I had one in my pocket and gave it to him. This was his excuse to speak.

"It isn't so suspicious-lookin' to talk now as it would be at night or in the cuddy—and in the cuddy there's no telling whose ears are about," he said. "I'll give you my scheme thought on since breakfast, and listen close, for I dursen't talk much: after this we must belay, or the men'll be set jawing. When we come to the Gulf of Mexico, you'll let me know how long it'll be afore we're fifty mile off the Mississippi. I helped to stow the cargo in this vessel, and she's choke-full, and there's only one place where they'll be able to get at to scuttle her, and that's right for'ard of the fore-hatch. I'll let that out to Stevens bit by bit, in an ordinary way, and he'll remember it. The night afore we heave to—you'll tell me when—I'll fall overboard and get drowned. That'll happen in your watch. We'll get one o' them packin'-cases full o' tin tacks up out o' the steerage and stow it away in one of the quarter-boats, and you'll let that drop over-board—d'ye see?—which'll sound like a man's body, and sink right away, and then you'll roar out that the boatswain's fallen overboard. Let 'em do what they like. I shall be stowed away for'ard, down in the fore-peak somewheres, and the man as comes there to bore a hole *I'll choke.* Leave the rest to me. If Stevens he sings out to know if it's done I'll say 'Yes,' and tell him to lower away the boats, and hold on for me. He'll take my voice for the fellow as is scuttling the ship. Now," he added, vehemently, "I'll lay any man fifty pound agin ten shillings that Stevens don't wait for the man he sends below. He'll get into the boat and shove off and lay by. You'll give me the signal, and I'll come up sharp, an' if there's a breath o' air we'll have the mainyards round somehow; and if the boats get in our road we'll run 'em down, and if there's no wind, and they try to board us—let 'em look out! for there'll be more bloodletting among 'em than ever they saw before, by God!"

He motioned with his hand that we should leave the poop, and walked away.

Miss Robertson looked at me and I at her for some moments in silence.

"Will it do, Mr. Royle?" she asked, in a low voice.

"Yes," I said.

"You think we shall be saved by this stratagem?"

I reflected before answering, and then said, "I do."

She went down the companion-ladder, and when we were in the cuddy she took my hand in both of hers and pressed it tightly to her heart, then hurried into her cabin.

CHAPTER XII

THE MORE I considered the boatswain's proposal, the better I liked it. All that day I turned it over and over in my mind. And, what was useful to me, I could sleep when I lay down in my watches below, which was a luxury I had feared, after the boatswain's disclosure at the breakfast-table, would be denied me.

I did not wish Miss Robertson to sit at the cuddy table at meal-hours, and when dinner-time came I took care that as good a meal should be taken to her and her father as the ship could furnish.

When Stevens joined me at the table, he sung out to the steward to "tell the old gent an' his darter that dinner vos a-vaitin'!" Whereupon I explained that the old gentleman was too ill to leave his bunk.

"Well, then, let the gal come," said he.

"She can't leave her father," I replied.

"Perhaps it ain't that so much as because I ain't genteel enough for her. It's the Vest End o' London as won't have nothen to do with Wapping. The tobaccy in my breath is too strong for her."

"Nothing of the kind. The old man is ill, and she must watch him. As to your manners, I dare say she is better pleased with them than you ought to be told. It is not every ship's carpenter that could talk and look like a skipper, and keep men under as you do."

"You're right there!" he exclaimed, with a broad grin. "Come, sarve us outa dollop o' that pork, will yer? Roast pork's never too fresh for me."

And he fell like an animal to the meat, and forgot, as I wished, all about Miss Robertson.

In the first watch, from eight in the evening until midnight, which was the boatswain's, I went and sat for an hour with the old gentleman and his daughter. Not a word was said about the peril we were in; he was quite ignorant of it, and, being better and stronger, was eager in his questions about the ship's progress.

I took notice that he appeared to forget all about the mutiny, and conversed as if I were captain. Nor did he show any strong recollection of the loss of his ship and the circumstances attending it. Indeed, it seemed that as he grew better his memory grew worse. *That* was the faculty injured by his sufferings, and when I listened to his questions, which took no cognizance of things of the past, though as recent as yesterday, I thought his memory would presently quit him wholly, for he was an old man, with a mind too feeble to hold on tightly.

I left them at half-past nine, and went on deck. I tried to see who was at the wheel, but could not make the man out. I think it was one of the Dutchmen. Better this man than Fish, Johnson, or some of the others, whose names I forget, who were thick with the carpenter, and before whom it would not be wise to talk with any suggestion of mystery with the boatswain.

However, there was not much chance of my being noticed, for the night was gloomy, and all about the decks quite dark. The ship was under top-sail and maintop-gallant-sails; the wind was east-south-east, blowing freshly with long seas. There was no appearance of foul weather, and the glass stood steady; but an under-sky of level cloud lay stretched across the stars; and, looking abroad over the ship's side, nothing was distinguishable but the foam of the waves breaking as they ran.

As I emerged from the companion, the boatswain hailed the forecastle, and told the man there to keep a good lookout. I had not had an opportunity of speaking to him since the morning. I touched him on the arm, and he turned and stared to see who I was.

"Ah, Mr. Royle," said he.

"Let's get under the lee of that quarter-boat," said I. "We can hear each other there. Who's at the wheel?"

"Dutch Joe."

"Come to the binnacle first, and I'll talk to you about the ship's course, and then we'll get under the quarter-boat, and he'll think I am giving you sailing directions."

We did this, and I gave the boatswain some instructions in the hearing of the Dutchman; and to appear very much in earnest, the boatswain and I hove the log while Dutch Joe turned the glass, which he could easily attend to holding a spoke with one hand, for the ship was steering herself.

We then walked to the quarter-boat and stood under the lee of it.

"Bo's'n," said I, "the more I think of your scheme the better I like it. Whatever may happen, your being in the hold will prevent any man from scuttling the ship."

"Yes, so it will; I'll take care of that. One blow must do the job—he mustn't cry out. The piano-fortes are amidships on merely two feet of dunnage; all for'ard the cases run large, and it's there they'll find space."

"My intention is not to wait until we come to the Gulf in order to carry this out," said I; "I'll clap on sixty, eighty, a hundred miles, just as I see my way, to every day's run, so as to bring the Gulf of Mexico close alongside the Bermuda Islands. Do you understand, bo's'n?"

"Yes, I understand. There's no use in waitin'. You're quite right to get it over. The sooner the better, says I."

"We shall average a run of three hundred miles every twenty-four hours, and I'll slip in an extra degree whenever I can. Who's to know?"

"Ne'er a man on this wessel, sir," he answered. "There's not above two as can spell words in a book."

"So I should think. Of course I shall have to prick off the chart according to the wind. A breeze like this may well give us three hundred miles. If it fall calm, I can make her drift sixty miles west-sou'-west, and clap on another eighty for steerage-way. I shall have double reckonings—one for the crew, one for myself. You, as chief, will know it's all right."

"Leave that to me," he answered, with a short laugh. "They've found out by this time that the ship's a clipper, and I'll let 'em understand that there never was a better navigator than you. It'll be for you and me to keep as much canvas on her as she'll carry in our watches, for the sake of appearance; and if I was you, sir, I'd trim the log-line afresh."

"A good idea," said I. "I'll give her a double dose. Twelve knots shall be nothing in a moderate breeze."

We both laughed at this: and then, to make my presence on deck appear reasonable, I walked to the binnacle.

I returned and said:

"In nine days hence we must contrive to be in longitude 62° and latitude 33°—somewhere about it. If we can average one hundred and eighty miles every day, we shall do it."

"What do you make the distance from where we are now to the Gulf?"

"In broad numbers, three thousand miles."

"No more."

"Averaging two hundred miles a day, we should be abreast of New Orleans in a fortnight. I said three weeks, but I shall correct myself to Stevens to-morrow, after I have taken observations. I'll show him a jump on the chart that will astonish him. I'll punish the scoundrels yet. I'll give them the direct course to Bermuda when they're in the boats, and if our plot only succeeds and the wind serves, one of us two will be ashore on the island before them, to let the governor know whom he is to expect."

"That may be done too," answered the boatswain; "but it'll have to be a dark night to get away from 'em without their seeing of us."

"They'll choose a dark night for their own sakes. Boatswain, give us your hand. Your cleverness has, in my opinion, as good as saved us, I felt a dead man this morning, but I never was more alive than I am now."

I grasped his hand, and went below, positively in better spirits than I had enjoyed since I first put my foot upon this ill-fated ship.

The first thing I did the next morning was to mark off the log-line afresh, having smuggled the reel below during my watch. I shortened the distances between the knots considerably, so that a greater number should pass over the stern while the sand was running than would be reeled off if the line were true.

At eight bells, when the boatswain went on deck, I asked him to take the log with him; and, following him presently, just as Stevens was about to leave the Poop, I looked around me, as if studying the weather, and said:

"Bo's'n, you must keep the log going, please. Heave it every hour, never less. I may have to depend upon dead-reckoning to-day, Mr. Stevens"; and I pointed to the sky, which was as thick as it had been all night.

"Shall I heave it now?" inquired the boatswain.

"Did you heave it in your watch, Mr. Stevens?" said I.

"No," he replied. "What are we doin' now? This has been her pace all along—ha'n't touched a brace or given an order since I came on deck."

He had come on deck to relieve me at four.

"Let's heave the log," I exclaimed, "I shall be better satisfied."

I gave the glass to Stevens, and while arranging the log-ship, I looked over the side, and said:

"By Jove, she's walking and no mistake!"

"I allow that we're going ten," said the man at the wheel.

"I give her thirteen good," said I.

"Call it fifteen, and you'll not be far out," observed the boatswain.

The carpenter cocked his evil eye at the water, but hazarded no conjecture.

"She *can* sail—if she can't do nothing else," was all he said.

I flung the log-ship overboard.

"Twin!" I cried out.

I saw the knots fibbing out like a string of beads. The reel roared in the boatswain's hands, and when Stevens roared "Stop!" I caught the line and allowed it to jam me against the rail, as though the weight of it, dragged through the water at the phenomenal speed at which we were supposed to be going, would haul me overboard.

"What's that knot there, Mr. Stevens?" I called out. "Bear a hand; the line is cutting my fingers in halves!"

He put down the sand-glass and laid hold of the line where the knot was, and began to count.

"Fifteen!" he roared.

"Well, I'm jiggered!" exclaimed the man steering.

I looked at Stevens triumphantly, as though I should say, "what do you think of that?"

"I told you you wur wrong, Mr. Royle," said the boatswain. "It's all fifteen. By jingo! it ain't sailing, it's engine-drivin'."

The true speed of the "Grosvenor" was about nine and a half knots—certainly not more; and whether the carpenter should believe the report of the log or not was nothing to me.

"Log it fifteen on the slate, bo's'n, and keep the log going every hour," I said, and went below again.

I saw, as was now my custom at every meal, that the steward took a good breakfast to the Robertsons' cabin, and then sat down with Stevens to the morning repast.

I took this opportunity of suggesting that if the wind held, and the vessel maintained her present rate of speed, we might hope to be in the Gulf of Mexico in a fortnight.

"How do you make that out? It was three weeks yesterday."

"And it might have been a month," I answered, "but a few days of this kind of sailing, let me tell you, Mr. Stevens, make a great difference in one's calculations."

"How fur off is the Gulf of Mexico?" he asked.

"About a couple of thousand miles."

"Oh, a couple of thousand miles. Well, and what reckoning do you get out o' that?"

"Suppose you put the ship's pace down at thirteen knots an hour."

"I thought you made it fifteen?" he queried, looking at me suspiciously.

"Yes, but I don't suppose we shall keep that up. For the sake of argument I call it thirteen."

"Well?" cramming his mouth as he spoke.

"In twenty-four hours we shall have run a distance of three hundred and twelve miles."

He nodded.

"Therefore, if we have the luck to keep up this pace of two knots less than we are now actually doing for fifteen days, we shall have accomplished—let me see."

I drew out a pencil, and commenced a calculation on the back of an old envelope.

"Three hundred and twelve multiplied by fifteen. Five times naught are naught; three naughts and two are ten; add two thousand, we shall have accomplished a distance of four thousand six hundred and eighty miles—that is, two thousand six hundred and eighty miles further than we want to go."

He was puzzled (and well he might be) by my fluent figures, but would not appear so.

"I understand," he said.

"Stop a bit," I exclaimed; "I want to show you something."

I entered the captain's cabin, procured a chart of the North and South Atlantic, including the eastern American coast, and spread it upon the table.

"The two thousand miles I have given you," said I, "would bring you right off the Mississippi. See here."

He rose and stooped over the chart.

"The short cut to the Gulf," I continued, pointing with my pencil, "is through the Florida Channel, clean through the Bahamas, where the navigation is very ugly."

"I see."

"I wouldn't trust myself there without a pilot on any consideration, and, of course," said I, looking at him, "we don't want a pilot."

"I should rayther think we don't," he answered, scowling at the chart.

"So," I went on, "to keep clear of ships and boats, which are sure to board us if we get among these islands, I should steer round the Carribees, do you see?—well away from them, and up through the Caribbean Sea, to the Gulf. Do you follow me?"

"Yes, yes—I see."

"Now, Mr. Stevens," said I, very gravely, "I want to do my duty to the crew, and put them and myself in the way of getting ashore and clear off from all bad consequences."

The scoundrel tried to meet my eyes, but could not; and he listened to me, gazing the while on the chart.

"But I don't think I should succeed if I got among those islands blocking up the entrance of the gulf; and as to the gulf itself, you may take your oath it's full of ships, some of which will pick you up before you reach the shore while others are pretty certain to come across the vessel you have abandoned, and then—look out!"

He swallowed some coffee hastily, stared at the chart, and said, in a surly voice, "What are you driving at?"

"Instead of our abandoning the ship in the Gulf of Mexico," I said, "My opinion is that, in order to assure our safety, and lessen the chance of detection, we ought to abandon her clear of these islands, to the nor'ard of them, off this coast here—Florida," pointing to the chart.

"You think so?" he said, doubtfully, after a long pause.

"I am certain of it. We ought to land upon some uninhabited part of the coast, and travel along it northward until we reach a town, and there represent ourselves as shipwrecked sailors. Ask your mates if I am not right."

"Perhaps you are," he replied, still very dubious, though not speaking distrustfully.

"If you select the coast of Florida, clear of all these islands, and away from the track of ships, I'll undertake, with good winds, to put the ship off in nine or ten days. But I'll not answer for our safety if you oblige me to navigate her into the Gulf of Mexico."

He continued looking at the chart for some moments, and I saw by the movements of his lips that he was trying to spell the names of the places written on the Florida coast outline, though he would not ask me to help him.

At last he said:

"It's Fish and two others as chose New Orleans. I have no fancy for them half an' half places. What I wanted was to get away into the Gulf of Guinea, and coast along down to Congo, or that way. I know the coast, but I never was in Ameriky, and," he added, fetching the chart a blow with his fist, "curse me if I like the notion of going there!"

"It won't do to be shifting about," said I, frightened that he would go and get the crew to agree with him to run down to the African coast, which would seriously prolong the journey, and end, for all I could tell, in defeating my scheme; "we shall be running short of water and eatable stores, and then we shall be in a fix. Make up your mind, Mr. Stevens, to the Florida coast; you can't do better. We shall fetch it in a few days, and once ashore, we can disperse in parties, and each party can tell their own yarn, if they are asked questions."

"Well, I'll talk to Fish and the others about it," he growled, going back to his seat. "I think you're right about them West India Islands. We must keep clear o' them. Perhaps some of 'em for'ard may know what this here Florida is like. I was never ashore there."

He fell to his breakfast again, and, finding him silent, and considering that enough had been said for the present, I left him.

I did not know how well I had argued the matter until that night, when he came to me on the poop, at half past eight, and told me that the men

were all agreed that it would be too dangerous to abandon the ship off
New Orleans, and that they preferred the notion of leaving her off the
Florida coast.

I asked him if I was to consider this point definitely settled, and on his
answering in the affirmative, I sung out to the man at the wheel to keep her
away a couple of points, and ordered some of the watch to haul in a bit on
the weather-braces, explaining to Stevens that his decision would bring our
course a trifle more westerly.

I then told him that, with a good wind, I would give the ship eight or
nine days to do the run in, and recommended him to let the crew know this,
as they must now turn to and arrange, not only how they should leave the
ship—in what condition, whether with their clothes and effects, as if they
had time to save them, or quite destitute, as though they had taken to the
boats in a hurry—but also make up their minds as to the character of the
story they should relate when they got ashore.

He answered that all this was settled, as, of course, I was very well
aware; but then my reason for talking to him in this strain was to convince
him that I had no suspicion of the diabolical project he was meditating
against my life.

You will, perhaps, find it hard to believe that he and the others should
be so ignorant of navigation as to be duped by my false reckonings and
misstatements of distances. But I can aver from experience that merchant-
seamen are, as a rule, as ignorant and thickheaded a body of men as any in
this world—and scarcely a handful in every thousand with even a small
acquaintance with the theoretical part of their calling. More than a knowledge of practical seamanship is not required from them; and how many are
proficient even in this branch? Of every ship's company more than half always seem to be learning their business; furling badly, reefing badly,
splicing, scraping painting, cleaning badly; turning to lazily; slow up aloft,
negligent, with an immense capacity of skulking.

I am persuaded that had I not shown Stevens the chart, I could have
satisfied him that a southerly course would have fetched the coast of
America. The mistake I made was in being too candid and honest with them
in the beginning. But then I had no plan formed. I dared not be tricky without plausibility, and without some definite end to achieve. Now that I had

got a good scheme in my head, I progressed with it rapidly, and I felt so confident of the issue, in the boatswain's pluck and my own energy, that my situation no longer greatly excited my apprehensions, and all that I desired was that the hour might speedily arrive when the boats with their cargo of rascals and cowards should put off and leave the ship.

CHAPTER XIII

HAVING NO other log-book than my memory to refer to, I pass over six days, in which nothing occurred striking enough for my recollection to retain.

This brought us to Sunday; and on that day at noon we were, as nearly as I can recall, in 37° north latitude and 50° west longitude.

In round numbers Bermuda lies in latitude 32° and longitude 65°. This is close enough for my purpose. We had consequently some distance yet to run before we should *heave to off the coast of Florida*. But we had for five days carried a strong following wind with us, and were now (heading west by south half south) driving eight or nine knots an hour under a fresh wind forward of the port beam.

I own I was very glad to be able to keep well to the nor'ard of 30°; for had the north-east trade-winds got hold of the ship, I should not have been able to accommodate the distances run to my scheme so well as I now could with shifting winds, blowing sometimes moderate gales.

The crew continued to behave with moderation. The carpenter, indeed, grew more coarse and offensive in manner as the sense of his importance and of his influence over the men grew upon him; and there were times when Johnson and Fish put themselves rather disagreeably forward; but I must confess I had not looked for so much decency of behavior as was shown by the rest of the men in a crew who were absolute masters of the vessel.

But, all the same, I was not to be deceived by their apparent tractable-ness and quiet exterior. I knew but too well the malignant purpose that underlay this reposeful conduct, and never addressed them but I felt that I was accosting murderers, who, when the moment should arrive, would watch their victims miserably drown, with horrid satisfaction at the success of their cruel remedy to remove all chance of their apprehension.

On this Sunday old Mr. Robertson came on deck, for the first time, accompanied by his daughter, who had not before been on the poop in the day-time.

It was my watch on deck; had it been the carpenter's, I should have advised them to keep below.

What I had feared had now come to pass. Mr. Robertson's memory was gone. He could recall nothing; but what was more pitiful to see, though it was all for the best, so far as he was concerned, he made no effort to recollect. Nothing was suggestive; nothing, that ever I could detect, put his mind in labor. His daughter spoke to me about this melancholy extinction of his memory, but not with any bitterness or sorrow.

"It is better," she said, "that he should not remember the horrors of that shipwreck, nor understand our present dreadful position."

It was indeed the sense of our position that took her mind away from too active contemplation of her father's intellectual enfeeblement. There was never a more devoted daughter, more tender, gentle, unremitting in her foresight of his wants; and yet, in spite of herself, the feeling of her helplessness would at times overpower her; that strong and beautiful instinct in women which makes them turn for safety and comfort to the strength of men whom they can trust, would master her. I knew, I felt through signs touching to me as love, how she looked to me out of her loneliness, out of the deeper loneliness created in her by her father's decay, and wondered that I, a rough sailor, little capable of expressing all the tenderness and concern and strong resolutions that filled my heart, should have the power to inspirit and pacify her most restless moods. In view of the death that might await us—for hope and strive as we might, we could pronounce nothing certain—it was exquisite flattery to me, breeding in me, indeed, thoughts which I hardly noted then, though they were there to make an epoch in my life, to feel her trust, to witness the comfort my presence gave her, to receive her gentle whispers that she had no fear now; that I was her friend; that she knew me as though our friendship was of old, old standing!

I say, God bless her for her faith in me I look back and know that I did my best. She gave me courage, heart, and cunning; and so I owed my life to her, for it was these things that saved it. She exactly knew the plans concerted by the boatswain and myself, and was eager to help us; but I could find no part for her.

However, this Sunday afternoon, while I stood near her, talking in a low voice, her father sitting in a chair that I had brought from the cuddy, full in the sun, whose light seemed to put new life into him—I said to her, with a smile:

"If to-night is dark enough, the boatswain must be drowned."

"Yes," she answered, "I know. It will not be too soon, you think?"

"No. I shall not be easy until I get him stowed away in the hold."

"You will see," she exclaimed, "that the poor fellow takes plenty to eat and drink with him!"

"A good deal more than he wants is already there," I answered. "For the last three days he has been dropping odds and ends of food down the fore-hatch. Let the worst come to the worst, he has smuggled in enough, he tells me, to last him a fortnight. Besides, the water-casks are there."

"And how will he manage to sleep?"

"Oh, he'll coil up and snug himself away anyhow. Sailors are never pushed for a bedstead: anything and everything serves. The only part of the job that will be rather difficult is the drowning him. I don't know anything that will make a louder splash, and sink quickly, too, than a box of nails. The trouble is to heave it overboard without the man at the wheel seeing me do it: and I must contrive to let him think that the boatswain is aft before I raise the splash, because if this matter is not ship-shape and carried out cleverly, the man, whoever he may be, that takes the wheel will be set thinking, and then get on to talking. Now not the shadow of a suspicion must attend this."

"May I tell you how I think the man who is steering can be deceived?"

"By all means."

She fixed her eyes on the sea and said:

"I must ask some questions first. When you come on deck, will it be the boatswain's or the carpenter's turn to go downstairs?

"The carpenter's. He must be turned in before I move."

"And will the same man be at the wheel who steered the ship during the carpenter's watch?"

"No. He will be relieved by a man out of the port watch."

"Now, I understand. What I think is, that the man who comes to take the other one's place at the wheel ought to see the boatswain as he passes along the deck. The boatswain should stand talking with you in full sight of this man—that is, near the wheel, if the night is dark—so that he can hear his voice, if he cannot distinguish his face; and when all is quiet in the fore-part of the ship, then you and he should walk away and stand yonder," pointing, as she spoke, to the break of the poop.

I listened to her with interest and curiosity.

"Some one must then creep up and stand beside you, and the boatswain must instantly slip away and hide himself. The case of nails ought to be ready in one of those boats; you and the person who takes the boatswain's place must then go to the boat, and one of you, under pretense of examining her, must get the box of nails out on to the rails ready to be pushed overboard. Then the newcomer must crouch among the shadows, and glide away off the poop, and when he is gone, you must push the box over into the sea and cry out."

"The plot is perfect!" I exclaimed, struck not more by its ingenuity than the rapidity with which it had been conceived. "There is only one draw-back—who will replace the bo's'n? I dare not trust the steward."

"You will trust me?" she said.

I could not help laughing as I asserted, "You do not look like the bo's'n."

"Oh, that is easily done," she replied, slightly blushing, and yet looking at me bravely. "If he will lend me a suit of his clothes, I will put them on."

To spare her the slightest feeling of embarrassment, I said:

"Very well, Miss Robertson. It will be a little masquerading, that is all. I will give you a small sou'wester that will hide your hair—though even that precaution should be unnecessary, for if the night is not dark the adventure must be deferred."

"It is settled!" she exclaimed, with her eyes shining. "Come! I knew I should be able to help. You will arrange with the boatswain, and let me know the hour you fix upon, and what signal you will give me to steal up on deck and place myself near you."

"You are the bravest girl in the world! You are fit to command a ship!" I emphatically affirmed.

She smiled as she answered, "A true sailor's compliment, Mr. Royle." Then, with a sudden sigh and a wonderful change of expression, making her beauty a sweet and graceful symbol of the ever-changing sea, she cried, looking at her father:

"May God protect us and send us safely home! I dare not think too much. I hope without thinking. Oh, Mr. Royle, how shall you feel when we are starting for dear England? This time will drive me mad to remember!"

CHAPTER XIV

I SHALL never forget the deep anxiety with which I awaited the coming on of the night, my feverish restlessness, the exultation with which I contemplated my scheme, the miserable anguish with which I foreboded its failure.

It was like tossing a coin—the cry involving life or death!

If Stevens detected the stratagem, my life was not worth a rush-light, and the thoughts of Mary Robertson falling a victim to the rage of the crew was more than my mind could be got to bear upon.

Stevens came on deck at four o'clock in the afternoon, and that I might converse with the boatswain without fear of incurring the carpenter's suspicion, I brought a chart from the captain's cabin and spread it on the cuddy table, right under the after sky-light; and while the boatswain and I hung over it, pretending to be engaged in calculations, we completed our arrangements.

He was struck with the boldness of Miss Robertson's idea, and said he would as soon trust her to take part in the plot as any stout-hearted man. He grinned at the notion of her wearing his clothes, and told me he'd make up a bundle of his Sunday rig, and leave it out for me to put into her cabin.

"She'll know how to shorten what's too lengthy," said he, "and you'd better tell her to take long steps ven she walks, for vimmen's legs travels twice as quick as a man's and that's how I alvays knows vich sex is hacting before me in the theayter; though, to be sure, some o' them do dress right up to the hammer, and vould deceive their own mothers."

"Are the hatches off for'ard?"

"You leave that to me, Mr. Royle. That'll be all right."

"What weapon have you got?"

"Only a bar of iron the size of my leg," he answered, grimly. "I shouldn't like to drop it on my foot by accident."

We brought our hurried conversation to a close by perceiving the carpenter staring at us steadfastly through the sky-light; and, whispering that everything now depended upon the night being dark, I repaired with my chart to the cabin I occupied.

I noticed at this time that the lid of one of the lockers stood a trifle open, sustained by the things inside it, which had evidently been tumbled and not put square again.

This, on inspecting the locker, I found to be the case; and, remembering that here was the bag of silver I had come across while searching for clothes for old Mr. Robertson, I thrust my hand down to find it. It was gone. "So, Mr. Stevens," thought I, "this is some of your doing, is it? A thief as well as a murderer! You grow accomplished." Well, if he had the silver in his pocket when he quitted the ship, it would only drown him the sooner, should he find himself overboard. There was comfort in that reflection, any way; and I should have been perfectly willing that the silver had been gold, could the rogue's death have been hastened by the transmutation.

A little before six o'clock, at which hour I was to relieve the boatswain in order to take charge of the ship through the second dog-watch, Stevens being in his cabin and all quiet in the after part of the vessel, I went quietly down the ladder that conducted to the steerage, this ladder being situated some dozen feet abaft the mizzen-mast.

All along the starboard side of the ship in this part of her were stowed upward of seven hundred boxes of tintacks, each box about twenty inches in length by twelve in breadth, and weighing pretty heavy. There was nothing else that I could think of that would so well answer the purpose of making a splash alongside as one of these boxes, and which combined the same weight in so handy and portable a bulk. Anything in wood must float; anything in iron might be missed. All these things had to be carefully considered, for, easy as the job of dropping a weight overboard to counterfeit the sound of a human body fallen into the water may seem, yet in my case the difficulty of accomplishing it successfully, and without the chance of subsequent detection, was immense, and demanded great prudence and foresight.

I conveyed one of these boxes to my cabin, and when four bells were struck (the hands kept the relief bells going for their own sakes, I giving them the time each day at noon), I smuggled it up in a top-coat, and stepped with an easy air on to the poop. The man who had been steering was in the act of surrendering the spokes to another hand, and I took advantage of one of them cutting off a piece of tobacco for the other, which kept them both occupied, to put my coat and the box inside it in the stern-sheets of the port quarter-boat, as though it were my coat only which I had deposited there out of the road, handy to slip on should I require it.

The boatswain observed my action without appearing to notice it; and as he passed me on the way to the cuddy, he said that his clothes would be ready by eight bells for the lady, and that I should find them in a bundle near the door.

He would not stay to say more; for I believe that the carpenter had found something suspicious in our hanging together over the chart, and had spoken to this effect to his chums among the men; and it therefore behooved the boatswain and me to keep as clear of each other as possible.

One stroke of fortune, however, I saw was to befall us. The night, unless a very sudden change took place, would be dark.

The sky was thick, with an even and unbroken ground of cloud which had a pinkish tint down in the western horizon, where the sun was declining behind it. The sea was rough, and looked muddy. The wind held steady, but blew very fresh, and had drawn a trifle further to the southward, so that the vessel was a point off her course. The motion of the ship was very uncomfortable, the pitching sharp and irregular, and she rolled as quickly as a vessel of one hundred tons would.

As the shadows gathered upon the sea, the spectacle of the leaden-colored sky and waves was indescribably melancholy. Some half dozen Mother Carey's chickens followed in our wake, and I watched their gray breasts skimming the surface of the waves until they grew indistinguishable on the running foam. The look of the weather was doubtful enough to have justified me in furling the maintop-gallant-sails and even single-reefing the two top-sails; but though this canvas did not actually help the ship's progress, as she was close to the wind, and it pressed her over and gave much leeway, yet I thought it best to let it stand, as it suggested an idea of speed to the men (which I took care the log should confirm), and I should require to make a long reckoning on the chart next day to prove to Stevens that we were fast nearing the coast of Florida.

At eight o'clock I called Stevens, and saw him well upon deck before I ventured to enter the boatswain's berth. I then softly opened the door, and heard the honest fellow snoring like a trooper in his bunk; but the parcel of clothes lay ready, and I at once took them, and knocked lightly on Miss Robertson's door.

She immediately appeared, and I handed her the clothes and also my sou'wester, which I had taken to my cabin after quitting the deck.

'What is to be the signal?' she asked.

"Three blows of my heel over your cabin. There is a spare cabin next door for you to use, as your father ought not to see you."

"I will contrive that he does not see me," she answered. "He fell asleep just now when I was talking to him. I had better not leave him, for if he should wake up and call for me, I should not like to show myself in these clothes for fear of frightening him; whereas if I stop here, I can dress myself by degrees, and can answer him without letting him see me."

"There is plenty of time," I said. "The bo's'n relieves the carpenter at midnight. I will join the bo's'n when the carpenter has left the deck. Here is my watch—you have no means of knowing the time without quitting your cabin."

"Is the night dark?"

"Very dark. Nothing could be better. Have no fear," I said, handing her my watch; "we shall get the bo's'n safely stowed below, and with him a crowbar. The carpenter will find it rather harder than he imagines to scuttle the ship. He—I mean the bo's'n—is sound asleep, and snoring like a field-marshal on the eve of glory. His trumpeting is wonderfully consoling, for no man could snore like that who forebodes a dismal ending of life."

I took her hand, receiving as I did so a brave smile from her hopeful, pretty face, and left her.

Without much idea of sleeping, I lay down under a blanket, but fell asleep immediately, and slept as soundly, if not as noisily, as the boatswain, until eleven o'clock.

The vessel's motion was now easier; she did not strain, and was more on an even keel, which either meant that the wind had fallen or that it had drawn aft.

I looked through the port-hole, to see if I could make anything of the night, but it was pitch-dark. I lighted a pipe to keep me awake, and lay down again to think over our plot, and find, if I could, any weakness in it, but felt more than ever satisfied with our plans. The only doubtful point was whether the fellow who went down to scuttle the ship would not get into the fore-peak; but if the boatswain could contrive to knock a hole in the bulkhead, he would have the man, whether he got down through the fore-castle or the fore-hatch; and this I did not question he would manage, for he was very well acquainted with the ship's hold and the disposition of the cargo.

I found myself laughing once when I thought of the fright the scoundrel (whoever it might be) would receive from the boatswain—he would think he had met the devil or a ghost; but I did not suppose the boatswain would give him much time to be afraid, if he could only bring that crowbar, as big as his leg, to bear.

The sound of eight bells being struck set my heart to beating rather quickly, and almost immediately I heard Stevens' heavy step coming down the companion-ladder.

I lay quiet, thinking he might look in, as it would better suit my purpose to let him think me asleep. He went and roused out the boatswain, and after a little the boatswain went on deck.

But Stevens did not immediately turn in. I cautiously abstracted the key, and looked through the key-hole, and observed him bring out a bottle of rum and a tumbler from the pantry, and help himself to a stiff glass. He swallowed the fiery draught with his back turned upon the main-deck, that the men, if any were about, should not see him; and drying his lips by running his sleeve the whole length of his arm over them, he replaced the bottle and glass and went to his cabin.

This was now my time. There was nothing to fear from his finding me on deck should he take it into his head to come up, since it was reasonable that I, acting as skipper, should at any and all hours be watching the weather and noting the ship's course, more particularly now, when we were supposed to be drawing near land.

Still, I left my cabin quietly, as I did not want him to hear me, and sneaked up through the companion on tip-toe.

The night was not so pitch-dark as I might have expected from the appearance of it through the port-hole; but it was quite dark enough to answer my purpose. For instance it was as much as I could do to follow the outline of the mainmast, and the man at the wheel and the wheel itself, viewed from a short distance, were lumped into a blotch, though there was a halo of light all around the binnacle.

The lamp that was alight in the cuddy hung just abaft the foremost sky-light, and I saw that it would be necessary to cover the glass. So I stepped up to the boatswain, who stood near the mizzen-mast.

"Are you all ready, bo's'n?"

"All ready."

"Not afraid of the rats?" I said, with a laugh.

"No, nor wuss than rats," he replied. "Has the lady got my clothes on yet? I *should* like to see her."

"She'll come when we are ready. That light shining on the sky-light must be concealed. I don't want to put the lamp out, and am afraid to draw the curtains for fear the rings should rattle. There's a tarpaulin in the starboard quarter-boat; take and throw it over the sky-light while I go aft and talk to the fellow steering. Who is he?"

"Jim Cornish."

He found the tarpaulin, and concealed the light, while I spoke to the man at the wheel about the ship's course, the look of the weather and so on.

"Now," said I, rejoining the boatswain, "come and take two or three turns along the poop, that Cornish may see us together."

We paced to and fro, stopping every time we reached the wheel to look at the compass.

When we were at the fore end of the poop, I halted.

"Walk aft," I said, "and post yourself right in the way of Cornish, that he sha'n't be able to see along the weatherside of the poop."

I followed him until I had come to the part of the deck that was right over Miss Robertson's cabin, and there struck three smart blows with the heel of my boot, at the same time flapping my hands against my breast so as to make Cornish believe that I was warming myself.

I walked to the break of the poop and waited.

In less time than I could count twenty a figure came out of the cuddy and mounted the poop-ladder, and stood by my side. Looking close into the face I could see that it was rather too white to be a sailor's, that was all. The figure was a man's, most perfectly so.

"Admirable!" I whispered, grasping her hand.

I posted her close against the screened sky-light, that her figure might be on a level with the mizzen-mast viewed from the wheel, and called to the boatswain.

The tone of my voice gave him his cue. He came forward just as a man would to receive an order.

"She is here," I said, turning him by the arm to where Miss Robertson stood, motionless. "For God's sake, get forward at once! Lose no time!"

He went up to her and said,

"I'm sorry I can't see you properly, miss. If this wur daylight I reckon you'd make a handsome sailor, just fit for the gals to go dreamin' an' ravin' about."

With which, and waving his hand, the plucky fellow slipped off the poop like a shadow, and I watched him glide along the main-deck until he vanished.

"Now," whispered I to my companion, "the tragedy begins. We must walk up and down that the man steering may see us. Keep on the left side of the deck; it is higher than where I shall walk, and will make you look taller."

I posted her properly, and we began to measure the deck.

Anxious as I was, I could still find time to admire the courage of this girl. At no sacrifice of modesty—no, not even to the awaking of an instant's mirth in me—was her noble and beautiful bravery illustrated. Her pluck was so grand an expression of her English character that no emotion but that of profound admiration of her moral qualities could have been inspired in the mind of any man who beheld her.

I took care not to go further than the mizzen-rigging, so that Cornish should distinguish nothing but our figures; and after we had paraded the deck awhile I asked her to stand near the quarter-boat, in which I had placed the box.

I then got on to the rail and fished out the box smartly, and stood it on the rail.

"Keep your hand upon it," said I, "that it may not roll overboard."

With which I walked right up to Cornish.

"Does she steer steady?"

"True as a hair."

"I left my coat this afternoon in one of the quarter-boats. Have you seen it?"

"No."

"Perhaps it's in the starboard boat."

I pretended to search, and then drawing close to Miss Robertson, said, quickly:

"Creep away now. Keep close to the rail and crouch low. Get to your cabin and change your dress. Roll the clothes you are wearing in a bundle and hide them for the present."

She glided away on her little feet, stooping her head to a level with the rail.

All was quiet forward—the main-deck deserted. I waited some seconds, standing with my hand on the box, and then I shoved it right overboard. It fell, just as I had expected, with a thumping splash.

Instantly I roared out, "Man overboard! Down with your helm! The bo's'n's gone!" and to complete the imposture, I bounded aft, cut away a life-buoy, and flung it far into the darkness astern.

Cornish obeyed me literally; put the helm right down, and in a few moments the sails were shaking wildly.

"Steady!" I shouted. "Aft here and man the port main-braces! Bear a hand! the bo's'n's overboard!"

My excitement made my voice resonant as a trumpet, and the men in both watches came scampering along the deck. The shaking of the canvas, the racing of feet, my own and the cries of the crew, produced, as you may credit, a fine uproar. Of course I had foreseen that there would be no danger in bringing the ship back. The wind, though fresh, was certainly not strong enough to jeopardize the spars; moreover, the sea had moderated.

Up rushed the carpenter in a very short time, rather the worse, I thought, for the dose he had swallowed.

"What's the matter? What the devil is all this?" he bellowed, lurching from side to side as the ship rolled, for we were now broadside on.

"The bo's'n has fallen overboard!" I shouted in his ear; and I had need to shout, for the din of the canvas was deafening.

"Do you say the bo's'n?" he bawled.

"Yes. What shall we do? Is it too dark to pick him up?"

"Of course it is!" he cried, hoarse as a raven. "What do you want to do? He's drowned by this time! Who's to find him? Give 'em the proper orders, Mr. Royle!" and he vociferated to the men, "Do you want the masts to carry away? Do you want to be over-hauled by the fust wessel as comes this road, and hanged, every mother's son of you, because the bo's'n's fallen over-board?"

I stood to leeward, gazing at the water and uttering exclamations to show my concern and distress at the loss of the boatswain.

Stevens dragged me by the arm.

"Give 'em the proper orders, I tell ye, Mr. Royle!" he cried, "I say that the bo's'n's drowned, and that no stopping the wessel will save him. Sing out to the men, for the Lord's sake! Let her fill again, or we're damned!"

"Very well," I replied, with a great air of reluctance, and I advanced to the poop-rail and delivered the necessary orders. By dint of flattening in the jib-sheets and checking the main-braces and brailing up the spanker and rousing the foreyards well forward, I got the ship to pay off. The carpenter worked like a madman, bawling all the while that if the ship was dismasted, all hands would certainly be hanged; and he so animated the men by his cries and entreaties, that more work was done by them in one quarter of an hour than they would have put into treble that time on any other occasion.

It was now one o'clock; so it had not taken us an hour to drown the boatswain, put the ship in irons, and get her clear again.

Stevens came off the main-deck on to the poop, greatly relieved in his mind, now that the sails were full and the yards trimmed, and asked me how it happened that the boatswain fell overboard.

I replied, very gravely, that I had come on deck at eight bells, being anxious to see what way the ship was making and how she was heading; that, remembering I had left an overcoat in one of the quarter-boats, I looked, but could not find it; that I spoke to the boatswain, who told me that he had seen the coat in the stern-sheets of the quarter-boat that afternoon, and got on to the poop-rail to search the boat; that I had turned my head for a moment, when I heard a groan, which was immediately followed by a loud splash alongside, and I perceived that the boatswain had vanished.

"So," continued I, "I pitched a life-buoy astern and sung out to put the helm down; and I must say, Mr. Stevens, that I think we could have saved the poor fellow had we tried. But you are really the skipper of this ship, and since you objected I did not argue."

"There's no use sayin' we *could* ha' saved him," rejoined Stevens, gruffly. "I say we couldn't. Who's to see him in the dark? We should have had to burn a flare for the boat to find us, and what with our driftin' and their lumpin' about, missing their road, and doing no airthly good, we should ha' ended in losin' the boat."

He did not notice the tarpaulin spread over the sky-light, though I had an explanation of its being there had he inquired the meaning of it.

He hung about the deck for a whole hour, though I had offered to take the boatswain's watch, and go turn and turn about with him (Stevens), and he had a long yarn with the man at the wheel, which I contrived to drop in upon after awhile, and found Cornish explaining exactly how the boatswain fell overboard, and corroborating my story in every particular.

Thus, laborious as my stratagem had been, it was, as this circumstance alone proved, in no sense too labored; for had not Cornish seen with his own eyes the boatswain and myself standing near the boat just before I gave the alarm, he would in all probability have represented the affair in such a way to Stevens as to set him doubting my story, and perhaps putting the men on to search the ship, to see if the boatswain *was* overboard. He went below at two o'clock.

The sea fell calm, and the wind shifted round to the nor'ard and westward, and was blowing a steady, pleasant breeze at six bells. The stars came out and the horizon cleared, and, looking to leeward, I beheld at a distance of about four miles the outline of a large ship, which, when I brought the binocular glasses to bear on her, I found under full sail.

She was steering a course seemingly parallel with our own, and as I watched her my brains went to work to conceive in what possible way I could utilize her presence.

At all events, the first thing I had to do was to make sail, or she would run away from me; so I at once called up the watch.

While the men were at work the dawn broke, and by the clearer light I perceived that the vessel was making a more westerly course than we, and was drawing closer to us at every foot of water we severally measured. She was a noble-looking merchantman, like a frigate with her painted ports with double top-sail and top-pliant yards, and with sky-sails set, so that her sails were a wonderful volume and tower of canvas.

The sight of her filled me with emotions I cannot express. As to signaling her, I knew that the moment the men saw me handling the signal-halyards they would crowd aft and ask me what I meant to do. I might, indeed, hail her if I could steer the "Grosvenor" close enough alongside for my voice to carry; but if they failed to hear me or refused to help, what would be my position? So surely as I raised my voice to declare our situation, so surely would the crew drag me down and murder me out of hand.

Presently Fish and Johnson came along the main deck, and while Fish entered the cuddy Johnson came up to me.

"Hadn't you better put the ship about?" he said. "You're running us rather close. The men don't like it."

Seeing that no chance would be given me to make my peril known to the stranger, I formed my resolution rapidly. I called out to the men:

"Johnson wants to 'bout the ship. Yonder vessel can see that we are making a free wind, and she'll either think we're mad or that there's something wrong with us if we 'bout ship with a beam wind. Now what am I to do?"

"Haul us away from that ship—that's all we want," answered one of them.

At this moment the carpenter came running up the poop-ladder, with nothing on but his shirt and a pair of breeches.

"Halloo!" he called out, fiercely, "what are you about? Do you want to put us alongside?"

And he bawled out fiercely, "Port your helm! run right away under her stern!"

"If you do that," I exclaimed, very anxious now to show how well-intentioned I was, "you will excite her suspicions. Steady!" I cried, seeing the ship drawing rapidly ahead; "bring her to again a point off her course."

Stevens scowled at me, but did not speak.

The crew clustered up the poop-ladder to stare at the ship, and I caught some of them casting such threatening looks at me that I wanted no better hint of the kind of mercy I should receive if I played them any tricks.

"Mr. Stevens," said I, "leave me to manage, and I'll do you no wrong. That ship is making more way than we are, and we shall have her dead on end presently. Then I'll show you what to do."

As I spoke the vessel which we had brought well on the port bow hoisted English colors. The old ensign floated gracefully, and stood out at the gaff end.

"We must answer her," I exclaimed to the carpenter. "You had better bend on the ensign and run it up."

I suppose he knew that there could be no mischievous meaning in the display of this flag, for he obeyed me, though leisurely.

The ship when she saw that we answered her, hauled her ensign down, and after awhile, during which she sensibly increased the distance between us, and had drawn very nearly stern on, hoisted her number.

"Run up the answering pennant," I exclaimed; "it will look civil, anyway, and it means nothing."

I pointed out the signal to the carpenter, who hoisted it; but I could see by his face that he meant to obey no more orders of this kind.

"Steady as she goes!" cried I, to the fellow steering. "A hand let go the weather mizzen-braces, and haul in, some of you, to leeward."

This maneuver laid the sails of the mizzen-mast aback; they at once impeded our way, nor, being now right ahead of us, could the people on board the ship see what we had done. The result was, the vessel drove away rapidly, I taking care to luff as she got to windward, so as to keep our flying jib-boom in a direct line with her stern.

To judge by the way the men glanced at me and spoke to one another, they evidently appreciated this stratagem; and Stevens condescended to say, "That's one for her."

"Better than going about," I answered, dryly.

"They've hauled down them signals," he said, blinding the point I raised by my remark.

"See. She doesn't mean to stop to ask any questions!"

The end of this was that in about twenty minutes the ship was three or four miles ahead of us; so not choosing to lose any more time, I swung the mizzen-yards, and got the "Grosvenor" on her course again.

Stevens went below to put on his coat and cap and boots, in order to relieve me, for it was now four o'clock. The dawn had broken with every promise of a fine day, and where the sun rose the sky resembled frost-work, layer upon layer of high delicate clouds, ranged like scale-armor, all glittering with silver brightness, and whitening the sea, over which they hung with a pale, pearly light.

I was thoroughly exhausted, not so much from the want of rest as from the excitement I had gone through. Still, I had a part to play before I turned in; so I stuck my knuckles in my eyes to rub them open, and waited for Stevens, who presently came on deck, having first stopped on the main-deck to grumble to his crony Fish over his not having had a quarter of an hour's sleep since midnight.

"I'm growed sick o' the sight o' this poop," he growled to me. "Sick o' the sight o' the whole wessel. Fust part o' the woyage I was starved for food. Now, with the bo's'n overboard, I'm starved for sleep. How long are we going to take to reach Floridy? Sink me if I shouldn't ha' woted for some nearer coast had I known this woyage wur going to last to the day o' judgment."

"If it don't fall calm," I answered, "I may safely promise to put you off the coast of Florida on Friday afternoon."

He thrust his hands into his breeches pockets, and stared aft.

"I am very much troubled about the loss of the bo's'n," said I.

"Are you?" he responded, ironically.

"He was a civil man and a good sailor."

"Yes; I dessay he was. But he's no use now."

"He deserved that we should have made an effort to save him."

"Well, you said that before, and I said no; and I suppose I know wot I mean when I says no."

"But won't the crew think me a heartless rascal for not sending a boat to the poor devil?" I demanded, pretending to lose my temper.

"The bo's'n was none so popular—don't make no mistake. He wasn't one of— Hell seize me! where are you drivin' to, Mr. Royle? Can't you let a drowned man alone?" he cried, with an outburst of passion. But immediately he softened his voice, and, with a look of indescribable cunning, said, "Some of the hands didn't like him, of course; and some did, and they'll be sorry. I am one of them as did, and would ha' saved him, if I hadn't feared the masts, and reckoned there'd be no use in the boat gropin' about in the dark for a drownin' man."

"No doubt of that," I replied, in a most open manner. "You know the course, Mr. Stevens? You might set the foretop-mast-stun'sail presently, for we shall have a fine day."

And with a civil nod I left him, more than ever satisfied that my stratagem was a complete success.

I bent my ear to Miss Robertson's cabin as I passed, to hear if she were stirring. All was still: so I passed on to my berth, and turned in just as I was, and slept soundly till eight o'clock.

CHAPTER XV

I ONLY saw Miss Robertson for a few minutes at breakfast time.

The steward, as usual, carried their breakfast on a tray to the door; and taking it in, she saw me and came forward.

"Is it all well?" she asked, quickly and eagerly.

"All well," I replied.

"He is in the hold," she whispered, "and no one knows?"

"He is in the hold, and the crew believe to a man that he is overboard."

"It is a good beginning," she affirmed, with a faint smile playing over her pale face.

"Thanks to your great courage! You performed your part admirably."

"There is that hateful carpenter watching us through the sky-light," she whispered, without raising her eyes. "Tell me one thing before I go—when will the ship reach the port she is to stop at?"

"I shall endeavor to make it Friday afternoon."

"The day after to-morrow!"

She clasped her hands suddenly, and exclaimed, with a little sob in her voice, "Oh, let us pray that God will be merciful and protect us!"

I had no thoughts for myself as I watched her enter her cabin. The situation was, indeed, a dreadful one for so sweet and helpless a woman to be placed in. I, a rough, sturdy fellow, used to the dangers of the sea, was scared at our position when I contemplated it. Truly might I say that our lives hung by a hair, and that whether we were to live or perish dismally would depend upon the courage and promptness with which the boatswain and I should act at the last moment.

It was worse for me that I did not know the exact plan of the mutineers.

I was aware that their intention was to scuttle the ship and leave her, with us on board, to sink; but *how* they would do this I did not know. I mean I could not foresee whether they would scuttle the ship while all the crew remained on board, stopping until they knew the vessel was actually sinking before taking to the boats, or whether they would get into the boats, leaving one man in the hold to scuttle the ship, and, lying by, to take him off when his work should have been performed.

Either was likely; but one would make our preservation comparatively easy; the other would make it almost impossible.

When I went on deck all hands were at breakfast. The carpenter quitted the poop the moment I showed myself, and I was left alone, none of the crew visible but the steersman.

The breeze was slashing; a splendid sailing wind; the fore-top-mast-stun'sail set, every sail round and hard as a drum-skin, and the water smooth; the ship bowled along like a yacht in a racing match. Nothing was in sight all round the horizon.

I made sure that the carpenter would go to bed as soon as he had done breakfast; but instead, about twenty minutes after he had left the poop, I saw him walk along the main-deck and disappear in the forecastle.

After an interval of some ten minutes he reappeared, followed by Johnson, the cook, and a couple of hands. They got upon the port side of the long-boat, and presently I heard the fluttering and screaming of hens.

I crossed the poop to see what was the matter, and found all four men wringing the necks of the poultry. In a short time about sixteen hens—all that remained—lay dead in a heap near the coop. The cook and Johnson gathered them up and carried them into the galley.

Soon after they returned, and clambered on to the top of the long-boat, the cover of which they pitched off and fell, each with a knife in his hands, upon the pigs. The noise now was hideous. The pigs squealed like human beings; but both men probably knew their work, for the screeching did not last above five minutes.

The cook, with his face, arms and breeches all bloody, flung the carcasses among the men, who had gathered round to witness the sport, and a deal of ugly play followed. They tossed the slaughtered pigs at each other, and men and pigs fell down with tremendous thuds; and soon there was not a man who did not look as though he had been rolled for an hour in the gutter of a shambles. Their hoarse laughter, their horrible oaths, their rage not more shocking than their mirth, the live men rolling over the dead pigs, their faces and clothes ghastly with blood—all this was a scene which made one abhor one's self for laughing at it, though it was impossible to help laughing sometimes. But occasionally my mirth would be checked by a sudden spasm of terror, when I caught a sight of a fellow with an infuriate face, monstrous with its crimson coloring, rush with his knife at another, and be struck down like a nine-pin by a dead pig hurled full at his head before he could deliver his blow.

The saturnalia came to an end, and the men, cursing, growling, groaning and laughing—some reeling half stunned, and all panting for breath —surged into the forecastle to clean themselves while the cook and Johnson carried the pigs into the galley.

I did not quite understand what this scene heralded, but had not long to wait before it was explained.

In twos and threes, after much delay, the men emerged and began to wash the decks down. Two got into the long-boat and began to clean her out. Then the carpenter came aft with Johnson, and I heard him swearing at the steward. After a bit, Johnson came forth, rolling a cask of cuddy bread along the deck; after him went the steward, bearing a limejuice jar, filled, of course with rum.

These things were stored near the foremast. Then all three came aft again (the carpenter superintending the work), and more provisions were taken forward; and when enough was collected, the whole was snugged and covered with a tarpaulin ready, as I now understand, to be shipped into the long-boat, when she should have been swung over the ship's side.

These preparations brought the reality of the position of myself and companions most completely home to me; yet I perfectly preserved my composure, and appeared to take the greatest interest in all that was going forward.

The carpenter came upon the poop presently, and went to the starboard quarter-boat and inspected it. He then crossed to the other boat, after which he walked up to me.

"How many hands," he asked, "do you think the long-boat 'ud carry, comfortable?"

I measured her with my eyes before answering.

"About twenty," I replied.

"One on top o' t'other, like cattle?" he growled. "Why, mate, there wouldn't be standin' room."

"Do you mean to put off from the ship in her?"

"In her and one of them others," he replied, meaning the quarter-boats.

"If you want my opinion, I should say that all hands ought to get into the long-boat. She has heaps of beam, and will carry us all well. Besides, she can sail. It will look better, too, to be found in her, should we be picked up before landing; because you can make out that both quarter-boats were carried away."

"We're all resolved," be answered, doggedly. "We mean to put off in the long-boat and one o' them quarter-boats. The quarter-boat can tow the long-boat if it's calm. Why I ax'd you how many the long-boat 'ud carry, was because we don't want to overload the quarter-boat. We can use her as a tender for stores and water, do you see, so that if we get to a barren place we sha'n't starve."

"I understand."

"Then two boats'll be enough, any ways."

"I should say so. They'd carry thirty persons between them," I answered.

To satisfy himself he went and took another look at the boats, and afterwards called Johnson up to him.

They talked together for some time, occasionally glancing at me, and Johnson then went away; but in a few minutes he returned with a mallet and chisel. Both men now got into the port-quarter-boat and proceeded, to my rage and mortification, to rip a portion of the planking out of her. In this way they knocked several planks away and threw them overboard, and Johnson then got out of her and went to the other boat, and fell to examining her closely to see that all was right; for they evidently had made up their minds to use her, she being the larger of the two.

The carpenter came and stood close beside me, watching Johnson. I dare say he expected I would ask him why he had injured the boat; but I hardly dared trust myself to speak to him, so great was my passion and abhorrence of the wretch, whose motive in rendering this boat useless was, of course, that we should not be able to save ourselves when we found the ship sinking.

When Johnson had done, some men came aft, and they went to work to provision the remaining quarter-boat, passing bags of bread, tins of preserved meat, kegs of water, and stores of that description, from hand to hand, until the boat held about a quarter as much again as she was fit to carry.

In the meantime others were busy in the long-boat, getting her fit for sailing with a spare top-gallant-stun'sail boom and top-gallant-stun'sail, looking to the oars and thole-pins, and so forth.

The morning passed rapidly, the crew as busy as bees, smoking to a man, and bandying coarse jokes with one another, and uttering loud laughs as they worked.

The carpenter never once addressed me. He ran about the decks, squirting tobacco-juice everywhere, superintending the work that was going forward, and manifesting great excitement, with not a few displays of bad temper.

A little before noon, when I made ready to take the sun's altitude, the men at work about the long-boat suspended their occupation to watch me, Stevens drew aft, and came snuffling about my heels.

When I sung out eight bells, and went below to work out my observations, he followed me into the cabin, and stood looking on. The ignorance of his distrust was almost ludicrous; I believe he thought I should work out a false reckoning if he were not by, but that his watching would prevent me from making two and two five.

"Now, Mr. Royle," said he, seeing me put down my pencil, "where are we?"

I unrolled the chart upon the table, and drew a line down a rule from the highly imaginary point to which I had brought the ship at noon on the preceding day to latitude 29°, longitude 74° 30'. "Here is our position at the present moment," I said, pointing to the mark on the chart.

"This here is Floridy, ain't it?" he demanded outlining the coast with his dirty thumb.

"That is Florida."

"Well, I calls it Floridy for short."

"Floridy then. I know what you mean."

"And you give us till the day arter to-morrow to do this bit o' distance in?"

"It doesn't look much on the chart. There's not much room for miles to show in on a square of paper like this."

"Well, we shall be all ready to lower away the boats when you give us the word," said he.

"Perhaps you'll sit down for five minutes, Mr. Stevens, and inform me exactly of your arrangements," I exclaimed; "for it is difficult for me to do my share in this job unless I accurately know what yours is to be."

He looked at me askant, his villainous eyes right in the corners of their sockets; but sat down, nevertheless, and tilted his cap over his forehead in order to scratch the back of his head.

"I thought you knew what our plans was?" he remarked.

"Why, I've got a kind of general notion of them, but I should like to understand them more clearly."

"Well, I thought they was clear—clear as mud in a wine-glass. Leastwise they're clear to all hands."

"For instance, why did you knock a hole in the quarter-boat this morning?"

"I didn't think you'd want that explained," he answered, promptly.

"But you see I do, Mr. Stevens."

"Well, we only want two boats, and it 'ud be a silly lookout to leave the third one sound and tight, to drift about with the 'Grosvenor's' name writ inside o' her."

"Why?"

"Because I say it would."

"How could she drift about if she were up at the davits?"

"How do I know?" he answered morosely. "I'm lookin' at things as may happen. It ain't for me to explain of them."

"Very well," said I, master enough of the ruffian's meaning to require no further information on this point.

"Anything more, Mr. Royle?"

"Yes. The next matter is this: You gave me to understand that we should heave the ship to at night?"

"Sartinly. As soon as ever it comes on dusk, so as we shall have all night before us to get well away."

"Do you mean to leave her with her canvas standing?"

"Just as she is when she's hove to."

"Some ship may sight her, and finding her abandoned, send a crew on board to work her to the nearest port."

I thought this might tempt him to admit that she was to be scuttled, which confession need not necessarily have involved the information that I and the others were to be left on board.

But the fellow was too cunning to hint at such a thing.

"Let them as finds her keep her," he said, getting up. "That's their consarn. Any more questions, Mr. Royle?"

"Are we to take our clothes with us?"

He grinned in the oddest manner.

"No. Them as has wallyables may shove 'em into their pockets; but no kits'll be allowed in the boats. We're a poor lot o' shipwrecked sailors—mariners, as the newspapers calls us—come away from a ship that was settlin' under our legs afore we had the 'arts to leave her. We just had time to wittol the boats and stand for the shore. We depend upon Christian kindness for 'elp; and if we falls foul o' a missionary, leave me alone to make him vurship our piety. The skipper he fell mad and jumped overboard. The chief mate he lost his life by springin' into vun o' the boats and missin' of it; and the second mate he manfully stuck to the ship for the love he bore her owners, and, we pree-sume, went down with her."

"Oh!" I ejaculated, forcing a laugh;"then I am not to admit that I am the second mate, when questioned?"

He stared at me as if he were drunk, and cried, "You!" then burst into a laugh, and hit me a slap on the back.

"Ah!" he exclaimed. "I forgot. Of course, you'll not be second mate when you get ashore."

"What then?"

"Why, a passenger—a parson—the ship's doctor. We'll tell you wot to say as we go along. Come, get us off this bloomin' coast, will you, as soon as you can," pointing to the chart. "All hands is growin' delikit with care and consarn; as Joe Sampson used to sing,

> "'Vith care and consarn
> Ve're a-vaisting avay.'

"And our nerviss systems is that wrought up with fear of our necks, that blowed if we sha'n't want two months o' strong physicking and prime livin', at the werry least, to make men of us ag'in arter we're landed."

And with a leering grin and an ugly nod he quitted the cabin.

CHAPTER XVI

I MADE up my mind, as Stevens left me, to bring this terrible time to an end on Friday afternoon, come what might. Let it fall a calm, let it blow a gale, on Friday afternoon I would tell the carpenter that the ship was off the coast of Florida, forty or fifty miles distant.

If, by the boatswain's ruse, I could keep the ship afloat and carry her to Bermuda, it would matter little whether we hove her to one hundred or even two hundred miles distant from the island. The suspense I endured, the horror of our situation, was more than I could bear. I believed that my health and strength would give way if I protracted the ship's journey to the spot where the men would leave her, even for twenty-four hours longer than Friday.

The task before me, then, was to prepare for the final struggle, to thoroughly mature my plans, to utilize the control I still had over the ship to the utmost advantage, and to put into shape all plausible objections and hints I could think upon, which would be helpful to me if adopted by the crew.

What I most felt was the want of fire-arms. The revolver I carried was indeed five-chambered, and there was much good-fortune in my having been the first to get hold of it. But could I have armed the boatswain, or even the steward, with another pistol, I should have been much easier in my mind when I contemplated the chances of a struggle between us and the crew.

However, there is no evil that is not attended by some kind of compensation, and I found this out; for taking it into my head that there might be a pistol among Duckling's effects, though I was pretty sure that the weapon he had threatened me with was the one in my possession, I entered his cabin with the intention to begin a search, but had no sooner opened the lid of his chest than I perceived that I had been forestalled; for the clothes were tossed any way, the pockets turned inside out, and articles taken out of wrappers, as I should judge from the paper coverings that lay among the clothes.

So now I could only hope that Duckling had not had a pistol, since whoever had rifled his box must have met with it. And that Stevens was the thief in this as in the case of the silver I had no doubt at all.

There being now only two of us to keep watch, Stevens and I did not meet at dinner. I took his place while he dined, and he then relieved me.

The steward told me they were having a fine feast in the forecastle; that upward of ten of the fowls that had been strangled in the morning had been put to bake for the men's dinner; that, in addition to this, they had cooked three legs of pork, and were drinking freely from a jar of rum, which the carpenter had ordered him to take forward.

I could pretty well judge that they were enjoying themselves by the loud choruses they were singing.

Believing they would end in becoming drunk, I knocked on Miss Robertson's door to tell her on no account to show herself on deck. She gave me her hand the moment she saw me, and gently brought me into the cabin and made me sit down, though I had not meant to stay.

The old gentleman stood with his back to the door, looking through the port-hole. Though he heard my voice, he did not turn, and only looked round when his daughter pulled him by the arm.

"How do you do, sir?" he asked, making me a most courtly bow. "I hope you are well? You find us, sir," with a stately wave of the hand, "in wretched accommodations; but all this will be mended presently. The greatest lesson of life is patience."

And he made me another bow, meanwhile looking hard at me and contracting his brows.

I was more affected by this painful change—this visible and rapid decay, not of his memory only, but of his mind—than I know how to describe. The mournful, helpless look his daughter gave him, the tearless melancholy in her eyes, as she bent them on me, hit me hard.

I did not know how to answer him, and could only fix my eyes on the deck.

"This prospect," he continued, pointing to the port-hole, "is exceedingly monotonous. I have been watching it I should say a full half hour—about that time, my dear, should you not think?—and find no change in it whatever. I witness always the same unbroken line of water, slightly darker, I observe, than the sky which bends to meet it. That unbroken line has a curious effect upon me. It seems to press like a substantial ligature, or binding, upon my forehead; positively," he exclaimed, with a smile almost as sweet as his child's, "as though I had a cord tied round my head."

He swept his hand over his forehead, as though he could remove the sensation of tightness by the gesture. It was pitiful to witness such a venerable and dignified old gentleman stricken thus in his mind by the sufferings and miserable horrors of shipwreck.

"I think, sir," I said, addressing him with all the respectfulness I could infuse into my voice, "that the uneasiness of which you complain would leave you if you would lie down. The eye gets strained by staring through a port-hole, and that eternal horizon yonder really grows a kind of craze in one's head if watched too long."

"You are quite right, sir," he replied, making me another bow; and, addressing his daughter, "The gentleman sympathizes with the peculiar inspirations of what I may call monotonous nature."

He looked at her with extraordinary and painful earnestness. Evidently some recollections had leaped into his mind and quitted him immediately, leaving him bewildered by it.

He then said, in a most plaintive voice:

"I will lie down. Your shoulder, my love."

He stretched out his trembling hand. I got up to help him, but he withdrew from me with an air of offended pride, and reared his figure to its full height.

"This is my daughter, sir," he exclaimed, with cold emphasis; and though I knew he was not accountable for his behavior, I shrunk back, feeling more completely snubbed than ever I remember being in my life.

With her assistance he got into the bunk, and lay there quite still.

She drew close to me, and obliged me to share the seat she made of the box which had contained the steward's linen.

"You are not angry with him?" she whispered.

"Indeed not."

"I shall lose him soon. He will not live long," she said, and tears came into her eyes.

"God will spare him to you, Miss Robertson. Have courage. Our trials are nearly ended. Once ashore, he will recover his health. It is this miserable confinement, this gloomy cabin, this absence of the comforts he had been used to, that are telling upon his mind. He will live to recall all this in his English home. The worst has never come until it is passed—that is my creed; because the worst may be transformed into good even when it is on us."

"*You* have the courage," she answered, "not I. But you give me courage. God knows what I should have done but for you."

I looked into her brave, soft eyes, swimming in tears, and could have spoken some deep thoughts to her then, awakened by her words.

I was silent a moment, and then said:

"You must not go on deck to-day. Indeed, I think you had better remain below until I ask you to join me."

"Why? is there any new danger?"

"Nothing you need fear. The men, who fancy themselves very nearly at their journey's end, threaten to grow boisterous. But my importance to them is too great to allow them to offend me yet. Still, it will be best for you to keep out of sight."

"I will do whatever you wish."

"I am sure you will. My wish is to save you—not my wish only—it is my resolution. Trust me wholly, Miss Robertson. Keep up your courage, for I may want you to help me at the last."

"You must trust me, too, as my whole trust is in you," she answered, smiling.

I smiled back at her and said:

"Now let me tell you what may happen—what all my energies are and have been engaged to bring about. On Friday afternoon I shall tell the carpenter that the ship is fifty or sixty miles off the coast of Florida. If the night is calm—and I pray that it may be—the ship will be hove to, that is, rendered stationary on the water; the long-boat will be slung over the side, and the quarter-boat lowered. All *this* is certain to happen. But now come my doubts. Will the crew remain on board until the man they send into the hold to scuttle the vessel rejoins them? or will they get into the boats and wait for him alongside? If they take to the boats and wait for the man, the ship is ours. If they remain on board, then our preservation will depend upon the bo's'n."

"How?"

"He will either kill the man who gets into the hold, or knock him insensible. He will then have to act as though *he* were the man he has knocked on the head."

"I see."

"If they call to him, he will have to answer them without showing himself. Perhaps he will call to them. They will answer him. They will necessarily muffle their voices, that we who are aft may not suspect what they are about. In that case the bo's'n may counterfeit the voice of the man he has knocked on the head successfully."

"But what will he tell them?"

"Why, that his job is nearly finished, and that they had best take to the boats and hold off for him, as he is scuttling her in half a dozen places, and the people aft will find her sinking and make a rush to the boats if they are not kept away. He will tell them that when he has done scuttling her he will run and jump overboard and swim to them. This, if done cleverly, may decide the men to shove off. We shall see."

"It is a clever scheme," she answered, musingly. "The boatswain's life depends upon his success, and I believe he will succeed in duping them."

"What can be done he will do, I am sure," I said, not choosing to admit that I had not her confidence in the stratagem, because I feared that the more the boatswain should endeavor to disguise his voice the greater would be the risk of its being recognized. "But let me tell you that this is the worst view of the case. It is quite probable that the men will take to the boats and wait for their mate to finish in the hold, not only because it will save time, but because they will imagine it an effectual way of compelling us to remain on the vessel."

"What villains! And if they take to the boats?"

"Then I shall want you."

"What can I do?"

"We shall see. There still remains a third chance. The carpenter is, or I have read his character upside down, a born murderer. It is possible that this villain may design to leave the man whom he sends into the hold to sink the ship. He has not above half a dozen chums, confidential friends, among the crew; and it will be his and their policy to rid themselves of the others as best they can, so as to diminish the number of witnesses against them. If, therefore, they contemplate this, they will leave the ship while they suppose the act of scuttling to be actually proceeding. Now, among the many schemes which have entered my mind, there was one I should have put in practice had I not feared to commit any action which might in the smallest degree imperil your safety. This scheme was to cautiously sound the minds of the men who were not in the carpenter's intimate confidence; ascertain how far they relish the notion of quitting the ship for a shore that might prove inhospitable, or on which their boats might be wrecked and themselves drowned; and discover, by what shrewdness I am master of, how many I might get to come over to my side if the boatswain and myself turned upon Stevens and killed him, shot down Johnson, and fell, armed with my revolver and a couple of belaying-pins, upon Cornish and Fish— these three men composing Stevens' cabinet. I say that this was quite practicable, and no very great courage required to execute it, as we should have killed or stunned these men before they would be able to resist us."

"There would be nine left."

"Yes; but I should have reckoned upon some of them helping me."

"You could not have depended upon them."

"Well, we have another plan; and I refer to this only to show you a specimen of some of the schemes which have come into my head."

"Mr. Royle, if you had a pistol to give me, I would help you to shoot them! Show me how I can aid you in saving our lives, and I will do your bidding!" she exclaimed, with her eyes on fire.

I put my finger on my lip and smiled.

She blushed scarlet, and said: "You do not think me womanly to talk so?"

"You would not hate me were you to know my thoughts," I answered, rising.

"Are you going, Mr. Royle?"

"Yes. Stevens, for all I know, may have seen me come in here. I would rather he should find me in my own cabin."

"We see very little of you, considering that we are all three in one small ship," she said, hanging her head.

"I never leave you willingly, and would be with you all day if I might. But a rough sailor like me is poor company."

"Sailors are the best company in the world, Mr. Royle."

"Only one woman in every hundred thinks so—perhaps one in every thousand. Well, you would see less of me than you do if I was not prepared to lay down my life for you. No! I don't say that boastfully. I have sworn in my heart to save you, and it shall cost me my life if I fail. That is what I should have said."

She turned her back suddenly, and I hardly knew whether I had not said too much. I stood watching her for a few moments, with my fingers on the handle of the door. Finding she did not move, I went quietly out, but as I closed the door I heard her sob. Now, what had I said to make her cry? I did not like to go in again, and so I repaired to my cabin, wishing, instead of allowing my conversation to drift into a personal current, I had confined it to my plans, which I had not half unfolded to her, but from which I had been as easily diverted as if they were a bit of fiction, instead of a living plot that our lives depended on.

During my watch from four to six, Stevens joined me, and asked how "Floridy" would bear from the ship when she was hove to?

I told him that Florida was not an island, but part of the main coast of

North America, and that he might head the boats any point from north-north-west to south-south-west, and from a distance of fifty or sixty miles, fetch some part of the Florida coast, which, I dared say, showed a seaboard ranging four hundred miles long.

This seemed new to him, which more than ever convinced me of his ignorance; for though I had repeatedly pointed out Florida to him, yet he did not know but that it was an island, which might easily be missed by steering the boats a point out of the course given.

He then asked me what compasses we had that we might take with us.

"We shall only want one in the long-boat," I replied; "and there is one on the table in the captain's cabin which will do. Have you got the long-boat all ready?"

"Ay, clean as a new brass farden, and provisioned for a month."

"Now, let me understand; when the ship is hove to, you will sling the long-boat over?"

"I explained all that before," he answered gruffly.

"Not that."

"You're hangin' on a tidy bit about them there boats. What do you think?"

"I suppose my life is as good as yours, and that I have a right to find out how we are to abandon this ship and make the shore," I answered with some show of warmth, my object being to get all the information from him that was to be drawn. "You'll get the long-boat alongside, and all hands will jump into her? Is that it?"

"Why, wot do you think we'd get the boat alongside for if we didn't get into her?" he replied, with a kind of growling laugh.

"Will anybody be left on the ship?"

"Anybody left on the ship?" he exclaimed, fetching a sudden breath. "Wot's put that in your head?"

"I was afraid that that yellow devil, the cook, might induce you to leave the steward behind to take his chance to sink or swim in her, just out of revenge for calling bad pork good," said I, fixing my eyes upon him.

"No, no, nothen of that sort," he replied quickly, and with evident alarm. "Curse the cook! d'ye think I's skipper to give them kind o' orders?"

"Now you see what I'm driving at," I said, laying my hand on his arm, and addressing him with a smile. "I really did think you meant to leave the poor devil of a steward behind. And what I wanted to understand was how you proposed to manage with the boats to prevent him boarding you—that is why I was curious."

The suspicious ruffian took the bait as I meant he should; and, putting on an unconcerned manner, which fitted him as ill as the pilot-jacket which he had stolen from the captain he had murdered, and which he was now wearing, inquired, "What I meant by that? If they left the steward behind— not that they was goin' to, but to say it, for the sake o' argyment—what would the management of the boats have to do with preventin' him boardin' of them? He didn't understand."

"Oh, nothing," I replied, with a shrug. "Since we are to take the steward with us, there's an end to the matter."

"Can't you explain, sir?" he cried, striving to suppress his temper.

"It is not worth the trouble," said I; "because, don't you see, if even you had made up your mind to leave the steward on the ship, you'd only have one man to deal with. What put this matter into my head was a yarn I read sometime ago about a ship's company wishing to leave their vessel. There were only two boats which were serviceable, and these wouldn't hold above two thirds of the crew. So the men conspired among themselves—do you understand me?"

"Yes, yes, I'm a-followin' you."

"That is, twelve men out of a crew composed of eighteen hands re- solved to lower the boats and get away, and leave the others to shift for themselves. But they had to act cautiously, because, don't you see, the fel- lows who were to be left behind would become desperate with the fear of death, and if any of them contrived to get into the boats, they might begin a fight, which, if it didn't capsize the boats, was pretty sure to end in a drowning match. Of course in our case, as I have said, even supposing you *had* made up your mind to leave the steward behind, we should have noth- ing to fear, because he would be only one man. But when you come to two or three, or four men driven mad by terror, then look out, if they get among you in a boat! for fear will make two as strong as six, and I shouldn't like to be in the boat where such a fight was taking place."

"Well, but how did them other chaps manage as you're tellin' about?"

"Why, they all got into the boats in a lump, and shoved off well clear of the ship. The others jumped into the water after them, but never reached the boats. But all this doesn't hit *our* case. You wished me to explain, and now you know my reasons for asking you how you meant to manage with the boats. Do not forget that there is a woman among us, and a fight at the last moment, when our lives may depend upon orderliness and coolness, may drown us all."

And so saying, I left him, under pretense of looking at the compass.

CHAPTER XVII

I HAD no reason to suppose that the hints I took care to wrap up in my conversation with Stevens would shape his actions to the form I wished them to take: but though they did no good, they would certainly do me no harm, and it was at least certain that my opinion was respected, so that I might hope that some weight would attach to whatever suggestions I offered.

Nothing now remained to be done but to wait the result of events; but no language can express an idea of my anxiety as the hours passed, bringing us momentarily closer to the dreaded and yet wished for issue.

Some of the men got intoxicated that afternoon, and I believe two of them had a desperate set-to; they sung until they were tired, and for tea had more hot roast pork and fowls.

But the majority had their senses, and kept those who were drunk under; so that their riot was all forward.

I wondered what the boatswain would think of the shindy over his head, and whether he had a watch to tell the time by. His abode was surely a very dismal one, among the coals in the fore-peak, and dark as night, with plenty of rats to squeak about his ears, and the endless creaking and complaining of the timbers under the water.

A terrible idea possessed me once. It was that he might be asleep when the man went down to scuttle the ship, who, of course, would take a candle with him and find him lying there.

But there was no use in *imagining* evil. I could only do what was possible. If we were doomed to die, why, we must meet our fate heroically. What more?

It blew freshly at eleven o'clock, and held all night. I kept all the sail on the ship that she would bear, and up to noon next day we spanked along at a great pace.

Then the wind fell light and veered round to the north; but this did not matter to me for I showed the carpenter a run on the chart which convincingly proved to him that, even if we did no more than four knots an hour until next day, we should be near enough to the coast of Florida to heave to.

This afternoon the men made preparations to swing the long-boat over the side, clapping on straps to the collar of the mainstay, and forward round the trestle-tree, ready to hook on the tackles to lift the boat out of her chocks. Their eagerness to get away from the ship was well illustrated by these early preparations.

All that day they fared sumptuously on roast pork, and whatever took their fancy among the cuddy stores, but drank little, or at all events not enough to affect them; though there was sufficient rum in the hold to kill them all off in a day, had they had a mind to broach the casks.

Toward evening we sighted no less than five ships, two standing to the south and the others steering north. The spectacle of these vessels fully persuaded Stevens that we were nearing the coast, he telling me he had no doubt they were from the West Indies, which he supposed were not more than four hundred miles distant.

I did not undeceive him.

I saw Miss Robertson for a few minutes that evening to repeat my caution to her not to show herself on deck.

The men were again at their pranks in the forecastle, skylarking, as they call it at sea, and though not drunk, they were making a tremendous noise. One of them had got a concertina, and sat tailor-fashion, on top of the capstan, and some were dancing, two having dressed themselves up as women in canvas bonnets, and blankets round them to resemble skirts.

Fun of this sort would have been innocent enough had there been any recognized discipline to overlook it; but from decent mirth to boisterous, coarse disorder is an easy step to sailors; and in the present temper of the crew the least provocation might convert the ship into a theater for exhibitions of horse-play which, begun in vanity, might end in criminal excesses.

During my brief conversation with Miss Robertson, I asked her an odd question— Could she steer a ship?

She answered, "Yes."

"You say 'yes' because you will try if you are wanted to do so," I said.

"I say 'yes' because I really understand how to use the wheel," she replied, seriously.

"Where did you learn?"

"During our voyage to the Cape of Good Hope. I used to watch the man steering, and observe him move the wheel so as to keep the compass-card steady. I told Captain Jenkins I should like to learn to steer, and he would often let me hold the wheel, and, for fun, give me orders."

"Which way would you pull the spokes if I told you to put the helm to the starboard?"

"To the left," she answered, promptly.

"And if I said 'hard over'?"

"If the wind was blowing on the left-hand side, I would push the wheel to the right until I could push it no further. You can't puzzle me, indeed. I know all the steering terms. *Really*, I can steer."

I quite believed her, though I should never have dreamed of her proficiency in this matter; and told her that if we succeeded in getting away from the boats, she would be of the utmost importance to us, because then there would be three men to work the ship, whereas two only would be at liberty if one had to take the wheel.

And now I come to Friday.

We kept no regular watches. Stevens, ever distrustful of me, was markedly so now that our voyage was nearly ended. He was incessantly up and down, looking at the compass, computing the ship's speed by staring at the passing water, and often engaged, sometimes on the poop, sometimes on the forecastle, in conversation with Fish, Cornish, Johnson and others.

He made no inquiries after Mr. or Miss Robertson; he appeared to have forgotten their existence. I also noticed that he shirked me as often as he could, leaving the deck when I appeared, and mounting the ladder the furthest from where I stood when he came aft from the main-deck.

The dawn had broken with a promise of a beautiful day; though the glass, which had been dropping very slowly all through the night, stood low at eight o'clock that morning. The sun, even at that early hour, was intensely hot, and here and there the pitch in the seams of the deck adhered to the soles of one's boots, while the smell of the paint-work rose hot in the nostrils.

There was a long swell, the undulations, moderate though wide apart, coming from the westward; the clouds were very high, and the sky a dazzling blue, and the wind about north, very soft and refreshing.

The men were quiet, and continued so throughout the day. Many of them, as well as the carpenter, incessantly gazed around the horizon, evidently fearing the approach of a vessel; and some would steal aft and look at the compass, and then go away again.

We were under all plain sail, and the ship, as near as I could tell, was making about five knots an hour, though the log gave us seven, and I logged it seven on the slate in case of any arguments arising.

When I came on deck with my sextant in hand to take sights, I was struck by the intent expressions on the faces of the crew, the whole of whom, even including the cook, had collected on the poop, or stood upon the ladders waiting for me.

When I saw them thus congregated, my heart for a moment failed me.

The tremendous doubt crossed my mind—were they acquainted with the ship's whereabouts? Did they know, had they known all through, that I was deceiving them?

No!

As I looked at them I became reassured. Theirs was an anxiety I should have been blind to misconstrue. The true expression on their faces represented nothing but eager curiosity to know whether our journey was really ended, or whether more time must elapse before they could quit the ship which they had rendered accursed with the crime of murder, and which, as I well knew, from what Stevens had over and over again let fall, they abhorred with all the terrors of vulgar conscience.

Having made my observations, I was about to quit the poop, when one of the men called out:

"Tell us what you make of it."

"I will when I have worked it out," I replied.

"Work it out here, while we looks on."

"Do any of you understand navigation?"

There was no reply.

"Unless you can count," said I, "you'll not be able to follow me."

"Two and two and one makes nine," said a voice.

"What do you mean by jokin'? You ought to be ashamed o' yourself!" exclaimed one of the men. And then there was a blow, and immediately after an oath.

"If you want me to work out these sights in your presence, I'll do so," said I.

And I went below to get the things I required, leaving my sextant on deck to show them that I meant to be honest.

When I returned, they were all around the sky-light gazing at the sextant as though it were an animal; no man taking the liberty to touch it, however.

They came, hustling each other about me as I sat on the sky-light working out my figures, and I promise you their proximity, coupled with my notion that they *might* suspect I had been deceiving them, did not sharpen my wits so as to expedite my calculations.

I carried two reckonings in my head—the false and the true; and, finding our actual whereabouts to be ninety-eight miles from Bermuda, the islands bearing west-south-west, as straight as a line, I unfolded the chart, and, giving them the imaginary longitude and latitude, put my finger upon the spot we were supposed to have reached, exclaiming:

"Now you can see where we are!"

"Just make a small mark there with your pencil, will you?" said Johnson; "then all hands can have a look."

I did so and quitted the sky-light, surrendering the chart to the men, who made a strange picture as they stood poring over it, pointing with their brown forefingers and arguing.

"There's no question I can answer, is there?" said I to the carpenter.

"Mates, is there anything you want to say to Mr. Royle?" he exclaimed.

"When are we going to heave the ship to?" asked Fish.

"That's for you to answer," I rejoined.

"Well, I'm for not standin' too close inshore," said Fish.

"How fur off do you say is this here Florida coast?" asked Johnson.

"About sixty miles. Look at the chart."

"And every minute brings us nearer," said a man.

"That's true," I replied. "But you don't want to leave the ship before dusk do you?"

The men looked at each other as though they were not sure that they ought to confide so much to me as an answer to my question would involve. I particularly took notice of this, and felt how thoroughly I was put aside by them in their intentions.

The carpenter said, "You'll understand our arrangements by and by, Mr. Royle. How's the wind?"

"About north," said I.

"Mates, shall we bring the yards to the masts and keep the leeches liftin' till we're ready to stop her?"

"The best thing as can happen," said Johnson.

"She'll lie to the west'ard at that, and'll look to be sailin' properly if a wessel sights her; and she'll make no headway neither," said Stevens.

"You can't do better," I exclaimed.

So the helm was put down, and as the men went to work I descended to my cabin.

The steward's head was at the pantry door, and I called to him, "Bring me a biscuit and the sherry."

I wanted neither, but I had something to say to him; and if Stevens saw him come to my cabin with a tray in his hand he was not likely to follow and listen at the door.

The steward put the tray down and was going away, when I took him by the arm and led him to the extremity of the cabin.

"Do you value your life?" I said to him, in a whisper.

He stared at me and turned pale.

"Just listen," I continued. "At dusk this evening the men are going to scuttle the ship first, that she may fill with water and sink. It is not their intention to take us with them."

"My God!" he muttered, trembling like a freezing man, "are we to be left on board to sink?"

"That is what they mean. But the bo's'n, who they believe to be drowned, is in the hold ready to kill the man who goes down to scuttle the ship. If we act promptly, we may save our lives and get away from the ruffians. There are only three of us, but we must fight as though we were twelve men, if it should come to our having to fight. Understand that. When once the men are in the boats, no creature among them must ever get on board again alive. Hit hard—spare nothing! If we are beaten, we are dead men; if we conquer, our lives are our own."

"I'll do my best," answered the steward, the expression upon whose face, however, was anything but heroical. "But you must tell me what to do, sir. I sha'n't know, sir. I never was in a fight, and the sight of blood is terrifying to me, sir."

"You'll have to bottle up your fears. Don't misunderstand me, steward. Every man left on board this ship to drown will look to his companions to help him to save his life. And, by all that's holy! if you show any cowardice, if you skulk, if you do not fight like forty men, if you do not stick by my side and obey my words like a flash of lightning, as sure as you breathe I'll put a bullet through your head! I'll kill you for not helping me!"

And I pulled out the pistol from my pocket and flourished it under his nose. He recoiled from the weapon his eyes half out of his head, and gasped:

"What am I to use, sir?"

"The first iron belaying-pin you can snatch up," I answered. "There are plenty to be found. And now be off. Not a look, not a word! Go to your work as usual. If you open your mouth you are a dead man."

He went away as pale as a ghost. However, cur as he was, I did not despair of his turning to at the last moment. Cowards will sometimes make terrible antagonists. The madness of fear renders them desperate, and in their frenzy they will do more execution than the brave, deliberate man.

I did not remain long off the poop, being too anxious to observe the movements of the crew.

I found the breeze slackening fast, with every appearance of a calm in the hot, misty blue sky and the glassy aspect of the horizon. The lower sails flapped to every motion of the ship, and, lying close to what little wind there was, we made no progress at all.

The promise of a calm, though favorable to the intentions of the men, in so far as it would keep the horizon clear of sailing ships, and so limit the probability of their operations being witnessed to the chance of a steamer passing, was a blow to me; as one essential part of my scheme—that of swinging the main yards round and getting way on the ship when the men had left her—would be impracticable.

The glass, indeed, stood low; but then this might betoken the coming of more wind than I should want—a gale that would detain the men on the ship, and force them to defer the scheme of abandoning her for an indefinite period.

They had gone to dinner, but were so quiet that the vessel seemed deserted, and nothing was audible but the clanking of the tiller-chains and the rattling of the sails against the masts.

Stevens was forward, apparently having his dinner with the men. In glancing through the sky-light, I saw Mary Robertson looking up at me. I leaned forward, so that my face was concealed from the man at the wheel— the only person on deck beside myself—and whispered:

"Keep up your courage, and be ready to act as I may direct."

"I am quite ready," she answered.

"Remain in your cabin," I said, "and don't let the men see you"; for it had flashed upon me that if the crew saw her they might force her to go along with them in their boats.

"I wanted a little brandy for papa," she answered. "He is very poorly and weak, and rambles terribly in his talk."

She turned to hide her tears from me, and prevent me witnessing her struggles to restrain them. She would feel their impotence, the mockery of them, at such a time; besides, dear heart, she would think I should distrust her courage if she let me see her weep.

The steward came forward under the sky-light as she entered her cabin, and said:

"I will fight for my life, sir."

"That is my advice to you."

"I will do my best. I have been thinking of my wife and child, sir."

"Hush!" I cried. "Not so loud. If your courage fails you, there is a girl in that cabin there who will show you how to be brave. Remember two things—act quickly and strike hard; and, for God's sake! don't fall to drinking to pull up your nerves! If I find you drunk, I will call upon the men to drown you."

And with this injunction I left the sky-light.

The men remained a great while in the forecastle, all so quiet that, I wondered whether some among them were not even now below scuttling the ship. But they would hardly act so prematurely. To be sure it would take a long time for the ship to fill, bored even in half a dozen places by an auger; but until the evening fell, and they were actually in the boats, they could not be sure that a wind would not spring up to oblige them to keep the ship.

I remained on deck, never thinking of dinner, watching the weather anxiously.

An ordinary seaman came aft to relieve the wheel; but finding that the ship had no steerage-way on her, he squatted himself on the taff-rail, pulled out a pipe and began to smoke. I took no notice of him.

Shortly afterward Stevens came along the main-deck and mounted the poop.

"A dead calm," said he, after sweeping the horizon with hand his over his eyes, "and blessedly hot."

"Is the ship to be left all standing?" I inquired.

"What do you think?" he replied, with an air of indifference, casting his eyes aloft.

"I should snug her, certainly."

"Why?" he demanded, folding his arms and staring at me as he leaned against the poop-rail.

"Because, should she drift, and be overhauled by another ship, it will look more ship-shape if she is found snug, as though she had been abandoned in a storm."

"There's something in that," he answered, without shifting his position.

"Shall I tell the men to shorten sail?"

"If you like," he replied, grinning in my face.

I pretended not to observe his odd manner, being very anxious to get in all the sail I could while there were men to do it. So I sung out, "All hands shorten sail!"

The men on the forecastle stared and burst into a laugh; and one of a group on the main deck, who were inspecting the provisions for the long-boat, which lay under a tarpaulin, exclaimed:

"Wot's goin' to happen?"

I glanced at the carpenter, who still surveyed me with a broad grin, and walked aft. I was a fool not to have anticipated this. What was it to the crew whether the ship sunk with all sails standing or all sails furled?

I was too restless to go below; but to dissemble my terrible anxiety as well as I could, I lighted a pipe and crouched in the shadow of the mizzen-mast out of the way of the broiling sun.

The breeze had utterly gone. The sea was glassy and white, and long wreaths of mist stood down in the south, upon the horizon. As I looked at the ship, at her graceful spaces of canvas lowering upon the fine and delicate masts, her white decks, her gleaming brass-work, the significance of the crime meditated by the crew was shocking to me. The awful cold-bloodedness with which they meant to sink the beautiful vessel, with the few poor lives who were to be left defenseless on board, overwhelmed me with horror and detestation. So atrocious an act I thought the Almighty would not surely permit.

Could not I count upon His mercy and protection? Remembering that I had not sought Him yet, I pulled off my cap, and without kneeling—for I durst not kneel with the eyes of the men upon me—I mutely invoked His heavenly protection. I pleaded with all the strength of my heart for the sweet and helpless girl whom, under His divine providence, I had already rescued from one dreadful fate, and whom, under His sure guidance, I might yet preserve from the slow and bitter death which the crew had planned that we should suffer.

It was not until six o'clock that the carpenter ordered the men to get the long-boat over. But just before he called out, I had noticed, with a leap of joy in me, that the water out in the north-west was dark as with a shadow of a cloud upon it.

Though this was no more than a cat's-paw, and traveled very slowly, I was certain, not only from the indications of the barometer, but from the complexion of the sky, that wind was behind.

The men did not appear to notice it, and when the carpenter sung out the order, all hands went to work briskly.

Some ran aloft with tackles, which they made fast to the starboard fore and main yard-arms; others hooked on tackles to the straps which were already round the trestle-tree and collar of the mainstay. But willingly as they worked, even these preliminary measures ran into a great deal of time; and before they had done, a light breeze had come down on the ship, and taken her aback.

The carpenter, seeing this, clapped some hands on to the fore and mizzen-braces, and filled the fore and after sails. The ship was therefore hove to with her head at west.

This done, he went to the wheel, put the helm amidship, and made it fast; and then went forward again to superintend the work.

I took up my position on the starboard side of the poop, close against the ladder, and there I remained. I scanned the faces of the men carefully, and found all hands present, including the cook. I thus knew that no man was below in the hold, and it was now my business to watch closely that I might not miss the man who should have the job to scuttle the ship.

The breeze died away, but in the same direction whence it had come was another shadow, more defined, and extending far to the north. The men had begun their work late, and as they knew that they had little or no twilight to count upon, labored hard at the difficult task of raising the long-boat out of her chocks, and swinging her clear of the bulwarks.

It was close upon seven o'clock before they were ready to hoist. They took the end of one fall to the capstan on the main-deck, the other they led forward through a block, and presently up rose the boat until it was on a level with the bulwarks. Then the yard-arm tackles were manned, the mid-ship falls slacked off, and the big boat sunk gently down into the water.

She was brought alongside at once, and three men jumped into her. Then began the process of storing the provisions. This was carried on by five men, while the remaining three came aft; and while one got into the quarter-boat, the other two lowered her.

At this moment I missed the carpenter.

I held my breath, looking into the boats and all around.

He was not to be seen.

I strained my ear at the foremost sky-light, conceiving that he might have entered the cuddy.

All was silent there.

Beyond the shadow of a doubt, he it was who had planned the scuttling of the ship, and he it was who had left the deck to do it.

It was a supreme moment. I had not contemplated that he would be the man who should bore the hole. If the boatswain killed him!

Great God! the hands were on deck—all about us! If he did not return they would seek him. He was their leader, and they were not likely to quit the ship without him.

The hair stirred on my head; the sweat stood in beads on my face. I bit my lip half through to control my features, and stood waiting for—I knew not what!

CHAPTER XVIII

THE MEN went on busily provisioning the long-boat, some whistling gay tunes, others laughing and passing jokes, all in good spirits, as though they were going on a holiday expedition.

The shadow on the horizon was broadening fast, and the sun was sinking quickly, making the ocean blood-red with its burning effulgence, and veining the well-greased masts with lines of fire.

What had happened?

Even now, as I thought, was the villain lying dead, the auger in his hand!

The minutes rolling past seemed eternal. Five, ten, twenty minutes came and went. The sun's lower limb was close against the water-line, sipping the ruddy splendor it had kindled. The breeze was now close at hand, but we still lay in a breathless calm, and the sails flapped softly to the tuneful motion of the deep.

Then some of the men who remained on deck went over the ship's side, leaving four of the crew on the main-deck close against the gangway. These men sometimes looked at me, sometimes into the cuddy, sometimes forward, but none of them spoke.

Now the sun was half hidden, and the soft breeze blowing upon the sails outlined the masts against those which were backed.

Suddenly—and I started as though I had beheld a ghost—the carpenter came round from before the galley, and walked quickly to the gangway.

"Over with you, lads," he cried.

Like rats leaping from a sinking hull they dropped, one after the other, into the long-boat, the carpenter going last. Their painter was fast to a chain-plate, and they cast it adrift. The quarter-boat was in tow, and in a few minutes both boats stood at some two or three cable lengths from the ship, the men watching her.

The last glorious fragment of the sinking sun fled, and darkness came creeping swiftly over the sea.

I had stood like one in whom life had suddenly been extinguished—too much amazed to act. Seeing the carpenter return, I had made sure that he had killed the boatswain; but his behavior contradicted this supposition. Had he been attacked by the boatswain and killed him, would he have quitted the ship without revenging himself upon me, whom he would know to be at the bottom of this conspiracy against his life?

What, then, was the meaning of his return, his collected manner, his silent exit from the ship? Had the boatswain lying hidden, died? The thought fired my blood. Yes, I believed that he had died—that the carpenter had performed his task unmolested without perceiving the corpse—and that, while I stood there, the water was rushing into the ship's hold!

I flung myself off the poop and bounded forward. In the briefest possible time I was peering down the forescuttle.

"Below there!" I cried.

There was no answer.

"Below there, I say, bo's'n!"

My cry was succeeded by a hallow, thumping sound.

"Below there!" I shouted for the third time.

I heard the sounds of a foot treading on something that crunched under the tread.

"I am Mr. Royle. Bo's'n, are you below? For God Almighty's sake answer, and let me know that you are living!"

"Have the skunks cleared out?" responded a voice, and, stumbling as he moved, the boatswain came under the forescuttle, and turned up his face.

"What have you done?" I cried, almost delirious.

"Why, plugged up two on 'em. There's only one more," he answered.

"One more what?"

"Leaks—holes—whatever you call 'em."

So saying he shouldered his way back into the gloom.

It was now all as clear as daylight to me. I waited some minutes, bursting with impatience and anxiety, during which I heard him hammering away like a calker. My fear was that the men would discover that they had omitted to put the compass in the boats, and that they would return for one. There were other things, too, of which they might perceive the omission, and row to the ship to obtain them before she sunk.

Just as I was about to cry out to him to bear a hand, the boatswain's face gleamed under the hatchway.

"Have you done?" I exclaimed.

"Ay, ay."

"Is she tight?"

"Tight as a cocoa-nut."

"Up with you, then! There is a bit of a breeze blowing. Let us swing the main-yards and get way upon the ship. They are waiting to see her settle before they up sail. It is dark enough to act. Hurry, now!"

He came up through the forecastle and followed me on to the main-deck.

Though not yet dark, the shadow of the evening made it difficult to distinguish faces even a short distance off. There was a pretty little wind up aloft rounding the royals and top-gallant-sails, and flattening the sails on the main-yards well against the masts.

I stopped a second to look over the bulwarks, and found that the boats still remained at about three cable-lengths from the ship. They had shipped the mast in the long-boat; but I noticed that the two boats lay side by side, four men in the quarter-boat, and the rest in the long-boat, and that they were handing out some of the stores which had been stowed in the quarter-boat to lighten her.

"We must lose no time, Mr. Royle," exclaimed the boatswain.

"How many hands can we muster?"

"Three."

"That'll do. We can swing the main-yards. Who's the third?—the steward? Let's have him out."

I ran to the cuddy and called the steward. He came out of the pantry.

"On the poop with you!" I cried. "Right aft—you'll find the bo's'n there. Miss Robertson!"

At the sound of her name she stepped forth from her cabin. "The men are out of the ship," I exclaimed. "We are ready to get way upon her. Will you take the wheel at once?"

She was running on to the poop before the request was well out of my mouth.

The boatswain had already let go the starboard main-braces; and as I rushed aft, he and the steward were hauling to leeward. I threw the whole weight of my body on the brace, and pulled with the strength of two men.

"Put the wheel to starboard!" I cried out; and the girl, having cast off the lashing with marvelous quickness, ran the spokes over.

"By God, she's a wonder!" cried the boatswain, looking at her.

And so was he. The muscles on his bare arms stood up like lumps of iron under the flesh as he strained the heavy brace.

The great yards swung easily: the top-sail, top-gallant, and royal yards came round with the main-yard, and swung themselves when the sails filled.

There was no time to gather in the slack of the lee braces. I ran to windward, belayed the braces, and raised a loud cry.

"They're after us, bo's'n!—they're after us!"

We might have been sure of that; for if we had not been able to see them, we could have heard them; the grinding of the oars in the rowlocks; the frothing of the water at the boat's bows, the cries and oaths of the men in the long-boat, inciting the others to overtake us.

Only the quarter-boat was in pursuit as yet; but in the long-boat they were rigging up the stun'sail they had shipped, meaning, as they were to windward, to bear down upon us.

There was no doubt that they guessed their scheme had been baffled, by discerning *three* men on deck. The carpenter at least knew that old Mr. Robertson was too ill to leave his cabin, and failing *him,* he would instantly perceive that a trick had been played, and though he could not tell, in that light and at that distance, who the third man was, he would certainly know that this third presence on board implied the existence of a plot to save the ship.

As the boat approached, I perceived that she was rowed by four men and steered by a fifth; and presently hearing his voice, I understood that this man steering was Stevens.

The ship had just got way enough upon her to answer her helm. Already we were drawing the long-boat away from our beam on to the quarter.

I shouted to Miss Robertson, "Steady! keep her straight as she is!" for even now we had brought the wind too far aft for the trim of the yards.

"Steward!" I cried, "whip out one of those iron belaying-pins, and stand by to hammer away!"

We then posted ourselves—the boatswain and the steward at the gangway, and I half-way up the poop ladder, each with a heavy belaying-pin in his hand—ready to receive the scoundrels who were making for the starboard main-chains.

The boat, urged furiously through the water, came up to us hand over fist, the carpenter cursing us furiously, and swearing that he would do for us yet.

I got my pistol ready, meaning to shoot the ruffian the moment he should be within reach of the weapon, but abandoned this intention from a motive of hate and revenge. I knew if I killed him as he sat there in the stern-sheets that the others would take fright and run away; and such was my passion, and the sense of our superiority over them from our position in the ship as against theirs in the boat, that I made up my mind to let them come alongside and get into the chains, so that we might kill them all as a warning to the occupants of the long-boat, who were now coming down upon us before the breeze.

I took one glance at Miss Robertson; her figure was visible by the side of the wheel. She was steering as steadily as any sailor, with an emotion of gratitude to God for giving us such help, and her so much courage at this supreme moment, I addressed all my energies to the bloody work before me.

The boat dashed alongside, and the men threw in their oars. The fellow in the bow grabbed hold of one of the chain-plates, passed the boat's painter around it, hauled it short, and made it fast with incredible activity and speed. Then, pulling their knives out of their sheaths, they all came clambering into the main-chains.

So close as they now were, I could make out the faces of the men. One was big Johnson, another Cornish, the third Fish, the fourth Schmidten.

I alone was visible. The boatswain and steward stood with uplifted arms ready to strike at the first head that showed itself.

The carpenter sprang on to the bulwark just where I stood.

He poised his knife to stab me under the throat.

"Now, you murderous, treacherous ruffian!" I cried, at the top of my voice, "say your prayers!" I leveled the pistol at his head, the muzzle not being a yard away from his face, and pulled the trigger. The bright flash illuminated him like a ray of lightning. He uttered a scream, shrill as a child's, but terrific in intensity, clapped his hands to his face, and fell like a stone into the main-chains.

"It is your turn now!" I roared to Johnson, and let fly at him. He was holding on to one of the main-shrouds in the act of springing on to the deck. I missed his head, but struck him on the arm, I think; for he let go the shroud with a deep groan, reeled backward, and toppled overboard, and I heard the heavy splash of his body as he fell.

But we were not even now, three to three, but three to one; for the boatswain had let drive with his frightful belaying-pin at Fish's head, just as that enormous protuberance had shown itself over the bulwark, and the wretch lay dead or stunned in the boat alongside; while the steward, who had secreted a huge carving-knife in his bosom, had stabbed the Dutchman right in the stomach, leaving the knife in him; and the miserable creature hung over the bulwark, head and arms hanging down toward the water, and, suddenly writhing as he hung, dropped overboard.

Cornish, of all five men, alone lived. I had watched him aim a blow at the boatswain's back, and fired, but missed him. But he too had missed his aim, and the boatswain, slewing round, struck his wrist with the heavy belaying-pin—whack! it sounded like the blow of hammer on wood—and the knife fell from his hand.

"Mercy! spare my life!" he roared, seeing that I had again covered him, having two more shots left.

The steward, capable, now that things had gone well with us, of performing prodigies of valor, rushed upon him, laid hold of his legs, and pulled him off the bulwark on to the deck.

I thought the fall had broken his back, for he lay groaning and motionless.

"Don't kill him!" I cried. "Make his hands fast and leave him for the present. We may want him by and by."

The boatswain whipped a rope's end round him and shoved him against the rail, and then came running up the poop-ladder, wiping the streaming perspiration from his face.

The breeze was freshening, and the boat alongside wobbled and splashed as the ship towed her through the water.

I ran aft and stared into the gloom astern. I could see nothing of the long-boat. I looked again and again, and fetched the night-glass, and by its aid, sure enough, I beheld her, a smudge on the even ground of the gloom, standing away close to the wind, for this much I could tell by the outline of her sail.

"Miss Robertson," I cried, "we are saved! Yonder is the long-boat leaving us. Our lives are our own!"

"I bless God for His mercy," she answered quietly. But then her pent-up feelings mastered her; she rocked to and fro, grasping the spokes of the wheel, and I extended my arms just in time to save her from falling.

"Bo's'n!" I shouted, and he came hurrying to me. "Miss Robertson has fainted! Reach me a flag out of that locker."

He handed me a signal-flag, and I laid the poor girl gently down upon the deck, with the flag for a pillow under her head.

"Fetch me some brandy, bo's'n. The steward will give you a wine-glassful."

And, with one hand upon the wheel to steady the ship, I knelt by the girl's side, holding her cold fingers, with so much tenderness and love for her in my heart that I could have wept like a woman to see her lying so pale and still.

The boatswain returned quickly, followed by the steward. I surrendered the wheel to the former, and taking the brandy succeeded in introducing some into her mouth. By dint of this, and chafing her hands and moistening

her forehead, I restored her to consciousness. I then, with my arm supporting her, helped her into the cuddy; but I did not stay an instant after
this, for there was plenty of work to be done on deck; and though we had
escaped one peril, yet here we might be running headlong into another,
for the ship was under full sail; we had but three men to work her, not
counting Cornish, of whose willingness or capacity to work after his
rough handling I as yet knew nothing. The glass stood low, and if a gale
should spring up and catch us as we were, it was fifty to one if the ship did
not go to the bottom.

"Bo's'n," I exclaimed, "what's to be done now?"

"Shorten sail while the wind's light, that's sartin," he answered. "But the
first job must be to get Cornish out of his lashin's and set him on his legs. He
must lend us a hand."

"Yes; we'll do that," I replied. "Steward, can you steer?"

"No, sir," responded the steward.

"Oh, d——n it!" vociferated the boatswain. "I'd rather be a guffy than a
steward," meaning by guffy a marine.

"Well," cried I, "you must try."

"But I know nothing about it, sir."

"Come here and lay hold of these spokes. Look at that card—no, by
Jove! you can't see it."

But the binnacle lamp was trimmed, and in a moment the boatswain
had pulled out a lucifer match, dexterously caught the flame in his hallowed
hands, and fired the mesh.

"Look at that card," I said, as the boatswain shipped the lamp.

"I'm a lookin', sir."

"Do you see that it points south-east?"

"Yes, sir."

"If those letters S. E. swing to the left of the lubber's point—that black
mark there—pull the spokes to the left until S. E. comes to the mark again.
If S. E. goes to the right, shove the spokes to the right. Do you understand?"

"Yes, I think I do, sir."

"Mind your eye, steward. Don't let those letters get away from you, or
you'll run the ship into the long-boat, and bring all hands on board again.

And leaving him holding on to the wheel with the fear and in the attitude of a cockney clinging for his life, the boatswain and I walked to the main-deck.

Cornish lay like a bundle against the rail. When he saw us he cried out:

"Kill me if you like, but for God's sake loosen this rope first! It's keepin' my blood all in one place!"

"How do you know we haven't come to drown you?" cried the boatswain, in an awful voice. "Don't jaw us about your blood. You won't want none in five minutes."

"Then the Lord have mercy upon my soul!" groaned the poor wretch, and let drop his head, which he had lifted out of the scuppers to address us.

"Drownin's too easy for the likes o' you," continued the boatswain. "You want whippin' and picklin' and then quarterin' arter-ward."

"We are willing to spare your life," said I, feeling that we had no time to waste, "if you will give us your word to help us to work this ship, and bring her into port, if we get no assistance on the road."

"I'll do anything if you'll spare my life," moaned he, "and loose this rope round my middle."

"Do you think he's to be trusted, Mr. Royle?" said the boatswain, in a stern voice, playing a part. "There's a bloodthirsty look on his countenance, and his eyes are full o' murder."

"Only try me!" groaned Cornish, faintly.

"He wur Stevens's chief mate," continued the boatswain; "an' I think it 'ud be wiser to leave him as he is for a few hours while we consider the advisability of trustin' of him."

"Then I shall be cut in halves!" moaned Cornish.

"Well," I exclaimed, pretending first to reflect, "we will try you; and if you act honestly by us you shall have no cause to complain. But if you attempt to play false, we will treat you as you deserve; we will shoot you as we shot your mates, and pitch your body overboard. So you'll know what to expect. Bo's'n, cast him adrift."

He was speedily liberated, and the boatswain hoisted him on to his feet, when, finding him very shaky, I fetched a glass of rum from the pantry, which he swallowed.

"Thank you, sir," said he, rubbing his wrist, which the boatswain had struck during the conflict. "I'll be honest and do what I can. You may trust me to work for you. This here mutiny belonged to all hands, and was no one man's, unless it were Stevens's; and I'd rather be here than in the long-boat."

"Bo's'n," said I, cutting the fellow short, "the carpenter made the port quarter-boat useless by knocking some planks out of her. We ought to get the boat alongside on board while the water's smooth—we may want her."

" Right you are, Mr. Royle," said he. "Pay us out a rope's end, will you, and I'll drop her under the davits."

And, active as a cat, he scrambled into the main-chains.

But on a sudden I heard a heavy splash.

"My God!" I cried, "he's fallen overboard!" And I was rushing toward the poop when I heard him sing out, "Halloo! here's another!" and this was followed by a second splash.

I got on to the bulwarks and bawled to him, "Where are you? What are you doing? Are you bathing?"

"The deuce a bit!" he answered. "It was one o' them blessed mutineers in the main chains, and here was another in the boat. I pitched 'em into the water. Now, then, slacken gently, and belay when I sing out."

In a few moments the boat was under the davits and both falls hooked on. Then up came the boatswain, and the three of us began to hoist, manning first one fall and then the other, bit by bit, the boat was up; but she was a heavy load, with her freight of provisions and water—too precious to us to lose—and we panted, I promise you, by the time she was abreast of the poop-rail.

"Mr. Bo's'n!" said Cornish, suddenly, "beggin' your pardon—I thought you was dead."

"Did you, Jim Cornish?"

"I thought you was drownded, sir."

"Well, I ain't the first drownded man as has come to life again."

"All hands, Mr. Bo's'n, thought you was overboard, lyin' drownded. You was overboard?"

"And do you think I'm going to explain?" answered the boatswain, contemptuously.

"It terrified me to see you, sir."

"Well, perhaps I ain't real, arter all. How do you know? Seein' ain't believin', so old women say."

"I don't believe in ghosts; but I thought you was one, Mr. Bo's'n, and so did big Johnson when he swore you was one of the three at the port main-braces."

"Well, I ain't ashamed o' bein' a shadder. Better men nor me have been shadders. I knew a ship-chandler as wos a church-warden and worth a mint o' money, who became a shadder, and kept his wife from marryin' William Soaper, o' the Coopid public-house, Love Lane, Shadwell High Street, by standin' at the foot of her bed every night at eight bells. He had a cast in wun eye, Mr. Royle, and that's how his wife knew him."

"Well, I say no more; but my hair riz when you turned an' hit me over the arm. I thought you couldn't be substantial like."

"'Cause you didn't get enough o' my belaying-pin," rejoined the boatswain, with a loud laugh. "Wait till you turn dusty ag'in, mate, and then you'll see wot a real ghost can do."

Just then Miss Robertson emerged from the companion. I ran to her and entreated her to remain below—though for an hour only.

"No, no," she answered, "let me help you. I am much better—I am quite well now. I can steer the ship while you take in some of the sails, for I know there are too many sails set, if the wind should come."

Then, seeing Cornish, she started and held my arm, whispering, "Who is he? Have they come on board?"

I briefly explained, and then renewed my entreaties that she should remain in her cabin; but she said she would not leave the deck, even if I refused her permission to steer, and pleaded so eloquently, holding my arm and raising her sweet eyes to my face, that I reluctantly gave way.

She hastened eagerly to take the steward's place, and I never saw a man resign any responsible position more willingly than he.

I now explained to the boatswain that the glass stood very low, and that we must at once turn to and get in all the sail we could handle.

I asked Cornish if he thought he was able to go aloft, and on his answering in the affirmative, first testing the strength of his wrist by hanging with his whole weight to one of the ratlines on the mizzen-rigging, he went to work to clew up the three royals.

I knew that the steward was of no use aloft, and never even asked him if he would venture his hand at it, for I was pretty sure he would lose his head and tumble overboard before he had mounted twenty feet, and he was too useful to us to lose right off in that way.

Cornish went up to stow the mizzen-royal, and the boatswain and I went aloft to the main-royal. The breeze was still very gentle, and the ship slipping smoothly through the black space of sea; but when we were in the main-royal yard I called the attention of the boatswain to the appearance of the sky in the north-west, for it was lightning faintly in that direction, and the pale illumination sufficed to expose a huge bank of cloud stretching far to the north.

"We shall be able to get the top-gallant-sails off her," he said, "and the jibs and staysails. But I don't know how we're going to furl the main-sail, and it'll take us all night to reef the top-sails."

"We must work all night," I answered, "and do what we can. Just tell me, while I pass this gasket, how you managed in the hold."

"Why," he answered, "you know I took a kind o' crowbar down with me, and I reckoned on splittin' open the head of the fust as should drop through the fore-scuttle. But, turnin' it over in my mind, I thought it 'ud be dangerous to kill the feller, as his mates might take it into their heads to wait for him. And so I determined to hide myself when I heerd the cove comin', and stand by to plug up the holes arter he wur gone."

Here he discharged some tobacco-juice from his mouth, and dried his lips on the sail.

"Werry well; I had my knife with me an' a box o' matches, and werry useful they wos. I made a bit of a flare by combing out a strand of yarns and settin' fire to it, and found wot was more pleasin' to my eye than had I come across a five-pun note—I mean a spare broomstick, which I found knocking about in the coal-hole; and I cut it up in pieces and pointed 'em ready to sarve. I knew whoever 'ud come would use an auger, and know'd the size hole it 'ud cut; and by and by—but the Lord knows how long it were afore it happened—I hears some one drop down the fore-scuttle and strike a match and light a bit o' candle-end. I got behind the bulkhead, where there was a plank out, and I see the carpenter working away with his auger, blowin' and sweatin' like any respectable hartizan earnin' of honest wages. By and by the water comes rushin' in; and then he bores another hole and the water comes through that; and then he bores another hole, arter which he blows out his candle and goes away, scramblin' up on the deck. My fingers quivered to give him one for hisself with the end o' my crowbar over the back of his head. However, no sooner did he clear out than I struck a match, fits in the bits of broomstick, and stops the leaks as neatly, as he made 'em. I thought they'd hear me drivin' them plugs in, and that was all I was afraid of. But the ship's none the worse for them holes. She's as tight as ever she wos: an' I reckon if she gets no more water in her than'll come through them plugs, she won't be in a hurry to sink." I laughed as we shook hands heartily.

I often think over that; the immense height we looked down from; the mystical extent of black water mingling with the far-off sky; the faint play of lightning on the horizon; the dark hull of the ship far below, with the dim radiance of the cuddy lamps upon the sky-lights; the brave, sweet girl steering us; and we two perched on a dizzy eminence, shaking hands!

CHAPTER XIX

CORNISH had stowed the mizzen-royal by the time we had reached the deck, and when he joined us we clewed up the foretop-gallant-sail, so that we might handle that sail when he had done with the royal.

I found this man quite civil and very willing, and in my opinion he spoke honestly when he declared that he had rather be with us than in the long-boat.

The lightning was growing more vivid upon the horizon; that is, when I looked in that direction from the towering height of the fore royal yard; and it jagged and scored with blue lines the great volume and belt of cloud that hung to the sea. The wind had slightly freshened, but still it remained a very gentle breeze, and urged the ship noiselessly through the water.

The stars were few and languishing, as you may have sometimes seen them on a summer's night in England when the air is sultry and the night dull and thunderous. All the horizon round was lost in gloom, save where the lightning threw out at swift intervals the black water against the gleaming background of cloud.

When we again reached the deck we were rather scant of breath, and I, being unused of late to this kind of exercise, felt the effects of it more than the others.

However, if it was going to blow a gale of wind, as the glass threatened, it was very advisable that we should shorten sail, now that it was calm; for assuredly three men, although working for their lives as we were, would be utterly useless up aloft when once the weather got bad.

We went into the cuddy and took, all three of us, a sup of rum to give us life, and I then said, "Shall we turn to and snug away aft, since we are here?"

They agreed; so we went on the poop and let go the mizzen-top-gallant and top-sail halyards, roused out the reef tackles, and went aloft, when we first stowed the top-gallant-sail, and then got down upon the top-sail yard.

It was a hard job tying in all three reefs, passing the ear-rings and hauling the reef-bands taut along the yard; but we managed to complete the job in about half an hour.

Miss Robertson remained at the wheel all this time, and the steward was useful on deck to let go any ropes which we found fast.

"It pains me," I said to the girl, "to see you standing here. I know you are worn out, and I feel to be acting a most unmanly part in allowing you to have your way."

"You cannot do without me. Why do you want to make your crew smaller in number than it is?" she answered, smiling, with the light reflected from the compass card upon her face. "Look at the lightning over there! I'm sailor enough to know that our masts would be broken if the wind struck the ship with all this sail upon her. And what is *my* work—idly standing here—compared to yours—you, who have already done so much, and are still doing the work of many men?"

"You argue too well for my wishes. I want you to agree with me."

"Whom have you to take my place here?"

"Only the steward."

"He cannot steer, Mr. Royle; and I assure you the ship wants watching."

I laughed at this nautical language in her sweet mouth, and said:

"Well, you shall remain here a little while longer."

"One thing," she exclaimed, "I will ask you to do—to look into our cabin and see if papa wants anything."

I ran below and peeped into the cabin. She had already lighted the lamp belonging to it, and so I was able to see that the old gentleman was asleep. I procured some brandy and water and biscuit, and also a chair, and returned on deck.

"Your father is asleep," said I, "so you may make your mind easy about him. Here are some refreshments; and see, if I put this chair here you can sit and hold the wheel steady with one hand: there is no occasion to remain on your feet. Keep that star yonder—right over the yard-arm," pointing it out to her. "That is as good a guide as a compass for the time being. We need only keep the sails full. I can shape no course as yet, though we shall haul round the moment we have stripped more canvass off her."

I now heard the voices of Cornish and the boatswain right away far out in the darkness ahead, and, running forward on to the forecastle, I found them stowing the flying jib.

To save time I let go the outer and inner jib-halyards, and, with assistance of the steward, hauled those sails down. He and I also clewed up the main top-gallant-sail, took the main-tack and sheet to the winch and got them up, rounded up the leech-lines and buntlines as well as we could, and then belayed and went forward again. I let go the fore-top-sail halyards and took the ends of the reef-tackles to the capstan; and while the two others were tackling the outer jib, the steward and I hauled down the main-top-mast-stay-sail, and snugged it as best we could in the netting.

Those tasks achieved, I got upon the bowsprit, and gave the two men a hand to stow the jibs.

"Now, mates," I cried, "let's get upon the fore-top-sail yard and see what we can do there."

And up we went, and in three quarters of an hour, with the help of a jigger, we had hauled out the ear-rings and tied every blessed reef-point in the sail.

But this was the finishing touch to our strength, and Cornish was so exhausted that I had to help him over the top down the fore-rigging.

We had indeed accomplished wonders; close-reefed two of the three top-sails, stowed the three jibs, the three royals, the top-gallant-sails and stay-sails. Our work was rendered three times harder than it need have been by the darkness: we had to fumble and grope, and by being scarcely able to see each other we found it extremely difficult to work in unison; that instead of hauling all together, we hauled at odd times, and rendered our individual strength ineffectual, when, could we have collectively exerted it, we should have achieved our purpose easily.

"I must sit down for a spell, sir," said Cornish. "I can't do more work yet."

"If we could only get that top-gallant-sail off her!" I exclaimed, looking longingly up at it. But, all the same, I felt that a whole regiment of bayonets astern of me could not have urged me one inch up the shrouds.

We dragged our weary limbs aft and squatted ourselves near the wheel, I for one scarcely able to stand.

"Mr. Royle," said Miss Robertson, "will you and the others go down into the cabin and get some sleep? I will keep watch, and promise faithfully to wake you the moment I think necessary."

"Bo's'n," I exclaimed, "do you hear that? Miss Robertson wants us to turn in. She will keep watch, she says, and call us if a gale comes!"

"God bless her!" said the boatswain. "I called her a wonder just now, and I'd call her a wonder again. So she is! and though she hears me speak, and may think me wantin' in good manners, I'll say this—an' tired as I am, I'd fight the man now as he stood who'd contradict me—that she's just one o' the best—mind, Jim, I say the best—o' the properest kind o' gals as God Almighty ever made; a regular real woman to the eye, and a sailor in her heart. And, by the livin' Moses, Jim, if you can tell me now to my face that you would ha' let her sink in this here wessel, I'll chuck you overboard, you willain'! So say it!"

"I don't want to say it," muttered Cornish, penitentially. "I never thought o' the lady. I forgot she were on board. Mr. Bo's'n, don't say no more about it, please. I've done my duty, I hope, Mr. Royle. I've worked werry hard, considerin' my bad wrist. I'd liefer fight for the lady than agin her, now that I see wot she's made of. 'By-gones is by-gones,' as the cock had his eye knocked out in a fight said when he looked about and couldn't see nothen of it; and if you call me a willain, well and good; I'll not arguey, fur I dare say you ain't fur wrong, mate."

"Mr. Royle, you have not answered me. Will you and the others lie down and sleep while I watch?"

"Not yet, Miss Robertson. By and by, perhaps. We have more work before us, and are only resting. Steward!"

He came from behind the companion, where I think he had fallen asleep.

"Yes, Mr. Royle, sir."

"Cut below and mix all hands a jug of brandy and water, and bring some biscuits. Here, bo's'n, is some tobacco. Smoke a pipe. Fire away, Cornish. It's more soothing than sleep, mates."

"The lightning's growin' rather powerful," said the boatswain, looking astern as he lighted his pipe.

"Don't it look as if it wur settin', away to the east'ard?" questioned Cornish.

"No," I replied, watching the lurid gleams lighting up the piled-up clouds. "It's coming after us dead on end, though slowly enough."

I pulled out my watch and held it close to the binnacle.

"Half-past two!" I cried, amazed at the passage of time. "Upon my word, I didn't think it was twelve o'clock yet. Miss Robertson, I know I can not induce you to go below, but you must allow me to relieve you for a spell at the wheel. I can sit and steer as well as you. You'll find this grating comfortable."

Saying which I pulled out some flags from the locker and made a kind of cushion for her back. I then took her chair, keeping the wheel steady with my foot.

There was less wind than there had been half an hour before; enough to give the vessel steerage-way, and that was all.

We were heading south-east, the wind, or what there was of it, upon the port quarter. There was every promise of a calm falling again, and this I should not have minded, nor the lightning either, which might well have been the play of a passing thunder-storm, had it not been for the permanent depression of the mercury.

The air was very warm, but less oppressive than it had been; the sea black and even, and the heavens with a stooping murky aspect.

It was some comfort to me, however, to look aloft, and see the amount of canvas we had taken off the ship. If we could only manage to pull up our strength again, we might well succeed in furling the top-gallant-sail, and reefing the top-sail before the change of weather came.

The steward made his appearance with the spirits and biscuit; and Miss Robertson went below, whispering to me as she passed, that she wished to look at her father, and that she would return in a few minutes.

"Now that the lady's gone, Mr. Royle," exclaimed the boatswain, as soon as she had left the deck, "let's talk over our situation and think what's to be done."

The steward squatted himself on his hams like a coolie, and posed himself in an attitude of eager attention.

"Quite right, bo's'n," I replied. "I have been thinking during the time we have been at work, and will tell you what my plans are. At noon yesterday—that will be fifteen hours ago—the Bermuda Islands bore as true as a hair west-half-south. We hove to with the ship's head to the nor'ard and westward and made some way at that, and taking the run we have made to-night, I allow that if we head the ship west by north we shall make the islands with anything like a breeze, some time on Monday morning."

"But, if we're just off the coast of Florida," said Cornish, "why couldn't we turn to and run for the West India Islands?"

"Which is nearest, I wonders," exclaimed the boatswain, "the West Hindie Islands or the kingdom of Jericho?"

"It's 'ardly a time for jokin'," remonstrated the steward.

"I don't know that I said anything funny," observed Cornish, warmly.

"Well, then, wot do you mean by talking about the West Hindia Islands?" cried the boatswain.

"Wot do I mean?" retorted the other; "why wot I says. Here we are off the coast of Floridy—"

"Off the coast o' your grandmother! Shut up, mate, and let Mr. Royle speak. You know nothing about it."

"The Bermudas are nearer to hand than the West Indies," I continued, not wishing to explain. "What we have to do, then, the moment we can use our legs, is to haul the ship round. How is the wind now? north-north-west. Well, she will lie properly. And as soon as ever it comes day-break, we must run up a signal of distress, and keep it flying. What more can we do?"

"I suppose," said the boatswain, doubtfully, sucking so hard at his pipe that it glowed like a steamer's red light under his nose, "you wouldn't like to wenture on a run to the English Channel, Mr. Royle? It would be airning some kind of fame, and perhaps a trifle o' money from the owners, if it wur to git about that three hands—well, I'll ax the steward's pardon and say four—that four hands brought this here blessed ship and her walleyble cargo out o' a rigular knock-down mutiny, all aways up the Atlantic Ocean, into the Henglish Channel, and landed her safe in the West Hindie docks. I never see my name in print in my life—"

"What's your true name, Mr. Bo's'n?" inquired the steward.

"Joshua, or Jo Forward, young feller; sometimes called Forrard, sometimes Jo and on Sundays, Mister."

"I know a Forward as lives at Blackwall," said the steward.

"Do yer? Well, then, now you knows two. Wot I was sayin', Mr. Royle, was, I never see my name in print in my life, and I should like to see it regular wrote down in the newspapers. Lloyd's is always my weekly penn'orth ashore."

He knocked the hot ashes into the palm of his hand, scrutinized it earnestly to see that there was no tobacco left in it, and tossed it away.

"A good deal, sir," said the steward, in a thin voice, "is to be said about the lady we saved. The saving of her alone would make 'eroes of us in the public mind."

"Wot do you call us—'eroes?" interrogated the boatswain.

"Yes, sir, 'eroes."

"What's the meaning of that word, Mr. Royle—any relation to earwigs?"

"He means heroes," I replied. "Don't you, steward?"

"I did more than mean it—I said it," exclaimed the steward.

"That's how the Chaneymen talk, and quarrel with you for not followin' of their sense. Wot do you think of my notion, Jim, of sailin' this wessel to England?" said the boatswain.

Cornish made no answer. I saw him, in the pale light diffused around the binnacle, wipe his mouth with the back of his hand, and shift uneasily on his seat. I could scarcely wonder that the boatswain's idea should make him feel uncomfortable.

"Your scheme," said I, "would be a capital one providing that every man of us four had six hands and six legs and the strength of three big Johnsons;

that we could do without sleep and split ourselves into pieces whenever we had occasion to reef top-sails. But, as I am only capable of doing one man's work, and require rest like other weakly mortals, I must tell you plainly that I for one should be very sorry to undertake to work this ship to the English Channel, unless you would guarantee that by dawn this morning we should receive a draft of at least six men out of a passing vessel."

"Well, well," said the boatswain, "it was only a thought; and I don't say it's to be done."

"Not to be thought on—much less done," exclaimed Cornish.

"Don't be too sartin, friend," retorted the boatswain, turning smartly on him. "'Where there's a will there's a way,' wos a sayin' when I was a lad."

"If it comes on to blow," I put in, "it may take us all we can do to fetch Bermuda. Don't dream of aiming for a further port."

At this moment Miss Robertson returned. I asked her how she found her father, and she replied, in a low voice, that he was sleeping, but that his breathing was very faint and uncertain, and that he sometimes talked in his sleep.

She could not disguise her anxiety, and I entreated her to go below and watch him and rest herself as well; but she answered that she would not leave the deck until I had finished taking in sail and doing what was necessary.

"You can not tell me that I am not of use," she added. "I will steer while you work, and if you wish to sleep I will watch for you. Why should I not do so? I can benefit papa more by helping you to save the ship than by leaving you to work alone while I sit with him. I pray God," she said, in her sweet, low, troubled voice, " all may go well with us. But I have been so near to death that it scarcely frightens me now. Tell me what to do and I will do it— though for your sake alone as you would have sacrificed your life for mine. I owe you what I can never repay; and how kind, how gentle, how good you have been to my father and me."

She spoke in so low a voice that it was impossible for any one to hear her but myself; and so greatly did her words affect me—I, who had now learned to love her, who could indeed have died a hundred-fold over for her dear sake, that I dared not trust myself to speak. Had I spoken I should have said what I was sure she would have disliked to hear from a rough sailor like me: nay, I even turned away from her, that I might be silent, recoiling from my own heart's language, that seemed but an impertinence, an unfair obtrusion of claims which, even though she admitted them by speaking of my having saved her life, I should have been unmanly to assert.

I quickly recovered myself, and said, forcing a laugh:

"You are as bad a mutineer as the others. But as you will not obey me, I must obey you."

And looking at the ponderous bank of cloud in the north-west, of which the gathering brightness and intensity of the lightning was illustrating its steady approach, I exclaimed: "Are we strong enough to turn to, mates?"

"We can douse that top-gallant-sail, I dare say," answered the boatswain. "Up on your pins, steward!"

And we trooped along to the main-deck.

The spell of rest, and perhaps the grog, not to mention the tobacco, had done us no harm. The three of us went aloft, carrying the jigger with us, which we left in the main-top, and furled the top-gallant sail, if not in man-of-war fashion and with a proper harbor bunt, at all events very securely.

But the main-top-sail was another matter. All three of us had to lay out to windward to haul taut one ear-ring; then skim along to the other end of the yard to the other ear-ring; and so up and down, and still more reef-points and still more ear-rings, until my legs and fingers ached.

This job over, we rested ourselves in the main-top, and then got upon the main-yard, and made shift to pass the yard-arm gaskets round the sail, and stow it after a fashion, though I had no doubt that the first gale of wind that struck it would blow it clear of its lashings in a minute.

Then on deck again with the main-top-sail halyards to the capstan; and the dawn found the ship under the three close-reefed top-sails, fore-sail, and fore-top-mast-stay-sail, the whole of the other canvas having been reefed and stowed away by three worn-out men, one of whom had been nearly knocked up by the fight with the mutineers, the second of whom was fresh from an imprisonment of three days in a close, stifling and rat-swarming coal-hole, while a third had received such a crack on his wrist as would have sent any man but an English sailor to his hammock, and kept him ill and groaning for a month.

CHAPTER XX

OUR NEXT job was to man the port-braces and bring the ship to a westerly course. But before we went to this work the boatswain and I stood for some minutes looking at the appearance of the sky.

The range of cloud, which had been but a low lying and apparently a fugitive bank in the north-west at midnight, was now so far advanced as to project nearly over our heads; and what rendered its aspect more sinister was the steely color of the sky, which it ruled with a line, here and there rugged, but for the most part singularly even, right from the confines of the north-eastern to the limits of the south-western horizon. All the central portion of this vast surface of cloud was of a livid hue, which, by a deception of the eye made it appear convex; and at frequent intervals a sharp shower of arrowy lightning whizzed from that portion of it furthest away from us; but as yet we could hear no thunder.

"When the rain's before the wind, then your top-sail halyards mind," chanted the boatswain. "There's rather more nor a quarter o' an inch o' rain there, and there's something worse nor rain astern of it."

The gloomiest feature of this approaching tempest, if such it were, was the slowness, at once mysterious and impressive, of its approach.

I was not, however, to be deceived by this into supposing that, because it had taken nearly all night to climb the horizon, there was no wind behind it. I had had experience of a storm of this kind, and remember the observations of one of the officers of the ship when speaking of it. "Those kind of storms," he said, "are not driven by the wind, but create it. They keep a hurricane locked up in their insides, and wander across the sea on the lookout for ships; when they come across something worth wrecking, they let fly. Don't be deceived by their slow pace and imagine them only thunderstorms. They'll burst like an earthquake in a dead calm over your head, and, whenever you see one coming, snug your ship right away down to the last reef in her, and keep your stern at it."

"I am debating, bo's'n," said I, "whether to bring the ship round or keep her before it. What do you think?"

"There's a gale of wind there. I can smell it," he replied; "but we're snug enough to lie close, aren't we?" looking up at the masts.

"That's to be proved," said I. "We'll bring her close, if you like; but I am pretty sure we shall have to run for it later on."

"It'll bowl us well away into mid-Atlantic, won't it, Mr. Royle?"

"Yes; I wish we were more to the nor'ard of Bermuda. However, we'll tackle the yards, and have a trial for the tight little islands."

"They're pretty nigh all rocks, aren't they? I never sighted 'em."

"Nor I. But they've got a dock-yard at Bermuda, I believe, where the Yankees refit sometimes, and that's about all I know of those islands."

I asked Miss Robertson to put the helm down, and keep it there until the compass pointed west; but the ship had so little way upon her, owing to the small amount of canvas she carried now and the faintness of the wind, that it took her as long to come round as if we had been warping her head to the westward by a buoy.

Having braced up the yards and steadied the helm, we could do no more; and resolving to profit as much as possible from the interval of rest before us, I directed Cornish to take the wheel, and ordered the steward to go forward and light the galley fire and boil some coffee for breakfast.

"Bo's'n," said I, "you might as well drop below and have a look at those plugs of yours. Take a hammer with you and this light," handing him the binnacle-lamp, "and drive the plugs in hard, for if the ship should labor heavily, she might strain them out."

He started on his errand, and then I told Miss Robertson that there was nothing now to detain her on deck, and thanked her for the great service she had rendered us.

How well I remember her as she stood near the wheel, wearing my straw hat, her dress hitched up to allow freedom to her movements; her small hands with the delicate blue veins glowing through the white clear skin, her yellow hair looped up, though with many a tress straying like an amber-colored feather; her marble face, her lips pale with fatigue, her beautiful blue eyes fired ever with the same brave spirit, though dim with the weariness of long and painful watching, and the oppressive and numbing sense of ever-present danger!

On no consideration would I allow her to remain any longer on deck; and though she begged to stay, I took her hand firmly, and led, her into the cuddy to her cabin door.

"You will faithfully promise me to lie down and sleep?" I said.

"I will lie down, and will sleep if I can," she answered with a wan smile.

"We have succeeded in saving you so far," I continued earnestly, "and it would be cruel, very cruel, and hard upon me to see your health break down for the want of rest and sleep, when both are at your command, now that life is bright again, and when any hour may see us safe on the deck of another vessel."

"You shall not suffer through me," she replied. "I will obey you; indeed I will do anything you want."

I kissed her hand respectfully, and said that a single hour of sound sleep would do her a deal of good; by that time I would take care that breakfast should be ready for her and her father, and then I held open the cabin door for her to enter, and returned on deck.

A most extraordinary and wonderful sight saluted me when I reached the poop.

The sun had risen behind the vast embankment of cloud, and its glorious rays, the orb itself being invisible, projected in a thousand lines of silver beyond the margin of the bank to the right and overhead, jutting out in visible threads, each as defined as a sunbeam in a dark room.

But the effect of this wonderful light was to render the canopy of cloud more horribly livid; and weird and startling was the contrast of the mild and far-reaching sunshine, streaming in lines of silver brightness into the steely sky, with the blue lightning ripping up belly of the cloud, and suffering the eye to dwell for an instant on the titanic stratum of gloom that stood ponderously behind.

Nor was the ocean at this moment a less somber and majestical object than the heavens; for upon half of it rested a shadow deep as night, making the water sallow and thick, and most desolate to behold under the terrible curtain that lay close down to it upon the horizon; while all on the right the green sea sparkled in the sunbeams, heaving slowly under the calm that had fallen.

Looking far away on the weather-beam, and where the shadow on the sea was deepest, I fancied that I discerned a black object, which might well be a ship with her sails darkened by her distance from the sun.

I pointed it out to Cornish, who saw it too, and I then fetched the telescope.

Judge of my surprise and consternation when the outline of a boat with her sail low down on the mast entered the field of the glass! I cried out, "It's the long-boat!"

Cornish turned hastily.

"My God!" he cried, "they're doomed men!"

I gazed at her intently, but could not be deceived, for I recognized the cut of the stun'sail, lowered as it was in anticipation of the breaking of the storm, and I could also make out the minute dark figures of the men in her.

My surprise, however, was but momentary, for considering the lightness of the wind that had prevailed all night, and the probability of her having stood to and fro in expectation of coming across us, or the quarter-boat which had attacked us, I had no reason to expect that they should have been far off.

The boatswain came along the quarter-deck, singing out, "It's all right below! No fear of a leak there!"

"Come up here," I cried. "There's the long-boat yonder!"

On hearing this he ran aft as hard as he could and stared in the direction I indicated, but could not make her out until he had the glass to his eye, on which he exclaimed:

"Yes, it's her, sure enough. Why, we may have to make another fight for it. She's heading this way, and if she brings down any wind, by jingo! she'll overhaul us."

"No, no," I answered. "They're not for fighting. They don't like the look of the weather, bo's'n, and would board us to save their lives, not to take ours."

"That's it, sir," exclaimed Cornish. "I reckon there's little enough mutineering among 'em, now Stevens is gone. I'd lay my life they'd turn to and go to work just as I have, if you'd lay by for 'em and take 'em in."

Neither the boatswain nor I made any reply to this.

For my own part, though we had been perishing for the want of more hands, I don't think I should have had trust enough in those rascals to allow them on board; for I could not doubt that when the storm was over, and they found themselves afloat in the "Grosvenor" once more, they would lay violent hands on me and the boatswain, and treat us as they treated Coxon and Duckling, revenging themselves in this way upon us for the death of

Stevens and the other leaders of the mutiny, and likewise protecting them-selves against their being carried to England and handed over to the authorities on shore as murderers.

The lightning was now growing very vivid, and for the first time I heard the sullen moan of thunder.

"That means," said the boatswain, "that it's a good bit off yet; and if that creature for'ard'll only bear a hand we shall be able to get something to eat and drink before it comes down."

However, as he spoke the steward came with a big coffee-pot. He set it on the sky-light, and fetched from the pantry some good preserved meat, biscuit, and butter, and we fell to the repast with great relish and hunger.

Being the first to finish, I took the wheel while Cornish breakfasted, and then ordered the steward to go and make some fresh coffee, and keep it hot in the galley, and prepare a good breakfast for the Robertsons, ready to serve when the young lady should leave her cabin.

"Bo's'n," said I, as he came slowly toward me, filling his pipe. "I don't like the look of that main-sail. It'll blow out and kick up a deuce of a shindy. You and Cornish had better lay aloft with some spare line and serve the sail with it."

"That's soon done," he answered, cheerfully. And Cornish left his break-fast and they both went aloft.

I yawned repeatedly as I stood at the wheel, and my eyes were sore for want of sleep.

But there was something in the aspect of that tremendous, stooping, quarter sphere of cloud abeam of us throwing a darkness most sinister to behold on half the sea, and vomiting quick lances of blue fire from its cav-erns, while now and again the thunder rolled solemnly, which was formidable enough to keep me wide awake.

It was growing darker every moment: already the sun's beams were obscured, though that portion of the great canopy of cloud which lay near-est to the luminary carried still a flaming edge.

A dead calm had fallen, and the ship rested motionless in the water.

The two men remained for a short time on the main-yard, and then came down, leaving the sail much more secure than they had found it. Cor-nish dispatched his breakfast, and the boatswain came to me.

"Do you see the long-boat now, sir?"

"No," I replied; "she is hidden in the rain yonder. By Heaven! it is coming down!"

I did not exaggerate; the horizon was gray with the rain; it looked like steam rising from the boiling sea.

"It'll keep 'em busy bailing," said the boatswain.

"Hold on here," I cried, "till I get my oilskins."

I was back again in a few moments, and he went away to drape himself for the downfall, and to advise Cornish to do the same.

I left the wheel for a second or two to close one of the sky-lights, and as I did so a flash of lightning seemed to set the ship on fire, and immediately came a deafening crash of thunder. I think there is something more awful in the roar of thunder heard at sea than on shore, unless you are among the mountains; you get the full intensity of it, the mighty outburst smiting the smooth surface of the water, which in itself is a wonderful vehicle of sound, and running onward for leagues without meeting any impediment to check or divert it.

I hastened to see if the lightning-conductor ran clear to the water, and finding the end of the wire coiled up in the port main-chains, flung it overboard and resumed my place at the wheel.

Now that the vast surface of cloud was well forward of overhead, I observed that its front was an almost perfect semi-circle, the extremities at either point of the horizon projecting like horns. There still remained, embraced by these horns, a clear expanse of steel-colored sky. *There* the sea was light, but all to starboard it was black, and the terrible shadow was fast bearing down upon the ship.

Crack! the lightning whizzed, and turned the deck, spars, and rigging into a net-work of blue fire. The peal that followed was a sudden explosion—a great dead crash, as though some mighty ponderous orb had fallen from the highest heaven upon the flooring of the sky and riven it.

Then I heard the rain.

I scarcely know which was the more terrifying to see and hear—the rain, or the thunder and lightning.

It was a cataract of water falling from a prodigious elevation. It was a dense, impervious, liquid veil, shutting out all sight of sea and sky. It tore the water into foam in striking it.

Then *boom!* down it came upon us.

I held on by the wheel, and the boatswain jammed himself under the grating. It was not rain only—it was hail as big as eggs; and the rain-drops were as big as eggs too.

There was not a breath of air. This terrific fall came down in perfectly perpendicular lines; and as the lightning rushed through it, it illuminated with its ghastly effulgence a broad sheet of water.

It was so dark that I could not see the card in the binnacle. The water rushed off our decks just as it would had we shipped a sea; and, for the space of twenty minutes I stood stunned, deaf, blind, in the midst of a horrible and overpowering concert of pealing thunder and rushing rain, the awful gloom being rendered yet more dreadful by the dazzling flashes which passed through it.

It passed as suddenly as it had come, and left us still in a breathless calm, drenched, terrified and motionless.

It grew lighter to windward, and I felt a small air blowing on my streaming face; lighter still, though to leeward the storm was raging and roaring, and passing with its darkness like some unearthly night.

I squeezed the water out of my eyes, and saw the wind come rushing toward us upon the sea, while all overhead the sky was a broad, lead-colored space.

"Now, bo's'n," I roared, "stand by!"

He came out from under the grating, and took a grip of the rail.

"Here it comes!" he cried; "and by the holy poker!" he added, "here comes the long-boat atop of it!"

I could only cast one brief glance in the direction indicated, where, sure enough, I saw the long-boat flying toward us on a surface of foam. In an instant the gale struck the ship and over she heeled, laying her port bulwark close down upon the water. But there she stopped.

"Had we had whole top-sails," I cried, "it would have been Amen!"

I waited a moment or two before deciding whether to put the helm up and run. If this was the worst of it, the ship would do as she was. But in that time the long-boat, urged furiously forward by the sail they still kept on her, passed close under our stern. Twice, before she reached us, I saw them try to bring her so as to come alongside, and each time I held my breath, for I knew that the moment they brought her broadside to the wind she would capsize.

May God forbid that ever I should behold such a sight again!

It was indescribably shocking to see them swept helplessly past within hail of us. There were seven men in her. Two of them cried out and raved furiously, entreating with dreadful, mad gesticulations as they whirled past. But the rest, some clinging to the mast, others seated with their arms folded, were silent, like dead men already, with fixed and staring eyes—a ghastly crew. I saw one of the two raving men spring on to the gunwale, but he was instantly pulled down by another.

But what was there to see? It was a moment's horror—quick-vanishing as some monstrous object leaping into sight under a flash of lightning, then instantaneously swallowed up in the devouring gloom.

Our ship had got way upon her, and was surging forward with her lee channels under water. The long-boat dwindled away on our quarter, the spray veiling her as she fled, and in a few minutes was not to be distinguished upon the immeasurable bed of foam and wave, stretching down to the livid storm that still raged upon the far horizon.

"My God!" exclaimed Cornish, who stood near the wheel unnoticed by me. "I might ha' been in her! I might ha' been in her!"

And he covered his face with his hands, and sobbed and shook with the horror of the scene, and the agony of the thoughts it had conjured up.

CHAPTER XXI

I HARDLY knew what to make of the weather; for though it blew very hard, the wind was not so violent as it had been during those three days which I have written of in another part of this story.

The ship managed to hold her own well, with her head at west; I mean that she went scraping through the water, making very little lee-way, and so far she could fairly well carry the three close-reefed top-sails; though I believe that had another yard of canvas more than was already exposed been on her, she would have lain down and never righted again, so violent was the first clap and outfly of the wind.

Nevertheless, I got the boatswain to take the wheel, and sent Cornish forward to stand in the fore-top-sail sheets, while I kept by the mizzen, for I was not at all sure that the terrific thunder-storm that had broken over us was not the precursor of a hurricane, to come down at any moment on the gale that was already blowing, and wreck the ship out of hand.

In this way twenty minutes passed, when, finding the wind to remain steady, I sung out to Cornish that he might come aft again. As I never knew the moment when a vessel might heave in sight, I bent on the small ensign and ran it half-way up at the gaff end, not thinking it judicious to exhibit a train of flag-signals in so much wind. I then took the telescope, and, setting it steady in the mizzen-rigging, slowly and carefully swept the weather horizon, and afterward transferred the glass to leeward, but no ship was to be seen.

"We ought to be in the track o' some sort o' wessels, too," exclaimed the boatswain, who had been awaiting the result of my inspections. "The steamers from Liverpool to New Orleans, and the West India mail-ships, 'ud come right across this way, wouldn't they?"

"Not quite so far north," I answered. "But there ought to be no lack of sailing-ships from all parts—from England to the southern ports of the United States and North America—from American ports to Rio and the eastern coast of South America. They can not keep us long waiting. Something must heave in sight soon."

"Suppose we sight a wessel, what do you mean to do, sir?"

"Ask them to let me have a few men to work the ship to the nearest port."

"But suppose they're short-handed?"

"Then they won't oblige us."

"I can't see myself, sir," said he, "why, instead o' tryin' to fetch Bermuda, we shouldn't put the helm up and square away for England. How might the English Channel lie as we now are?"

"A trifle to the east'ard of north-east."

"Well, this here's a fair wind for it."

"That's true; but will you kindly remember that the ship's company consists of three men?"

"Of four, countin' the steward, and five, countin' Miss Robertson."

"Of three men, I say, capable of working the vessel."

"Well, yes; you're right. Arter all, there's only three to go aloft."

"I suppose you know," I continued, "that it would take a sailing-ship, properly manned, four or five weeks to make the English Channel."

"Well, sir."

"Neither you, nor I, nor Cornish could do without sleep for four or five weeks."

"We could keep regular watches, Mr. Royle."

"I dare say we could; but we should have to let the ship remain under reefed top-sails. But instead of taking four or five weeks, we should take four or five months to reach England under close-reefed top-sails, unless we could keep a gale of wind astern of us all the way. I'll tell you what it is, bo's'n, these exploits are very pretty and appear very possible, in books, and persons who take anything that is told them about the sea as likely and true believe they can be accomplished. And on one or two occasions they have been accomplished. Also I have heard on one occasion a gentleman made a voyage from Timor to Bathurst Island on the back of a turtle. But the odds, in my unromantic opinion, are a thousand to one against our working the ship home as we are, unless we can ship a crew on the road, and very shortly. And how can we be sure of this? There is scarce a ship goes to sea now that is not short-handed. We may sight fifty vessels, and get no help from one of them. They may all be willing to take us on board if we abandon the 'Grosvenor'; but they'll tell us that they can give us no assistance to work her. Depend upon it, our wisest course is to make Bermuda. There, perhaps, we may pick up some hands. But if we head for England in this trim—a deep ship, with heavy gear to work, and but two seamen to depend upon, if the third has to take the wheel, trusting to chance to help us, I repeat that the odds against our bringing the ship home are one thousand to one. We shall be at the mercy of every gale that rises, and end in becoming a kind of phantom ship, chased about the ocean just as the wind happens to blow us."

"Well, sir," said he, "I daresay you're right, and I'll say no more about it. Now, about turnin' in. I'll keep here, if you like to go below for a couple of hours. Cornish can stand by to rouse you up."

I had another look to windward before making up my mind to go below. A strong sea was rising, and the wind blew hard enough to keep one leaning against it. There was no break in the sky, and the horizon was thick, but the lookout was not worse than it had been half an hour before.

We were, however, snug enough aloft, if not very neat; the bunt of the mainsail, indeed, looked rather shaky, but the other sails lay very secure upon the yards; and this being so, and the gale remaining steady, I told the boatswain to keep the ship to her present course, and went below, yawning horribly and dead wearied.

I had slept three-quarters of an hour when I was awakened by the steward rushing into my cabin and hauling upon me like a madman. Being scarcely conscious, I imagined that the mutineers had got on board again, and that here was one of them falling upon me; and having sense enough, I suppose, in my sleepy brain to make me determine to sell my life at a good price, I let fly at the steward's breast and struck him so hard that he roared out, which sound brought me to my senses at once.

"What is it?" I cried.

"Oh, sir," responded the steward, half dead with terror and loss of breath occasioned by my blow, "the ship's sinking, sir! We're going down! I've been told to fetch you up. The Lord have mercy upon us!"

I rolled on to the deck in my hurry to leave the bunk, and ran with all my speed up the companion-ladder; nor was the ascent difficult, for the ship was on a level keel, pitching heavily, indeed, but rolling slightly.

Scarcely, however, was my head up through the companion when I thought it would be blown off my shoulders. The fury and force of the wind was such as I had never before in all my life experienced.

Both the boatswain and Cornish were at the wheel, and, in order to reach them, I had to drop upon my hands and knees and crawl along the deck. When near them, I took a grip of the grating and looked around me.

The first thing I saw was the main-sail had blown away from most of the gaskets, and was thundering in a thousand rags upon the yard. The fore-sail was split in halves, and the port mizzen-top-sail sheet had carried away, and the sail was pealing like endless discharges of musketry.

All the spars were safe still. The lee-braces had been let go, the helm put up, and the ship was racing before a hurricane as furious as a tornado, heading south-east, with a wilderness of foam boiling under her bows.

This, then, was the real gale which the thunderstorm had been nearly all night bringing up. The first gale was but a summer breeze compared to it.

The clouds lay like huge fantastic rolls of sheet lead upon the sky; in some quarters of the circle drooping to the waterline in patches and spaces ink-black. No fragment of blue heaven was visible; and yet it was lighter than it had been when I went below.

The ensign, half-masted, roared over my head; the sea was momentarily growing heavier, and as the ship pitched, she took the water in broad sheets over her forecastle.

The terrible beating of the mizzen-top-sail was making the mizzenmast, from the mast-coat to the royal mast-head, jump like a piece of whalebone. Although deafened, bewildered, and soaked through with the screaming of the gale, the thunder of the torn canvas, and the spray which the wind tore out of the sea and hurled through the air, I still preserved my senses; and, perceiving that the mizzen-top-mast would go if the sail were not got rid of, I crawled on my hands and knees to the foot of the mast and let go the remaining sheet.

With appalling force, and instantaneously, the massive chain was torn through the sheave-hole, and in less time than I could have counted ten, one half the sail had blown into the main-top, and the rest streamed like the ends of whip-cord from the yard.

I crawled to the fore-end of the poop to look at the main-mast; that stood steady; but while I watched the fore-mast, the fore-sail went to pieces, and the leaping and plunging of the heavy blocks upon it made the whole mast quiver so violently that the top-gallant and royal-mast beat to and fro like a bow strung and unstrung quickly.

I waited some moments, debating whether or not to let go the foretop-sail sheets; but, reflecting that the full force of the wind was kept away from it by the main-top-sail, and that it would certainly blow to pieces if I touched a rope belonging to it, I dropped on my hands and knees again and crawled away aft.

"I saw it coming!" roared the bo's'n in my ear. "I had just time to sing out to Cornish to slacken the lee-braces and put the helm hard over."

"We shall never be able to run!" I bellowed back. "She'll be pooped, as sure as a gun, when the sea comes! We must heave her to while we can. No use thinking of the fore-top-sail—it must go!"

"Look there!" shouted Cornish, dropping the spokes with one hand to point.

There was something indeed to look at; one of the finest steamers I had ever seen, brig-rigged, hove to under a main-stay-sail. She seemed, so rapidly were we reeling through the water, to rise out of the sea.

She lay with her bowsprit pointing across our path, just on our starboard bow. Lying as she was, without way on her, we should have run into her had the weather been thick, as surely as I live to say so.

We slightly starboarded the helm, clearing her by the time we were abreast by not more than a quarter of a mile. But we dared not have hauled the ship round another point; for, with our braces all loose, the first spilling of the sails would have brought the yards aback, in which case, indeed, we might have called upon God to have mercy on our souls, for the ship would not have lived five minutes.

There was something fascinating in the spectacle of that beautiful steamship, rolling securely in the heavy sea, revealing as she went over to starboard her noble, graceful hull to within a few feet of her keel. But there was also something unspeakably dreadful to us to see help so close at hand, and yet of no more use than had it offered a thousand miles away.

There was a man on her bridge, and others doubtless watched our vessel unseen by us; and God knows what sensations must have been excited in them by the sight of our torn and whirling ship blindly rushing before the tempest, her sails in rags, the half-hoisted ensign bitterly illustrating our miserable condition, and appealing, with a power and pathos no human cry could express, for help which could not be given.

"Let us try and heave her to now!" I shrieked, maddened by the sight of this ship whirling fast away on our quarter. "We can lie by her until the gale has done, and then she will help us!"

But the boatswain could not control the wheel alone: the blows of the sea against the rudder made it hard for even four pairs of hands to hold the wheel steady. I rushed to the companion and bawled for the steward, and when, after a long pause, he emerged, no sooner did the wind hit him than he rolled down the ladder.

I sprung below, hauled him up by the collar of his jacket, and drove him with both hands to his stern up to the wheel.

"Hold onto these spokes!" I roared. And then Cornish and I ran staggering along the poop.

"Get the end of the starboard main-brace to the capstan!" I cried to him. "Look alive! ship one of the bars ready!"

And then I scrambled as best I could down to the main-deck, and went floundering forward through the water, that was now washing higher than my ankle, to the fore-top-sail halyards, which I let go.

Crack! whiz! away went the sail, strips of it flying into the sea like smoke.

I struggled back again on to the poop, but the violence of the wind was almost more than I could bear; it beat the breath out of me; it stung my face just as if it were filled with needles; it roared in my ears; it resembled a solid wall; it rolled me off my knees and hands and obliged me to drag myself against it, bit by bit, by whatever came in my road to hold on to.

Cornish lay upon the deck with the end of the main-brace in his hands, having taken the necessary turn with it around the capstan.

I laid my weight against the bar and went to work, and scrambling and panting, beaten half dead by the wind, and no more able to look astern without protecting my eyes with my hands than I could survey any object in a room full of blinding smoke, I gradually got the mainyard round, but found I had not the strength to bring it close to the mast.

I saw the boatswain speak to the steward, who left the wheel to help me with his weight against the capstan bar.

I do think at that moment that the boatswain transformed himself into an immovable figure of iron. Heaven knows from what measureless inner sources he procured the temporary strength; he clenched his teeth, and the muscles in his hands rose like bulbs as he hung to the wheel and pitted his strength against the blows of the seas upon the rudder.

Brave, honest fellow! a true seaman! a true Englishman! Well would it be for sailors were there more of this kind among them to set them examples of honest labor, noble self-sacrifice, and duty ungrudgingly performed!

The seas struck the ship heavily as she rounded to. I feared that she would have too much head-sail to lie close, for the fore-sail and fore-top-sail were in ribbons—they might show enough roaring canvas when coupled with the fore-top-mast-stay-sail to make her pay off, we having no after-sail set to counterbalance the effect of them.

However, she lay steady, that is, as the compass goes, but rolled fearfully, wallowing deep like a ship half full of water, and shipped such tremendous seas that I constantly expected to hear the crash of the galley stove in.

I now shaded my eyes to look astern; not hoping, indeed to see the steamer near, but expecting at least to find her in sight. But the horizon was a dull blank: not a sign of the vessel to be seen, nothing but the rugged line of water, and the nearer deep dark under the shadow of the leaden pouring clouds.

CHAPTER XXII

IN BRINGING the ship close to the wind in this terrible gale, without springing a spar, we had done what I never should have believed practicable to four men, taking into consideration the size of the ship and the prodigious force of the wind; and when I looked aloft and considered that only a few hours before, so to speak, the ship was carrying all the sail that could be put upon her, and that three men had stripped her of it and put her under a close-reefed main-top-sail fit to encounter a raging hurricane, I could not help thinking that we had a right to feel proud of our endurance and spirit.

There was no difficulty now in holding the wheel, and, had no worse sea than was now running been promised us, the helm might have been lashed and the vessel lain as comfortably as a smack with her foresail over to windward.

The torn sails were making a hideous noise on the yards forward, and as there was no earthly reason why this clamor should be suffered to last, I called to Cornish to get his knife ready and help me to cut the canvas away from the jackstays. We hauled the braces tight to steady the yards, and then went aloft, and in ten minutes severed the fragments of the fore-sail and top-sail, and they blew up into the air like paper and were carried nearly half a mile before they fell into the sea.

The wind was killing up aloft, and I was heartily glad to get on deck again, not only to escape the wind, but on account of the foretop-mast and top-gallant-mast, both of which had been heavily tried, and now rocked heavily as the ship rolled, and threatened to come down with the weight of the yards upon them.

But neither Cornish nor I had strength enough in us to stay the masts more securely: our journey aloft and our sojourn on the yards, and our fight with the wind to maintain our hold, had pretty well done for us; and in Cornish I took notice of that air of lassitude and dull indifference which creeps upon shipwrecked men when worn out with their struggles, and which resembles, in its way, the stupor which falls upon persons who are perishing of cold.

It was fair, however, since I had some rest, that I should now take a spell at the wheel, and I therefore told Cornish to go to the cabin lately occupied by Stevens, the ship's carpenter, and turn in, and then crawled aft to the poop and desired the boatswain to go below and rest himself, and order the steward, who had not done one-tenth of the work we had performed, to stand by ready to come on deck if I should call to him.

I was now alone on deck, in the center, so it seemed when looking around the horizon, of a great storm, which was fast lifting the sea into mountains.

I took a turn round the spokes of the wheel and secured the tiller ropes to steady the helm, and held on, crouching to windward, so that I might get some shelter from the murderous force of the wind by the slanting deck and rail.

I could better now realize our position than when at work, and the criticalness of it struck and awed me like a revelation. I cast my eyes upon the main-top-sail, and inspected it anxiously, as on this sail our lives might depend. If it blew away, the only sail remaining would be the fore-top-mast-stay-sail. In all probability the ship's head would at once pay off, let me keep the helm jammed down as hard as I pleased; the vessel would then drive before the seas, which, as she had not enough canvas on her to keep her running at any speed, would very soon topple over her stern, sweep the decks fore and aft, and render her unmanageable.

There was likewise the further danger of the fore-top-mast going, the whole weight of the stay-sail being upon it. If this went, it would take that sail with it, and the ship would round into the wind's eye and drive away astern.

Had there been more hands on board, I should not have found these speculations so alarming. My first job would have been to get some of the cargo out of the hold and pitch it overboard so as to lighten the ship, for the dead weight in her made her strain horribly. Then, with men to help, it would have been easy to get the storm-try-sail on if the top-sail blew away, clap preventer back stays on to the fore-mast and fore-top-mast, and rouse them taut with tackles, and send down the royal and top-gallant-yards, so as to ease the masts of the immense leverage of these spars.

But what could four men do—one of the four being almost useless, and all four exhausted not by the perils and labor of the storm only, but by the fight they had had to make for their lives against fellow beings?

Alone on deck, with the heavy seas splashing and thundering, and precipitating their volumes of water over the ship's side, with the gale howling and roaring through the skies, I grew bitterly despondent. It seemed as if God himself were against me; that I was the sport of some remorseless fate, whereby I was led from one peril to another, from one suffering to another, and no mercy to be shown me until death gave me rest.

And yet I was sensible of no revolt and inward rage against what I deemed my destiny. My being and individuality were absorbed and swallowed up in the power and immensity of the tempest like a raindrop in the sea. I was overwhelmed by the vastness of the danger which surrounded me, by the sense of the littleness and insignificance of myself and my companions in the midst of this spacious theatre of warring winds, and raging seas, and far-reaching sky of pouring cloud. I felt as though all the forces of nature were directed against my life; and those cries which my heart would have sent up in the presence of dangers less tumultuous and immense were silenced by a kind of dull amazement, of heavy, passive bewilderment, which numbed my mind, and forced upon me an indifference to the issue without depriving me of the will and energy to avert it.

I held my post at the wheel, being anxious that the boatswain and
Cornish should recruit their strength by sleep, for if one or the other of
them broke down, then, indeed our case would be deplorable.

The force of the wind was stupendous, and yet the brave main-top-sail
stood it; but not an hour had passed since the two men went below when
a monster wave took the ship on the starboard bow and threw her up, rolling at the same time an immense body of water onto the decks; her stem
where I was crouched, sunk in the hollow level with the sea, then, as the
leviathan wave rolled under her counter, the ship's bows fell into a prodigious trough with a sickening, whirling swoop. Ere she could recover,
another great sea rolled right upon her, burying her forecastle, and rushing
with the fury of a cataract along the main-deck.

Another wave like that, and our fate was sealed.

But happily these were exceptional seas; smaller waves succeeded, and
the struggling, straining ship showed herself alive still.

Alive, but maimed. That tremendous swoop had carried away the
jib-boom and the fore-top-gallant-masts—the one close against the bowsprit
head, the other a few inches above the top-gallant-yard. The mast, with the
royal-yard upon it, hung all in a heap against the fore-top-mast, but fortunately kept steady, owing to the yard-arm having jammed itself into the
fore-top-mast rigging. The jib-boom was clean gone adrift, and was washing
away to leeward.

This was no formidable accident, though it gave the ship a wrecked
and broken look. I should have been well pleased to see all three top-gallant
masts go over the side, for the weight of the yards, swaying to and fro at
great angles, was too much for the lower masts, and not only strained the
decks, but the planking to which the chain-plates were bolted.

My great anxiety now was for the fore-top-mast, which was sustaining
the weight of the broken mast and yard, in addition to the topgallant-yard,
still standing, and the heavy pulling of the fore-top-mast-stay-sail.

Dreading the consequences that might follow the loss of this sail, I
called to the steward at the top of my voice, and on his thrusting his head
up the companion, I bade him rouse up Cornish and the boat-swain, and
send them on deck.

In a very short time they both arrived, and the boatswain, on looking
forward, immediately comprehended our position and anticipated my order.

"The top-mast'll go!" he roared in my ear. "Better let go the stay-sail-halyards, and make a short job o' it."

"Turn to and do it at once," I replied. Away they skurried. I lost sight of them when they were once off the poop, and it seemed an eternity before they showed themselves again on the forecastle.

No wonder! They had to wade and struggle through a rough sea on the main-deck, which obliged them to hold on, for minutes at a time, to whatever they could put their hands to.

I wanted them to bear a hand in getting rid of the stay-sail, for, with the wheel hard down, the ship showed a tendency to fall off. But it was impossible to make my voice heard—I could only wave my hand; the boatswain understood the gesture, and I saw him motion to Cornish to clear off the forecastle. He then ran over to leeward and let go the fore-top-mast-stay-sail sheet and halyards, and, this done, he could do no more but take to his heels.

The hullabaloo was frightful—the thundering of the sails, the snapping and cracking of the sheets.

Boom! I knew it must follow. It was a choice of two evils—to poop the ship or lose a mast.

Down came the top-mast, splintering and crashing with a sound that rose above the roar of the gale, and in a minute was swinging against the shroud—an awful wreck to behold in such a scene of raging sea and buried decks.

I knew well now what ought to be done, and done without delay; for the stay-sail was in the water, ballooning out to every wave, and dragging the ship's head round more effectually than had the sail been set.

But I had a wonderful ally in the boatswain—keen, unerring, and intrepid, a consummate sailor. I should never have had the heart to give him the order; and yet there he was, and Cornish by his side, at work, knife in hand, cutting and hacking away for dear life.

A long and perilous job indeed—now up aloft, now down, soaked by the incessant seas that thundered over the ship's bows, tripping over the raffle that encumbered the deck, actually swarming out on the bowsprit with their knives between their teeth, at moments plunged deep in the sea, yet busy again as they were lifted high in the air.

I draw my breath as I write. I have the scene before me; I see the ropes parting under the knives of the men. I close my eyes as I behold once more the boiling wave that buries them, and dare not look, lest I should find them gone. I hear the hooting of the hurricane, the groaning of the over-loaded vessel, and over all the faint hurrah those brave spirits utter as the last rope is severed and the unwieldly wreck of spars and cordage falls overboard and glides away upon a running sea, and the ship comes to again under my hand, and braves, with her bows almost at them, the merciless onslaught of the huge green waves.

Only the day before, one of these men was a mutineer, blood-stained already, and prepared for new murders!

Strange translation! from base villainy to actions heroical! But those who know sailors best will least doubt their capacity of gauging extremes.

CHAPTER XXIII

BY THE loss of the fore-top-mast the ship was greatly eased. In almost every sea that we had encountered since leaving England. I had observed the immense leverage exerted over the deep-lying hull by the weight of her lofty spars; and by the effect which the carrying away of the fore-top-mast had produced, I had no doubt that our position would be rendered far less critical, while the vessel would rise to the waves with much greater ease, if we could rid her of a portion of her immense top weight.

I waited until the boatswain came aft, and then surrendered the wheel to Cornish; after which I crouched with the boatswain under the lee of the companion, where, at least, we could hear each other's voices.

"She pitches easier since that fore-top-mast went, bo's'n. There is still too much top-hanger. The main-royal-stay is gone, and the mast can't stand long, I think, unless we stay it for'ard again. But we mustn't lose the top-mast."

"No, we can't do without him. Yet there's a risk of him goin' too, if you cut away the top-gall'nt backstays. What's to prevent him?" said he, looking up at the mast.

"Oh, I know how to prevent it," I replied, "I'll go aloft with a hand-saw and wound the mast. What do you think? Shall we let it carry away?"

"Yes," he replied, promptly. "She'll be another ship with them masts out of her. If it comes on fine we'll make shift to bend on the new fore-sail, and get a jib on her by a stay from the lower mast-head to the bowsprit end. Then," he continued, calculating on his fingers, "We shall have the main-top-mast-stays'l, mizzen, mizzen-tops'l—six and two makes height—height sails on her—a bloomin' show o' canvas!"

He ran his eye aloft and said, emphatically.

"I'm for lettin' of 'em go, most sartinly."

I got up, but he caught hold of my arm.

"I'll go aloft," said he.

"No, no," I replied, "it's my turn. You stand by to cut away the lanyards to leeward, and then get to windward and wait for me. We must watch for a heavy lurch, for we don't want the spars to fall amidships, and drive a hole through the deck."

Saying which, I got off the poop and made for the cabin lately shared between the carpenter and the boatswain, where I should find a saw in the tool-chest.

I crept along the main-deck to leeward, but was washed off my feet in spite of every precaution, and thrown with my head against the bulwark, but the blow was more bewildering than hurtful. Fortunately, everything was secure, so there were no pounding casks and huge spars, driving about like battering-rams, to dodge.

I found a saw, and also laid hold of the sounding-rod, so that I might try the well, being always very distrustful of the boatswain's plugs in the fore-hold; but on drawing up the rod out of the sounding pipe, I found there were not above five to six inches of water in her, and, as the pumps sucked at four inches, I had not only the satisfaction of knowing that the ship was tight in her hull, but that she was draining in very little water from her decks.

This discovery of the ship's soundness filled me with joy, and, thrusting the saw down my waistcoat, I sprang into the main-rigging with a new feeling of life in me.

I could not help thinking, as I went plowing and clinging my way up the ratlines, that the hurricane was less furious than it had been an hour ago; but this, I dare say, was more my hope than my conviction, for, exposed as I now was to the full force of the wind, its power and outcry were frightful. There were moments when it jammed me so hard against the shrouds that I could not have stirred an inch—no, not to save my life.

I remember once reading an account of the wreck of a vessel called the "Wager," where it was told that so terrible was the appearance of the sea many of the sailors went raving mad with fear at the sight of it, some throwing themselves overboard in their delirium, and others falling flat on the deck and rolling to and fro with the motion of the ship, without making the smallest effort to help themselves.

I believe that much such a fear as drove those poor creatures wild was spread below me now, and I can only thank Almighty God for giving me the courage to witness the terrible spectacle without losing my reason.

No words that I am master of could submit the true picture of this whirling, mountainous, boiling scene to you. The waves, foreshortened to my sight by my elevation above them, drew, nevertheless, a deeper shadow into their caverns, so that, so lively was this deception of coloring, each time the vessel's head fell into one of these billows it seemed as though she were plunging into a measureless abysm, as roaring and awful as a maelstrom, from which it would be almost impossible for her to rise in time to lift to the next great wave that was rushing upon her.

When, after incredible toil, I succeeded in gaining the cross-trees, I paused for some moments to recover breath, during which I looked, with my fingers shading my eyes, carefully all round the horizon, but saw no ship in sight.

The top-mast was pretty steady, but the top-gallant-mast rocked heavily, owing to the main-royal-stay being carried away; moreover, the boatswain had already let go the royal and top-gallant-braces, so that they might run out when the mast fell, and leave it free to go overboard; and the yards swinging in the wind and to the plunging of the ship, threatened every moment to bring down the structure of masts, including all or a part of the top-mast, so that I was in the greatest peril.

In order, therefore, to lose no time, I put my knife in my teeth, and shinned up the top-gallant rigging, where, holding on with one hand, I cut the top-gallant-stay adrift, though the strands were so hard that I thought I should never accomplish the job. This support being gone, the mast jumped wildly, insomuch that I commended my soul to God, every instant believing that I should be shaken off the mast or that it would go overboard with me.

However, I succeeded in sliding down again into the cross-trees, and having cut away the top-gallant rigging to leeward, I pulled out my saw and went to work at the mast with it, sawing the mast just under the yard, so that it might go clean off at that place.

When I had sawed deep enough, I cut away the weather rigging and got down into the main-top as fast as ever I could, and sung out to the boat-swain to cut a way to leeward.

By the time I reached the deck all was adrift to leeward, and the mast was now held in its place by the weather backstays. I dropped into the chains and there helped the boatswain with my knife, and watching an opportunity when the ship rolled heavily to leeward, we cut through the lanyards of the top-gallant backstay, and the whole structure of spar, yards, and rigging went flying overboard.

Encouraged by the success of these operations, and well knowing that a large measure of our safety depended upon our easing the ship of her top-hamper, I sung out that we would now cut away the mizzentop-gallant-mast, and once more went aloft, though the boatswain begged hard to take my place this time.

This spar, being much lighter and smaller, did not threaten me to dangerously as the other had done, and in a tolerably short space of time we had sent it flying overboard after the main-top-gallant-mast; and all this we did without further injury to ourselves than a temporary deprivation of strength and breath.

The ship had now the appearance of a wreck; and yet in her mutilated condition was safer than she had been at any moment since the gale first sprung up. The easing her of all this top weight seemed to make her as buoyant as though we had got a hundred tons of cargo out of her. Indeed, I was now satisfied, providing everything stood, and the wind did not increase in violence, that she would be able to ride out the gale.

Cornish (as well as the boatswain and myself) was soaked through and through; we therefore arranged that the boatswain and I should go below and shift our clothes, and that the boatswain should then relieve Cornish.

So down we went, I, for one, terribly exhausted, but cheered all the same by an honest hope that we should save our lives and the ship, after all.

I stepped into the pantry to swallow a dram, so as to get my nerves together, for I was trembling all over with the weariness in me, and, cold as ice on the skin from the repeated dousings I had received, then changed my clothes; and never was anything more comforting and grateful than the feel of the dry flannel and the warm stockings and sea-boots which I exchanged for shoes that sopped like brown paper and came to pieces in my hand when I pulled them off.

The morning was far advanced, a little past eleven. I was anxious to ask Miss Robertson how she did, and reassure her as to our position before going on deck to take observations, and therefore went to her cabin door and listened, meaning to knock and ask her leave to see her if I heard her voice in conversation with her father.

I strained my ear, but the creaking and groaning of the ship inside, and the bellowing of the wind outside, were so violent, that, had the girl been singing at the top of her voice, I do not believe I should have heard her.

I longed to see her, and shook the handle of the door, judging that she would distinguish this sound amid the other noises which prevailed, and, sure enough, the door opened, and her sweet face looked out.

She showed herself fully when she saw me, and came into the cuddy, and was going to address me, but a look of agonizing sorrow came into her face; she dropped on her knees before the bench at the table and buried her head, and never was there an attitude of grief more expressive of piteous misery than this.

My belief was that the frightful rolling of the ship had crazed her brain, and that she fancied I had come to tell her we were sinking.

Not to allow this false impression to affect her an instant longer than could be helped, I dropped on one knee by her side, and at once told her that the ship had been eased, and was riding well, and that the gale, as I believed, was breaking.

She shook her head, still keeping her face buried, as though she would say that it was not the danger we were in that had given her that misery.

"Tell me what has happened?" I exclaimed. "Your troubles and trials have been very, very great—too great for you to bear, brave and true-hearted as you are. It unmans me and breaks me down to see you in this attitude. For your own sake, keep up your courage for a little longer. The first ship that passes when this gale abates will take us on board; and there are three of us still with you who will never yield an inch to any danger that may come while their life holds out and you remain to be saved."

She upturned her pale face, streaming with tears, and said the simple words, but in a tone I shall never forget—"Papa is dead!"

Was it so, indeed?

And was I so purblind as to wrong her beautiful and heroic character by supposing her capable of being crazed with fears for her own life?

I rose from her side and stood looking at her in silence. I had nothing to say.

However dangerous our situation might have been, I should still have known how to comfort and encourage her.

But—her father was dead!

This was a blow I could not avert—a sorrow no labor could remit. It struck home hard to me.

I took her hand and raised her, and entered the cabin hand in hand with her. The moisture of the deck dulled the transparency of the bull's-eye, but sufficient light was admitted through the port-hole to enable me to see him. He was as white as a sheet, and his hair frosted his head, and made him resemble a piece of marble carving. His under-jaw had dropped, and that was the great and prominent signal of the thing that had come to him.

Poor old man! lying dead under the coarse blanket, with thin hands folded, as though he had died in prayer, and a most peaceful, holy calm in his face!

Was it worth while bringing him from the wreck for this?

"God was with him when he died," I said, and I closed his poor eyes as tenderly as my rough hands would let me.

She looked at him, speechless with grief, and burst into an uncontrollable fit of crying.

My love and tenderness, my deep pity of her lonely helplessness, were all so great an impulse in me, that I took her in my arms and held her while she sobbed upon my shoulder. I am sure that she knew my sorrow was deep and real, and that I held her to my heart that she might not feel her loneliness.

When her great outburst of grief was passed, I made her sit; and then she told me that when she had left the deck, she had looked at her father before lying down, and thought him sleeping very calmly. He was not dead then. Oh, no! she had noticed by the motion of the covering on him that he was breathing peacefully. Being very tired, she had fallen asleep quickly and slept soundly. She awoke, not half an hour before she heard me trying the handle of the door. The rolling and straining of the ship frightened her, and she heard one of the masts go overboard. She got out of bed, meaning to call her father, so that he might be ready to follow her, if the ship were sinking (as she believed it was), on to the deck, but could not wake him. She took him by the arm, and this bringing her close to his face, she saw that he was dead. She would have called me, but dreaded to leave the cabin lest she should be separated from her father. Meanwhile she heard the fall of another mast alongside, and the ship at the moment rolling heavily, she believed the vessel actually sinking, and flung herself upon her father's body, praying to God that her death might be mercifully speedy, and that the waves might not separate them in death.

At this point she broke down, and cried again bitterly.

When I came to think over what she had gone through during that half hour—the dead body of her father before her, of him whose life a few hours before she had no serious fear of, and the bitterness of death which she had tasted in the dreadful persuasion that the vessel was sinking, I was too much affected to speak. I could only hold her hands and caress them, wondering in my heart that God, who loves and blesses all things that are good and pure, should single out this beautiful, helpless, heroic girl for suffering so complicated and miserable.

After a while I explained that it was necessary I should leave her, as I was desirous of observing the position of the sun, and promised, if no new trouble detained me on deck, to return to her as soon as I had completed my observations.

So without further words I came away and got my sextant, and went on deck.

I found Cornish still at the wheel and the boatswain leaning over the weather side of the ship about half-way down the poop, watching the hull of the vessel as she rolled and plunged. I might have saved myself the trouble of bringing the sextant with me, for there was not only no sign of the sun now, but no promise of it showing itself even for a minute. Three impenetrable strata of cloud obscured the heavens: the first, a universal mist or thickness, tolerably bright as it lay nearest the sun; beneath this, ranges of heavier clouds, which had the appearance of being stationary, owing to the speed at which the ponderous smoke-colored clouds composing the lowest stratum were swept past them. Under this whirling, gloomy sky the sea was tossing in mountains, and between sea and cloud the storm was sweeping with a stupendous voice, and with a power so great that no man on shore who could have experienced its fury there would believe that anything afloat could encounter it and live.

I remained until noon anxiously watching the sky, hoping that the outlines of the sun might swim out, if for a few moments only, and give me a chance to fix it.

I was particularly wishful to get sights, because, if the wind abated, we might be able to wear the ship and stand for the Bermudas, which was the land the nearest to us that I knew of. But I could not be certain as to the course to be steered unless I knew my latitude and longitude. The "Grosvenor," now hove to in this furious gale, was drifting dead to leeward at from three to four knots an hour. Consequently, if the weather remained thick and this monstrous sea lasted, I should be out of my reckoning altogether next day. This was the more to be deplored, as every mile was of serious consequence to persons in our position, as it would represent so many hours more of hard work and bitter expectation.

The boatswain had by this time taken the wheel, to let Cornish go below to change his clothes, and, as no conversation could be carried on in that unsheltered part of the deck, I reserved what I had to say to him for another opportunity, and returned to the cuddy.

I could not bear to think of the poor girl being alone with her dead father in the darksome cabin, where the grief of death would be augmented by the dismaying sounds of the groaning timbers and the furious wash of the water against the ship's side.

I went to her and begged her to come with me to my own cabin, which, being to windward, and having two bull's-eyes in the deck, was lighter and more cheerful than hers.

"Your staying here," I said, "cannot recall your poor father to life; and I know if he were alive, he would wish me to take you away. He will rest quietly here, Miss Robertson, and we will close the cabin door and leave him for a while."

I drew her gently from the cabin, and when I had got her into the cuddy, I closed the door upon the old dead man, and led her by the hand to my own cabin.

"I intend," I said, "that you shall occupy this berth, and I will remove to the cabin next to this."

She answered in broken tones that she could not bear the thought of being separated from her father.

"But you will not be separated from him," I answered, "even though you should never see him more with your eyes. There is only one separation, and that is when the heart turns and the memory forgets. He will always be with you in your thoughts, a dear friend, a dear companion and father, as in life; not absent because he is dead, since I think that death makes those whom we love doubly our own, for they become spirits to watch over us, let us journey where we please, and their affection is not to be chilled by worldly selfishness. Try to think thus of the dead. It is not a parting that should pain us. Your father has set out on his journey before us; death is but a short leave-taking, and only a man who is doomed to live forever could look upon death as on eternal separation."

She wept quietly, and once or twice looked at me as though she would smile through her tears, to let me know that she was grateful for my poor attempts to console her; but she could not smile. Rough and idle as my words were, yet, in the fullness of my sympathy, and of my knowledge of her trials, and my sense of the dangers which, even as I spoke, were raging round us, my voice faltered, and I turned to hide my face.

It happened then that my eye lighted upon the little Bible I had carried with me in all my voyages since I had gone to sea, and I felt that now, with the old man lying dead, and his poor child's grief, and our own hard and miserable position, was the fitting time to invoke God's mercy, and to pray to Him to watch over us.

I spoke to that effect to Miss Robertson, and said that if she consented, I would call in Cornish and the steward and ask them to join us; that the boatswain was at the wheel and could not leave his post, but we might believe that the Almighty would accept the brave man's faithful discharge of his duty as a prayer, and would not overlook him, if our prayers were accepted, because he could not kneel in company with us.

"Let him know that we are praying," she exclaimed, eagerly, "and he will pray too."

I saw that my suggestion had aroused her, and at once left the cabin and went on deck, and, going close to the boatswain, I said:

"Poor Mr. Robertson is dead, and his daughter is in great grief."

"Ah, poor lady!" he replied. "I hope God'll spare her. She's a brave young woman, and seen a sight more trouble within the last fort-night than so pretty a gell deserves."

"Bo's'n, I am going to call in Cornish and the steward, and read prayers and ask God for His protection. I should have liked you, brave old messmate, to join; but as you can't leave the deck, pray with us in your heart, will you?"

"Ay, ay, that I will, heartily; an' I hope for the lady's sake that God Almighty'll hear us, for I'd sooner die myself than she should, poor gell! for I'm older, and it's my turn afore hers by rights."

I clapped him on the back and went below, where I called to the steward and Cornish, both of whom came aft upon hearing my voice.

During my absence, Miss Robertson had taken the Bible and laid it open on the table; and when the two men came in I said:

"My lads, we are in the hands of God, who is our Father; and I will ask you to join this lady and me in thanking Him for the mercy and protection He has already vouchsafed us, and to pray to Him to lead us out of present peril and bring us safely to the home we love."

The steward said "Yes, sir," and looked about him for a place to sit or kneel, but Cornish hung his head and glanced at the door shamefacedly.

"You need not stop unless you wish, Cornish," said I. "But why should you not join us? The way you have worked, the honest manner in which you have behaved, amply atone for the past. From no man can more than hearty repentance be expected, and we all stand in need of each other's prayers. Join us, mate."

"Won't it be makin' a kind of game o' religion for the likes o' me to pray?" he answered. "I was for murderin' you an' the lady and all hands as are left on board this wessel—what 'ud be the use o' *my* prayers?"

Miss Robertson went over to him and took his hand.

"God," said she, "has told us that there is more joy in heaven over one sinner that repenteth than over ninety-and-nine just persons who need no repentance. But who is good among us, Cornish? Be sure that as you repent so are you forgiven. My poor father lies dead in his cabin, and I wish you to pray with me for him, and to pray with us for our own poor lives. Mr. Royle," she said, "Cornish will stay."

And, with an expression on her face of infinite sweetness and pathos, she drew him to one of the cushioned lockers and seated herself by his side.

I saw that her charming, wonderful grace, her cordial, tender voice, and her condescension, which a man of his condition would feel, had deeply moved him.

The steward seated himself on the other side of her, and I began to read from the open book before me, beginning the chapter which she had chosen for us during my absence on deck. This chapter was the eleventh of St. John, wherein is related the story of that sickness "which was not unto death, but for the glory of God, that the Son of God might be glorified thereby."

I read only to the thirty-sixth verse, for what followed that did not closely apply to our position; but there were passages preceding it which stirred me to the center of my heart, knowing how they went home to the mourner, more especially those pregnant lines, "Martha saith unto him, I know that He shall rise again in the resurrection at the last day. Jesus said unto her, I am the resurrection and the life: he that believeth in Me, though he were dead, yet shall he live," which made me feel that the words I had formerly addressed to her were not wholly idle.

I then turned to St. Matthew, and read from the eighth chapter those few verses wherein it is told that Christ entered a ship with his disciples, and that there arose a great storm. Only men in a tempest at sea, their lives in jeopardy, and worn out with anxiety and the fear of death, know how great is the comfort to be got out of this brief story of our Lord's power over the elements, and His love of those whom He died to save; and, taking this as a kind of text, I knelt down, the others imitating me, and prayed that He who rebuked the sea and the wind before His doubting disciples, would be with us who believed in Him in our present danger.

Many things I said (feeling that He whom I addressed was our Father, and that He alone could save us) which have gone from my mind, and tears stood in my eyes as I prayed; but I was not ashamed to let the others see them, even if they had not been as greatly affected as I, which was not the case. Nor would I conclude my prayer without entreating God to comfort the heart of the mourner, and to receive in heaven the soul of him for whom she was weeping.

I then shook Cornish and the steward heartily by the hand, and I am sure, by the expression in Cornish's face, that he was glad he had stayed, and that his kneeling in prayer had done him good.

"Now," said I, "you had best get your dinner, and relieve the boatswain; and you, steward, obtain what food you can, and bring it to us here, and then you and the bo's'n can dine together."

The two men left the cabin, and I went and seated myself beside Miss Robertson, and said all that I could to comfort her.

She was very grateful to me for my prayers for herself and her father, and already, as though she had drawn support from our little service, spoke with some degree of calmness of his death. It would have made her happy, she said, could she have kissed him before he died, and have been awake to attend to any last want.

I told her that I believed he had died in his sleep, without a struggle; for, so recent as his death was, less placidity would have appeared in his face had he died awake or conscious. I added that secretly I had never believed he would live to reach Valparaiso, had the ship continued her voyage. He was too old a man to suffer and survive the physical and mental trials he had passed through; and, sad though his death was, under the circumstances which surrounded it, yet she must think it had only been hastened a little; for he was already an old man, and his end might have been near, even had all prospered and he had reached England in his own ship.

By degrees I drew her mind away from the subject by leading her thoughts to our own critical position. At another time I should have softened my account of our danger; but I thought it best to speak plainly, as the sense of the insecurity of our lives would in some measure distract her thoughts from her father's death.

She asked me if the storm was not abating.

"It is not increasing in violence," I answered, "which is a good sign. But there is one danger to be feared which must very shortly take me on deck. The wind may suddenly lull and blow again hard from another quarter. This would be the worst thing that could happen to us, for we should then have what is called a cross sea, and the ship is so deeply loaded that we might have great difficulty in keeping her afloat."

"May I go on deck with you?"

"You would not be able to stand. Feel this!" I exclaimed, as the ship's stern rose to a sickening height and then came down, down, down, with the water roaring about her as high as our ears.

"Let me go with you!" she pleaded.

"Very well," I replied, meaning to keep her under the companion, half way up the ladder.

I took a big top-coat belonging to the captain and buttoned her up in it, and also tied his fur cap over her head, so that she would be well protected from the wind, while the coat would keep her dress close against her.

I then slipped on my oilskins, and taking a strong grip of her hand to steady her, led her up the companion-ladder.

"Do not come any further," said I.

"Wherever you go I will go," she answered, grasping my arm.

Admiring her courage and stirred by her words, which were as dear to me as a kiss from her lips would have been, I led her right on to the deck over to the windward, and made her sit on a small coil of rope just under the rail.

The sea was no heavier than it had been since the early morning, and yet my short absence below had transformed it into a sublime and stupendous novelty.

You will remember that not only was the "Grosvenor" a small ship, but that she lay deep, with a free board lower by a foot and a half than she ought to have shown.

The height from the poop-rail to the water was not above twelve feet;

and it is therefore no exaggeration to say that the sea, running from fifteen to twenty feet high, stood like walls on either side of her.

To appreciate the effect of such a sea upon a ship like the "Grosvenor," you must have crossed the Atlantic in a hurricane, not in an immense and powerful ocean steamer, but in a yacht.

But even this experience would not enable you to realize our danger; for the yacht would not be overloaded with cargo; she would probably be strong, supple and light; whereas the "Grosvenor" was choked to the height of the hold with seven hundred and fifty tons of dead weight, and was a Nova Scotia soft-wood ship, which means that she might start a butt at any moment, and go to pieces in one of her frightful sweeps downward.

Having lodged Miss Robertson in a secure and sheltered place, I crawled along the poop on to the main-deck and sounded the well again. I found a trifle over six inches of water in her, which satisfied me that she was still perfectly tight, and that the extra leakage was owing to the drainings from the decks.

I regained the poop and communicated the good news to the boat-swain, who nodded; but, I noticed that there was more anxiety in his face than I liked to see, and that he watched the ship very, closely each time she pitched with extra heaviness.

Miss Robertson was looking up at the masts with alarmed eyes: but I pointed to them and smiled, and shook my head to let her know that their wrecked appearance need not frighten her. I then took the telescope, and, making it fast over my back, clambered into the mizzen-top, she watching my ascent with her hands tightly clasped.

The ensign still roared some half dozen feet below the gaff end; it was a brave bit of bunting to hold on as it did. I planted myself firmly against the rigging and carefully swept the weather-horizon, and finding nothing there, pointed the glass to leeward; but all that part of the sea was likewise a waste of foaming waves, with never a sign of a ship in all the raging seas.

I was greatly disappointed, for though no ship could have helped us in such a sea, yet the sight of one hove to near us—and no ship afloat, sailer or steamer, but must have hove to in that gale—would have comforted us greatly, as a promise of help at hand and rescue to come when the wind should have gone down.

CHAPTER XXIV

ALL THAT day the wind continued to blow with frightful force, and the sky to wear its menacing aspect. On looking, however, at the barometer at four o'clock in the afternoon, I observed a distinct rise in the mercury; but I did not dare to feel elated by this promise of an improvement; for, as I have before said, the only thing the mercury foretells is a change of weather, but what kind of change you shall never be sure of until it comes.

What I most dreaded was the veering of the gale to an opposite quarter, whereby, a new sea being set running right athwart, or in the eye of the already raging sea, our decks would be helplessly swept and the ship grow unmanageable.

A little after eight the wind sensibly decreased, and, to my great delight, the sky cleared in the direction whence the gale was blowing, so that there was a prospect of the sea subsiding before the wind shifted—that is, if it shifted at all.

When Cornish, who had been below resting after a long spell, came on deck and saw the stars shining, and that the gale was moderating, he stared upward like one spellbound, and then, running up to me, seized my hand and wrung it in silence.

I heartily returned this mute congratulation, and we both went over and shook hands with the boatswain; and those who can appreciate the dangers of the frightful storm that had been roaring about us all day, and feel with us in the sentiments of despair and helplessness which the peril we stood in awoke in us, will understand the significance of our passionate silence as we held each other's hand and looked upon the bright stars, which shone like the blessing of God upon our forlorn state.

I was eager to show Mary Robertson these glorious harbingers, and ran below to bring her on deck.

I found her again in the cabin in which her father lay, bending over his body in prayer. I waited until she turned her head, and then exclaimed that the wind was falling, and that all the sky in the northwest was bright with stars, and begged her to follow me and see them.

She came immediately, and, after looking around her, cried out in a rapturous voice:

"Oh, Mr. Royle! God has heard our prayers!" and in the wildness of her emotions, burst into a flood of tears.

I held her hand as I answered:

"It was your grief that moved me to pray to Him, and I consider you our guardian angel on board this ship, and that God who loves you will spare our lives for your sake."

"No, no; do not say so; I am not worthier than you—not worthier than the brave boatswain, and Cornish, whose repentance would do honor to the noblest heart. Oh, if my poor father had but been spared to me!"

She turned her pale face and soft and swimming eyes up to the stars and gazed at them intently, as though she witnessed a vision there.

But though the wind had abated, it still blew a gale, and the sea boiled and tumbled about us and over our decks in a manner that would have been terrifying had we not seen it in a greater state of fury.

I sent the steward forward to see if he could get the galley-fire to burn, so as to boil us some water for coffee, for though the ship was in a warm latitude, yet the wind, owing to its strength, was at times piercingly cold, and we all longed for a hot drink—a cup of hot coffee or cocoa being infinitely more invigorating, grateful, and warming than any kind of spirits drunk cold.

All that the steward did, however, was to get wet through; and this he managed so effectually that he came crawling aft, looking precisely as if he had been fished out of the water with grappling-hooks.

I lighted a bull's-eye lamp, and went to the pumps and sounded the well.

On hauling up the rod I found, to my consternation, that there were nine inches of water in the ship.

I was so much startled by this discovery that I stood for a moment motionless; then, bethinking me that one of the plugged auger-holes might be leaking, I slipped forward without saying a word to the others, and getting a large mallet from the tool-chest, I entered the forecastle, so as to get into the fore-peak.

I had not been in the forecastle since the men had left the ship, and I cannot describe the effect produced upon me by this dark, deserted abode, with its row of idly swinging hammocks glimmering in the light shed by the bull's-eye lamp; the black chests of the seamen which they had left behind them; here and there a suit of dark oilskins suspended by a nail and looking like a hanged man; the hollow place resonant with the booming thunder of the seas and the mighty wash of the water swirling over the top-gallant deck.

The whole scene took a peculiarly ghastly significance from the knowledge that of all the men who had occupied those hammocks and bunks, one only survived; for four of them we ourselves had killed, and I could not suppose that the long-boat had lived ten minutes after the gale had broken upon her.

I made my way over the cable-ranges, stooping my head to clear the hammocks, and striking my shins against the sea-chests, and swung myself into the hold.

Here I found myself against the water-casks, close against the cargo, and just beyond was the bulkhead behind which the boatswain had hidden when Stevens bored the holes.

Carefully throwing the light over the walls, I presently perceived the plugs or ends of the broom-stick protruding; and going close to them I found they were perfectly tight, that no sign of moisture was visible around them.

It may seem strange that this discovery vexed and alarmed me. And yet this was the case.

It would have made me perfectly easy in my mind to have seen the water gushing in through one of these holes, because not only would a few blows of the mallet have set it to rights, but it would have acquainted me with the cause of the small increase of water in the hold.

Now that cause must be sought elsewhere.

Was it possible that the apprehensions I had felt each time the ship had taken one of her tremendous headers were to be realized?—that she had strained a butt or started a bolt in some ungetatable place?

Here where I stood, deep in the ship, below the waterline, it was frightful to hear her straining, it was frightful to feel her motion.

The whole place resounded with groans and cries, as if the hold had been filled with wounded men.

What bolts, though forged by a Cyclops, could resist that horrible grinding—could hold together the immense weight which the sea threw up as a child a ball, leaving parts of it poised in air, out of water, unsustained save by the structure that contained it, then letting the whole hull fall with a hollow, horrible crash into a chasm between the waves, beating it first here, then there, with blows the force of which was to be calculated in hundreds of tons?

I scrambled up through the fore-scuttle, and, perceiving Cornish smoking a pipe under the break of the poop, I desired he would go and relieve the boatswain at the wheel for a short while and send him to me, as I had something particular to say to him.

I waited until the boatswain came, as here was the best place I could choose to conduct conversation.

Beyond all question the wind was falling; and though the ship still rolled terribly, she was not taking in nearly so much water over her sides.

I retrimmed the lamp in my hand, and in a few minutes the boatswain joined me.

I said to him at once:

"I have just made nine inches of water in the hold."

"When was that?" he inquired.

"Ten minutes ago."

"When you sounded the well before, what did you find?"

"Between five and six inches."

"I'll tell you what it is, sir," said he. "You'll hexcuse me sayin' of it, but it's no easy job to get at the true depth of water in a ship's bottom when she's tumblin' about like this here."

"I think I got correct soundings."

"Suppose," he continued, "you drop the rod when she's on her beam-ends. Where's the water? Why, the water lies all on one side, and the rod'll come up pretty near dry."

"I waited until the ship was level."

"Ah, *you* did, because you knows your work. But it's astonishin' what few persons there are as really *does* know how to sound the pumps. You'll hexcuse me, sir, but I should like to drop the rod myself."

"Certainly," I replied, "and I hope you'll make it less than I."

In order to render my description clear to readers not acquainted with such details, I may state that in most large ships there is a pipe that leads from the upper deck, alongside the pumps, down to the bottom, or within a few inches of the bottom of the vessel. The water in the hold necessarily rises to the height of its own level in this pipe; and in order to gauge the depth of water, a dry rod of iron, usually graduated in feet and inches, is attached to the end of a line and dropped down the tube, and when drawn up the depth of water is ascertained by the height of the water on the rod.

It is not too much to say that no method for determining this essential point in a ship's safety could well be more susceptible of inaccuracy than this.

The immersed rod, on being withdrawn from the tube, wets the sides of the tube; hence, though the rod be dry when it is dropped a second time, it is wetted in its passage down the tube; and as the accuracy of its indication is dependent on its exhibiting the mark of the level water, it is manifest that if it becomes wetted before reaching the water, the result it shows on being withdrawn must be erroneous.

Secondly, as the boatswain remarked to me, if the well be sounded at any moment when the vessel is inclined at any angle on one side or the other, the water must necessarily roll to the side to which the vessel inclines, by which the height of the water in the well is depressed, so that the rod will not report the true depth.

Hence, to use the sounding-rod properly, one must not only possess good sense, but exercise very great judgment.

I held the lamp close to the sounding-pipe, and the boatswain carefully dried the rod on his coat preparatory to dropping it.

He then let it fall some distance down the tube, keeping it, however, well above the bottom, until the ship, midway in a roll, stood for a moment on a level keel.

He instantly dropped the rod, and, hauling it up quickly, remarked that we had got the true soundings this time.

He held the rod to the light, and I found it a fraction over nine inches.

"That's what it is, anyway," said he, putting down the rod.

"An increase of three inches since the afternoon."

"Well, there's nothen to alarm us in that, is there, Mr. Royle?" he questioned. "Perhaps it's one o' my plugs as wants hammerin'."

"No, they're as tight as a new kettle," I answered. "I have just come from examining them."

"Well, all we've got to do is to pump the ship out; and, if we can, make the pumps suck all right. That'll show us if anything's wrong."

This was just the proposition I was about to make; so I went into the cuddy and sung out for the steward; but he was so long answering that I lost my temper and ran into the pantry, where I found him shamming sleep.

I started him on to his legs and had him on the main-deck in less time than he could have asked what the matter was.

"Look here!" I cried, "if you don't turn to and help us all to save our lives, I'll just send you adrift in that quarter-boat with the planks out of her bottom! What do you mean by pretending to be asleep when I sing out to you?"

And after abusing him for some time to let him know that I would have no skulking, and that if his life were worth having he must save it himself, for we were not going to do his work and our own as well, I bade him lay hold of one of the pump-handles, and we all three of us set to work to pump the ship.

If this were not the heaviest job we had yet performed, it was the most tiring; but we plied our arms steadily and perseveringly, taking every now and then a spell of rest, and shifting our posts so as to vary our postures; and after pumping I scarcely know how long, the pumps sucked, whereat the boatswain and I cheered heartily.

"Now, sir," said the boatswain, as we entered the cuddy to refresh ourselves with a dram of brandy and water after our heavy exertions, "we know that the ship's dry, leastways, starting from the ship's bottom; if the well's sounded again at half past ten—it's now half past nine—that'll be time enough to find out if anything's gone wrong."

"How about the watches? We're all adrift again. Here's Cornish at the wheel, and it's your watch on deck."

As I said this, Miss Robertson came out of the cabin where her father lay—do what I might I could not induce her to keep away from the old man's body—and, approaching us slowly, asked why we had been pumping.

"Why, ma'am," replied the boatswain, "it's always usual to pump the water out o' wessels. On dry ships it's done sometimes in the mornin'

watch, and t'others they pumps in the first dog-watch. All accordin'. Some
wessels as they call colliers require pumpin' all day long; and the 'Heagle,'
which was the fust wessel as I went to sea in, warn't the only Geordie as
required pumpin' not only all day long, but all night long as well. Every
blessed wessel has her own custom, but it's a werry dry ship indeed as don't
want pumpin' wunce a day."

"I was afraid," she said, "when I heard the clanking of the pumps, that
water was coming into the ship."

She looked at me earnestly, as though she believed that this was the
case, and that I would not frighten her by telling her so. I had learned to
interpret the language of her eyes by this time, and answered her doubts as
though she had expressed them.

"I should tell you at once if there was any danger threatened in that
way," I said. "There was more water in the ship than I cared to find in her, so
the three of us have been pumping her out."

"About them watches, Mr. Royle?" exclaimed the boatswain.

"Well, begin afresh, if you like," I replied. "I'll take the wheel for two
hours, and then you can relieve me."

"Why will you not let me take my turn at the wheel?" said Miss
Robertson.

The boatswain laughed.

"I have proved to you that I know how to steer."

"Well, that's right enough," said the boatswain.

"All three of you can lie down then."

I smiled and shook my head.

Said the boatswain: "If your arms wur as strong as your sperrit, miss,
there'd be no reason why you shouldn't go turn and turn about with us."

"But I can hold the wheel."

"It 'ud fling you overboard. Listen to its kicken'. You might as well try
to prewent one o' Barclay Perkins's dray hosses from bustin' into a gallop by
catchin' hold o' its tail. It 'ud be a poor lookout for us to lose you, I can tell
yer. What," continued the boatswain, energetically, "we want to know is, that
you're sleepin', and forgettin' all this here excitement in pleasin' dreams. To
see a lady like you knocked about by a gale o' wind is just one o' them
things I have no fancy for. Mr. Royle, if I had a young and beautiful darter,

and a dook or a barryonet worth a thousand a year, if that ain't sayin' too much, wos to propose a marriage to her, an' ax her to come and be married to him in some fur-off place, wich 'ud oblige her to cross the water, blowed if I'd consent. No flesh an' blood o' mine as I had any kind o' feeling for should set foot on board ship without fust having a row with me. Make no mistake. I'm talkin' o' females, miss. I say the sea ain't a fit place for women and gells. It does middlin' well for the likes of me and Mr. Royle here, as aren't afraid o' carryin' full-rigged ships and other agreeable dewices in gun-powder and Hindian ink on our harms, and is seasoned, as the sayin' is, to the wexations o' the mariner's life. But when it comes to young ladies crossin' the ocean, an' I don't care wot they goes as—as passengers or skippers' wives, or stewardishes, or female hemigrants—then I say it ain't proper; and if I'd ha' been a lawyer I'd ha' made it agi'n the law, and contrived such a Act of Parleyment as 'ud make the gent as took his wife, darter, haunt, cousin, grandmother, female nephey, or any relations in petticoats, to sea along with him, wish hisself hanged afore he paid her passage-money."

I was so much impressed by this vehement piece of rhetoric, delivered with many convulsions of the face and a great deal of handsawing, that I could not forbear mixing him some more brandy and water, which he drank at a draught, having first wished Miss Robertson and myself long life and plenty of happiness.

His declamation had quite silenced her, though I saw by her eyes that she would renew her entreaties the moment she had me alone.

"Then you'll go on deck, sir, and relieve Cornish, and I'll turn in?" observed the boatswain.

"Yes."

"Right," said he, and was going.

I added:

"We must sound the well again at half past ten."

"Ay, ay!"

"I sha'n't be able to leave the wheel, and I would rather you should sound than Cornish. I'll send the steward to rouse you."

"Very well," said he. And after waiting to hear if I had anything more to say, he entered his cabin, and in all probability was sound asleep two minutes after.

Miss Robertson stood near the table, with her hands folded and her eyes bent down.

I was about to ask her to withdraw to her cabin and get sleep.

"Mr. Royle, you are dreadfully tired and worn out, and yet you are going on deck to remain at the wheel for two hours."

"That is nothing."

"Why will you not let me take your place?"

"Because—"

"Let the steward keep near that ladder there, so that I can call to him if I want you."

"Do you think I could rest with the knowledge you were alone on deck?"

"You refuse because you believe I am not to be trusted," she said, gently, looking down again.

"If your life were not dependent on the ship's safety, I should not think of her safety, but of yours. I refuse for your own sake, not for mine—no, I will not say that. For *both* our sakes, I refuse. I have one dear hope—well, I will call it a great ambition, which I need not be ashamed to own: it is, that I may be the means of placing you on shore in England. This hope has given me half the courage with which I have fought on through danger after danger since I first brought you from the wreck. If anything should happen to you now, I feel that all the courage and strength of heart which have sustained me would go. Is that saying too much? I do not wish to exaggerate," I exclaimed, feeling the blood in my cheeks, and lamenting, without being able to control, the impulse that had forced this speech from me, and scarcely knowing whether to applaud or detest myself for my candor.

She looked up at me with her frank beautiful eyes, but on a sudden averted them from my face to the door of the cabin where her dead father lay. A look of indescribable anguish came over her, and she drew a deep, long, sobbing breath.

Without another word, I took her hand and led her to the cabin, and I knew the reason why she did not turn and speak to me was that I might not see she was weeping.

But it was time for action, and I dare not let the deep love that came to me for her divert thoughts from my present extremity.

I summoned the steward, who tumbled out of his cabin smartly enough, and ordered him to bring his mattress and lay it alongside the companion-ladder, so as to be within hail.

This done, I gained the poop and sent Cornish below.

CHAPTER XXV

AS I STOOD at the wheel I considered how I should act when the storm had passed. And I was justified in speculating, because now the sky was clear right away round, and the stars large and bright, though a strong gale was still blowing and keeping the sea very heavy.

Indeed, the clearness of the sky made me think that the wind would go to the eastward, but as yet there was no sign of it veering from the old quarter.

We had been heading west ever since we hove to, and traveling broad-side on dead south-south-east. Now, if wind and sea dropped our business would be to make sail, if possible, and, with the wind holding north-north-west, made an eight hours' board north-easterly and then round and stand for Bermuda.

This, of course, would depend upon the weather.

It was, however, more than possible that we should be picked up very soon by some passing ship. It was not as though we were down away in the South Pacific, or knocking about in the poisonous Gulf of Guinea, or up in the North Atlantic at 60°. We were on a great ocean highway, crossed and recrossed by English, American, Dutch, and French ships, to and from all parts of the world: and bad indeed would our fortune be, and baleful the star under which we sailed, if we were not overhauled in a short time and assistance rendered us.

A great though unexpressed ambition of mine was to save the ship and navigate her myself, not necessarily to England, but to some port whence I could communicate with her owners and ask for instructions.

As I have elsewhere admitted, I was entirely dependent on my profession, my father having been a retired army surgeon, who had died extremely poor, leaving me at the age of twelve an orphan, with no other friend in the world than the vicar of the parish we dwelt in, who generously sent me to school for two years at his own expense and then, after sounding my inclinations, apprenticed me to the sea.

Under such circumstances, therefore, it would be highly advantageous to my interests to save the ship, since my doing so would prefer some definite claims upon the attention of the owners, or perhaps excite the notice of another firm more generous in their dealings with their servants, and of a higher commercial standing.

While I stood dreaming in this manner at the wheel, allowing my thoughts to run on until I pictured myself the commander of a fine ship, and ending in allowing my mind to become engrossed with thoughts of Mary Robertson, whom I believed I should never see again after we had bidden each other farewell on shore, and who would soon forget the young second mate whom destiny had thrown her with for a little time of trouble and suffering and death, I beheld a figure advance along the poop, and on its approach, I perceived the boatswain.

"I've been sounding the well, Mr. Royle," said he. "I roused up on a sudden and went and did it, as I woke up anxious; and there's bad news, sir—twelve inches o' water."

"Twelve inches!" I cried.

"It's true enough. I found the bull's-eye on the cuddy table and the rod don't tell no lies when it's properly used."

"The pumps suck at four inches, don't they?"

"Yes, sir."

"Then that's a rise of eight inches since half-past nine o'clock. What time is it now?"

"Twenty minutes arter ten."

"We must man the pumps at once. Call Cornish. You'll find the steward on a mattress against the companion-ladder."

He paused a moment to look round him at the weather, and then went away.

I could not doubt now that the ship was leaky, and after what we had endured, and my fond expectation of saving the vessel—and the miserable death after all our hopes, that might be in store for us—I felt that it was very hard on us, and I yielded to a fit of despair.

What struck most home to me was that my passionate dream to save Mary Robertson might be defeated. The miseries which had been accumulated on her wrung my heart to think of. First her shipwreck, and then the peril of the mutiny, and then the dreadful storm that had held us face to face with death throughout the fearful day, and then the death of her father, and now this new horror of the ship whereon we stood filling water beneath our feet.

Yet hope—and God be praised for this mercy to all men!—springs eternal, and after a few minutes my despair was mastered by reflection. If the ship made no more water than eight inches in three-quarters of an hour, it would be possible to keep her afloat for some days by regular spells at the pumps, and there were four hands to work them if Miss Robertson steered while we pumped. In that time it would be a thousand to one if our signal of distress were not seen and answered.

Presently I heard the men pumping on the main-deck, and the boatswain's voice singing to encourage the others. What courage that man had! I, who tell this story, am ashamed to think of the prominence I give to my own small actions when all the heroism belongs to him. I know not what great writer it was who, visiting the field of the battle of Waterloo, asked how it was that the officers who fell in that fight had graves and monuments erected to them, when the soldiers—the privates by whom all the hard work was done, who showed all the courage and won the battle—lay nameless in hidden pits? And so, when we send ships to discover the North Pole, we have little to say about poor Jack, who loses his life by scurvy, or his toes and nose by frost-bites, who labors manfully, and who makes all the success of the expedition, so far as it goes. Our shouts are for Jack's officer; we title him, we lionize him—*his* was all the work, all the suffering, all the anxiety, we think. I who have been to sea say that Jack deserves as much praise as his skipper, and perhaps a little more; and if honor is to be bestowed let Jack have his share; and if a monument is to be raised, let poor Jack's name be written on the stone as well as the other's, for be sure that Jack could have done without the other, but also be sure that the other couldn't have done without Jack.

Chained to my post, which I dared not vacate for a moment, for the ship pitched heavily and required close watching as she came to and fell off upon the swinging seas I grew miserably anxious to learn how the pumping progressed, and felt that, after the boatswain, my own hands would do four times the work of the other two.

It was our peculiar misfortune that of the four men on board the ship three only should be capable; and that as one of the three men was constantly required at the wheel, there were but two available men to do the work. Had the steward been a sailor, our difficulties would have been considerably diminished, and I bitterly deplored my want of judgment in allowing Fish and the Dutchman to be destroyed, for though I would not have trusted Johnson and Stevens, yet the other two might have been brought over to work for us, and I have no doubt that the spectacle of the perishing wretches in the long-boat, as she was whirled past us, would have produced as salutary an effect upon them as it had upon Cornish; and with two extra hands of this kind we could not only have kept the pumps going, but have made shift to sail the ship at the same time.

The hollow, thrashing sounds of the pump either found Miss Robertson awake or aroused her, for soon after the pumping had commenced she came on deck, swathed in the big, warm overcoat and fur cap.

Such a costume for a girl must make you laugh in the description; and yet, believe me, she lost in nothing by it. The coat dwarfed her figure somewhat, but the fur cap looked luxurious against her fair hair, and nothing could detract from the exquisite femininity of her face, manner, and carriage. I speak of the impression she had made on me in the day-time; the starlight only revealed her white face now to me.

"Is the water still coming into the ship?" she asked.

"The bo's'n had reported to me that eight inches deep have come into her since half past nine."

"Is that much?"

"More than we want."

"I don't like to trouble you with my questions, Mr. Royle; but I am very, very anxious."

"Of course you are; and do not suppose that you can trouble. Ask me what you will. I promise to tell you the truth."

"If you find you can not pump the water out as fast as it comes, in, what will you do?"

"Leave the ship."

"How?" she exclaimed, looking around her.

"By that quarter-boat there."

"But it would fill with water and sink in such waves as these."

"These waves are not going to last, and it is quite likely that by this time to-morrow the sea will be calm."

"Will the ship keep afloat until to-morrow?"

"If the water does not come in more rapidly than it does at present the ship will keep afloat so long as we can manage to pump her out every hour. And so," said I, laughing to encourage her, "we are not going to die all at once, you see."

She drew quite close to me, and said:

"I shall never fear death while you remain on board, Mr. Royle. You have saved me from death once, and, though I may be wicked in daring to prophesy, yet I feel *certain—certain,*" she repeated, with singular emphasis, "that you will save my life again."

"I shall try very hard, be sure of that," I answered.

"I believe—no, it is not so much a belief as a strong conviction, with which my mind seems to have nothing to do—that, whatever dangers may be before us, you and I will not perish."

She paused, and I saw that she was looking at me earnestly.

"You will not think me superstitious if I tell you that the reason of my conviction is a dream? My poor father came and stood beside me; he was so *real!* I stretched out my arms to him, and he took my hand and said, 'Darling, do not fear! He who has saved your life once will save it again. God will have mercy upon you and him for the prayers you offered to Him.' He stooped and kissed me and faded away, and I started up and heard the men pumping. I went look at him, for I thought—I thought he had really come to my side. Oh, Mr. Royle, his spirit is with us!"

Though my mind was of too prosaic a turn to catch any significance in a dream, yet there was a strange, deep, solemn tenderness in her voice and manner as she related this vision that impressed me. It made my heart leap to hear her own sweet lips pronounce her faith in me, and my natural hopes and longings for life gathered a new light and enthusiasm from her own belief in our future salvation.

"Shipwrecked persons have been saved by a dream before now," I replied, gravely. "Many years ago a vessel called the 'Mary' went ashore on some rocks to the southward of one of the Channel Islands. A few of the crew managed to gain the rocks, where they existed ten or twelve days without water or any kind of food save limpets, which only increased their thirst without relieving their hunger. A vessel bound out of Guernsey passed the rocks at a distance too far away to observe the signals of distress made by the perishing men. But the son of the captain had twice dreamed that there were persons dying on those rocks, and so importuned his father to stand close to them that the men with great reluctance consented. In this way, and by a dream, those sailors were saved. Though I do not as a rule believe in dreams, I believe this story to be true, and I believe in your dream."

She remained silent, but the ship presently giving a sudden lurch she put up her hand on my arm to steady herself, and kept it there. Had I dared I should have bent my head and kissed the little hand. She could not know how much she made me love her by such actions as this.

"The boatswain has told me," she said, after a short silence, "that you want to save the ship. I asked him why. Are you angry with me for being curious?"

"Not in the least. What did he answer?"

"He said that you thought that the owners would recompense you for your fidelity, and promote you in their service."

"How could he know this? I have never spoken such thoughts to him."

"It would not be difficult to guess such a wish."

"Well, I don't know that I have any right to expect promotion or recompense of any kind from owners who send their ship to sea so badly provisioned that the men mutiny."

"But if the water gains upon the ship, you will not be able to save her."

"No, she must sink."

"What will you do then?"

"Put you on shore or aboard another ship," I replied, laughing at my own evasion, for I knew what she meant.

"Oh, of course, if we do not reach the shore we shall none of us be able to do anything," she said, dropping her head, for she stood close enough to the binnacle-light to enable me to see her movements and almost catch the expression of her face. "I mean what will you do when we get ashore?"

"I must try to get another ship."

"To command?"

"Oh, dear, no! as second mate, if they'll have me."

"If command of a ship were given you would you accept it?"

"If I could, but I can't."

She asked quickly, "Why not?"

"Because I have not passed an examination as master."

She was silent again, and I caught myself listening eagerly to the sound of the pumping going on on the main-deck, and wondering at my own levity in the face of our danger. But I could not help forgetting a very great deal when she was at my side.

All at once it flashed upon me that her father owned several ships, and that her questions were preliminary to her offering me the command of one of them.

I give you my honor that all recollection of who and what she was, of her station on shore, of her wealth as the old man's heiress, had as absolutely gone out of my mind as if the knowledge had never been imparted. What she was to me—what love and the wonderful association of danger and death had endeared her to me as—was what she was as she stood by my side, a sweet and gentle woman, whom my heart was drawing closer and closer to every hour, whose life I would have died to preserve, whose danger made my own life a larger necessity to me than I should have felt it.

A momentary emotion of disappointment, a resentment whereof I knew not the meaning, through lacking the leisure or the skill to analyze it, made me turn and say—

"Would you like me to command one of your ships, Miss Robertson?"

"Yes," she answered, promptly.

"As a recompense for my humane efforts to preserve you from drowning?"

She withdrew her hand from my arm and inclined her head to look me full in the face.

"Mr. Royle, I never thought you would speak to me like that."

"I want no recompense for what I have done, Miss Robertson."

"I have not offered you any recompense."

"Let me feel," I said, "that you understand it is possible for an English sailor to do his duty without asking or expecting any manner of reward. The Humane Society's medals are not for him."

"Why are you angry with me?" she exclaimed, sinking her head, and speaking with a little sob in her voice.

I was stirred to the heart by her broken tones, and answered:

"I am not angry. I could not be angry with you. I wish you to feel that what I have done, that whatever I may do—is—"

I faltered and stopped—an ignominious breakdown! though I think it concealed the true secret of my resentment.

I covered my confusion by taking her hand and resting it on my arm again.

"Do you mean," she said, "that all you have done has been for my sake only—out of humanity—that you would do as much for anybody else?"

"No," said I, boldly.

Again she withdrew her hand and remained silent, and I made up my mind not to interrupt her thoughts.

After a few moments she went to the ship's side and stood there; sometimes looking at the stars and sometimes at the water that stretched away into the gloom into heavy breaking seas.

The wind was singing shrilly up aloft, but the sounds of the pumping ceased on a sudden.

I awaited the approach of the boatswain with inexpressible anxiety. After an interval I saw his figure come up the poop-ladder.

"Pumps suck!" he roared out.

"Hurrah!" I shouted. "Down with you for grog all round!" for the other two were following the boatswain. But they all came aft first and stood near the wheel, blowing like whales, and Miss Robertson joined the group.

"If it's no worse than this, bo's'n," I asserted, "she'll do."

"Ay, she'll do, sir; but it's hard work. My arms feel as though they wos tied up in knots."

"So do mine," said the steward.

"Shall I take the wheel?" asked Cornish.

"No; go and get some grog and turn in, all of you. I am as fresh as a lark, and will stay here till twelve o' clock," I replied.

The steward at once shuffled below.

"Boatswain, ask Mr. Royle to let me take the wheel," said Miss Robertson. "He has been talking to me for the last half hour, and sometimes held the wheel with one hand. I am sure I can hold it."

"As you won't go below, Miss Robertson, you shall steer, but I will stop by you," I said.

"That will be of no use!" she exclaimed.

Cornish smothered a laugh and walked away.

"Now, bo's'n, down with you!" I cried. "I'll have you up again shortly to sound the well. But half an hour's sleep is something. If you get knocked up, I lose half the ship's company—two-thirds of it."

"All right, sir," he replied, with a prodigious yawn. "You an' the lady'll know how to settle this here business of steering."

And off he went.

"You see how obedient these men are, Miss Robertson. Why will you not obey orders, and get some sleep?"

"I have offended you, Mr. Royle, and I am very, very sorry."

"Let us make peace, then," I said, holding out my hand.

She took it; but when I had got her hand, I would not let it go for some moments.

She was leaving the deck in silence, when she came back and said: "If we should have to leave this ship suddenly, I should not like—it would make me unhappy forever to think of poor papa left in her."

She spoke, poor girl! with a great effort.

I answered immediately.

"Any wish you may express shall be carried out."

"He would go down in this ship without a prayer said for him! she exclaimed, sobbing.

"Will you leave this with me? I promise you that no tenderness, no reverence, no sincere sorrow shall be wanting."

"Mr. Royle, you are a dear good friend to me. God knows how lonely I should have been without you; and yet—I made you angry."

"Do not say that. What I do I do for your safety—for your ultimate happiness; so that when we say farewell to each other on shore, I may feel that the trust which God gave me in you was honorably and faithfully discharged. I desire, if our lives are spared, that this memory may follow me when all this scene is changed, and we behold it again only in our dreams. I should have told you my meaning just now, but one cannot always express one's thoughts."

"You have told me your meaning, and I shall not forget it. God bless you!" she implored, in her calm, earnest voice, and went slowly down into the cuddy.

CHAPTER XXVI

THE WIND still continued a brisk gale and the sea very heavy. Yet overhead it was a glorious night; and as the glass had risen steadily, I was surprised to find the wild weather holding on so long.

I busied my head with all kinds of schemes to save the ship, and believed it would be no hard matter to do so if the water did not come into her more quickly than she was now making it.

Unfortunately, there were only two parts of the ship's hold which we could get into—namely, right forward in the fore-peak, and right aft down in the lazarette. If she had strained a butt, or started any part of her planking or outer skin, amid-ships or anywhere in her bottom between these two points, there would be no chance of getting at the leak unless the cargo were slung out of her.

But the leak could not be considered very serious that did not run a greater depth of water into the ship than under a foot an hour; and with the Bermudas close at hand and the weather promising fair, I could still dare to think it possible, despite the hopes, and fears which alternately depressed and elevated me, to bring the vessel to port, all crippled and under-manned as she was.

These speculations kept me busily thinking until half-past eleven, on which I bawled to the steward, who got up and called the boatswain and Cornish, though I only wanted the boatswain. Cornish thought it was midnight and his turn to take the wheel, so he came aft. I resigned my post, being anxious to get on the main-deck, where I found the boatswain in the act of sounding the well, he having lost some time in relighting the lamp, which had burnt out.

He dropped the rod carefully, and found the water thirteen inches deep —that was, nine inches high in the pumps.

"Just what I thought," said he; "she's takin, of it at a foot an hour, no better and no worse."

"Well, we must turn to," I exclaimed. "We mustn't let it above a foot, as every inch will make our work longer and harder."

"If it stops at that, good and well," said the boatswain. "But there's always a hif in these here sinkin' cases. However, there's time enough to croak when the worst happens."

He called to the steward, and we all three went to work and pumped vigorously, and kept the handles grinding and clanking, with now and again a spell of a couple of minutes' rest between, until the pumps gave out the throaty sound which told us that the water was exhausted.

Though this was proved beyond a doubt that, providing the leak remained as it was, we should be able to keep the water under, the prospect before us of having to work the pumps every hour was extremely disheartening; all four of us required sleep to put us right, and already our bones were aching with weariness. Yet it was certain that we should be able to obtain, at the very best, but brief snatches of rest; and I, for one, did not even promise myself so much, for I had strong misgivings as to the condition of the ship's bottom, and was prepared, at any moment, to find the water gaining more rapidly upon us than we could pump it out, though I kept my fears to myself.

I had been on deck now for four hours at one stretch; so, leaving Cornish at the wheel, I lay down on the steward's mattress in the cuddy, while he seated himself on the bench with his head upon the cuddy table, and snored in that posture.

But we were all aroused again within an hour by Cornish, who called to us down the companion, and away we floundered, with our eyes gummed up with sleep, to the pumps, and wearily worked them like miserable automatons.

The dawn found me again at the wheel, having been there half an hour.

I scanned the broken, desolate horizon in the pale light creeping over it, but no ship was in sight. The sea, though not nearly so dangerous as it had been, was terribly sloppy, short, and quick, and tumbled very often over the ship's side, making the decks, with the raffle that encumbered them, look wretched.

I had not had my clothes off me for some days, and the sense of personal discomfort in no small degree aggravated the profound feeling of weariness which ached like rheumatism in my body and absolutely stung in my legs. The skin of my face was hard and dry with long exposure to the terrible wind and the salt water it had blown and dried upon it; and though my underclothing was dry, yet it produced all the sensation of dampness upon my skin, and never in all my life had I felt so uncomfortable, weary and spiritless as I did standing at the wheel when the dawn broke, and I looked abroad upon the rugged fields of water and found no vessel in sight to inspire me with a moment's emotion of hope.

I was replaced at the wheel by the boatswain, and took another turn at the pumps. When this harassing job was ended, I went into the forecastle, making my way thither with much difficulty.

I had a sacred duty to perform, and now that the daylight was come, it was proper I should go to work.

On entering the forecastle, I looked around me on the empty hammocks swinging from the deck, and finding one that looked new and clean, took it down and threw the mattress and blankets out of it and folded it up as a piece of canvas.

I then searched the carpenter's berth for a sail needle, twine, and palm, which things, together with the hammock, I took aft.

On reaching the cuddy, I called Cornish, whose services in this matter I preferred to the steward's, and bade him follow me into the cabin where the old man's body lay.

When there, I closed the door and informed him that we should bury the poor old gentleman when the morning was more advanced, and that I wished him to help me to sew up the body in the hammock.

God knows I had rather that any man should have undertaken this job than I; but it was a duty I was bound to perform, and I desired, for Miss Robertson's sake, that it should be carried out with all the reverence and tenderness that so rude and simple a burial was susceptible of, and nothing done to cause the least violence to her feelings.

We spread the hammock open on the deck, and lifted the body and placed it on the hammock, and rolled a blanket over it. A very great change had come over the face of the corpse since death, and I do not think I should have known it as the kindly, dignified countenance, reverent with its white hair and beard, that had smiled at me from the bunk and thanked me for what I had done.

For what I had done! Alas! how mocking was this memory now! With what painful cynicism did that lonely face illustrate the power of man over the great issues of life and death!

I brought the sides of the hammock to meet over the corpse, and held them while Cornish passed the stitches. I then sent him to find me a big holy-stone or any pieces of iron, so as to sink the body, and he brought some pieces of the stone which I had secured in the clews at the foot of the hammock.

We left the face exposed, and raised the body on to the bunk and covered it over; after which I dispatched Cornish for a carpenter's short-stage I had noticed forward, and which was in use for slinging the men over the ship's side for scraping or painting her. A grating would have answered our purpose better, but the hatches were battened down, the tarpaulins over them, and there was no grating to be got at without leaving the hatchway exposed.

I dressed this short-stage in the big ensign, and placed it on the upper bunk ready to be used, and then told Cornish to stand by with the steward, and went aft and knocked at Miss Robertson's door.

My heart was in my throat, for this mission was even more ungrateful to me than the sewing up of the body had been, and I was afraid that I should not be able to address her tenderly enough, and show her how truly I mourned for and with her.

As I got no answer, I was leaving, wishing her to obtain all the sleep she could; but when I had gone a few paces she came out and followed me.

"Did you knock just now, Mr. Royle?" she asked.

I told her yes, but could not immediately summon up courage enough to tell her why I had knocked.

She looked at me inquiringly, and I began to reproach myself for my weakness, and still I could not address her; but, seeing me glance toward her father's cabin, she understood all on a sudden, and covered her face with her hands.

"I have left his face uncovered for you to kiss," I said, gently laying my hand on her arm.

She went at once into his cabin, and I closed the door upon her and waited outside.

She did not keep me long waiting. I think, brave girl that she was, even amid all her desolating sorrow, that she knew I would wish the burial over, so that we might address ourselves again to the ship.

"I leave him to you now," she said.

I thought she meant that she would not witness the funeral and was glad that she had so resolved, and I accordingly took her hand to lead her away to her cabin.

"Let me be with you!" she exclaimed. "Indeed, indeed, I am strong enough to bear it. I should not be happy if I did not know the moment when he left me, that I might pray to God for him then."

"Be it so," I answered. "I will call you when we are ready."

She left me; and Cornish and the steward and I went into the cabin to complete the mournful preparations.

I cased the body completely in the hammock, and we then raised it up and laid it upon the stage, which we had made to answer for a stretcher, and over it I threw a sheet, so that only the sheet and the ensign were visible.

This done, I consulted with Cornish as to what part of the deck we should choose in order to tilt the body overboard. It is generally the custom to rest the body near the gangway, but the ship was rolling too heavily to enable us to do this now, and the main-deck was afloat; so we decided on carrying the body right aft, and thither we transported it, lodging the foot of the stretcher on the rail abaft the port quarter-boat.

The boatswain removed his hat when he saw the body, and the others imitated him.

I went below and told Miss Robertson that all was ready, and took from among the books belonging to the captain an old thin volume containing the Office for the Burial of Dead at Sea, printed in very large type. It was fortunate that I had noticed this slip of a book when overhauling Captain Coxon's effects, for my own prayer-book did not contain the office, and there was no church service among the captain's books.

I entreated Miss Robertson to reflect before resolving to witness the burial. I told her that her presence could do no good, and faithfully assured her that prayers would be read, and the sad little service conducted as reverently and tenderly as my deep sympathy and the respect which the others felt for her could dictate.

She only answered that it would comfort her to pray for him and herself at the moment he was leaving her, and put her hand into mine, and gently and with tearless eyes, though with a world of sorrow in her beautiful pale face, asked me to take her on deck.

Such grief was not to be argued with—indeed, I felt it would be cruel to oppose any fancy, however strange it seemed to me, which might really solace her.

She started and stopped when she saw the stretcher and the white sheet and the outlines beneath it, and her hand clasped mine tightly; but she recovered herself and we advanced, and then, resolving that she should not see the body leave the stretcher, I procured a flag and placed it near the after sky-light, and said she could kneel there; which she did with her back turned upon us.

I then whispered Cornish to watch me and take note of the sign I should give him to tilt the stretcher, and to do it quickly; after which I placed myself near the body and began to read the service.

It was altogether a strange, impressive scene—one that in a picture would, I am sure, hold the eye for a long time, but in the reality create an ineffaceable memory.

The insecurity—the peril, I should prefer to say—of our situation heightened my own feelings, and made me behold in the corpse we were about to commit to the deep, a sad type and melancholy forerunner of our own end. The ship, with her broken masts, her streaming decks, her jib-boom gone, her one sail swollen by the hoarse gale, lunging and rolling amid the tumultuous seas that foamed around and over her; the strong man

at the wheel, bareheaded, his hair blown about by the wind, looking downward with a face full of blunt and honest sorrow, and his lips moving as they
repeated the words I read; the motionless, kneeling girl; the three of us
standing near the corpse; the still, dead burden on the stretcher, waiting to
be launched; the blue sky and sun kindling into glory as it soared above the
eastern horizon—all these were details which formed a picture the wildness
and strangeness of which no pen could describe. They are all, as a vision,
before me as I write; but they make me know how poor are words, and
eloquence how weak, when great realities and things which have befallen
many men are to be described.

When I came to that part of the office wherein it is directed that the
body shall be let fall into the sea, my heart beat anxiously, for I feared that
the girl would look around and see what was done.

I gave the sign, and instantly Cornish obeyed, and I thank God that the
sullen splash of the corpse was lost in the roar of a sea bursting under the
ship's counter.

Now that it was gone, the worst was over; and in a short time I brought
the service to an end, omitting many portions which assuredly I had not
skipped had not time been precious to us.

I motioned to Cornish and the steward to carry the stretcher away, and
waited for Miss Robertson to rise; she remained for some minutes on her
knees, and when she rose the deck was clear.

She gave me her hand, and smiled softly, though with a heartbroken
expression in her eyes, at the boatswain by way of thanking him for his
sympathy, and I then conducted her below and left her at the door of the
cabin, saying:

"I have no words to tell you how I feel for you. Pray God that those who
are still living may be spared, and be sure that in His own good time He will
comfort you."

CHAPTER XXVII

ALL THAT morning the gale continued fresh and the sea dangerous. We found that the ship was regularly making nine to ten inches of water an hour; and after the funeral we turned to and pumped her out again.

But this heavy work, coupled with our extreme anxiety and the perils and labor we had gone through, was beginning to tell heavily upon us. The steward showed signs of what strength he had coming to an end, and Cornish's face had a worn and wasted look, as of a man who had fasted long. The boatswain supported this fatigue best, and always went cheerfully to work, and had encouraging words for us all. As for me, what I suffered most from was, strange to say, the eternal rolling of the ship. At times it completely nauseated me. Also it gave me a racking headache, and occasionally the motion so bewildered me that I was obliged to sit down and hold my head in my hands until the dizziness had passed.

I believe this feeling was the result of overwork, long wakefulness, and preying anxiety which was hourly sapping my constitution. Yet I was generally relieved by even a quarter of an hour's sleep, but presently was troubled again, and I grew to dread the time when I should take the wheel, for right aft the motion of the ship was intensely felt by me, so much so that on that morning, the vessel's stern falling heavily into a hollow, I nearly fainted, and only saved myself from rolling on the deck by clinging convulsively to the wheel.

At a quarter past eleven I had just gone into the cuddy, after having had an hour's spell at the pumps with the boatswain and the steward, when I heard Cornish's voice shouting down the companion, "A sail! A sail!"

But a minute before I had felt so utterly prostrated that I should not have believed myself capable of taking half a dozen steps without a long rest between each. Yet those magical words sent me rushing up the companion-ladder with as much speed and energy as I should have been capable of after a long night's refreshing slumber.

The moment Cornish saw me he pointed like a madman to the horizon on the weather-beam, and the ship's stern rising at that moment, I clearly beheld the sails of a vessel, though in what direction she was going I could not tell by the naked eye.

Both the boatswain and the other had come running aft on hearing Cornish's exclamation, and the steward, in the madness of his eagerness, had swung himself on to the mizzen rigging, and stood there bawling, "Yonder's the ship! yonder's the ship! Come up here, and you'll see her plain enough!"

I got the telescope and pointed it at the vessel, and found that she was heading directly for us, steering due south, with the gale upon her starboard quarter.

On this I cried out, "She's coming slap at us, boys! Hurrah! Cornish, you were the first to see her; thank you! thank you!"

I grasped his hand and shook it wildly. I then seized the telescope and inspected the vessel again, and exclaimed, while I held the glass to my eye:

"She's a big ship, bo's'n. She's carrying a main-top-gallant-sail, and there's a single reef in her fore-top-sail. She can't miss us! She's coming right at us, hand over fist, boys! Steward, go and tell Miss Robertson to come on deck. Down with you, and belay that squalling! Do you think we're blind?"

The small ensign was still alive, roaring away just as we had hoisted and left it; but in my excitement I did not think the signal importunate enough, though surely it was so; and rushing to the flag-locker, I got out the book of signals, and sung out to the boatswain to help me to bend on the flags which I threw out, and which would represent that we were sinking.

We hauled the ensign down and ran up the string of flags, and glorious they looked in our eyes, as they streamed out in a semi-circle, showing their brilliant colors against the clear blue sky.

Again I took the telescope, and set it on the rail, and knelt to steady myself.

The hull of the ship was now half risen, and as she came rolling and plunging over the seas I could discern the vast space of froth she was throwing up at her bows. Dead on as she was, we could not tell whether she had hoisted any flag at her peak, and I hoped, in mercy to us, that she would send up an answering pennant to the royal-mast-head, so that we might see it and know that our signal was perceived.

But this was a foolish hope, only such a one as bitter, eager anxiety could coin. She was coming right at us; she *could* not fail to see us; what need to answer us yet, when a little patience, only a little patience, and she would be within a biscuit's throw of us?

Miss Robertson came on deck without any covering on her head, and the wind blew her hair away from its fastenings and floated it out like a cloud of gold. She held on to the rail and stared at the coming ship with wide eyes and a frowning forehead; while the steward, who had fallen crazy with the sight of the ship, clambered once more into the mizzen rigging, and shouted and beckoned to the vessel as a little child would.

It did not take me long, however, to recover my own reason, the more especially as I felt we might require all the sense we had when the ship rounded and hove to. I could not, indeed, hope that they would send a boat through such a sea; they would lie by us and send a boat when the sea moderated, which, to judge by the barometer and the high and beaming sky, we might expect to find that night or next morning; and then we should require our senses, not only to keep the pumps going, but to enter the boat calmly and in an orderly way, and help our rescuers to save our lives.

The boatswain leaned against the companion-hatchway with his arms folded, contemplating the approaching ship with a wooden face. Variously and powerfully as the spectacle of the vessel had affected Cornish and Miss Robertson, and myself and the steward, on the boatswain it had scarcely produced any impression.

I know not what kind of misgiving came into my mind as I looked from the coming ship to his stolid face.

I had infinite confidence in this man's judgment and bravery, and his lifelessness on this occasion weighted down upon me like a heavy presentiment, in so much that the cheery, congratulatory words about to address to Miss Robertson died away on my lips.

I should say that we had sighted this vessel's upper sails when she was about seventeen miles distant, and, therefore, coming down upon us before a strong wind, and helped onward by the long running seas, in less than half an hour her whole figure was plain to us upon the water.

I examined her carefully through the glass, striving to make out her nationality by the cut of her aloft. I thought she had the look of a Scotch ship, her hull being after the pattern of the Aberdeen clippers, such as I remembered them in the Australian trade, painted green, and she was also rigged with sky-sail-poles and a great breadth of canvas.

I handed the glass to the boatswain, and asked him what country he took her to be of. After inspecting her, he said he did not think she was

English; the color of her canvas looked foreign, but it was hard to tell; we should see her colors presently.

As she approached, Miss Robertson's excitement grew very great; not demonstrative—I mean, she did not cry out nor gesticulate like the steward in the rigging; it was visible, like a kind of madness, in her eyes, in her swelling bosom, in a strange, wonderful, brilliant smile upon her face, such as a great actress might wear in a play, but which we who observed it know to be forced and unreal.

I ran below for the fur cap and coat, and made her put them on, and then drew her away from the ship's side and kept close to her, even holding her by the hand for some time, for I could not tell what effect the sight of the ship might produce upon her mind, already stung and weakened by privations and cruel sorrow and peril.

The vessel came rolling and plunging down toward us before the wind, carrying a sea on either quarter as high as her main-brace bumpkins, and spreading a great surface of foam before and around her.

When she was about a couple of miles off they let go the main-top-gallant-halyards and clewed up the sail; and then the helm was star-boarded, which brought her bows astern of us and gave her a sheer, by which we saw that she was a fine bark of at least eight hundred tons burden.

At the same moment she hoisted Russian colors.

I was bitterly disappointed when I saw that flag. I should have been equally disappointed by the sight of any other foreign flag, unless it were the Stars and Stripes, which floats over brave hearts, and is a signal to Englishmen as full of welcome and promise, almost, as their own loved bit of bunting.

I had hoped, God knows how earnestly, that we should behold the English ensign at the gaff-end. Our chances of rescue by a British ship were fifty to one as against our chances of rescue by a foreigner. Cases, indeed, have been known of ships commanded by Englishmen sighting vessels in distress and leaving them to their fate; but, to the honor and glory of our calling, I say that these cases make so brief a list that no impartial-minded man will allow them to weight with him a moment when he considers the vast number of instances of pluck, humanity, and heroism which illustrate and adorn the story of British naval life.

It is otherwise with foreigners. I write not with any foolish insular prejudice against wooden shoes and continental connections: we can not dispute good evidence. Though I believe that the Russians make fair soldiers and fight bravely on sea, why was it that my heart sank when I saw that flag? I say that the British flag is an assurance to all distressed persons that what can be done for them will be done for them; and foreigners know this well, and would sooner sight it when they are in peril than their own colors, be those colors Dutch, or French, or Spanish, or Danish, or Italian, or Russian. But he must be a confident man indeed who hopes anything from a vessel sailing under a foreign flag when life is to be saved at the risk of the lives of the rescuers.

"He's goin' to round to!" exclaimed the boatswain, who watched the movements of the ship with an unconcern absolutely phenomenal to me even to recall now, when I consider that the lives of us all might have depended upon the stranger's actions.

She went gracefully swooping and swashing along the water, and I saw the hands upon the deck aft standing by at the main-brace to back the yards.

"Bo's'n," I cried, "she means to heave to—she won't leave us."

He made no answer, but continued watching her with an immovable face.

She passed under our stem not more than a quarter of a mile distant, perhaps not so far. There was a crowd of persons near the wheel, some looking at us through binocular glasses, others through telescopes. There were a few women and children among them.

Yet I could detect no hurry, no eagerness, no excitement in their movements; they appeared as imperturbable as Turks or Hollanders, contemplating us as though we were rather an object of curiosity than in miserable, perishing distress.

I jumped upon the grating abaft the wheel, and waved my hat to them and pointed to our signals. A man standing near their starboard quarter-boat, whom, by the way he looked aloft, I judged to be the captain, flourished his hand in reply.

I then, at the top of my voice and through my hands shouted, "We're sinking! for God's sake stand by us!" On which the same person held up his hand again, though I do not believe he understood or even heard what I said.

Meanwhile they had braced up the fore-yards, and as the vessel came round parallel with us, at a distance of about two-thirds of a mile, they backed the main-yards, and in a few moments she lay steady, riding finely upon the water and keeping her decks dry, though the seas were still splashing over us freely.

Seeing now, as I believed, that she meant to stand by us, all my excitement broke out afresh. I cried out that we were saved, and fell upon my knees and thanked God for his mercy. Miss Robertson sobbed aloud, and the steward came down out of the rigging and danced about the deck, exclaiming wildly and extending his arms toward ship. Cornish retained his grasp of the wheel, but could not move his eyes from the ship; the boatswain alone remained perfectly tranquil, still, and even angered me by his hard, unconcerned face.

"Good God!" I cried, "do you not value your life? Have you nothing to say? See, she is lying there, and will wait till the sea moderates, and then fetch us on board."

"Perhaps she may," he answered, "and it'll be time enough for me to go mad when I *am* saved."

And he then folded his arms afresh, and leaned against the rail, contemplating the ship with the same extraordinary indifference.

They now hauled down the flag, and I waited anxiously to see if they would hoist the answering pennant to let us know they understood our signal; but they made no further sign that way, nor could I be sure, therefore, that they understood the flags we hoisted; for though in those days Marryat's Code was in use among ships of all nations, yet it often happened (as it does now) that vessels, both British and foreign, would, through the meanness of their owners, be sent to sea with merely the flags indicating their own number on board, so that speaking one of these vessels was like addressing a dumb person.

The movements of the people on the Russian bark were quite discernible by the naked eye; and we all now, saving the boatswain, watched her with wrapt eagerness, the steward stopping his mad antics to grasp the poop-rail and gaze with devouring eyes.

We did not know what they would do, and, indeed, we scarcely knew what we had to expect; for it was plain to us all that a boat would stand but a poor chance in that violent sea, and that we should run a greater risk of losing our lives by quitting the ship than by staying in her.

But would they not give us some sign, some assurance, that they meant to stand by us?

The agony of my doubts of their intentions was exquisite.

For some time she held her ground right abreast of us; but our topsail being full, while the Russian was actually hove to, we slowly began to reach ahead of her.

Seeing this I cried out to Cornish to put the helm hard down, and keep the sail flat at the leech; but he had already anticipated this order, though it was a useless one; for the ship came to and fell off with every sea, though the helm was hard down; and before we could have got her to behave as we wished, we should have been obliged to clap some after-sail upon her, which I did not dare do, as we had only choice of the mizzen and cross-jack, and either of these sails (both being large) would probably have slued her head round into the sea, and thrown her dead and useless on our hands.

Seeing that we were slowly bringing the Russian on to our lee quarter, I called out, in the hope of encouraging the others, "No matter! she will let us draw ahead, and then shorten sail and stand after us."

"Are they goin' to lower that boat?" exclaimed the boatswain, suddenly starting out of his apathetic manner.

There was a crowd of men round the starboard davits where the quarter-boat hung, but it was not until I brought the telescope to bear upon them that I could see they were holding an animated discussion.

The man who had motioned to us, and whom I took to be master of the ship, stood aft, in company with two others and a woman, and gesticulated very vehemently, sometimes pointing at us and sometimes at the sea.

His meaning was intelligible enough to me, but I was not disheartened; for though it was plain that he was representing the waves as too rough to permit them to lower a boat, which was a conclusive sign, at least, that those whom he addressed were urging him to save us, yet his refusal was no proof that he did not mean to keep by us until it should be safe to send a boat to our ship.

"What will they do, Mr. Royle?" exclaimed Miss Robertson, speaking in a voice sharpened by the terrible excitement under which she labored.

"They will not leave us," I answered. "They are men—and it is enough that they should have seen you among us to make them stay. Oh!" I cried, "it is hard that those waves do not subside! But patience! The wind is lulling—we have a long spell of daylight before us. Would to God she were an English ship! I should have no fear then." I again pointed the glass at the vessel.

The captain was still declaiming and gesticulating; but the men had withdrawn from the quarter-boat, and were watching us over the bulwarks. Since the boat was not to be lowered, why did he continue arguing?

I watched him intently, watched him until my eyes grew bleared and the metal rim of the telescope seemed to burn into the flesh around my eye.

I put the glass down, and turned to glance at the flags streaming over my head.

"There she goes! I knew it! They never shows no pity!" exclaimed the boatswain, in a deep voice.

I looked and saw the figures of the men hauling on the lee main-braces.

The yards swung round; the vessel's head paid off; they squared away forward, and in a few minutes her stern was at us, and she went away, solemnly rolling and plunging; the main-top-gallant-sail being sheeted home and the yard hoisted as she surged forward on her course.

We remained staring after her—no one speaking—no one believing in the reality of what he beheld.

Of all the trials that had befallen us, this was the worst.

Of all the terrible, cruel disappointments that can afflict suffering people, none, *none* in all the hideous catalogue, is more deadly, more unendurable, more frightful to endure, than that which it was our doom then to feel. To witness our salvation at hand and then to miss it; to have been buoyed up with hope unspeakable; to taste, in the promise of rescue, the joy of renovated life; to believe that our suffering was at an end, and that in a short time we should be among sympathetic rescuers, looking back with shudders upon the perils from which we had been snatched—to have felt all this, and then to be deceived!

I thought my heart would burst. I tried to speak, but my tongue clove to the roof of my mouth.

When the steward saw that we were abandoned he uttered a loud scream and rushed headlong down into the cuddy.

I took no notice of him.

Cornish ran from the wheel, and, springing on to the rail, shook his fist at the departing vessel, raving, and cursing her with horrible blasphemous words, black in the face with his mad and, useless rage.

The boatswain took his place, and grasped the wheel, never speaking a word.

I was aroused from the stupor that had come over me, the effect of excessive emotion, by Miss Robertson putting her hand in mine.

"Be brave!" she whispered, with her mouth close to my ear. "God is with us still. My dead father would not deceive me. We shall be saved yet. Have courage, and be your own true self again."

I looked into her shining eyes, out of which all the excitement that had fired them while the Russian remained hove to had departed. There was a beautiful tranquillity, there was a courage Heaven-inspired, there was a soft and hopeful smile upon her pale face, which fell upon the tempest in my breast and stilled it.

God had given her this influence over me, and I yielded to it as though He himself had commended me.

All her own troubles came before me, all her own bitter trials, her miserable bereavement; and as I heard her sweet voice bidding me have courage, and beheld her smiling upon me out of her deep faith in her simple, sacred dream, I caught up both her hands and bent my head over them and wept.

"Cornish!" I cried, recovering myself, and seizing the man by the arm as he stood shouting at the fast-lessening ship, "what is the use of those oaths? Let them go their ways—the pitiless cowards! We are Englishmen, and our lives are still our own. Come, brave companions we have all undergone too much to permit this trial to break us. See this lady! she swears that we shall be saved yet. Be of her heart and mind and the bo's'n there, and help us to make another fight for it. Come!"

He suffered me to pull him off his perilous perch, and then sat himself down upon a coil of rope, trembling all over, and hid his face in his hands.

But a new trouble awaited me.

At this moment the steward came staggering up the companion-ladder, his face purple, his eyes protruding, and talking loudly and incoherently. He clasped the sea-chest belonging to himself, which certainly was of greater weight than he in his enfeebled state would have been able to bear had he not been mad. The chest was corded, and he had no doubt packed it.

He rushed to the ship's side and pitched it overboard, and was in the act of springing on to the rail, meaning to fling himself into the sea, when I caught hold of him, and, using more force than I was conscious of, dragged him backward so violently that his head struck the deck like a cannon shot, and he lay motionless and insensible.

"That's the best thing that could have happened to him," exclaimed the boatswain. "Let him lie a bit. He'll come to and may be leave his craze behind him. It wouldn't be the fust time I've seen a daft man knocked sensible."

And then, coolly biting a chew out of a stick of tobacco, which he very carefully replaced in his breeches pocket, he added:

"Jim, come and lay hold of this here wheel, will yer, while me and Mr. Royle pumps the ship out?"

Cornish got up and took the boatswain's place.

"I can help you to pump, Mr. Royle," said Miss Robertson.

The boatswain laughed.

"Lor' bless your dear 'art, miss, what next?" he cried. "No, no; you stand by here ready to knock this steward down ag'in if he shows hisself anxious to swim arter the Roosian. We'll see what water the ship's a-makin'; and if she shows herself obstinate, as I rayther think she will, why, we'll all turn to and leave her. For you've got to deal with a bad ship as you would with a bad wife: use every genteel persuasion fust; and if that won't alter her, there's nothen for it but to grease your boots, oil your hair, and po-litely walk out."

CHAPTER XXVIII

THERE BEING but two of us now to work the pumps, it was more than we could do to keep them going. We plied them, with a brief spell between, and then my arms fell to my side, and I told the boatswain I could pump no more.

He sounded the well and made six inches.

"There's only two inches left that we can get out of her," said he; "and they'll do no harm."

On which we quitted the main-deck and came into the cuddy.

"Mr. Royle," he said, seating himself on the edge of the table, "we shall have to leave this ship if we aren't taken off her. I reckon it'll require twelve feet o' water to sink her, allowin' for there being a deal o' wood in the cargo; and may be she won't go down at that. However, we'll say twelve feet, and supposin' we lets her be she'll give us, if you like, eight or nine hours afore settlin'. I'm not saying as we ought to leave her; but I'm lookin' at you, sir, and see that you're very nigh knocked up; Cornish is about a quarter o' the man he was; an' as to the bloomin' steward, he's as good as drowned, no better and no worse. We shall take one spell too many at them pumps and fall down under it an' never get up agin. Wot we had best do is to keep a look all around for wessels, get that there quarter-boat ready for lowerin', and stand by to leave the ship when the sea calms. You know how Bermuda bears, don't you, sir?"

"I can find out to-night. It is too late to get sights now."

"I think," he returned "that our lives'll be as safe in the boat as they are on board this ship, an' a trifle safer. I've been watching this wessel a good deal, and my belief is that wos another gale to strike her, she'd make one o' her long plunges and go to pieces like a pack o' cards, when she got to the bottom o' the walley o' water. Of course if this sea don't calm we must make shift to keep her afloat until it do. You'll excuse me for talkin' as though I wos dictatin'. I'm just givin' you the thoughts that come into my head while we wos pumpin'."

"I quite agree with you," I replied; "I am only thinking of the size of the quarter-boat—whether she isn't too small for five persons?"

"Not she! I'll get a bit of a mast rigged up in her, and it'll go hard if we don't get four miles an hour out of her somehows. How far might the Bermuda Islands be off?"

I answered, after reflecting some moments, that they would probably be distant from the ship between two hundred and fifty and three hundred miles.

"We should get pretty near 'em in three days," said he, "if the wind blew that way. Will you go an' tell the young lady what we're thinkin' o' doin', while I overhauls the boat an' see what's wantin' in her? One good job is, we sha'n't have to put off, through the ship's sinkin' all a heap. There's a long warning given us, and I can't help thinkin' that the stormy weather's blown hisself out, for the sky looks to me to have a regular-set fair blue in it."

He went on to the main-deck. I inspected the glass, which I found had risen since I last looked at it. This, coupled with the brilliant sky and glorious sunshine and the diminishing motion of the ship, cheered me somewhat, though I looked forward with misgiving to leaving the ship, having upon me the memory of sufferings endured by ship-wrecked men in this lonely condition, and remembering that Mary Robertson would be one of us, and have to share in any privations that might befall us.

At the same time, it was quite clear to me that the boatswain, Cornish, and myself, would never, with our failing strength, be able to keep the ship afloat; and for Miss Robertson's sake, therefore, it was our duty to put a cheerful face upon the melancholy alternative.

When I reached the poop, the first thing I beheld was the Russian bark, now a square of gleaming white upon the southern horizon.

I quickly averted my eyes from the shameful object, and saw that the steward had recovered from his swoon, and was squatting against the companion, counting his fingers and smiling at them.

Miss Robertson was steering the ship, while Cornish lay extended along the deck, his head pillowed on a flag.

The wind (as by the appearance of the weather I might have anticipated, had my mind been free to speculate on such things) had dropped suddenly, and was now a gentle breeze, and the sea was subsiding rapidly. Indeed, a most golden, glorious afternoon had set in, with a promise of a hot and breathless night.

I approached Miss Robertson, and asked her what was the matter with Cornish.

"I noticed him reeling at the wheel," she answered, "with his face quite white. I put a flag for his head, and told him to lie down. I called to you, but you did not hear me; and I have been waiting to see you that you might get him some brandy."

I found that the boatswain had not yet come aft, and at once went below to procure a dram for Cornish. I returned and knelt by his side, and was startled to perceive that his eyeballs were turned up, and his hands and teeth clinched, as though he were convulsed. Sharp tremors ran through his body, and he made no reply nor appeared to hear me, though I called his name several times.

Believing that he was dying, I shouted to the boatswain, who came immediately.

The moment he looked at Cornish he uttered an exclamation.

"God knows what ails the poor creature!" I cried. "Lift his head that I may put some brandy into his mouth."

The boatswain raised him by the shoulders, but his head hung back like a dead man's. I drew out my knife and inserted the blade between his teeth, and by this means contrived to introduce some brandy into his mouth, but it bubbled back again, which was a terrible sign, I thought; and still the tremors shook his poor body, and the eyes remained upturned, making the face most ghastly to see.

"It's his heart broke!" exclaimed the boatswain, in a tremulous voice. "Jim! what's the matter with 'ee, mate? You're not goin' to let the sight o' that Roosian murderer kill you? Come, come! God Almighty knows we've all had a hard fight for it, but we're not beat yet, lad. 'Tis but another spell o' waitin', and it'll come right presently. Don't let a gale o' wind knock the breath out o' you. What man as goes to sea but meets with reverses like this here? Swaller the brandy, Jim! My God, Mr. Royle, he's dyin'!"

As he said this Cornish threw up his arms and stiffened out his body. So strong was his dying action that he knocked the glass of brandy out of my hand and threw me backward some paces. The pupils of his eyes rolled down and a film came over them; he uttered something in a hoarse whisper, and lay dead on the boatswain's knee.

I glanced at Miss Robertson. Her lips were tightly compressed, otherwise the heroic girl showed no emotion.

The boatswain drew a deep breath, and let the dead man's head fall gently on the flag.

"For Miss Robertson's sake," I whispered, "let us carry him forward."

He acquiesced in silence, and we bore the body off the poop and laid it on the fore-hatch.

"There will be no need to bury him," said I.

"No need and no time, sir. I trust God'll be merciful to the poor sailor when he's called up. He was made bad by them others, sir. His heart wasn't wrong," replied the boatswain.

I procured a blanket from the forecastle and covered the body with it, and we then walked back to the poop slowly and without speaking.

I felt the death of this man keenly. He had worked well, confronted danger cheerfully; he had atoned, in his untutored fashion, for the wrongs he had taken part in; besides, the fellowship of peril was a tie upon us all, not to be sundered without a pang, which our hearts never would have felt had fate dealt otherwise with us.

I stopped a moment with the boatswain to look at the steward before joining Miss Robertson. To many, I believe, this spectacle of idiocy would have been more affecting than Cornish's death. He was tracing figures, such as circles and crosses, with his forefinger on the deck, and smiling vacantly meanwhile, and now and then looking around him with rolling, unmeaning eyes.

"How is it with you, my man?" I said.

He gazed at me very earnestly, rose to his feet, and taking my arm, drew me a short distance away from the boatswain.

"A ship passed us just now, sir," he exclaimed, in a whisper, and with a profoundly confidential air. "Did you see her?"

"Yes, steward, I saw her."

"A word in your ear, sir—*mum!* that's the straight tip. Do you see? I was tired of this ship, sir—tired of being afraid of drowning. I put myself on board that vessel, *and there I am now, sir.* But hush! do you know I cannot talk to them—they're furriners! Roosians, sir, by the living cock!—that's my oath—and it crows every morning in my back garden."

He struck me softly on the waistcoat, and fell back a step, with his finger on his lip.

"Ah," said I, "I understand. Sit down again and go on drawing on the deck, and then they'll think you're lost in study and not trouble you."

"Right, my lord—your lordship's 'umble servant," answered the poor creature, making me a low bow; and with a lofty and dignified air he resumed his place on the deck near the companion.

"Wot was he sayin'?" inquired the boatswain.

"He is quite imbecile. He thinks he is on board the Russian," I replied.

"Well, that's a comfort," said the boatswain. "He'll not be tryin' to swim arter her agin."

"Miss Robertson," I exclaimed, "you need not remain at the wheel. There is so little wind now that the ship may be left to herself."

Saying which I made the wheel fast and led her to one of the sky-lights.

"Bo's'n," said I, "will you fetch us something to eat and drink out of the pantry? Open a tin of meat, and get some biscuit and wine. This may be our last meal on board the 'Grosvenor,'" I added, to Miss Robertson, as the boatswain left us.

She looked at me inquiringly, but did not speak.

"Before we knew," I continued, "that poor Cornish was dying, the boatswain and I resolved that we should all of us leave the ship. We have no longer the strength to man the pumps. The water is coming in at the rate of a foot an hour, and we have found latterly that even three of us cannot pump more at a time out of her than six or seven inches, and every spell at the pumps leaves us more exhausted. But even though we had hesitated to leave her, yet, now that Cornish is gone and the steward has fallen imbecile, we have no alternative."

"I understand," she said, glancing at the boat and compressing her lips.

"You are not afraid—you who have shown more heart and courage than all of us put together?"

"No—I am not much afraid. I believe that God is looking down upon us and that He will preserve us. But," she cried, taking a short breath, and clasping her hands convulsively, "it will be very, very lonely on the great sea in that little boat."

"Why more lonely in that little boat than on this broken and sinking ship? I believe, with you, that God is looking down upon us, and He has given us that pure and beautiful sky as an encouragement and a promise. Contrast the sea now with what it was this morning. In a few hours hence it will be calm; and believe me when I say that we shall be a thousand-fold safer in that boat than we are in this strained and leaking ship. Even while we talk now the water is creeping into the hold, and every hour will make her sink deeper and deeper until she disappears beneath the surface. On the other hand, we may have many days together of this fine weather. I will steer the boat for the Bermuda Islands, which we can not miss by heading the boat west, even if I should lack the means of ascertaining our exact whereabouts, which you may trust me will not be the case. Moreover, the chance of our being rescued by a passing ship will be much greater when we are in the boat than it is while we remain here; for no ship, though she were commanded by a savage, would refuse to pick a boat up and take its occupants on board; whereas vessels, as we have already seen to our cost, will sight distressed ships and leave them to shift for themselves."

"I do not doubt you are right," she replied, with a plaintive smile. "I should not say or do anything to oppose you. And believe me," she exclaimed, earnestly, "that I do not think more of my own life than that of my companions. Death is not so terrible but that we may meet it if God wills, calmly. And I would rather die at once, Mr. Royle, than win a few short years of life on hard and bitter terms."

She looked at the steward as she spoke, and an expression of beautiful pity came into her face.

"Miss Robertson," I said, "in my heart I am pledged to save your life. If you die, we both die!—of that be sure."

"I know what I owe you," she answered, in a low and broken voice. "I know that my life is yours, won by you from the very jaws of death, soothed and supported by you afterward. What my gratitude is only God knows. I have no words to tell you."

"Do you give me the life I have saved?" I asked, wondering at my own breathless voice as I questioned her.

"I do," she replied, firmly, lifting up her eyes and looking at me.

"Do you give it to me because your sweet and generous gratitude makes you think it my due—not knowing I am poor, not remembering that my station in life is humble, without a question as to my past?"

"I give it to you because I love you!" she answered, extending her hand.

I drew her toward me and kissed her forehead.

"God bless you, Mary, darling, for your faith in me! God bless you for your priceless gift of your love to me! Living or dead, dearest, we are one!"

And she, as though to seal these words, which our danger invested with an entrancing mysteriousness, raised my hand to her spotless lips, and then held it some moments to her heart.

The boatswain, coming up the poop-ladder, saw her holding my hand. He approached us slowly and in silence; and, putting down the tray, which he had heaped, with sailor-like profusion, with food enough for a dozen persons, stood looking on us thoughtfully.

"Mr. Royle," he said, in a deliberate voice, "you'll excuse me sayin' of it, but, sir, you've found her out?"

"I have, bo's'n."

"You've found her out, sir, as the truest-hearted gell as ever did duty as a darter?"

"I have."

"I've watched her, and know her to be British—true oak, seasoned by God Almighty, as does this sort o' work better nor Time! You've found her out, sir?"

"It is true, bo's'n."

"And you, miss," he exclaimed, in the same deliberate voice, "have found *him* out."

She looked downward with a blush.

"Mr. Royle, and you, miss," he continued, "I'm not goin' to say nothen agin this being the right time to find each other out in. It's Almighty Providence as brings these here matters to pass, and it's in times o' danger as love speaks out strongest, turnin' the heart into a speakin'-trumpet and hailin' with a loud and tremendous voice. Wot I wur goin' to say is this: that in Mr. Royle I've seen the love for a long while past burnin' and strugglin', and sometimes hidin' of itself, and then burstin' up afresh like a flare aboard o' a sinkin' ketch on a windy night; and in you, miss, I've likewise seen tokens as 'ud ha' made me up and speak my joy days an' days ago, had it been *my* consarn to attend to 'em. I say, that now as we're sinkin' without at all meanin' to drown, with no wun but God Almighty to see us, this is the properest time for you to have found each other out in. Mr. Royle, your hand, sir; miss, yours. I say, God bless you! While we have breath we'll keep the boat afloat; and if it's not to be, still I'll say, God bless you!"

He shook us heartily by the hand, looked hard at the poor steward, as though he would shake hands with him too; then walked aft, hauled down the signals, stepped into the cuddy, returned with the large ensign, bent it on to the halyards, and ran it up to the gaff-end.

"That," said he, returning and looking up proudly at the flag, "is to let them as it may consarn know that we're not dead yet. Now, sir, shall I pipe to dinner?"

CHAPTER XXIX

I THINK the boatswain was right.

It was no season for love-making; but it was surely a fitting moment "for finding each other out in."

I can say this—and God knows, never was there less bombast in such a thought than there was in mine—that when I looked round upon the sea and then upon my beloved companion, I felt that I would rather have chosen death, with her love to bless me in the end, than life without knowledge of her.

I put food before the steward and induced him to eat; but it was pitiful to see his silly, instinctive ways—no reason in them, nothing but a mechanical guiding, with foolish, fleeting smiles upon his pale face.

I thought of that wife of his whose letter he had wept over, and his child, and scarcely knew whether it would not have been better for him and them that he should have died than return to them a broken-down, puling imbecile.

I said as much to Mary, but the tender heart would not agree with me.

"While there is life there is hope," she answered, softly. "Should God permit us to reach home, I will see that the poor fellow is well cared for. It may be that when all these horrors have passed, his mind will recover its strength. Our trials are *very* hard. When I saw that Russian ship, I thought my own brain would go."

She pressed her hand to her forehead, and an expression of suffering, provoked by memory, came into her face.

We dispatched our meal, and I went on to the main-deck to sound the well. I found two feet of water in the hold, and I came back and gave the boatswain the soundings, who recommended that we should at once turn to and get the boat ready.

I said to him, as he clambered into the boat for the purpose of over-hauling her, that I fully believed that a special Providence was watching over us, and that we might confidently hope God would not abandon us now.

"If the men had not chased us in this boat," I continued, "what chance should we have to save our lives? The other boat is useless, and we should never have been able to repair her in time to get away from the ship. Then look at the weather! I have predicted a dead calm to-night, and already the wind is gone."

"Yes, everything's happened for the best," he replied. "I only wish poor Jim's life had been saved. It's a'most like leavin' of him to drown, to go away without buryin' him; and yet I know there'd be no use in puttin' him over-board. There's been a deal o' precious human life wasted since we left the Channel; and who are the murderers? Why, the owners. It's all come of their sendin' the ship to sea with rotten stores. A few dirty pounds 'ud ha' saved all this."

We had never yet had the leisure to inspect the stores with which the mutineers had furnished the quarter-boat, and we now found, in spite of their having shifted a lot of provisions out of her into the long-boat before starting in pursuit of us, that there was still an abundance left: four kegs of water, several tins of cuddy bread, preserved meats and fruits, sugar, flour, and other things, not to mention such items as boxes of lucifer matches, fishing-tackle, a burning glass, a quantity of tools and nails; in a word, every-thing which men in the condition they had hoped to find themselves in might stand in need of to support life. Indeed, the foresight illustrated by the provisioning of this boat was truly remarkable, the only things they had omitted being a mast and sail, it having been their intention to keep this boat in tow of the other. I even found that they had furnished the boat with the oars belonging to the disabled quarter-boat in addition to her own.

However, the boat was not yet stocked to my satisfaction. I therefore repaired to my cabin and procured the boat's compass, some charts, a sextant, and other necessary articles, such as the "Nautical Almanac," and pencils and paper wherewith to work out my observations, which I placed very carefully in the locker in the stern-sheets of the boat.

I allowed Mary to help me, that the occupation might divert her mind from the overwhelming thoughts which the gradual settling of the ship on which we stood must have excited in the strongest and bravest mind; and, indeed, I worked busily and eagerly to guard myself against any terror that might come upon me. She it was who suggested that we should provide ourselves with lamps and oil; and I shipped a lantern to hoist at our mast-head when the darkness came, and the bull's-eye lamp to enable me to work out my observations of the stars, which I intended to make when the night fell. To all these things, which sounded numerous, but in reality occupied but little space, I added a can of oil, meshes for the lamps, top-coats, oilskins, and rugs to protect us at night, so that the afternoon was well advanced before we had ended our preparations. Meanwhile, the boatswain had stepped a top-gallant-stun'sail boom to serve us for a mast, well stayed, with a block and halyards at the masthead to serve for hoisting a flag or lantern, and a spare top-gallant-stun'sail to act as a sail.

By this time the wind had completely died away; a peaceful deep blue sky stretched from horizon to horizon; and the agitation of the sea had subsided into a long and silent swell, which washed up against the ship's sides, scarcely causing her to roll, so deep had she sunk in the water.

I now thought it high time to lower the boat and bring her alongside, as our calculation of the length of time to be occupied by the ship in sinking might be falsified to our destruction by her suddenly going stern down with us on board.

We therefore lowered the boat, and got the gangway-ladder over the side.

The boatswain got into the boat first to help Mary into her. I then took the steward by the arms and brought him along smartly, as there was danger in keeping the boat washing against the ship's side. He resisted at first, and only smiled vacantly when I threatened to leave him; but on the boatswain crying out that his wife was waiting for him, the poor idiot got himself together with a scramble, and went so hastily over the gangway that he narrowly escaped a ducking.

I paused a moment at the gangway and looked around, striving to remember if there was anything we had forgotten which would be of some
use to us. Mary watched me anxiously, and called to me by my Christian
name, at the same time extending her arms. I would not keep her in suspense a moment, and at once dropped into the boat. She grasped and
fondled my hand, and drew me close beside her.

"I should have gone on board again had you delayed coming," she whispered.

The boatswain shoved the boat's head off, and we each shipped an oar
and pulled the boat about a quarter of a mile away from the ship; and then,
from a strange and wild curiosity to behold the ship sink, and still in our
hearts clinging to her, not only as the home where we had found shelter for
many days past, but as the only visible object in all the stupendous reach of
waters, we threw in the oars and sat watching her.

She had now sunk as deep as her main-chains, and was but a little
higher out of the water than the hull from which we had rescued Mary and
her father. It was strange to behold her even from a short distance and notice her littleness in comparison with the immensity of the deep on which
she rested, and recall the terrible seas she had braved and triumphed over.

Few sailors can behold the ship in which they have sailed sinking before their eyes without the same emotion of distress and pity, almost, which
the spectacle of a drowning man excites in them. She has grown a familiar
name, a familiar object; thus far she has borne them in safety; she has been
rudely beaten and yet has done her duty; but the tempest has broken her
down at last; all the beauty is shorn from her; she is weary with the long and
dreadful struggles with the vast forces that nature arrayed against her; she
sinks, a desolate, abandoned thing, in mid-ocean, carrying with her a thousand memories which surge up in the heart with the pain of a strong man's
tears.

I looked from the ship to realize our own position. Perhaps not yet
could it be keenly felt, for the ship was still a visible object for us to hold on
by; and yet, turning my eyes away to the far reaches of the horizon at one
moment borne high on the summit of the ocean swell, which appeared
mountainous when felt in and viewed from the boat, then sinking deep in
the hollow, so that the near ship was hidden from us—the supreme loneli-

ness of our situation, our helplessness, and the fragility and diminutiveness of the structure on which our lives depended, came home to me with the pain and wonder of a shock.

Our boat, however, was new this voyage, with a good beam, and showing a tolerably bold side, considering her dimensions and freight. Of the two quarter-boats with which the "Grosvenor" had been furnished, this was the larger and the stronger built, and for this reason had been chosen by Stevens. I could not hope, indeed, that she would live a moment in anything of a sea; but she was certainly stout enough to carry us to the Bermudas, providing that the weather remained moderate.

It was now six o'clock. I said to the boatswain:

"Every hour of this weather is valuable to us. There is no reason why we should stay here."

"I should like to see her sink, Mr. Royle; I should like to know that poor Jim found a regular coffin in her," he answered. "We can't make no headway with the sail, and I don't recommend rowin' for the two or three miles we can fetch with the oars. It 'ud be wurse nor pumpin'."

He was right. When I reflected, I was quite sure I could not, in my exhausted state, be able to handle one of the big oars for even five minutes at a stretch; and, admitting that I *had* been strong enough to row for a couple of hours, yet the result to have been obtained could not have been important enough to justify the serious labor.

The steward all this time sat perfectly quiet in the bottom of the boat, with his back against the mast. He paid no attention to us when we spoke, nor looked around him, though sometimes he would fix his eyes vacantly on the sky as if his shattered mind found relief in contemplating the void. I was heartily glad to find him quiet, though I took care to watch him, for it was difficult to tell whether his imbecility was not counterfeited, by his madness, to throw us off our guard, and furnish him with an opportunity to play us and himself some deadly trick.

As some hours had elapsed since we had tasted food, I opened a tin of meat and prepared a meal. The boatswain ate heartily, and so did the steward: but I could not prevail upon Mary to take more than a biscuit and sherry and water.

Indeed, as the evening approached, our position affected her more deeply, and often, after she had cast her eyes toward the horizon, I would see her lips whispering a prayer, and feel her hand tightening on mine.

The ship still floated, but she was so low in the water that I every minute expected to see her vanish. The water was above her main-chains, and I could only attribute her obstinacy in not sinking to the great quantity of wood—both in cases and goods—which composed her cargo.

The sun was now quite close to the horizon, branding the ocean with a purple glare, but itself descending into a cloudless sky. I can not express how majestic and wonderful the great orb looked to us who were almost level with the water. Its disk seemed vaster than I had ever before seen it, and there was something sublimely solemn in the loneliness of its descent. All the sky about it, and far to the south and north, was changed into the color of gold by its luster; and over our heads the heavens were an exquisite tender green, which melted in the east into a dark blue.

I was telling Mary that ere the sun sank again we might be on board a ship, and whispering any words of encouragement and hope to her, when I was startled by the boatswain crying, "Now she's gone! Look at her!"

I turned my eyes toward the ship, and could scarcely credit my senses when I found that her hull had vanished, and that nothing was to be seen of her but her spars, which were all aslant sternward.

I held my breath, as I saw the masts sink lower and lower. First the cross-jack yard was submerged, the gaff with the ensign hanging dead at the peak, then the main-yard; presently only the main-top-mast cross-trees were visible, a dark cross upon the water; they vanished. At the same moment the sun disappeared behind the horizon; and now we were alone on the great, breathing deep, with all the eastern sky growing dark as we watched.

"It's all over!" said the boatswain, breaking the silence, and speaking in a hollow tone. "No livin' man 'll ever see the 'Grosvenor' again!"

Mary shivered and leaned against me. I took up a rug and folded it round her, and kissed her forehead.

The boatswain had turned his back upon us, and sat with his hands folded, I believe in prayer. I am sure he was thinking of Jim Cornish, and I would not have interrupted that honest heart's communion with its Maker for the value of the ship that had sunk.

Darkness came down very quickly, and, that we might lose no chance of being seen by any distant vessel, I lighted the ship's lantern and hoisted it at the mast-head. I also lighted the bull's-eye lamp and set it in the stern-sheets.

"Mary," I whispered, "I will make you up a bed in the bottom of the boat. While this weather lasts, dearest, we have no cause to be alarmed by our position. It will make me happy to see you sleeping, and be sure that while you sleep there will be watchful eyes near you."

"I will sleep as I am here, by your side; I shall rest better so," she answered. "I could not sleep lying down."

It was too sweet a privilege to forego; I passed my arm around her and held her close to me; and she closed her eyes like a child, to please me.

Worn out as I was, enfeebled both intellectually and physically by the heavy strain that had been put upon me ever since that day when I had been ironed by Captain Coxon's orders, I say—and I solemnly believe in the truth of what I am about to write—that had it not been for the living reality of this girl, encircled by my arm, with her head supported by my shoulder; had it not been for the deep love I felt for her, which localized my thoughts, and, so to say humanized them down to the level of our situation, forbidding them to trespass beyond the prosaic limits of our danger, of the precautions to be taken by us, of our chances of rescue, of the course to be steered when the wind should fill our sail—I should have gone mad when the night came down upon the sea and enveloped our boat (a lonely speck on the gigantic world of water) in the mystery and fear of the darkness. I know this by recalling the fancy that for a few moments possessed me in looking along the water, when I clearly beheld the outline of a coast, with innumerable lights winking upon it; by the whirling, dizzy sensation in my head which followed the extinction of the vision; by the emotion of wild horror and unutterable disappointment which overcame me when I detected the cheat. I pressed my darling to me, and looked upon her sweet face, revealed by the light shed by the lantern at the mast-head, and all my misery left me; and the delight which the knowledge that she was my own love, and that I held her in my arms, gave me, fell like an exorcism upon the demons of my stricken imagination.

She smiled when I pressed her to my side, and when she saw my face close to hers, looking at her; but she did not know that she had saved me from a fate more dreadful than death, and that so strong as I seemed, so earnest as I had shown myself in my conflicts with fate, so resolutely as I had striven to comfort her—had been rescued from madness by her whom I had a thousand times pitied for her helplessness.

She fell asleep at last, and I sat for nearly two hours motionless, that I should not awaken her. The steward slept with his head in his arms, kneeling—a strange, mad posture. The boatswain sat forward, with his face turned aft and his arms folded. I addressed him once, but he did not answer. Probably I spoke too low for him to hear, being fearful of waking Mary; but there was little we had to say. Doubtless he found his thoughts too engrossing to suffer him to talk.

Being anxious to "take a star," as we say at sea, and not knowing how the time went, I gently drew out my watch and found the hour a quarter to eleven. In replacing the watch I aroused Mary, who raised her head and looked round her with eyes that flashed in the lantern light.

"Where are we?" she exclaimed, and bent her head to gaze at me, on which she recollected herself. "Poor boy!" she said, taking my hand, "I have kept you supporting my weight. You were more tired than I. But it is your turn now. Rest your head on my shoulder."

"No, it is still your turn," I answered, "and you shall sleep presently. But since you are awake, I will try to find out where we are. You shall hold the lamp for me while I make my calculations and examine the chart."

Saying which, I drew out my sextant and got across the thwarts to the mast, which I stood up alongside of to lean on; for the swell, though moderate enough to pass without notice on a big vessel, lifted and sank the boat in such a way as to make it difficult to stand steady.

I was in the act of raising the sextant to my eye, when the boatswain suddenly cried, "Mr. Royle, listen!"

"What do you hear?" I asked.

"Hush! listen now!" he answered, in a breathless voice.

I strained my ear, but nothing was audible to me but the wash of the water against the boat's side.

"Don't you hear it, Mr. Royle?" he cried, in a kind of agony, holding up his finger. "Miss Robertson, don't you hear something?"

There was another interval of silence, and Mary answered: "I hear a kind of throbbing."

"It is so!" I exclaimed. "I hear it now! it is the engines of a steamer!"

"A steamer? Yes! I heard it! where is she?" shouted the boatswain, and he jumped on to the thwart on which I stood.

We strained our ears again.

That throbbing sound, as Mary had accurately described it, closely resembling the rhythmical running of a locomotive-engine heard in the country on a silent night at a long distance, was now audible; but so smooth was the water, so breathless the night, that it was impossible to tell how far away the vessel might be; for so fine and delicate a vehicle of sound is the ocean in a calm, that, though the hull of a steamship might be below the horizon, yet the thumping of her engines would be heard.

Once more we inclined our ears, holding our breath as we listened.

"It grows louder!" cried the boatswain. "Mr. Royle, bend your bull's-eye lamp to the end o' one o' the oars and swing it about, while I dip this mast-head lantern."

Very different was his manner now from what it had been that morning when the Russian hove in sight.

I lashed the lamp by the ring of it to an oar and waved it to and fro. Meanwhile the boatswain had got hold of the masthead halyards, and was running the big ship's lantern up and down the mast

"Mary," I exclaimed, "lift up the seat behind you, and in the left-hand corner you will find a pistol."

"I have it," she answered, in a few moments.

"Point it over the stem and fire!" I cried.

She leveled the little weapon and pulled the trigger; the white flame leaped, and a smart report followed.

"Listen now!" I said.

I held the ear steady, and the boatswain ceased to dance the lantern. For the first few seconds I heard nothing, then my ear caught the throbbing sound.

"I see her!" cried the boatswain; and, following his finger (my sight being keener than my hearing), I saw not only the shadow of a vessel down in the south-west, but the smoke from her funnel pouring along the stars.

"Mary," I cried, "fire again!"

She drew the trigger.

"Again!"

The clear report whizzed like a bullet past my ear.

Simultaneously with the second report a ball of blue fire shot up into the sky. Another followed, and another.

A moment after a red light shone clear upon the sea.

"She sees us!" I cried. "God be praised! Mary, darling, she sees us!"

I waved the lamp furiously. But there was no need to wave it any longer. The red light drew nearer and nearer; the throbbing of the engines louder and louder, and the revolutions of the propeller sounded like a pulse beating through the water. The shadow broadened and loomed larger. I could hear the water spouting out of her side and the blowing off of the safety-valve.

Soon the vessel grew a defined shape against the stars, and then a voice, thinned by the distance, shouted, "What light is that?"

I cried to the boatswain: "Answer, for God's sake! My voice is weak."

He hollowed his hands and roared back: "We're shipwrecked seamen adrift in a quarter-boat!"

Nearer and nearer came the shadow, and now it was a long, black hull, a funnel pouring forth a dense volume of smoke, spotted with fire-sparks, and tapering masts and fragile rigging, with the stars running through them.

"Ease her!"

The sound of the throbbing grew more measured. We could hear the water as it was churned up by the screw.

"Stop her!"

The sounds ceased, and the vessel came looming up slowly, more slowly, until she stopped.

"What is that?—a boat?" exclaimed a strong bass voice.

"Yes!" answered the boatswain. "We've been shipwrecked, we're adrift in a quarter-boat."

"Can you bring her alongside?"

"Ay, ay, sir!"

I threw out an oar, but trembled so violently that it was as much as I could do to work it. We headed the boat for the steamer and rowed toward her. As we approached, I perceived that she was very long, bark-rigged, and raking, manifestly a powerful, iron-built ocean steamer. They hung a red light on the forestay and a white light over her port quarter, and lights flitted about her gangway.

A voice sang out: "How many are there of you?"

The boatswain answered: "Three men and a lady."

On this the same voice called, "If you want help to bring that boat alongside, we'll send to you."

"We'll be alongside in a few minutes," returned the boatswain.

But the fact was, the vessel had stopped her engines when farther off from us than we had imagined; being deceived by the magnitude of her looming hull, which seemed to stand not a hundred fathoms away from us, and by the wonderful distinctness of the voice that had spoken us.

I did not know how feeble I had become until I took the oar; and the violent emotions excited in me by our rescue, now to be effected after our long and heavy trials, diminished still the little strength that was left in me; so that the boat moved very slowly through the water and it was full twenty minutes, starting from the time when we had shipped oars, before we came up with her.

"We'll fling you a rope's end," said a voice; "look out for it."

A line fell into the boat. The boatswain caught it, and sung out, "All fast!"

I looked up the high side of the steamer: there was a crowd of men assembled round the gangway, their faces visible in the light shed not only by our own mast-head lantern (which was on a level with the steamer's bulwarks), but by other lanterns which some of them held. In all this light we, the occupants of the boat, were to be clearly viewed from the deck; and the voice that had first addressed us said:

"Are you strong enough to get up the ladder? If not, we'll sling you on board."

I answered that if a couple of hands would come down into the boat so as to help the lady and a man (who had fallen imbecile) over the ship's side, the other two would manage to get on board without assistance.

On this a short gangway-ladder was lowered, and two men descended and got into the boat.

"Take that lady first," I said, pointing to Mary, but holding on, as I spoke, to the boat's mast, for I felt horribly sick and faint, and knew not, indeed, what was going to happen to me; and I had to exert all my power to steady my voice.

They took her by the arms, and watching the moment when the wash

of the swell brought the boat against the ship's side, landed her cleverly on
the ladder and helped her on to the deck.

"Bo's'n," I cried, huskily, "she—she is—saved! I am dying, I think. God
bless her! and—and—your hand, mate—"

I remember uttering these incoherent words, and seeing the boatswain
spring forward to catch me. Then my senses left me with a flash.

CHAPTER XXX

I REMAINED, as I was afterward informed, insensible for four days, during
which time I told and retold, in my delirium, the story of the mutiny and our
own sufferings, so that, as the ship's surgeon assured me, he became very
exactly acquainted with all the particulars of the "Grosvenor's" voyage, from
the time of her leaving the English Channel to the moment of our rescue
from the boat; though I, from whom he learned the story, was insensible as
I related it. My delirium even embraced so remote an incident as the running down of the smack.

When I opened my eyes I found myself in a small, very comfortable
cabin, lying in a bunk; and, being alone, I had no knowledge of where I was,
nor would my memory give me the slightest assistance. Every object my eye
rested upon was unfamiliar, and that I was on board a ship was all that I
knew for certain. What puzzled me most was the jarring sound caused by
the engines. I could not conceive what this meant nor what produced it;
and the vessel being perfectly steady, it was not in my power to realize that
I was being borne over the water.

I closed my eyes and lay perfectly still, striving to master the past and
inform myself of what had become of me; but so hopelessly muddled was
my brain that had some unseen person, by way of a joke, told me in a sepul-
chral voice that I was dead, and apprehending the things about me only by
means of my spirit, which had not yet had time to get out of my body, I
should have believed him; though I don't say that I should not have been

puzzled to reconcile my very keen appetite and thirst with my non-existent condition.

In a few minutes the door of the cabin was opened, and a jolly, red-faced man, wearing a scotch cap, looked in. Seeing me with my eyes open, he came forward and exclaimed, in a cheerful voice:

"All alive-o! Staring about you full of wonderment! Nothing so good as curiosity in a sick man. Shows that the blood is flowing."

He felt my pulse, and asked me if I knew who he was.

I replied that I had never seen him before.

"Well, that's not my fault," he said; "for I've been looking at you a pretty tidy while, on and off, since we hoisted you out of the brine.

> *"Guid speed an' furder to you, Johnny;*
> *Guid health, hale han's an' weather bonnie;*
> *May ye ne'er want a stoup o' brandy,*
> > *To clear your head!*

"Hungry?"

"Very," said I.

"Thirsty?"

"Yes."

"How do you feel in yourself?"

"I have been trying to find out. I don't know. I forget who I am."

"Raise your arm and try your muscles."

"I can raise my arm," I said, doing so.

"How's your memory?"

"If you'll give me a hint or two, I'll see."

He looked at me very earnestly and with much kindness in the expression of his jovial face, and debated some matter in his own mind.

"I'll send you in some beef-tea," he said, "by a person who'll be able to do you more good than I can. But don't excite yourself. Converse calmly, and don't talk too much."

So saying he went away.

I lay quite still, and my memory remained as helpless as though I had just been born.

After an interval of about ten minutes the door was again opened, and

Mary came in. She closed the door and approached me, holding a cup of beef-tea in her hand, but however she had schooled herself to behave, her resolution forsook her; she put the cup down, threw her arms round my neck, and sobbed with her cheek against mine.

With my recognition of her, my memory returned to me.

"My darling," I cried, in a weak voice, "is it you, indeed? Oh, God is very merciful to have spared us! I remembered nothing just now; but all has come back to me with your dear face."

She was too overcome to speak for some moments; but, raising herself presently, she said, in broken tones:

"I thought I should never see you again, never be able to speak to you more. But I am wicked to give way to my feelings, when I have been told that my excitement must be dangerous to my darling. Drink this, now—no, I will hold the cup to your lips. Strength has been given me to bear the sufferings we have gone through, that I may nurse you and bring you back to health."

I would not let go her hand; but when I attempted to prop myself up, I found my elbow would not sustain me; so I lay back and drank from the cup which she held to my mouth.

"How long is it," I asked her, "since we were taken on board this vessel?"

"Four days. Do you know that you fell down insensible in the boat the moment after I had been carried on to the deck of this ship? The men crowded around me and held their lanterns to my face, and I found that most of them were Scotch by their exclamations. A woman took me by the hand to lead me away, but I refused to move one step until I saw that you were on board. She told me that you had fainted in the boatswain's arms, and others cried out that you were dead. I saw them bring you up out of the boat, and told the woman that I must go with you and see where they put you, and asked if there was a doctor on board. She said yes, and that he was the man in the Scotch cap and great-coat, who was helping the others to take you down-stairs. I took your poor senseless hands and cried bitterly over them, and told the doctor I would go on my knees to him if he would save your life. But he was very kind—very kind and gentle."

"And you, Mary? I see you keep up your wonderful courage to the last."

"I fainted when the doctor took me away from you," she answered, with one of her sweet wistful smiles. "I slept far into the next day, and I rose well yesterday morning, and have been by your side nearly ever since. It is rather hard upon me that your consciousness should have returned when I had left the cabin for a few minutes."

I made her turn her face to the light that I might see her clearly, and found that though her mental and physical sufferings had left traces on her calm and beautiful face, yet, on the whole, she looked fairly well in health; her eyes bright, her complexion clear, and her lips red, with a firm expression on them. I also took notice that she was well dressed in a black silk, though probably I was not good critic enough just then in such matters to observe that it fitted her ill, and did no manner of justice to her lovely shape.

She caught me looking at the dress, and told me, with a smile, that it had been lent to her by a lady passenger.

"Why do you stand?" I said.

"The doctor only allowed me to see you on condition that I did not stay above five minutes."

"That is nonsense I cannot let you go, now you are here. Your dear face gives me back all the strength I have lost. How came I to fall down insensible? I am ashamed of myself. I, as a sailor, supposed to be inured to all kinds of privation, to be cut adrift from my senses by a shipwreck! Mary, you are fitter to be a sailor than I. After this, let me buy a needle and thread, and advertise for needlework."

"You are talking too much. I shall leave you."

"You cannot, while I hold your hand."

"Am I not much stronger than you are?"

"In all things stronger, Mary. You have been my guardian angel. You interceded for my life with God, and He heard you when He would not have heard me."

She placed her hand on my mouth.

"You are talking too much, I say. You reproach yourself for your weakness, but try to remember what you have gone through; how you had to baffle the mutineers, to take charge of the ship, to save our lives from their terrible designs. Remember, too, that for days together you scarcely closed your eyes in sleep—that you did the work of a whole crew during the storm. Dearest, what you have gone through would have broken many a man's heart or driven him mad. It has left you your own true self for me to love and cherish while God shall spare us to each other."

She kissed me on the mouth, drew her hand from mine, and with a smile full of tender affection left the cabin.

I was vexed to lose her even for a short time; and still chose to think myself a poor creature for falling ill and keeping to my bed, when I might be with her about the ship, and telling the people on board the story of her misfortunes and beautiful courage.

It was a mistake of the doctor's to suppose that her conversation could hurt me.

I had no idea of the time, and stared hard at the bull's-eye over my head, hoping to discover by the complexion of the light that it was early in the day, so that I might again see Mary before the night came. I was even rash enough to imagine that I had the strength to rise, and made an effort to get out of the bunk, which gave me just the best illustration I could wish that I was as weak as a baby. So I tumbled back with a groan of disappointment, and, after staring fixedly at the bull's-eye, I fell asleep.

This sleep lasted some hours. I awoke, not as I had first awakened from insensibility, with tremors and bewilderment, but easily, with a delicious sense of warmth and rest and renewing vigor in my limbs.

I opened my eyes upon three persons standing near the bunk; one was Mary, the other the doctor, and the third a thin, elderly, sunburned man, in a white waistcoat with gold buttons and a blue cloth loose coat.

The doctor felt my pulse, and letting fall my hand, said to Mary:

"Now, Miss Robertson, Mr. Royle will do. If you will kindly tell the steward to give you another basin of broth, you will find our patient able to make a meal."

She kissed her hand to me behind the backs of the others, and went out with a beaming smile.

"This is Captain Craik, Mr. Royle," continued the doctor, motioning to the gentleman in the white waistcoat, "commanding this vessel, the 'Peri.'"

I at once thanked him earnestly for his humanity, and the kindness he was showing me.

"Indeed," he replied, "I am very pleased with my good fortune in rescuing so brave a pair of men as yourself and your boatswain, and happy to have been the instrument of saving the charming girl to whom you are betrothed from the horror of exposure in an open boat. I have had the whole of your story from Miss Robertson, and I can only say that you have acted very heroically and honorably."

I replied that I was very grateful to him for his kind words; but I assured him that I only deserved a portion of his praise. The man who truly merited admiration was the boatswain.

"You shall divide the honors," he said, smiling. "The bo's'n is already a hero. My crew seem disposed to worship him. If you have nothing better for him in your mind, you may hand him over to me. I know the value of such men nowadays, and so much is left to the crimp."

Saying this, he went to the door and called; and immediately my old companion, the boatswain, came in. I held out my hand, and it was clutched by the honest fellow and held with passionate cordiality.

"Mr. Royle, sir," he exclaimed, in a faltering voice, "this is a happy moment for me. There was a time when I never thought I should ha' seen you alive again; and it went to my heart, and made me blubber like any old woman when I thought o' your dyin' arter all the trouble you've seen, and just when, if I may be so bold as to say it, you might be hopin' to marry the brave, high-spirited gell as you saved from drownin', and who belongs to you by the will o' God Almighty. Captain Craik, sir—I speak by your favor, and ax pardon for the liberty—this gen'man and me has seen some queer starts together since we first shipped aboard the 'Grosvenor' in the West Hindie docks, and," he cried, with vehemence, "I'd sooner ha' lost the use o' my right arm an' leg—yes, an' you may chuck my right eye in along with them—than Mr. Royle should ha' died just as he was goin' to live properly and set down on the bench o' matrimony an' happiness with a bold and happy wife!"

This eloquent harangue he delivered with a moist eye, addressing us all three in turn. I thanked him heartily for what he had said, but limited my reply to this; for though I could have complimented him more warmly than he had praised me, I considered that it would be more becoming to hold over all mutual admiration and you-and-me glorification until we should be alone.

I observed that he wore a velvet waistcoat, and carried a shiny cloth cap with a brilliant peak, very richly garnished with braid; and as such articles of raiment could only emanate from the forecastle, I concluded that they were gifts from the crew, and that Captain Craik had reason in thinking that the boatswain had become a hero.

The doctor shortly after this motioned him to go, whereupon he gave a ship-shape salute by tweaking an imaginary curl on his forehead, and went away.

I now asked what had become of the steward. Captain Craik answered that the man was all right so far as his health went; that he wandered about the decks very harmlessly, smiling in the faces of the men, and seldom speaking.

"One peculiarity of the poor creature," said he, "is that he will not taste any kind of food but what is served out to the crew. I have myself tried him with dishes from the saloon table, but could not induce him to touch a mouthful. The first time I tried him in this way he fell from me as though I had offered to cut his throat, the perspiration poured from his forehead, and he eyed me with looks of the utmost horror and aversion. Can you account for this?"

"Yes, sir," I replied. "The steward was in the habit of serving out the ship's stores to the crew of the 'Grosvenor.' He rather sided with the captain, and tried to make the best of what was outrageously bad. When the men mutinied they threatened to hang him if he touched any portion of the cuddy stores, and I dare say they would have executed their threat. He was rather a coward before he lost his reason, and the threat affected him violently. I myself never could induce him to taste any other food than the ship's rotten stores while the men remained in the vessel, and I dare say the memory of the threat still lives in his broken mind."

"Thanks for your explanation," said the doctor, "I shall sleep the better for it; for, upon my word, the man's unnatural dislike of good food—of *entrées*, man, and curried fowl and roast goose, for I tried him myself—has kept me awake bothering my head to understand."

"May I ask what vessel this is?" I said, addressing Captain Craik.

"The 'Peri' of Glasgow, homeward bound from Jamaica," he answered.

"I know the ship now, sir. She belongs to the———Line."

"Quite right. We shall hope to put you ashore in seven days hence. It is curious that I should have known Mr. Robertson, your lady's father. I called upon him a few years since in Liverpool, on business, and had a long conversation with him. Little could I have dreamed that his end would be so sad, and that it should be reserved for me to rescue his daughter from an open boat in mid-Atlantic!"

"Ah, sir," I exclaimed, "no one but I can ever know the terrible trials this poor girl has passed through. She has been twice shipwrecked within three weeks; she has experienced all the horrors of a mutiny; she has lost her father under circumstances which would have killed many girls with grief; she has been held in terror of her life, and yet never once has her noble courage flagged, her splendid spirit failed her."

"Yes," answered Captain Craik, "I have read her character in her story and in her way of relating it. You are to be congratulated on having won the love of a woman whose respect alone would do a man honour."

"He deserves what he has got," said the doctor, laughing. "Findings is keepings."

"I did find her, and I mean to keep her," I exclaimed.

"Well, you have picked up a fortune," observed Captain Craik. "It is not every man who finds a shipwreck a good investment."

"I know nothing about her fortune," I answered. "She did indeed tell me that her father was a ship-owner; but I have asked no questions and only know her as Mary Robertson, a sweet, brave girl, whom I love, and please God, mean to marry, though she possessed nothing more in the world than the clothes I found her in."

"Come, come!" said the doctor.

"You're not a sailor, doctor," remarked Captain Craik, dryly.

"But, my dear sir, you'll not tell me that a gold pound's not better than a silver sixpence?" cried the doctor. "Did you never sing this song:

Awa wi' your witchcraft o' beauty's alarms,
The slender bit beauty you grasp in your arms;
Oh, gie me the lass that has acres o' charms,
Oh, gie me the lass wi' the well-stockit farms.
Then hey for a lass wi' a tocher! then hey for a lass wi'
*   a tocher!*
Then hey for a lass wi' a tocher! the nice yellow guineas
*   for me.*

Is not an heiress better than a poor wench?"

"I don't see how your simile of the pound and the sixpence applies," answered Captain Craik. "A good woman is a good woman all the world over, and a gift that every honest man will thank God for.

> *Mark yonder pomp of costly fashion*
>   *Round the wealthy titled bride;*
> *But when compared with real passion,*
>   *Poor is all that princely pride.*

That's one of Robbie's, too, doctor, and I commend your attention to the whole song as a wholesome purge."

As the conversation was rather too personal to be much to my liking, I was very glad when it was put an end to by Mary coming in with a basin of soup for me.

CHAPTER XXXI

THANKS TO my darling's devotion, to her unwearied attentions, to her foresight and care for me, I was strong enough to leave my cabin on the third day following my restoration to consciousness.

During that time many inquiries were made after my health by the passengers, and Mary told me that the greatest curiosity prevailed fore and aft to see me. So misfortune had made a little ephemeral hero of me, and this, perhaps, was one stroke of compensation which I should have been very willing to dispense with.

The second officer of the ship, a man of about my height and build, had very kindly placed his wardrobe at my disposal, but all that I had chosen to borrow from him was some linen, which, indeed, I stood greatly in need of; but my clothes, though rather the worse for salt water, were in my opinion, quite good enough for me to wear until I should be able to buy a new outfit ashore.

At twelve o'clock, then, on the third day, I rose and leisurely dressed myself, and then sat waiting for Mary, whose arm to lean on I preferred to any one's else.

She came to the cabin presently, and when she had entered I folded her in my arms with so deep a feeling of happiness and love and gratitude in me that I had no words to speak to her.

It was when I released her that she said: "Since God has heard our prayers, dearest, and mercifully preserved us from death, shall we thank Him, now that we are together, and say one prayer for my dear father, who, I firmly believe, looks down upon us and has still the power to bless us?"

I took her hand, and we knelt together, and, first thanking her for reminding me of my bounden duty, I lifted up my heart to Almighty God, Father of all men, who had guarded us amid our perils, who had brought us to the knowledge and love of Him and of each other by the lesson, of hard trials and sorrowful privation.

And I would ask you to believe that I do not relate such circumstances as these from any ostentatious wish to parade my piety, of which, God knows, I have not so large a store that I need be vain of showing it; but that I may in some poor fashion justify many good men in my own profession who, because they are scandalized by persons among us that are bad, are confounded with these by people ashore, who imagine the typical sailor to be a loose, debauched fellow, with his mouth full of bad language and his head full of drink. I say earnestly that this is not so; that a large and generous soul animates many sailors; that they love God, pray to him, and in many ways—too rough, may be, to commend them to fastidious piety, but not surely the less honest for the roughness—strive to act up to a just standard of goodness; and that even among the bad—bad, I mean, through the looseness of their morals and the insanity of their language—there is often found a hidden, instinctive religion and veneration and fear of God not to be discovered in the classes ashore to which you may parallel them. Nor, indeed, do I understand how this can fail to be; for no familiarity with the mighty deep can lessen its ever appealing grandeur to them as a symbol of heavenly power and majesty; and the frequent fear of their lives in which sailors go— the fury of tempests, the darkness of stormy nights, the fragility of the ship in comparison with the mountainous waves which menace her, the horror of near and iron coasts—I say that such things, which are daily presented to them, must inevitably excite and sustain contemplations which very few events that happen on shore are calculated to arouse in the minds of the ignorant classes with whom such sailors as I am speaking of are on a level.

When I quitted the cabin, supported by Mary, I found myself in a very spacious saloon, most handsomely furnished and decorated, and striking me more by the contrast it offered to the plain and small interior of the "Grosvenor's" cabin.

The table was being prepared for lunch: smartly dressed steward and under-stewards trotted to and fro; there were flowers on the table, vases of gold-fish swinging from the deck, a rich thick carpet underfoot, comfortable and handsome sofas; a piano-forte stood against the mizzen-mast, which was covered with a mahogany skin and gilded; two rows of lamps went the length of the saloon; and what with the paintings on the cabin doors, the curtains, the rich brass-work about the spacious sky-lights, the bright sun-shine streaming in upon the whole scene and kindling a brilliance in the polished wood-work, the crystal on the table, the looking-glasses at the fore end of the saloon—I fairly paused with amazement, scarcely conceiving it possible that this airy, sunshiny, sumptuous drawing-room was actually the interior of a ship, and that we were on the sea, steaming at the rate of so many miles an hour toward England.

There were a couple of well-dressed women sewing or doing some kind of needle-work and conversing on one of the sofas, and on another sofa a gentleman sat reading. These, with the stewards, were all the people in the saloon.

The gentleman and the ladies looked at us when we approached, and all three of them rose.

The ladies came and shook hands with Mary, who introduced me to them; but I forget their names.

They began to praise me; the gentleman struck in and asked permission to shake me by the hand. They had heard my story—it was a beautiful ro-mance: in short, they overpowered me with civilities, and made me so nervous that I had scarcely the heart to go on deck.

Of course it was all very kindly meant; but, then, what were my ex-ploits? Nothing to make money out of, nothing to justify my appearance on the boards of a London theatre, nothing to furnish a column of wild writing to a newspaper, nothing to merit even the honor of a flattering request from a photographic company. I very exactly knew what I *had* done, and was keenly alive to the absurdity of any heroizing process.

However, I had sense enough to guess that what blushing honors were thrust upon me would be short-lived. Who does not thank God some time or other in his life that there is such a thing as oblivion?

So we went on deck, I overhearing one of the ladies talk some non-sense about her never having read or heard of anything more delicately romantic and exciting than the young sailor rescuing a pretty girl from a wreck and falling in love with her.

"Did you hear that, Mary?" I whispered.

"Yes," she answered.

"Was it romantic?"

"I think so."

"And exciting?"

"Dreadfully."

"And did they live happily ever afterward?"

"We shall see."

"Darling, it *is* romantic and it *is* exciting, to us, and to no one else. Yes, very romantic, now that I come to think of it; but all has come about so gradually that I have never thought of the romance that runs through our story. What time did we have to think? Mutineers out of Wapping are no polite garnishers of a love story; and romance must be pretty stoutly bolt-roped not to be blown into smithereens by a hurricane."

There were a number of passengers on deck—men, women and chil-dren; and when I ran my eye along the ship (the "Grosvenor" would have made a neat long-boat for her) and observed her dimensions, I thought that a city might have gone to sea in her without any inconvenience arising from overcrowding. In a word, she was a magnificent Clyde-built iron boat of some four thousand tons burden, and propelled by eight hundred horse-power engines; her decks white as a yacht's, a shining awning for-ward and aft; a short, yellow funnel, towering mast and broad yards, and embodying every conceivable latest improvement in compasses, capstans, boat-lowering gear, blocks, gauges, logs, windlass, and the rest of it. She was steaming over a smooth sea and under a glorious blue sky at the rate of thirteen knots or nearly fifteen miles an hour. Cool draughts of air circled under the awning, and fanned my hollow cheeks, and invigorated and re-freshed me like cordials.

The captain was on deck when we arrived, and the moment he saw me he came forward and shook my hand, offering me many kindly congratula-tions on my recovery; and with his own hands, placed chairs for me and

Mary near the mizzen-mast. Then the chief officer approached, and most, indeed I think all, of the passengers; and I believe that, had I been as cynical as old Diogenes, I should have been melted into a hearty faith in human nature by the sympathy shown me by these kind people.

They illustrated their goodness best, perhaps, by withdrawing after a generous salutation, and resuming their various employments or discussions, so as to put me at my ease. The doctor and the chief officer stayed a little while talking to us; and then presently the tiffin-bell rang, and all the passengers went below, the captain having previously suggested that I should remain on deck, so as to get the benefit of the air, and that he would send a steward to wait upon me. Mary would not leave my side; and the officer in charge taking his station on the bridge before the funnel, we, to my great satisfaction, had the deck almost to our selves.

"You predicted, Mary," I said, "that our lives would be spared. Your dream has come true."

"Yes; I knew my father would not deceive me. Would to God he had been spared!"

"Yet God has been very good to us, Mary. What a change is this from the deck of the 'Grosvenor—the seas beating over us, the ship laboring as though at any moment she must go to pieces—ourselves fagged to death, and each of us in our hearts for hours and hours beholding death face to face! I feel as though I had no right to be alive after so much hard work. It is a violation of natural laws, and an impertinent triumphing of vitality over the whole forces of nature."

"But you are alive, dear, and that is all I care about."

I pressed her hand, and after looking round me, asked her if she knew whether this vessel went direct to Glasgow.

"Yes."

"Have you any friends there?"

"None. But I have friends here. The captain has asked me to stay with his wife until I hear from home."

"To whom shall you write?"

"To my aunt in Leamington. She will come to Glasgow and take me home. And you—"

"I?"

I looked at her and smiled.

"I? Why your question puts a matter into my head that I must think over."

"You are not strong enough to think. If you begin to think, I shall grow angry."

"But I must think, Mary."

"I must think how I am to get to London, and what I am to do when I get there."

"When we were on the 'Grosvenor,' she said, "you did all the thinking for me, didn't you? And now that we are on the 'Peri,' I mean to do all the thinking for you. But I need not say that I have thought my thoughts out. I have done with them."

"Look here, Mary, I am going to be candid—"

"Here comes one of the stewards to interrupt you."

A very civil fellow came with a tray, which he placed on the sky-light, and stood by to wait on us. I told him he need not stay, and addressing Mary, I exclaimed:

"This recalls our farewell feast on the 'Grosvenor.'"

"Yes; and there is the boatswain watching us, as if he would like to come to us again and congratulate us on having found each other out. Do catch his eye, dear, and wave your hand. He dare not come here."

I waved my hand to him, and he flourished his cap in return, and so did three or four men who were around him.

"I am going—" I began.

"You will eat your lunch first," she interrupted.

"But why will you not listen?"

"Because I have made my arrangements."

"But I wish to speak of myself, dear."

"I am speaking of you—my arrangements concern you—and me."

I looked at her uneasily, for somehow the sense of my own poverty came home to me very sharply, and I had a strong disinclination to hear what my foolish pride might smart under as a mortification.

She read my thoughts in my eyes; and blushing, yet letting me see her sweet face, she said in a low voice:

"I thought we were to be married?"

"I hope so. It is my dearest wish, Mary. I have told you I love you. It would break up my life to lose you now."

"You shall not lose me—but neither will I lose you. I shall never release you more."

"Mary, *do* let me speak my thoughts out. I am very poor. The little that I had has gone down in the 'Grosvenor.' I could not marry you as I am. I could only offer you the hand of a pauper. Let me tell you my plans. I shall write, on reaching Glasgow, to the owners of the 'Grosvenor,' relate the loss of the ship, and ask for payment of the wages that are due to me. With this money I will travel to London and go to work at once to obtain a berth on another ship. Perhaps, when the owners of the 'Grosvenor' hear my story, they will give me a post on board one of their other vessels. At all events, I must hope for the best. I will work very hard—"

"No, no! I can not listen!" she exclaimed, impetuously. "You are going to tell me that you will work very hard to become captain and save a little money; and you will then say that several years must pass before your pride will suffer you to think yourself in a proper position to make me your wife."

"Yes, I was going to say that."

"Oh, where is your clever head which enabled you to triumph over the mutineers? Has the shipwreck served you as it has the poor steward?"

"My darling—"

"Were you to work twenty years, what money could you save out of this profession of the sea that would justify your pride—your cruel pride?"

I was about to speak.

"What money could you save that would be of service when you know that I am rich, when you know that what is mine is yours?"

"Not much," said I.

"Would you have loved me the less had you known me to be poor? Would you not have risked your life to save mine though I had been a beggar? You loved me, because—because I am Mary Robertson; and I love you because you are Edward Royle—dear to me for your own dear sake, for my poor dead father's sake, because of my love for you. Would you go away and leave me because you are too proud to make us both happy? I will give you all I have—I will be a beggar and you shall be rich, that you need not leave me. Oh, do not speak of being poor! Who is poor that acts as you have done? Who is poor that can enrich a girl's heart as you have enriched mine?"

She had raised her voice unconsciously, and overhearing herself, as it were, she stopped on a sudden, and bowed her head with a sob.

"Mary," I whispered, "I will put my pride away. Let no man judge me wrongly. I talk idly—God knows how idly—when I speak of leaving you. Yes, I could leave you—but at what cost? at what cost to us both? What you have said—that I loved you as Mary Robertson—is true. I know in my own heart that my love can not dishonor us—that it can not gain nor lose by what the future may hold in store for me with you, dear one, as my wife."

"Now you are my own true sailor boy!" was all she said.

I began this story on the sea, and I desire to end it on the sea; and though another yarn, which should embrace my arrival at Glasgow, my introduction to Mary's aunt, my visit to Leamington, my marriage, and divers other circumstances of an equally personal nature, could easily be spun to follow this, yet the title of this story must limit the compass of it, and with the "Wreck of the Grosvenor" my tale should have had an end.

And yet I should be doing but poor justice to the faithful and beautiful nature of my dear wife, if I did not tell you that the plans which she had unfolded to me, and which I have made to appear as though they only concerned myself, included the boatswain and the poor steward. For both a provision was contemplated which I knew her too well to doubt that she would remember: a provision, that on the one hand, would bring the boatswain alongside of us even in our own home, and make him independent of his calling, which to say the least, considering the many years he had been at sea, had served him but ill, and still offered him but a scurvy outlook; while, on the other hand, it would enable the steward to support himself and his wife and child, without in the smallest degree taxing that unfortunate brain which we could only hope the shipwreck had not irreparably damaged.

Thus much, and this bit of yarn is spun.

And now I ask myself, is it worth the telling? Well, however it goes as a piece of work, it may teach a lesson—that good sailors may be made bad and bad sailors may be made outrageous, and harmless men may be converted into criminals, by the meanness of ship-owners. Every man knows, thanks to one earnest, eloquent and indefatigable voice that has been raised among us, what this country thinks of the rascals who send rotten ships to sea. And it is worth while to acquaint people with another kind of rottenness that is likewise sent to sea, which, in its way, is as bad as rotten timbers—a rottenness which is even less excusable, inasmuch as it costs but a trifling sum of money to remedy, than hulls: I mean rotten food.

Sailors have not many champions, because I think their troubles and wrongs are not understood. You must live and suffer their lives to know their lives. Go aloft with them, man the pumps with them, eat their biscuit and their pork, and drink their water with them; lodge with crimps along with them; be of their nature, and experience their shore-going temptations, the harpies in trousers and petticoats who prey upon them, who drug them and strip them.

And however deficient a man may be in those qualifications of mind which go to the making of popular novels, I hope no person will charge such a writer with impertinence for drawing a quill in behalf of a race of men to whom Britain owes the greatest part of her wealth and prosperity; who brave death; who combat the elements; who lead in numerous instances the lives of mongrel dogs; who submit, with a few murmurs that scarcely ever reach the shore-going ear, to privations which blanch the cheeks to read, that our tables and our homes may be abundantly furnished, our banking balances large, and our national importance supreme.

THE END

"Few, if any, sea writers have exhibited such a remarkable power of description; and the book will stand for many years as one of the most accurate pictures of West Indian life, both afloat and on shore, during the early part of the nineteenth century."

—*Reader's Digest of Books*

"Most excellent."

—**Samuel Taylor Coleridge**

"[Scott's novels] contain some of the best fighting fun, tropical scenery, and description. . ."

—**George E. Saintsbury**,
One Thousand Best Books

"Said to rank with or surpass. . . Cooper and Marryat."

—**Asa Don Dickinson**,
The World's Best Books

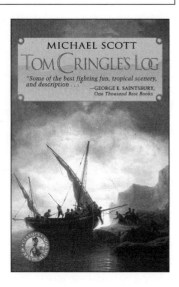

AMONG the dozen or so masterpieces of the sea, none will start young blood quicker or give a more real and fascinating picture of early 19th century sea life than this famous log by Michael Scott. The hero of the tale, Tom Cringle, is, in the opening chapter, an English midshipman thirteen years old. Assigned at first to service in home waters, he is soon transferred to the West Indies where war, piracy, smuggling, and slave-running are the order of the day. Tom later advances to captain with a command of his own—the audacious little *Wasp*.

Born in 1789, Michael Scott was an esteemed but anonymous Scottish novelist, receiving critical acclaim for the two novels he penned. Before settling in his native Glasgow, Scott lived for some years as an estate manager in Jamaica. Originally published as a series of essays in *Blackwood's* magazine, *Tom Cringle's Log* draws heavily on Scott's own Caribbean adventures.

Available at your favorite bookstore, or call toll-free: 1-888-BOOKS-11 (1-888-266-5711).

More classic sea stories (including three books by Captain Frederick Marryat) are available in the McBooks Press Classics of Nautical Fiction Series. To request a complimentary catalog, call 1-888-BOOKS-11.

TOM CRINGLE'S LOG
BY MICHAEL SCOTT
512 PAGES
$14.95, TRADE PAPERBACK
ISBN: 0-935526-51-X